To Re
Hope you enjoy it (handwritten)

M000290372

DEAR KILLER

A Marley Clark Mystery

Linda Lovely (signature)

Linda Lovely

2nd Paperback Edition, 2018, Windtree Press
Cover by Julie Kennedy, Digital City Designs, Austin, TX
Interior Design by LHI

1st Paperback Edition, 2011, L&L Dreamspell
Mass Market Edition, 2012, Harlequin Worldwide Mystery

This is a work of fiction, and is produced from the author's imagination. People, places and things mentioned in this novel are used in a fictional manner.

ACKNOWLEDGEMENTS

Thanks to my husband, Tom Hooker, sister, Rita Mann, and nieces, Tammy Nowling and Brenda Mann, for reading early drafts. Also, a shout-out to my great-nephew, Braden Mann, for allowing me to pinch his distinctive name.

Major (Retired) Arlene Underwood, a dear friend since kindergarten, deserves thanks for contributing details to help flesh out my heroine's Army experience. Also, a salute to Lowcountry friends Sue Collins, the Haught family, Sally Hendricks, La Rose Smith, and Sandy Foster for introducing me to coastal treasures.

I owe a ton of gratitude to my critique partners. Maya Reynolds, who's stuck with me the longest, deserves an extra star for plot suggestions, as does Robin Weaver, who is a genius at weaving in romance. Donna Campbell, Danielle Dahl, Polly Iyer, Howard Lewis, Jean Robbins, Helen Turnage, and Ellis Vidler helped enormously with their astute comments and red pencils.

DEDICATION

For Tom Hooker,
My husband and steadfast partner
in life's many adventures.
I couldn't ask for a better friend.

ONE

The wrought-iron gates stood open—again. The college kids assigned to lock up were zero for three this week. I sighed, switched on my flashlight, and walked toward the swimming pools. One more chink in the resort's security armor for vandals to exploit.

I noticed a smudge of light on the horizon and a twinge of unease crept over me. Hilton Head Island snaked into the ocean about twenty miles south, as a pelican flies, and its neon glitz cast a yellow pall over the velvet blackness. Normally our resort has too many competing halogens to detect a neighbor's light pollution.

Three lights in the Dolphin Club were out. It was too dark. Goose bumps raced up my arms. Something was hinky. Frozen in a cabana archway, I listened for any sound, some hint an intruder lurked in the shadows. Only gurgling water and a chorus of tree frogs broke the silence.

Sweeping my beam over the three-pool terrain, I strained to catch any movement. All was still. A second pass spotlighted an anomaly: clothing piled on a chair beside the Jacuzzi.

I walked closer, then paused as a shadowy blot rippled the surface of the water. It took a second to grasp someone floated face down. I sprinted. My feet made crunching noises as my shoes pulverized glass from the broken lamps.

No, no, no. Please don't let him be dead.

I thought "him" even though it was impossible to tell if the body belonged to a man or woman. A shock of hair streamed from the submerged head. Pale bony shoulders gleamed in the moonlight. When I grabbed the body under the armpits and hoisted it over the hot tub's lip, the man's head lolled backward.

Oh, God.

Stew Hartwell's gray eyes were wide open, though

1

sightless. I felt for a pulse. Nothing. I went on autopilot, pinching his nostrils shut, using two fingers to feel for any obstructions in his mouth.

I put my lips to his. They were warm. The Jacuzzi's one-hundred-four-degree water had left them soft and yielding. I blew, paused, blew. A rhythm. *Breathe, dammit, breathe, dammit, breathe.*

Nothing. My heart raced.

I rolled Stew on his stomach and pounded his back to expel water in his lungs. I flipped him and attacked his chest with my fist, trying to kick-start his heart. I put my lips to his once more. His mouth felt clammy now. Still, I tried to force more of my ragged gasps into his unresponsive lungs.

Come on, breathe.

Nothing. After five minutes, I gave up. Sweat trickled down my back. My face was damp and I realized I was crying. My breath came in labored pants. *Oh, Stew. I'm sorry.*

Years ago, my husband, Jeff, struck up a friendship with Stew. Whenever we visited the island, the two got together—poker, golf, Sunday football on Stew's big-screen. He was one of the good guys.

Now he's dead. Like Jeff.

My hot breath—wasted breath—rose in white puffs and mingled with the steam escaping the bubbling cauldron. The cool ocean breeze quickly wicked all warmth away.

I pulled a radio from my pocket and called Gary, the security guard on the front gate. "It's Marley Clark. I'm at the Dolphin. We have a drowning. I tried to revive him, but he's gone. Call EMS anyway."

"Who drowned?" Gary asked. "Is it a kid?"

I didn't answer. Though it was three in the morning, some sleepless codger might be amusing himself, listening to a police scanner. It wasn't rational, but I hesitated to say Stew's name aloud. If I kept quiet, maybe he wouldn't be dead.

"Sorry, Gary. I can't talk now. Get someone to wake up

Chief Dixon. The front entrance is wide open. I'll stay with the body."

Before Gary could ask more questions, I clicked the radio off.

Enough questions assaulted my brain. Stew was totally nude. What a way for your dead body to be discovered.

Of course, he was long past caring about decorum. That made the plume of sandy hair drifting from his head seem even sadder. The man let the baby-fine hair on one temple grow long for a classic comb-over. The result, like every comb-over, made me wonder if men who favored this camouflage technique shared a vampire's aversion to mirrors.

What possessed you to go skinny-dipping alone in the middle of the night?

During my resuscitation attempts, I'd dragged Stew most of the way out of the hot tub. However, his hips still rested on the Jacuzzi's curved ledge, and his legs dangled in the swirling water, giving them an eerie animation. His limp penis, withered from its extended submersion, showed no such life. It looked forlorn nested in its mat of brown pubic hair.

I was tempted to cover Stew. Provide him with some final dignity. But I knew better than to mess further with the scene. My attempts to resuscitate Stew had mucked things up enough. The unusual circumstances would certainly qualify the drowning as a suspicious death.

I looked away from Stew's torso. His feet continued to bob and the obscene jig drew my attention to the hot tub's water.

What the hell? I saw a carrot first. Orange and large, it bobbed to the surface by his toes. I watched in disbelief as the roiling water spit up celery stalks, whole onions and what looked like bay leaves. Gradually I realized a potpourri of vegetables simmered in the bubbling pot.

Sweet Jesus. What is this—a sick joke?

I looked wildly about to make sure I was alone. I'd been kneeling, and as I stumbled to my feet, I saw blood on the

3

concrete. My own. Shards of broken glass protruded from my knees and blood soaked the khaki slacks of my guard uniform.

That's when I noticed the towels, folded to form an arrow. It pointed to a patch of sand.

The Dolphin's designers had inserted sand and palm oases to break up the sea of concrete that cradled the complex's swimming pools. A crude message was scratched in the nearest greenery-and-dune pod.

Just one word: "STEWED."

My mind went numb. Nothing made sense. Had some psycho drowned Stew just to make a gruesome pun?

I remembered angry-looking punctures on Stew's back when I rolled him. Seizing his left shoulder, I eased his body up. Four marks embossed his pale back. Two close together, another two six inches away.

"Goddammit."

Nausea swept over me. I could barely imagine Stew's terror if my hunch proved correct. The crimson pricks looked like fresh stun jabs. I'd seen similar marks on my own body. When the Dear Island security officers were issued Tasers, our training required a demonstration. I'd been "volunteered" and knew firsthand the pole-axed feeling of having my limbs turn to jelly, of being aware of everything yet having a total disconnect between mind and body. I shivered, wondering if Stew had been fully cognizant of his fate, his brain frantically screaming at unresponsive muscles as his killer prepared to drown him.

I lowered Stew's shoulder, backed out of the crime scene along my original entry route, and prepared to intercept Chief Dixon and the EMS paramedics. They needed to understand the circumstances to avoid adding contaminants.

The wait would be brief. Dear Island's only five miles long and one and one-half miles wide. It took less than ten minutes to drive between any two points. And, yes, Dear Island is spelled D-E-A-R. Pre-1970 maps showed it as Deer Island. That was before it succumbed to a developer's spelling disorder or cuteness fetish. Having met my share of Lowcountry developers, either theory seemed plausible.

My manhandling of Stew's body had drenched me. My teeth clattered like castanets, and my knees throbbed. Congealed blood plastered my trousers to my legs. I plucked slivers of broken glass from the fabric. Anything to keep from looking at Stew. I fast-walked in tight circles, rubbing my hands to conjure up heat.

Paramedic Bill O'Brien was the first to charge on the scene. "Where's the victim?" he yelled as he hustled in my direction.

"He's dead," I answered. "No pulse. I tried mouth-to-mouth. Nothing."

"I'll give it a go anyway. Lead the way."

"Okay but this isn't a routine drowning. Stew Hartwell's been murdered. We need to think about the crime scene."

"Murdered? Are you sure?"

Bill's tone telegraphed skepticism. Residents took smug pride in the fact that Dear Island didn't have enough crime to warrant keeping statistics. There was the occasional theft as well as a smattering of complaints about inebriated idiots, usually vacationers or "tourons" in island speak. But a murder? Never.

Chief Dixon arrived in time to hear our exchange. "What in hell are you saying, Marley?" Dixon demanded.

We stood under the nearest functioning lamppost about twenty feet from Stew's body. The pooled light haloed Dixon's frizzy white hair, making him look like Ronald McDonald's grizzled grandpa.

While I summed up the situation, Bill tiptoed to the steamy six-person Jacuzzi. As a paramedic, he was qualified to pronounce Stew dead. After doing so, he studied the body and pointed out some bruising around Stew's wrists.

"Zip ties?" the chief wondered. "D'you suppose the killer tied his wrists while he was out for the count and cut 'em loose once he was dead?"

5

Bill nodded. "That's my guess."

Dixon rang the Hollis County Sheriff's Department to say we needed help pronto.

The chief's ruddy face looked more mottled than usual, - hinting at a bout of drinking or elevated blood pressure. He shook his head, hawked one up, and started to spit before he thought better of it. "Jesus H. Christ, you think someone fried Stew with a stunner in order to drown him? That's just dandy. Suppose that'll make all our boys prime suspects."

The same notion had crossed my mind—though I didn't think of Dear's security force as "our boys." It was no secret the chief preferred to hire men. Yet he figured my military career trumped my gender, so he overlooked my inability to scratch my nuts with the rest of his boys.

I paced off fifteen feet and circled the Jacuzzi, scanning the barren concrete. "Chief, the killer didn't use a Taser. Even civilian models eject those confetti-like markers that I.D. each weapon. Our murderer couldn't have picked them all up. Fortunately, that rules our weapons out."

"Eh? Speak up, will you?" An ex-Marine, Dixon blamed his poor hearing on close encounters with exploding shells. The counterfeit waterfall's gurgling wasn't helping him. "Who else packs stunners—just other cops, right?"

I raised my voice a notch. "Anyone willing to part with a few hundred bucks can buy stun guns or Tasers on the Internet. But I haven't a clue about all the options."

Dixon looked back at the body and cracked his knuckles. "Stew Hartwell. Who on earth would want to kill him?" The chief's interest in the body seemed strictly clinical; someone else would have to mourn the loss.

Poor Stew. My stomach did another samba. Then a white-hot anger flared in my gut. Stew didn't deserve to die like this— a gothic comic book ending.

"If only I'd patrolled this area sooner..."

"Forget it, Marley, you couldn't have saved him," the chief

said. "If you'd come earlier, you might be dead, too."

Until the chief answered, I hadn't realized I'd spoken aloud.

"You may have been one hot shot Army colonel, but even you can't bring back the dead."

Well, yes, once I could.

I was sixteen, a lifeguard. The boy was nine, chubby. When I hauled him from the depths, his lips were tinged with blue, as if the aqua water had dyed them. I breathed life into him. His fat cheeks turned from blue to pink like Mom's hydrangeas after she added lime.

Life seemed effortless then. I could cheat death. No longer. The living slipped away.

I blinked away the vision to concentrate on Dixon's monologue. "You know if someone hadn't gotten cute, we might've figured he was an unlucky drunk who drowned 'cause he was three sheets to the wind." He ran a hand through his hair. "Stew was known to knock back a few, and the hot tub sign is plastered with warnings for boozers. Guess the vegetables were meant to clue us in. Whoever killed Stew knew him, or at least his name."

The churning murderer's cauldron bubbled away without a conscience. How had the killer jimmied the timer to keep the Jacuzzi jets active? Tendrils of steam drifted from the super-sized hot tub.

"Jesus," I muttered. "What kind of sicko would dream this up?"

Dixon shrugged. "I suppose those are Stew's clothes. What possessed him to strip? Or do you think the killer undressed him?"

From our vantage point, we could see the clothing piled on the chair nearest his body. Car keys and a wallet sat atop Bermuda shorts.

"Say, is Stew's car parked out front?" Dixon asked.

"I'll go check." An urge to escape the insanity for a moment drove me to volunteer. "There's a tan Volvo parked on the far side of the lot. It could be Stew's."

***

After verifying the solitary car belonged to the victim, we cordoned off the crime scene and set up emergency floodlights to illuminate the area.

Three guards had joined Dixon and me. Two were fuzzy-cheeked youngsters, locals who wanted a job where they wouldn't stink of fish or have to kowtow to tourists. Carrying a gun was a big bonus. I was the same age as their mommas so they ma'amed me to death. Dirty jokes tended to die on their lips as I approached. Tonight their nervous laughter teetered toward hysteria. Laughing at death is a reflex as well as a cliché.

Dixon grimaced when a cacophony of sirens announced the arrival of the Hollis County Sheriff and his mainland coterie. "Think they'd have more sense," he mumbled. "Might as well have used a bullhorn. This racket is bound to bring out all the Nosey Parkers."

Sure enough, lights clicked on in a smattering of the pricey homes hovering above the poolscape. Perched atop stilt-like piers, the silhouetted bungalows resembled scrawny cranes.

Chief Dixon swaggered over to greet Sheriff Winston Conroy and engaged in a ritual good ol' boy greeting.

"Hey, Chief, hear you got something a tad more interesting than the usual heart attack," said Sheriff Conroy. "Gives me a chance to show your raggedy-ass island to our new officer. Meet Deputy Braden Mann."

The newcomer deputy appeared to be in his thirties. Old for a Lowcountry recruit. The lean, angular planes of his face were a bit weather-beaten, yet his limber physique spoke of resilient muscles and youthful energy. A straight back and commanding presence suggested he was used to giving the orders.

"Braden was a homicide cop in Atlanta," said the sheriff. "Likes to fish and hunt though, so he can't be all bad." He

8

motioned toward the road. "Coroner should pull in any minute. He was right behind us over the bridge. So what we got?"

As Dixon elaborated, the sheriff's face clouded. "Well, I'll be. How'd you find the body?"

Dixon nodded my way. "Marley here noticed the front gate unlocked and saw lights were out. Came round to investigate."

The sheriff stole a sideways glance at me. His quizzical look took in my uniform and age—twenty-five years senior to Dear Island's only other female officer, who was currently on-maternity leave.

"Who do we have here, Chief, another city slicker in hiding? Don't believe I've had the pleasure, ma'am."

"Marley Clark. I work part-time for Chief Dixon." We shook hands.

"Marley comes to us from the Pentagon, a colonel in Army Intelligence, no less." The chief sounded as if he wanted to one-up the sheriff.

"Just a lieutenant colonel," I corrected, not coveting a bogus promotion.

Dixon continued as though I hadn't uttered a peep. "I told Marley she was too dang young to play retiree. Besides I like having someone my own age to talk to."

The sheriff laughed. "Marley looks at least two decades younger than you, Dixon. Going to Clemson University did you in. You've aged like that bleu cheese the Ag school peddles."

"Yeah, yeah," Dixon harrumphed. "Let's get on with it."

The sheriff's sole CSI practitioner and the coroner went to work. I stood off to the side, huddled beside a lifeguard stand. The sharpened wind knifed through my soggy shirt. Massaging my arms to knead in warmth, I tried to recall my last conversation with Stew. When hands grazed my neck, I whirled, startled.

"It's Marley, right?" the deputy asked. "I'm Braden." He'd draped a jacket around my shoulders. My jitters knocked it to the ground. "Didn't mean to scare you." He smiled. "You look like you're freezing."

Before I could respond, he retrieved the jacket and wrapped me in it. "Thanks, but I can't take your coat."

"Nonsense. I'm not wet—and bleeding. How bad are those cuts?" He motioned toward my bloody knees.

"It's nothing." I was surprised he'd noticed. In all the hubbub, no one else had. "A little alcohol and a few Band-aids and I'll be fine."

"Sit down and I'll fetch a first-aid kit." He vanished before I could object.

I'm not used to being fussed over, especially by a stranger. But arguing required too much energy. Besides, until the coroner finished, Braden and I had little to do beyond shivering. A poolside lounge chair beckoned, its cushions cold and wet with dew. I was too weary to be persnickety.

In a minute, Braden returned. He knelt and rolled up the legs of my trousers. Thankfully, I'd shaved my legs, a hit or miss proposition for a woman living alone. He bit open a wet gauze pack and daubed at the cuts with a square of white cotton. The alcohol stung, but his hands felt warm, his fingers gentle. Despite the pain and cold, I began to relax. By the time he pressed down the last bandage I almost wished there were more cuts for him to doctor.

Braden snapped the first-aid kit closed and stood.

"Thanks again." I looked up and noticed Chief Dixon hovering. He dipped his chin toward Braden. "Sheriff wants you."

Then Dixon inclined his head in the direction of several bathrobe-clad residents clustered at the clubhouse entrance. He shooed me their way. "Marley, go deal with 'em, will ya?"

I slipped my arms into the deputy's loaner jacket and walked toward the residents. Recognizing the ringleader—Joe Reddick—I groaned inwardly. Recently elected to the board of the Dear Owners' Association, the former schoolteacher was puffed up with self-importance. He'd retired early after a "pain-

and-suffering" lawsuit yielded a hefty insurance settlement. My hunch was the little Napoleon had been unable to control his classroom and still itched to prove he could be boss.

"It's four a.m. I demand to know what's going on," Reddick blustered, grandstanding for the gathered throng.

"There's been a drowning." My tone straddled the territory between icy and polite. "We don't know what happened yet."

Reddick stuck out his lower jaw and crossed his arms over a protruding gut. "Well, I plan to find out. That's the sheriff, isn't it? You can't keep us in the dark. We're entitled to hear what's what. I'm going to talk to him."

I stepped directly in the fifty-year-old's path and tried reason. "This is police business. The coroner is here, and the area's off-limits."

"We'll see." Reddick attempted to dart around me.

My reaction was instantaneous and calamitous—for Reddick, that is. To counter his feint, I raised my arm like a traffic cop. He ran straight into it. His own momentum undid him. He stumbled and fell in a heap, clutching his throat as if he'd been garroted.

"Sorry," I muttered and offered a hand up. He wheezed and waved me off.

"Did you see her?" he stammered, showboating for his pajama-clad cohorts. "There's no room on our security force for thugs." His dentures lost their grip, and his attempts to click them back into place failed. "I'll p-p-press charges."

My initial chagrin at accidentally decking the guy turned to disgust. I thought of poor Stew lying dead and this jerk hoping to capitalize on the drama.

"That's right, you're the lawsuit king. Well, other folks work for a living, and that means the sheriff's still too busy to talk to you."

Reddick's performance must have convinced the rest of the rabble-rousers I was a deadly Kung Fu master. Quaking, they backed away like Chihuahuas facing a pit bull.

"The excitement's over for tonight. Go back to bed. That would help the authorities most."

God knows we need all the help we can get.

TWO

While the microwave zapped the sludge, I retrieved a Diet Coke, flipped the tab, and sighed at the energizing fizz. Pop and coffee are my two-fisted breakfast drinks. Army friends accused me of pumping caffeine to scare newcomers to my command. Truth is, my caffeine immunity is genetic. Mom drank it right before bed—to relax.

My mug tipped on its way out of the microwave. Hot coffee sloshed over the rim. "Ouch. Dammit."

Already swearing. Not a promising start to the day. My reflection in a glass cabinet door agreed. Auburn curls askew, my eyes cloaked in shadows like a cruelly aged Orphan Annie. I glanced at the clock. Ten minutes until my meeting with Deputy Braden Mann.

Crapola. No time for breakfast. I opened a jar of Jif and drubbed out a finger-full of peanut butter. Living alone had done wonders for my social graces.

Again, I mulled over my assignment as Braden's island guide. Dixon claimed my understanding of Dear's social terrain made me the logical pick. Younger officers, who couldn't afford to live on the island, were clueless. The chief also knew Dear's power structure didn't awe me. I'd taken a security job for my sanity, not to keep the wolf from my door.

Dixon had his reasons. But why had I accepted?

Catching the son-of-a-bitch who killed Stew was well worth losing a little shuteye. If local knowledge of our Mayberry by-the-sea could give Braden a head start on nailing the bastard, I was all for it.

But I had to admit there was more. The prospect of spending time with an intelligent, good-looking male wasn't repugnant. Especially since Braden was neither young enough to be my son nor old enough to recite cholesterol counts.

Conversations with fellow guards were often predictable. The men typecast me as Ann Landers with a holster.

I slurped down a final swallow of coffee, topped it with a pop chaser and hustled outside. Movement across the street snagged my attention as my neighbor Janie opened her living room blinds. Had news of Stew's murder reached her?

Janie briefly dated Stew. Then one night, he'd attempted romance and found farce. Poured wine and lit a dozen candles prearranged to surround his waterbed. The ambiance disintegrated when his wispy hair fanned out and caught fire. To extinguish the flames, Janie doused Stew with water from a handy bud base. A single rose stuck in his singed hair. Additional dates seemed out of the question.

Why Stew? I wondered for the umpteenth time. He was middle-aged and affable. As a real estate appraiser, he made a decent living. Yet he wasn't wealthy enough to be knocked off for money. For the life of me, I couldn't conjure up motives of passion or revenge. He'd routinely hit on women from the age of thirty to AARP cardholders. Yet his survival instincts were strong—married ladies remained off limits.

Though Stew was divorced, he was a proud dad who enthusiastically squired his twenty-year-old daughter around the island on every college break. Was her name Sharon? I said a silent prayer for the young woman.

Only five cars were parked in the paved lot adjacent to the Dear Owners' Association building. Whoever named the quasi-governmental body hadn't thought much about its DOA acronym, which prompted some employees to refer to it as the Deads. DOA oversees island necessities such as roads, the swing bridge that links us to our nearest island neighbor, and security. Much to his chagrin, the chief occupied an office plunked smack in the middle of the Deads' administrative fiefdom. I ran up the stairs and entered the reception area slightly out of breath.

I truly looked forward to spending time with Braden. His soft voice, calloused fingers and boyish grin exerted a magnetic pull. The single aesthetic flaw was a slightly crooked front tooth. The fact that he'd not spent money to cap it told me he wasn't obsessed with his appearance—or he had credit card debt.

I found him sitting on a cheery chintz sofa, reading an Audubon-blessed brochure on nature sanctuaries, a designation Dear began to tout shortly after its first developer shot the last wild boar. The officer looked almost preppy and seemed absorbed in his reading and courtesy coffee.

"Ready for the grand tour, Deputy Mann?"

He stood and smiled. Tan skin bunched around his brown—no, hazel—eyes. His gaze seemed both appraising and friendly. "I'm all yours, ma'am." He captured my hand in a snug grip.

"Well, call me anything but ma'am." My own smile matched his.

Dang, he hadn't used the "m" word once last night. One demerit. Perhaps it's an age-culture-geography thing, but most Midwesterners in my age group tend to prefer the screech of fingernails on a blackboard to a lazy chorus of ma'ams.

Braden correctly interpreted my unspoken subtext and laughed. "No more ma'ams, I promise. You clearly don't hail from these parts."

"Iowa," I answered. "One of those square states in the middle."

I pointed through the spotless window to my red Mustang. "We'll be less conspicuous if we're not tooling around in one of Dear's bubble tops. If it's okay with you, I'll drive."

"*Very* nice." Braden nodded admiringly at my '77 classic. "Do you let your husband drive it?"

I startled. *Let my husband drive?*

Oh, his gaze had settled on my plain gold wedding band.

15

"My husband died more than a year ago. A car accident." I never could call myself a widow. The word conjured up images of withered husks, women waiting to die.

"I'm sorry," Braden said. "I noticed your ring..."

"I should take it off. But I broke that finger. They'll have to cut the ring."

Why hadn't I bothered? Plain old inertia or something else?

When we reached the car, Braden caressed the shiny hood. "Dad bought a '77 Mustang when I was in first grade. We had that car for ten years. My father loved her."

Jeez, this guy was learning his ABCs when I was heading to college.

I'd purchased the used Mustang—in cherry condition—early in my military stint. The impulse buy spent most of its pampered life in an Iowa barn while I bounced from Augsburg to Fort Bragg and from Turkey to the Pentagon. The odometer had less than twenty thousand miles.

As my key slid into the ignition, I glanced at the deputy. He resembled a folded accordion, his knees practically tickling his chin. The seat wasn't set for his rugged, six-foot-four frame.

"Sorry." I grinned. "My last passenger was an ailing computer wedged against the dash for a ride to a repair shop. Adjust the seat any way you'd like."

Braden fiddled with a lever, stretched back, and sighed in relief. Given the comment about his dad's car, I recalculated my estimate of his age. Last night I'd pegged him as mid-thirties. Now my guess ratcheted slightly upward to early forties. He just looked younger. Athletic, trim. He even smelled good. Like a new leather purse.

He appeared to take his workouts seriously. However, they'd been powerless to halt the march of one age-related enemy—hair loss. Braden's black hair had thinned. A fact he didn't try to hide. His brush cut looked surprisingly good. Hey, spend enough time in the Army and men with long hair look a bit prissy. Jude Law excepted.

Once we reached the scene of last night's murder, I parked directly in front of the Dolphin entrance, disregarding the diminutive parking lines that decreed I was hogging two golf cart slots. While I pulled out keys to open the decorative wrought-iron grill that served as an admission gate, Braden read the posted hours.

"Is this the only way in?" he asked.

"No. It would be easy to slip in from the beach at low tide though we're talking pluff mud rather than sand for maybe three hundred feet. That muck can suck the paint right off your toenails. So Stew and the killer probably entered this way. The gate was open when I arrived.

"The young lady scheduled to lock up *thought* she'd done so. No guarantee there. Facilities are left unlocked all the time. Then again someone could have opened the gate later. Lots of people have keys."

"Including Stew?"

"No, but he knew plenty of folks who did. The fire station has a complete set of keys and another set hangs at the real estate office so agents can show off club facilities if they're closed. Dozens of club employees and all the security guards have keys, too. Helpful, huh? A list of the keyless might be shorter."

In the sparkling sunlight, the Dolphin, with its cheerful Caribbean face paint of banana yellow and hibiscus pink, looked an unlikely spot for murder. An open breezeway bisected the first floor of the two-story clubhouse, pulling visitors through to a smashing view of Mad Inlet and the Atlantic beyond. Sunrise Island lay to the right, its sugar-white beaches accessorized with the bleached bones of storm-felled trees. With the sensuous beauty of driftwood, the giant oak carcasses guarded the lush subtropical greenery to their back.

"What a view. Anyone live over there?" Braden nodded at

Sunrise.

"No. It's uninhabited. The University of South Carolina owns it and uses it primarily for sea turtle research. Sunrise was part of Dear Island before it broke in two."

"What do you mean, broke in two?"

"Hurricane Gracie made a direct hit in 1959, and today's Dear is the western half of the original island. The eastern half is Sunrise. Real estate agents gloss over this tidbit since it might prompt prospects to wonder what'll happen come the next big blow."

"That'd make me think twice," Braden agreed.

"At low tide, you can practically wade to Sunrise. But, believe me, you don't want to swim there when the tide's running strong. Every couple of years someone ignores our riptide warnings and drowns."

A blur of purple caught my eye as a figure crouched behind a lounge chair rose and sprinted toward the beach. "Hey, stop!" I took off running.

The culprit was easy to I.D. Not too many Dear residents sport purple mohawks.

"Henry Cuthbert, I'm putting in your reservation for juvie jail," I yelled after the fleeing teen. With no prayer of catching him, I braked, panting, at the edge of the concrete. Henry had three factors going for him—a head start, youth and bare feet. The pluff mud would have swallowed my size-ten cop shoes on the first tread.

Once Henry reached the water's edge, he turned to waggle both middle fingers in our direction. Then a skiff roared to his side and he dove into its well. A dune had blocked the waiting getaway boat from view. Brother Jared was driving. The whine of the motor didn't drown out their laughter.

Braden, who'd reached for his gun, re-holstered and grinned. "I take it those boys like to yank your chain."

"Yeah. Not worth chasing the pimply-faced weasels.

They're not your killers."

"Who are they?"

"Identical twins. Henry sports the purple hair. Jared tinted his plume green. We call them vampires because they usually strike between midnight and daybreak. Truth be known, we've all longed to drive stakes through their puny hairless chests. They smash mailboxes with ball bats, throw lawn furniture in pools, and mark their territory with beer cans and urine. It's gotten worse lately. Now they're terrorizing elderly residents too afraid to complain."

"Wonder what they were doing here," Braden said.

"Nothing good."

I glanced toward the Jacuzzi. The yellow caution tape had vanished—along with Stew, of course, and the vegetable potpourri. An "Out of Order" sign leaned against the dial for the hot tub's jets.

"If I hadn't been here, I'd never believe someone was murdered."

Braden shrugged. "Sheriff Conroy pushed to finish all on-site forensic work before daybreak. The last crew left at six a.m. Dear's developer must have political juice. Called in favors with SLED—the South Carolina Law Enforcement Division. He didn't want any grisly reminders of murder greeting guests this morning."

For the next half hour, we wandered the grounds and peered into every clubhouse portal. We circled the baby pool, where a hollow see-through whale made tykes long to be swallowed by a giant fish. Then we meandered among the fake outcroppings and caves crafted to make the freeform pools and fountains appear part of a natural paradise. While the plaster-of-Paris sculptures didn't quite achieve the intended ambiance, the hidden misters were a hit with children, who never failed to spy pirates lurking in the artificial fog.

Today the haze whispered against my skin like a gray

Linda Lovely

shroud. I kept glancing behind me, expecting something more lethal to materialize out of the cave's dank reaches. At the cavern's exit, the deputy stopped short. I walked right up his heels, ricocheted and wound up on my rump. Braden managed a more graceful gymnast's landing and sprang upright. He reached down and hauled me up with ease.

"You okay?" he asked.

"Yeah." I dusted off my rump. How embarrassing. "Sorry."

"Don't be. Can't remember the last time a woman fell for me."

His sly smile and lifted eyebrow made me blush. Did he think I planned my little trip?

"Glad you have a sense of humor. The last guy who landed at my feet threatened to sue."

"He must have been crazy." Braden reached over and tugged gently on one of my curls. "A piece of moss." He showed me the speck of furry green he'd extracted.

A light-headed moment ensued. Jeez. Was he flirting? How did you tell?

I'd been a chunky teen, shy around boys. The years most girls spent learning to flirt, I'd aced advanced placement classes, played clarinet in the marching band, and won the Iowa State debate championships. I hadn't exactly flunked flirting, just never matriculated in how-to-date school. Once basic training rendered my baby fat to muscle, who needed to flirt? The Army's male-to-female ratio erased any deficiency.

Braden pointed toward the Jacuzzi. "The murderer could have stood inside this overhang and been invisible," he said. "There's a direct line of sight. I did a little research last night. In Russia and some East European countries, police use stunners that can be fired twenty feet from the target, and there's no telltale confetti. It's possible our victim never saw his killer."

I frowned. "Stew may not have seen his killer, but my bet is he knew him. I can't imagine Stew skinny-dipping alone.

20

Probably meeting someone—the 'someone' who murdered him. Otherwise, we'd have two dead bodies or a hysterical witness. He knew his killer."

"You have a candidate?"

"No. Stew's life seemed pretty dull." I shared the scarce details that circulated the island about the man's job, occasional dates, and his golf and fishing hobbies.

When Braden questioned me, I named the women Stew occasionally squired, but couldn't come up with a single male confidante. He'd been friendly with everyone, good friends with no one. If it weren't for my neighbor, Janie Spark, I might have rowed in the same sad boat. But Janie was determined to rescue me from my tendency to hibernate.

"Okay. Let's try another tack," the deputy said. "The chief said you could give me a rundown on the island's shadier characters. Could Stew have crossed one of them?"

"Honestly, I can't think of anyone vicious enough to be a murderer. And I hate to repeat rumors. They flourish like weeds on Dear. Ninety-percent are pure baloney or plain malicious."

Braden looked me in the eye. "Look, I promise to keep my mouth shut. I grew up in a small town. If you dig in the local dirt, you find worms. But I've never come across a weirder murder, and I need all the help I can get."

The man's honest admission of his clueless state had definite appeal. Unfortunately I inhabited the same unaware zip code. "Okay, get ready for a scintillating busman's tour of Dear, complete with gossip commentary.

"Since you've met the two youngest members of the household, let's start with the Cuthberts."

***

Sitting at the southern terminus of Dear Drive, the manicured lawns of the Cuthbert estate practically oozed money. The green played against a backdrop of vivid blue sea and white-hot dunes.

After we parked, Braden let out an appreciative whistle at the spectacular home that straddled a trio of ocean lots. "Wow. This little getaway cost some serious change."

The elegant exterior featured acres of bronzed glass with columns of muted tabby—crushed seashells imprisoned in a web of mortar.

"Grace Cuthbert built it for four million," I said as we climbed out of the car. "Bet it's worth twice as much now."

"So why are we here? Is there a skeleton in her closet?"

"Well, it's gospel—not gossip—that Grace is an alcoholic. We've met a handful of times, once when I caught her twins cruising the island at four a.m. Grace lives with Hugh Wells, a former Las Vegas lounge lizard, reputed to have mob connections. But even if Hugh had wise guy contacts in the past, he appears to be enjoying early retirement courtesy of Grace's largesse."

Braden frowned. "The murder doesn't have a mob signature. Still, I'll check him out."

"Chief Dixon worries more about Grace's sons than her lover," I added. "They're a two-headed plague. Thank heaven they're corralled in a boarding school most of the year. They're on spring break now."

"Are they screwed up enough to murder someone?"

"No." I didn't need to think about my response. "They're just obnoxious punks. A surplus of hormones and cash."

"How would Stew have known these folks?"

"He wasn't exactly a friend of the family," I replied, "though he fished with Hugh occasionally and appraised property for the Cuthbert trust. Grace has lots of investments. She fronted twenty million to finance the island's newest development, Beach West."

"No kidding. What's the lady worth?"

"Gossips claim $500 million. Inherited. Her family holds thousands of shares of Leapgene. Her great-grandfather founded the company."

Braden scuffed at some sand in the rutted cul de sac. His bunched eyebrows suggested puzzlement. "Do many multi-millionaires hang their hats here? I don't mean to insult, but Dear Island doesn't look, well...ritzy enough."

"Few fulltime residents are truly wealthy, though more and more second homeowners qualify. Arthur Zantoc, the famous artist, hibernates here, but with four ex-wives, he probably has less disposable income than I do."

The timbre of Braden's laugh hinted that he might be making alimony payments. Hmm, no wedding band. Too bad I'm not ten years younger and hot to trot. Oh well, it was nice to enjoy a baritone laugh.

While I *knew* he was too young for me, I felt certain Janie would love to make Braden's acquaintance. When it came to dating, my neighbor, who was actually a month older than me, refused to discriminate on any basis—race, creed, social status or age.

I shook my head to chase away incipient fantasies. Had to be lack of sleep. Or failure to invest in batteries.

"You're right about the island lacking glitz. Besides, if rich folks want seclusion, they buy their own islands. A sultan owns one maybe fifteen minutes from here by boat."

"What about the developer?" Braden asked. "Stew must have dealt with him."

"There are actually two developers. Partners. We'll drive by Gator's place next."

We climbed in the Mustang and retraced our route at a twenty-five-mile-per-hour crawl. That's the island speed limit except on gravel roads, where it drops to fifteen. The funereal pace surely mortified my Mustang.

I idled my car just short of a lavender McMansion with an ocean view. "There's Gator Caldwell."

We watched as a short fireplug of a man injected his untidy

body into a sleek Ferrari.

"I assume Gator's a nickname. Does he wrestle them or something?"

I laughed. "He went to the University of Florida. Though he flunked out freshman year, he became a rabid football fan."

I didn't mention that Gator's pointy little teeth could have inspired the moniker. While they looked undersized, there seemed to be too many jagged incisors for the size of his mouth.

"Is the guy loaded?" Braden asked as the Ferrari purred to life.

"Depends who's talking. I hear vendors grouse that the Dear Company is way behind in paying bills. Stew did a lot of business with Gator. Used to join him at the marina bar for happy hour."

"What's Gator's background?"

"When he dropped out of college, he went home to Alabama. Made a mint as a paving contractor. Then he met up with B.J. Falcon, who put together the investment group to buy Dear after the last real estate slump pushed it into foreclosure."

"So is B.J. the brains of the outfit?"

"Well, it's no longer B.J. He literally got caught with his pants down. His ex-wife, Sally, now owns his shares in the Dear Company. She's vice president and director of marketing."

Gator zoomed around his circular drive. Even from a distance, his scowl was noticeable.

"Doesn't appear to be a happy man," Braden remarked. "Does it gall him, having a female partner?"

"Surprisingly, I don't think so. Sally's smoother than her ex and shrewd. Worked in her hubby's office fifteen years. She hatched the ideas; B.J. took the credit. She's much better than B.J. at schmoozing with high-roller types. She lives on the island with a ten-year-old daughter and her mom, who keeps house."

Braden made a note to arrange interviews with both Dear Company execs.

We gave Gator's exhaust fumes time to dissipate before we toddled in his wake. As we approached the intersection of Dear Drive and Egret Way, Jack Bride's golf cart pulled onto the verge beside of the road. Virulent slogans plastered the man's distinctive ride: "Stop Dear's Ecology Killers," "Cousteau Would Weep," "Crimes Against Nature."

Jack's arms waved wildly as he harangued two guys preparing to fell a huge live oak in the side yard of a vacation bungalow.

Braden swiveled in his seat to watch the histrionics as we drove past. "I was about to inquire about mentally unbalanced islanders. Do I have a candidate?"

"That's Jack Bride. I don't recall him having any beef with Stew." I instantly grimaced at my unintended pun. "God, I didn't mean it to come out that way. Dr. Bride's an ecology extremist. Got very upset when they broke ground for Beach West. The parcel's mostly swamp and jungle—or as the P.R. flacks put it, 'magnificent marsh and unspoiled subtropical forest.'

"Last week, when workers started toppling trees, Jack swung a discarded piece of rebar like a baseball bat. Banged up some equipment but didn't hit anyone. He's been a nuisance, screaming at Gator, defacing signs. There's a restraining order to keep him off company property. He's quite vocal about Dear's developers being ecology scumbags and crooks."

"Is he dangerous?"

"No. He's actually quite sweet."

Braden smiled. "You're a softie. Is there anything to his accusations?"

"No comment. I've heard Gator boast that any developer worth his salt has gone bankrupt at least three times. And his background is salty enough to advertise himself as a country ham. I don't know whether he achieved bankruptcy the old-fashioned way—stupidity and greed—or if some illegal scam caught up with him."

I turned the car onto Blue Heron. The street runs parallel to several holes on the golf course's back nine. We'd almost reached my own driveway when a chubby, gray-haired lady darted through an opening in the pines on a vacant lot.

"Help me. Help me," she screamed as she ran into the road.

Braden jumped out of the car before the Mustang shuddered to a stop.

"What's wrong?" he yelled as he ran toward a disheveled Mrs. Barnwell.

"An alligator...it's eating my baby." She was hysterical. "Oh my poor Candi. Please help. Hurry."

I abandoned the car and blew by the woman. I'd closed on Braden's heels when he drew his gun. "Braden, you can't shoot. Alligators are protected."

"Are you crazy," he fired back at me. "It's killing a child."

"Candi's her poodle," I wheezed.

As we neared the edge of the lagoon, there was a pitiful squeal and a fluffy patch of white sank out of sight. In an instant, all signs of life—alligator and poodle—disappeared. A thick carpet of duckweed slime resealed itself above the opening where we'd witnessed Candi's last gasp. The brackish water went still. No ripples to indicate movement below.

"Jesus Christ." Braden holstered his gun and stared at a little six-foot gator sunning itself a few feet away. This reptile clearly wasn't the culprit. "Did her poodle fall in the water? Surely these things can't chase down a dog."

"Don't bet on it. They've been clocked at thirty-five miles an hour for short bursts. Come on. Let's collect Mrs. Barnwell and take her home."

Since I was driving, Braden assumed the role of grief counselor, bundling the elderly woman into the back seat and patting her hand on the ride to her condo. He talked so softly I couldn't distinguish his words, but whatever he said soothed her. A nice guy. When we reached Mrs. Barnwell's condo, he sat with her while I knocked on doors to find a neighbor willing to assume our comforting duties.

As we watched the ladies mount the front steps, Braden shook his head. "I've been on Dear Island—what?—three hours tops, and I've gone for my gun twice. Unbelievable. In Atlanta's worst neighborhoods, I could go months without touching my piece."

I chuckled. "You just haven't figured out all our idiosyncrasies."

"Hard to believe. Not a car in sight. It's quiet as a tomb. Yet we've got a weirdo murder, vampire teens and alligator attacks. I heard Hollywood sometimes uses Dear Island as a movie set. Sure they're not making *Curse of the Voodoo* and forgot to tell you?"

I started the car. "Have to admit this is more excitement than usual."

"How many people live here full time?" he asked.

"Under a thousand. The island's sparsely populated in spring. Except for Easter. The holiday bumps the population up to three thousand with tourists and second homeowners. We don't see Hilton Head's traffic, but we get our share in summer. Upwards of ten thousand over the Fourth of July. It's a wonder the island doesn't sink. That's when most residents flee north."

I headed the car toward the front gate.

"Residents are mostly Yankees?" Braden asked, unconsciously seasoning his "Yankee" pronunciation with a dash of bitters.

"Are you asking about *damn Yankees*?" I teased, eyebrows lifted.

"Hey, I didn't say that. I married a New Yorker."

"My apologies." *Really.* Why wasn't he wearing *his* wedding band? "We transplants need to stick together. Give her my best."

"Doubtful. We only speak when I pick up my sons. I'm divorced."

"Sorry."

Unsure how to smooth over this conversational speed bump, I kept my mouth closed until we reached our final destination, the island's Disney-esque security gate.

"Thought you'd like to see the visitor logs. I'll run in and get them."

"Mind if I come along? I'd like to see your security setup."

"Not at all, but there's not much to see. It's all form, no function. Something tangible to foster a private island cachet. Mom used to say we had a one-butt kitchen. Our guardhouse qualifies as a two-butt affair."

Braden laughed. I opened a side door facing the exit-the-island lane and spoke to the young guard on duty as we squeezed inside. "Hey, Joey. Don't mind us."

Joey stood facing incoming traffic, the top half of his Dutch door open to dole out visitor passes.

A computer console corralled Braden and me on our side of the gatehouse. Our bodies touched. His breath warmed the back of my neck. He placed his hands on my shoulders, stroked down with his thumbs. "In quarters this tight, I figured you'd want to know where my hands are," he whispered, giving my shoulders a squeeze.

The contact triggered decidedly impure thoughts. *Hope he isn't a mind reader.* Braden didn't seem to notice my quickened pulse.

"How hard is it to get onto this island?" Braden shuffled through a stack of car passes waiting to be filled out. "How private is private?"

"Not very," I admitted. "In theory, only homeowners with auto decals, their guests, and renters with resort passes can enter. No deterrent for a smart thief—or murderer. If I wanted in, I'd pick a name and address out of the phone book. Then I'd call security saying I was Jill Schmo of 544 Turtle Cay, expecting my aunt, Dana Schmo. An hour later I'd drive up, flash a grin, and claim to be Dana Schmo. The guard would smile, hand over a pass, and wish me a nice visit."

To make my point, Joey sang out "Have a nice day" and waved on a carload of tourists.

"Here's yesterday's log." I held out the book. "Dixon said he'd fax a copy of the paperwork to the sheriff. We'll canvass every owner who supposedly called in guests. Of course, dozens of folks come on island every day in vans with contractor decals. Guards just wave them through. No one pays attention to the working blokes inside. Someone could even sneak in by boat. Our security sieve has too many leaks to narrow your suspect list."

Braden glanced at his watch. "Shoot. I need to be in Charleston by two for the autopsy. I'd better scoot."

We bid Joey goodbye and filed outside. I drove Braden back to his car. He thanked me for the tour and asked for my cell number in case he had questions.

"I'm one of North America's last holdouts—no cell." I scribbled my landline home number on the back of a security office business card.

"Will you be home tonight?" he asked.

I hesitated. "A friend asked me to attend a real estate banquet. But I'm in no mood."

"Real estate? Bet they'll talk plenty about Stew."

"I guess. Developers, agents, bankers, Dear's financial backers—they all knew him."

"Then you should go. You might hear something. Unlike me, you'll blend in. I could call tomorrow, see if you picked up any interesting tidbits."

Janie, you've got a date. My sudden change of heart would delight my neighbor, who didn't need to know the reason for my three-sixty.

Braden was pleasant company despite the somber circumstances. The contrast between his lazy accent and no-nonsense manner intrigued me. He was a straight shooter. He told you what he was thinking, and expected you to do the same. An admirable trait.

I tried not to think about his clean leather scent, those strong hands, or whether he was always so quick on the draw.

THREE

With more than an hour to kill before my next official duty, I headed home to grab a Diet Coke. The nearness of home—always right around the corner—was one of Dear Island's nicest features.

En route, I noticed the island's oversized flag hanging at half-staff in Stew's honor. Security lowered the flag whenever an islander died. Then residents stopped at the guard gate to learn the identity of the Dear departed. Given the island's geriatric profile, the flag languished in a mourning slump far too often. Today's tribute made me especially sad. By island standards, fifty-five-year-old Stew had been a mere youngster, way too young to die.

A ringing telephone prompted me to unlock my door in a hurry. A click sounded and the line went dead. I tightened my grip, strangling the silent plastic. The flag. All those deaths. The white noise pulled me back to another phone call. Another empty silence.

"Hello, who's speaking, please? Is this Mrs. Sherman?"

"No," I answered, annoyed. I figured the solicitous voice wanted to sell me a time-share. Friends and family knew I'd kept my maiden name.

"Could I please speak to Mrs. Sherman?" the voice persisted.

"There is no Mrs. Sherman, but I'm Jeff Sherman's wife, who's calling?" My tone was ice-cold. Intended to freeze any salesman's zeal.

"I'm sorry. Your husband's been in an accident. Could you please come to St. Mark's hospital?"

"Accident? Jeff's hurt? What happened?"

"I'm sorry I don't have details. Please come to the hospital," the monotone voice continued.

"Wait, just tell me. How badly is Jeff hurt?"

31

My heart raced. I heard a click. The bastard never said goodbye. Just hung up.

"Goddammit!" *I screamed into the silence.*

I realized the phone in my death grip was hundreds of miles and thirteen months removed from the one in Virginia. My stomach did a flip and cold sweat beaded my forehead. I breathed deeply remembering the call's aftermath. The nurse shepherded me into the hospital's family room. When the doctor walked in, he didn't need to say a word.

I chalked up the flashback to stress, lack of sleep, and another death picking at the scab of my memory. Sitting on my bed, I rolled my neck to unkink tight muscles. Then I phoned Janie and told her she had a "date" for the evening's banquet.

On Dear, most social activities came with implied Noah's Ark invites: you were expected to arrive in twos. So, as uncoupled women, Janie and I often served as ersatz dates for each other when we couldn't squirm out of obligatory appearances. Janie had no shot at wiggling out of tonight's bash. As Gator's right hand, she'd planned this soiree.

With my evening plans cemented, I headed to the fire station and found the training room packed. I sank into a folding chair at the back as my boss stomped to the podium.

"Listen up," Chief Dixon began. "I've been locked up all morning with Gator, Sally and the DOA board. Miracle of miracles, they agree. They want security beefed up till the sheriff figures out if Stew's death is some isolated incident or if we've got some weirdo stalking islanders. Until further notice, all days off are canceled."

Moans and groans floated up from the audience.

"Yeah, yeah. But you'll get double pay for overtime."

An audible sigh greeted the news.

"Gator and the Deads agree on something else," he added. "We're gonna zipper up on this murder. Not one word to an islander, not a peep to outsiders. Stew's death happened too late to make today's *Hollis Times*, but you can bet half the island already knows."

Half? I'd have wagered more like ninety percent, given the breathless news report on WGCO, a golden oldies station with a loyal island following.

"Sheriff Conroy doesn't want details of the murder to become public," the chief added. "So if anyone asks, Stew drowned, period. Say the investigating ball's in the sheriff's court. Tell anyone who asks that we're adding patrols. Hell, tell 'em even if they don't ask. Okay, that's it. New shifts are posted."

I stood. The chief foiled my attempt at a fast getaway. "Hey, Marley, wait up."

Drat. He probably wanted to chat about Joe Reddick's knockdown. At the time of our little set-to, Dixon was huddled with Sheriff Conroy and missed the theatrics.

"How did things go with the detective? Does the guy know what he's doing?"

I gave a short, positive report on Braden, then tried once more to vamoose.

"Not so fast. What in Sam Hill did you do to Reddick? The idiot came by this morning with his throat swathed in so many bandages I thought he was wearing a neck brace. Swears you beat up on him."

I rolled my eyes. "Oh, for Pete's sake. I stuck out my arm and the imbecile stormed into it. I was trying to keep him out of a roped-off crime scene."

"Well, Reddick claims he suffered public humiliation. Wants you to write an apology and get anger management counseling. Says if you don't, he'll sue."

"Do you really think he'd stand up in court and say a woman beat the crap out of him? His testimony would be a lot more humiliating than falling on his behind. But maybe I do need anger management 'cause I'm sure as hell teed-off now." I took a deep breath. "I don't need this, and neither do you. I'll resign."

"Oh, no, you won't," Dixon snapped. "If you quit, Reddick wins. This'll blow over. Just stay out of his way. I can't afford to lose you."

"Okay. I'll play it by ear. But make no mistake: I'll resign before I'll kowtow to that blowhard."

The chief's shoulders slumped. "All right, all right."

I turned and walked to the posted assignment roster. My next shift began at midnight. *Whoopee.* Now that I had a dinner date, I had just enough time for a short run and a catnap.

***

Ladies over fifty get horny.

I don't recall this topic being covered in Biology 101. Of course, at age sixteen, such news would have had the same relevance as learning that Martians eat tacos. Back then who dreamt we'd ever reach our dotage, living more than four decades?

I was having a hard time shaking my naptime vision. It had been quite real and Braden's role disturbingly vivid. He sat on the side of the Jacuzzi, just like Stew might have before he got zapped. Like Stew, Braden was buck-naked.

But the rangy detective of my dreams was very much alive when he stood and beckoned me with an enticing smile and something grander south of the border.

Get a grip, girlfriend. Braden undoubtedly thinks of you as an island geezer. This is strictly business. Of course, a little fantasy never hurt a soul.

I turned the shower on full force and waited until steam wafted around the curtain. Standing beneath the spray, I didn't hear the doorbell if, indeed, it sounded. The creaking bathroom door scared me silly.

"Hey, it's me," Janie called. "How long till you're ready?"

My D.C.-area habit of bolting all doors had not lost its grip.

34

That meant Janie had let herself in, using a key provided for emergencies. For a moment, the temptation to snatch it away made my fingers twitch. But my annoyance dissolved quickly. My neighbor was too good-hearted. I couldn't stay mad at her.

"You about gave me cardiac arrest. Never sneak up on a lady in the shower. Hitchcock's *Psycho*, remember? Don't you suffer from the showerus-interruptus syndrome?"

"Not me," Janie chirped and tossed her hair—a tawny gold following this week's beauty parlor consult. "I'm constantly hoping someone *will* join me in the shower."

She had to be the most cheerful fifty-something on the planet. She'd married disastrously in her twenties. After two years of wedlock, she found her husband in bed with her younger sister. Since then, Janie had courted an image as a carefree vamp who preferred independence and her cat to any permanent live-in male.

The gossip she'd endured as a result of her family's predilections—her older sister ran a "gentleman's club"—inoculated her against the vicissitudes of public opinion. She didn't give an eyelash what anyone said about her lifestyle or appearance.

While Janie took great care with makeup and clothes, the results often appeared chaotic. With her current retro-fifties/sixties look, she sported a June Allyson-style pageboy and wore shirtwaists to the office and hot pink palazzo pants out on the town.

"Go away," I ordered. "I'll be out of the shower in two shakes of my booty."

Ten minutes later, I joined my friend in the living room. She sat in my recliner, feet up, sorting my mail. Initially Janie's brashness grated. But I'd gotten past it. We were fellow island outcasts and nearly the same age. More importantly, she was my one and only Dear confidant. She was more than a poster child for individuality; she was nonjudgmental. A rare treasure.

"Want to pay my bills, too?" I asked.

"You ought to see my stack." She looked up and voiced a good-natured harrumph. "It's not fair. You look like a million with no makeup. Sigourney Weaver, eat your heart out."

Ever since the first *Alien* movie, I've been kidded about being Sigourney's look-alike. I'm tallish—five-foot-nine—with curly, okay unruly, auburn hair and dark brown eyes. More importantly, Sigourney and I both know how to hold a big-ass gun—a resemblance my Intel compatriots chortled over.

Janie Spark managed the real estate office, figured commissions, kept Gator's calendar, wrote his letters and performed—with apparent good cheer—chores that would have steamed me. I mean, who shops for the boss's wife in this day? Who shrugs off pats on the rump? Janie, that's who.

Whenever I mouthed off about Gator's male chauvinism, she reminded, "Hey, it pays the bills and I get a piece of the action."

For her duties, she claimed one-quarter of a percent of all real estate commissions—a chunk of change growing into a plump nest egg as selling prices for Dear homes rebounded after the last mortgage implosion. Many properties were once again stickered with million-dollar-plus price tags.

"I came early so you could fill me in. I'm sick about Stew. He wasn't my type, but I really liked him. Does the sheriff have any idea who killed him?"

"Can't tell you a thing you don't already know. First, because the chief would kill me. Second, because you undoubtedly know more than I do. It's a safe bet you eavesdropped on every word of your boss's powwow with security and the cops."

Janie winked. "Closed doors mean diddly if you know your air ducts. Mostly Gator shouted about the need to restore calm before the Easter holiday. He tongue-lashed Chief Dixon pretty good. Told him to do whatever it took to make people feel safe.

'Course, Gator's got reason to be testy. Easter week is a rental sellout and a real estate bonanza, and my bosses have piles of unpaid bills."

I rolled my eyes. "Unfortunately that harangue by your boss means I have to make it an early and utterly sober evening. I go on patrol at midnight."

"Yeah, what a hardship for a boozer like you. When you're feeling frisky, you knock back a light beer. Good thing I can drink for the both of us."

Janie stopped in front of my hallway mirror to poof up her hair.

"Keep those Vulcan ears of yours cocked tonight," I said. "Let's see if anyone mentions Stew arguing with an irate client. I promised Braden to play detective and pass along any clues."

Janie chuckled. "Ah, Braden is it? I heard the deputy's a hunk. You calling dibs?"

I shook my head dismissively, but the id component of my brain waffled.

Yeah, maybe I am.

***

When we ventured outside, an impenetrable, white fog blinded us. In the spring, chilly ocean currents and warm, fragrant air often skirmished over the season, cloaking many evenings in a white shroud.

"Let's take my golf cart," Janie suggested. "We won't be moving as fast if we hit something."

"Yeah, and we won't have seat belts either."

Like many islanders, Janie put more miles on her golf cart than her car. Not me. I was able-bodied enough to walk anywhere on the island in daylight and less than keen about after-dark golf cart rambles. I always fretted that the SUV riding my bumper would squash me like one of the island's million-plus palmetto bugs—*cockroaches* to a native Iowan.

"It'll be easier to find parking," she persisted.

Linda Lovely

"You've just forgotten how to parallel park your Caddy," I accused.

Resigned, I followed her to a golf cart that boasted a Mercedes-style hood ornament and—to my Yankee consternation—a horn that blared the opening bars of "Dixie."

As we doddered down the curbless roads, ocean breezes crocheted the mist, yielding startling black holes that defined the fog's lacework. The result seemed both fragile and menacing. We inched ahead in the amber cocoon created by our headlights. Mist dampened the normal April symphony of tiny tree frogs, each one smaller than a thumbnail.

A deep-throated roar penetrated the gloom—the primeval mating call of a bull alligator.

"You hear that?" I shuddered. As temperatures warmed, so did the blood and appetites of alligators, creatures that abstained from sex as well as food during winter. Come spring they were horny and voracious.

"Yeah, I heard an alligator provided a floor show for that law enforcement hunk you squired around today." She tented an eyebrow. "Of course, I've always suspected you see the alligators as a help in enforcing leash laws."

"Hey, I'm not that callous," I objected, shuddering as I imagined the terror Mrs. Barnwell's poodle felt when it was hauled beneath the green ooze.

It was unfair to label me as anti-pooch. I reserved my ire for owners who let their petite Fidos or jumbo Plutos poop on sand dunes, stick wet noses in my crotch, or make a growling charge at me with teeth bared. Twice canines sank teeth into my ankles while I ran on the beach.

"If only people would keep dogs on leashes at the beach. Maybe we should advertise that alligators sometimes lurk in the surf."

My first sighting of an alligator out for an ocean dip shocked me. I'd thought the prehistoric reptiles confined

38

themselves to fresh water. I even asked a ranger at Wilderness Point Park if I'd hallucinated. He said alligators aren't crazy about saltwater and have no salt glands for prolonged stays, but will take the plunge to shed parasites, heal wounds, or simply travel from point A to point B.

"Great, Marley, spread tales about surfing gators and I'll never retire. This is paradise. We don't mention alligators, flesh-eating no-see-ums or palmetto bugs big enough to saddle."

"Don't lecture me, friend. You started this with your crack about a gator floor show."

"Okay, we're here. I'll behave if you will."

Here was the entrance to the Dear Club, a thirty-year-old edifice. The latest island developer had spent four hundred thousand dollars on a facelift, but the major surgery yielded disappointing results. The cosmetic tucks and stitches remained obvious. Rain wept through ill-fitting windows and pooled in carpeted sinkholes, breeding oases for mold spores. However, if you kept your eyes on the intricate crown moldings, starched white linens and swanky delicacies served at soirées, the Dear Club made a passing stab at elegance.

I spied Jack Bride's golf cart blocking the entrance. With shoulders hunched, the avid gardener busily shoveled material from a wooden cargo bed fastened in the space typically reserved for ferrying golf clubs.

"Oh crap," I muttered, knowing I'd precisely summed up the problem. "Let me out. I'll try to cajole Dr. Bride into going home before someone calls security."

I approached the angry septuagenarian with faked nonchalance. The retired professor of etymology and his wife, Claire, moved to the island when deer outnumbered people. Six months ago, he'd buried Claire, a lovely lady who succumbed to Alzheimer's. A lot of people dismissed Bride as a nutter, but I admired him. He insisted on caring for his wife at home, even though his devotion took a heavy toll.

His white-hot hatred of Dear's developer stemmed from a letter he received a year ago revoking the couple's club membership. To maintain a semblance of normal life, Dr. Bride occasionally took his wife out for supper. One night, she hallucinated the waiters were armed gunmen and briefly freaked. The club's tactless response earned an ardent enemy.

The manure in the back of Dr. Bride's buggy heavily scented the air. As he inserted his shovel in the steamy pile, I placed a hand on his shoulder. He spun toward me, his shovel raised like a club. For a moment, I feared he'd bonk me. His greasy gray hair looked like it hadn't seen a comb in days. His bloodshot eyes darted wildly as if searching for unseen demons.

"Jack, please don't do this. If they call the sheriff, he'll cart you to jail."

Dr. Bride lowered his smelly load. "Oh, it's you." His gaze bored into mine.

He looked me up and down, taking in my purple pantsuit, considerably uptown from my usual T-shirt and shorts attire. "You're not joining them, are you? I heard they were having some fancy banquet. Celebrating their butchery of our island. Gathering to shovel more crapola. So I decided to do likewise. Let the bastards step in it. Let 'em reek."

I touched the hand gripping the shovel. "You're angry. But, Jack, if you go to jail, who's left to apply pressure? Try to keep them honest? There are better ways to protest. Sic DHEC on them. Get the university involved."

I squeezed his hand.

"It's Claire's birthday," he said softly. A tear rolled down his cheek.

"Think what Claire would have wanted. Go home, Jack."

He nodded, head down, shoulders stooped. Slowly he got in his cart and slipped away, leaving only a few shovels' worth of manure to decorate the marble-tiled portico.

"You're a wonder." Janie grinned. "What did you say to the

old coot?"

"Hey, how about a little compassion?" I snapped. "He's not an old coot, just distraught. His crusade's a way to deal with his grief."

"Sorry. I didn't mean to be flip. Let's find someone to hose off the tile."

Figuring we might nab some kitchen workers taking a smoke break, we meandered around to the side entrance. We hadn't walked far when Janie grabbed my arm.

"Look over there. What in hell has gotten into everyone? It looks like Sally may take off one of her stilettos and hammer it through Gator's head."

A spotlight used to accent the club's frou-frou landscaping spilled light on Sally's rage-reddened face. Often she played the Southern belle, shamelessly flattering her senior partner. Tonight, though, she was giving Gator what-for, poking a red-lacquered fingernail in his chest and adopting his curse-laced lexicon. The "Goddammit" and "Summabitch" seasonings rang clear across the yard, but not the conversational meat.

Janie collared an unlucky club employee and sent him to scoop the poop.

"Let's get to the banquet room," she muttered. "This better not be a preview. I didn't work my fanny off organizing this shindig for them to pull this crap."

We entered the lounge adjacent to the banquet room. Though things seemed peaceful, Janie stiffened and moaned. "Oh great, Gator brought his wife. Bea was supposed to be out of town. Wait till Sally sees her. If you thought she was mad before..."

"Don't you like Sally? I thought you two got along."

"We do," Janie answered. "For a while, Bea carped at Gator to fire me. Didn't want him to spend so much time with *another woman*. Said a male assistant lent more prestige. Sally stood up for me. Hell, if a catfight does break out, I'll dive right in and claw on Sally's behalf."

Janie snagged two caviar-smeared crackers from a wandering server before she continued. "Bea is none too keen about Sally being a company officer. But Gator's explained the facts of life—he doesn't have the money to buy Sally out. Plus I think Little-Miss-Trophy-Wife finally decided Sally and I were too decrepit to be competition. As if either of us would share a bed with Gator. Yuck."

Bea accepted a tall pink drink from the bartender. While the bottle redhead was young—late twenties—I suspected her rebuilt chassis had high-mileage. According to the island rumor mill, a steamy extramarital affair had allowed the former masseuse to trade up the husband ladder from the roofer she'd left behind. That was three years ago.

Bea, like the clubhouse, had been treated to a makeover. Women who'd met Bea in her former life swear the woman once sported a nose like Cyrano and had difficulty filling a "B" cup. Now her nose was bobbed so short I wondered how she kept on sunglasses. Conversely her boobs had ballooned to the size of blue-ribbon eggplants.

The overhaul hadn't improved the woman's disposition. I'd never seen a spontaneous smile. Maybe Botox injections made her lips incapable of one.

Janie leaned close and whispered in my ear. "The last time Sally dropped by, she asked if I knew why Bea didn't wear underpants. When I shook my head, she provided the answer—'To get a better grip on her broom.'"

Janie chortled so hard she choked on her canapé.

As we walked toward the bar, Gator and Sally arrived, smiles plastered on their faces. However, Sally's complexion remained mottled by anger. The minute Gator came into grabbing range, Bea snagged his arm and clung to him like kudzu.

Sally spied us and strode purposely our way. The woman

was an enigma. Bright, decisive, articulate, funny. Yet when men gathered round, she regressed into a simpering belle routine. Janie labeled it camouflage: the good old boys paid her less attention if she conformed to stereotype. The strategy let her siphon information she could put to good use.

"Hey, Janie, Marley," she said. "I want y'all to do me a tiny favor. Don't make a fuss when you see I shuffled the place cards. I put you two at the table with Bea and Gator and switched me 'cross the room. Now I could have fun sittin' by Bea and taking potshots, but most whiz over her pointy little head, and I promised I'd lay off Princess Titsy tonight."

"Okay, but that's no tiny favor," Janie replied. "Remind my boss that I'm worth twice my salary."

"You got it." Sally winked and snagged a glass of wine from a waiter.

For the next half hour, we milled. Janie chatted; I eavesdropped. As a known quantity with no stake in the island's real estate games, I functioned as sound-absorbing wallpaper. But, while everyone talked about Stew, not a soul speculated on enemies or motives. His colleagues seemed as puzzled as the cops.

When Sally finally strode to the podium, I was quite ready to heed her request that everyone take a seat. Janie and I slid into chairs at a round, eight-person table. Gator and Bea sat directly across from us.

Gator had prematurely gray hair, a florid face, and jagged teeth yellowed from nicotine. According to Janie, he had the attention span of a gerbil, a host of nervous tics, and was pure good ol' boy, though his friendship code required no sanctions for backstabbing.

Watching Bea pet him was enough to make a grown woman gag. You'd have thought Gator was a matinee idol. Apparently Bea wasn't about to let another young hussy steal her prize. Having massaged Gator's tired muscles—all of them—when he was wed to the first Mrs. Caldwell, the lady knew how easy it was to tempt her man to stray.

Bea was famous for verbally abusing the help and loudly criticizing anyone who didn't show her deference. Employing the royal "we," she also issued proclamations about proper club attire. I suspected Bea engineered the club's ouster of Dr. Bride. Of course, if she'd actually written the letter, it wouldn't have been so lucid. Her verbs and nouns fought like cats and dogs. Remedial English would have been a better investment than her boob job.

As we pulled our chairs into the table, Janie introduced me to the only stranger, Woodrow—Woody—Nickel, the company's new real estate sales manager.

"Nice to meet you." His killer smile sported enough white enamel to coat a soup kettle. Yet there was no warmth in his dental grimace.

Janie said he was a fraternity brother of Gator's brought on board to prepare for the Beach West sales push. My friend already despised him. She'd called secretaries at his former workplace to check him out. They described Woody as a macho cad who believed all women had pea brains. Janie figured it would be interesting to watch Sally demolish him.

In fairness, Woody was handsome in a male-model, gel-haired vein. But even without prior coaching, his name-dropping chatter would have left me cold. It was "I-this" and "I-that." His buttering of Gator made me want to toss my cookies. However, since Nickel didn't bother to converse with me, there was no need to make nice.

Throughout dinner, the agents talked ad nauseam about real estate. They were giddy at the thought of pent-up demand for Beach West lots—sorry, *homesites*. Janie reminded me regularly that "homesites" sold for double the money of "lots."

A map of the new development, displayed by the podium, showed 160 parcels in Beach West's Phase One. The new homesites were about one-third the size of lots on the "mature" side of the island where my house sat. Yet asking prices were double those for resale lots. Go figure.

Across the table, Bea recounted her victory of the day. She'd ordered the starter at the golf course to eject the Cuthbert twins for wearing T-shirts. Horror of horrors.

"Everyone knows we require collared shirts," she sniffed.

Gator squirmed. It's seldom politic to enforce dress codes for kids when you depend on their heiress mom to write million-dollar checks.

The developer deliberately snubbed his wife and turned the conversational tide back to Stew. The agents sang the victim's praises. "Nice guy." "Honest." "Easy to work with."

Gradually, the tributes meandered into a discussion of the "accident's" potential sales impact. "It was so unseemly," Bea piped up. "Stewart being disrobed. That's not the upscale image we want. We're just starting to attract class peoples."

Janie nudged my elbow and whispered, "Wonder if Bea thinks we're 'class peoples'?"

For an instant, I pitied Bea. I could imagine her as a flat-chested, gum-smacking teen. A poor Alabama cracker who longed for a prom invite from the bank president's son and instead sulked on a date with a gas-station greaser.

My sympathy evaporated when she launched into a diatribe about her maid's incompetence. From Janie, I knew the Dear Company's resort wing constantly rotated housekeepers through the Caldwell household. Any sane maid would quit if forced to endure the assignment longer than a week.

Given that most Dear maids were black, being tagged to work in the Caldwell household meant a double whammy. Bea and Gator were low-rent rednecks who had no compunction about telling racist jokes within earshot of black employees.

By the time our crème brûlée arrived, table conversation had boomeranged to the group's hope for strong spring sales.

Bea, who knew zilch about the market, lifted a spoon and twirled it backward to check her reflection in the makeshift convex mirror.

"I can't look forward to spring," she sniffed. "Though flowers inspire my profession."

Bea pulled down fifty thou a year as the resort's "stylist." To earn her salaried skim, she flipped through magazines and consulted an expert in feng shui. Her pronunciation made it rhyme with chop suey.

The trophy wife prattled on, making googly eyes at Nickel. "Here I am blessed with the name Bea, and bees scare me silly. I've been telling Gator we need to defecate all the bees on Dear—right along with those nasty red fire ants. I'm allergic to them, too."

Janie kicked my shin when my giggles bubbled to the surface. I assumed the woman wanted to *decimate* the bee population.

"I told our new chef not to use any peanuts. If a food even touches peanut oil, I could die. It's a curse, havin' my delicate constitution." Bea batted her eyelids with a fervor that stirred more air than the room's ceiling fans.

"Unless we find a new pollination scheme, bees and flowers go hand-in-hand," I said, trying to filter my sarcasm. "But I'm no fan of fire ants. I didn't realize a single ant could sting repeatedly until I stumbled on a mound."

Janie shuddered. "Yeah, fire ants set anchors in your skin so they can swivel their stingers and inject venom again and again. Hurts like hell. That's one reason I don't go tramping around Beach West. I saw one fire ant hill that looked like an elephant took a dump. It had to be three feet high."

I nudged my tablemate. "A great image to help digestion."

Conversation faded as the tuxedoed wait staff cleared dessert dishes and refilled coffee cups. Then Sally resumed her emcee duties. Gator always ceded public speaking to the pixyish blonde. A natural orator, she wasn't bad to look at either. Just a smidgen over five foot two, Sally had an hourglass figure and dressed to emphasize it. She wore stilettos and, though her silk suits were tasteful, their plunging necklines showcased ample décolletage. Her snug skirts hugged buns of steel.

"On behalf of our agents, I'm delighted to present bouquets to the 'flowers' of our operation—our delightful secretaries. These ladies put the bloom on the rose of Dear sales," Sally cooed and clapped daintily to initiate a round of applause. "Come on up, ladies."

"Good thing Sally's not diabetic," I muttered to Janie.

Sally air-kissed the admin trio as they crushed oversized arrangements of orchids, roses and baby's breath to their bosoms.

"It's worse than you think," my friend whispered back. "See beaming Bonnie? She gets the axe Monday."

"You're kidding. Isn't there some rule against cruel and unusual termination?"

Janie shrugged. "Not the way Gator and Sally see it. The firing's not personal. Besides, it'll be my job to let Bonnie go. If Gator sees Bonnie a month from now he'll act as if she's his long lost friend. What's amazing is he'll truly be hurt if she doesn't reciprocate."

"So what award are you getting? Do you have crib notes for your acceptance speech?"

"Hell, no," Janie replied. "I threatened bodily harm if anyone called me to the stage."

With no interest in Sally's pat-on-the-back poppycock, I let my mind and my gaze roam. Grace Cuthbert and boyfriend Hugh were seated two tables away. Grace was not yet fifty—a couple years younger than me. Her placid cow eyes gave me the willies. They were bloodshot and blank. The wrinkled flesh on her neck and arms looked like a chicken's gullet, basted in sun, tobacco fumes and liquor.

Having heard about the couple's odd relationship, I wasn't surprised to watch Grace slurp wine from a glass her helpmate kept filled to the brim. An indiscriminate sommelier, Hugh poured from whatever bottle was handy. Red one time, white the next. While the jewelry-encrusted Hugh was only ten years younger than Grace, the worn-out lady looked like his mother.

"And what can we say about Grace Cuthbert's vision and generosity…" Sally said.

When Grace missed her cue for a queenly wave, Hugh nudged the heiress to start her bobble-head nodding. Unfortunately the nudge undid her queasy equilibrium. With all eyes fixed on her, she slithered off her chair and under the table. Hugh's efforts to halt the slide proved ineffective. He was left holding one of her arms like a ref awarding victory to a dazed prizefighter.

The floor show ended in minutes. The help bundled the inebriated heiress outside with a minimum of fuss. Watching, I felt a surge of pity for her hoodlum sons—a mother missing in action and a smarmy sycophant calling the shots. What a home life.

"I'm sure it was the excitement," Sally said, attempting to recover momentum. She then proceeded to present multimillion-dollar-sales awards and laud Gator's bulldozing talents. Next she noted Nickel's addition to the team.

"Woody Nickel comes from the Keys, where he sold out a classy development in less than nine months. 'Course we don't expect him to be 'round here for long either. At least we hope not—cause that'll mean we've sold out. Next week we'll be selling homesites faster than pancakes on Shrove Tuesday. We're counting on Woody to take Dear Island to the next level.

"Now for tonight's final surprise." She upped the wattage of her smile. "What could possibly make a real estate agent happier—or richer—than an opportunity to sell Beach West?

How about a sister development on Emerald Cay?"

What the hell is Emerald Cay? My tablemates appeared equally baffled, with three smug exceptions—Woody, Gator and Bea.

With a flourish, Sally plucked the oversized artist's rendering of Beach West from its easel to expose another plat hiding in its shadow.

"We bought Hogsback Island," she announced proudly, "and rechristened it Emerald Cay. As y'all know, Hogsback—I mean Emerald Cay—sits diagonally across the channel from our marina. This unspoiled paradise is less than three minutes by boat. Ferry service will connect our islands. Emerald Cay homesites and amenities will be spectacular—an equestrian center, one-acre lots, palatial homes. But the icing on the cake will be the island's *green* appeal. We're harnessing wind, ocean tides and sun to provide all of Emerald's power."

The agent to my right moaned with orgasmic anticipation.

Sally thrust her hands forward to stay the applause. "I know you're dying to hear more. But we closed the deal too late to have details ready tonight. Next week we'll have complete info on both offerings. True synergy. Major marketing dollars. Hey, I'm betting all of y'all will join our million-dollar club next year. Hell, we may need to start a billion-dollar club."

Sally whipped up enthusiasm to a fare-thee-well. Clapping crescendoed, wave upon wave, but Janie's hands never left the table. She twisted her napkin like she was wringing a neck.

"Holy bat wings," Janie muttered. "When the hell did they get this wild hair? And who's the new fairy godmother? I can't believe they convinced Gracie to fork over enough for two projects plus mucho marketing bucks."

As soon as Sally lowered her microphone, Janie grabbed my wrist with an iron grip and sprinted for the door. "Come on," she said, teeth gritted.

We emerged from the club's interior ahead of the milling

masses. Janie shook her head with metronome regularity all the way to her golf cart, muttering "damn" every other beat.

"Last I knew, Gator was wrapping pennies to scrape together payroll," she grumped. "The owner of Hogsback wrote six months ago asking ten million for his island. Sure Gator drooled, but he dictated a letter saying 'we pass.' Banks are still skittish about pricey resort real estate. Sally must be banging some bank president to pull off a loan this size."

I chuckled at Janie's nonstop diatribe. "You can't stand it that Gator didn't confide in you before tonight's bash."

"Damn straight," she replied, absent her usual grin. "That's a first, and it worries me—especially since Woody and Bea knew. Woody's a horse's patoot, and Bea's a stupid witch. How could he tell them and not me?"

I had no answer. If Janie was this troubled, she had reason. Maybe she worried that her head—like Bonnie's—might be destined for the chopping block, and she'd be the last to know.

We rode in silence the rest of the way home.

FOUR

At the witching hour, I started my security watch of the south end of the island. At least the skies had cleared. Patrolling in fog was as much fun as swimming in pea soup. We seldom ride in pairs, and tonight was no exception.

Only a handful of streetlights dotted the main drag while total darkness cloaked any side street lined exclusively with undeveloped lots and vacant houses. The gloom made me appreciate the world our ancestors glimpsed by starlight. Swaying shapes, shadowy movements, the red eyes of animals glowing like fiery embers.

At times, the island nightscape appeared serene and lovely. I searched the heavens for falling stars and conversed with Jeff, imagining him winking at me from above. However, this was not a night for communing. It had an eerie edge.

By one a.m., I completed two slow circuits of the small residential feeder streets, some paved, some gravel, branching off Dear Drive. Since most of the island's seniors played Taps long before midnight, the number of houses lit up like Halloween pumpkins surprised me. It seemed Stew's death would have a definite impact on electric bills.

His murder, just twenty-four hours old, made the undeveloped Beach West terrain seem even spookier than Dear's side streets. Entering this black hole made me superstitious. But, at two a.m., it was past time to bump down the logger's lane that sliced into our island's last bastion of jungle.

Twisting vines, thicker than a well-fed python, stitched the palmettos, oaks and pines into a forbidding tapestry. Here and there, trees felled by storms, insects or bulldozers provided visual breaks in the dense growth.

A reddish light flickered through one of these windows. *A*

smoldering rubbish pile? I radioed the guard working the gate to let him know I planned to leave my vehicle to investigate.

Absent a Bobcat, there was no way to drive to the glowing beacon. So I picked my way through underbrush, wishing my feet were encased in knee-high clodhoppers instead of lace-up work shoes. Last month Gator had to be rushed to the E.R. after a water moccasin, residing in the general vicinity of my shoe treads, sank its fangs into his ankle.

Uh-oh. The light spilled from a lantern. Scorched palm fronds weren't to blame. *Crapola, who was out here?* The fine hairs at the base of my neck rose to attention. I sucked in a deep calming breath. *Should I creep back to my car and call for backup? Might a delay magically improve my night vision? Would standing still give a snake time to slither up my pants leg?*

The call to action won. I'd get close enough to see who was there, then decide on the appropriate flight or fight response.

Through the bramble, a hand appeared. It gripped a goblet that glittered in the lantern's beam. Blood red contents. *Holy moly.* For courage, I brushed the gun at my hip. Did I really need to find out *who* inhabited the clearing by my lonesome? My brain waved a white flag.

Get out of this freaking swamp and summon backup.

My plan to retreat changed when my toe met a vine. Freefalling into the clearing, I yelled, "Freeze," like a reincarnated Elliot Ness. My order prompted a girlish scream from a member of the interrupted party.

Years of military training served me well. I hit the ground, drew my gun, and recovered my feet in one fluid motion.

If you're going to make an entrance, might as well go whole hog.

I'm not sure what evil I expected, but it wasn't the Cuthbert twins. Jared stood still, a crimson decanter raised toward the heavens. Henry paused mid-step in a shadow dance. His prop was a monster-sized serrated hunting knife.

The spell broke. Jared fumbled the container. Its viscous

contents splashed over the rim, and bloody splatters exploded across his chest. Henry's gleaming weapon spiraled to the ground like a kamikaze glider.

My heart sank. The Cuthbert boys weren't alone. Chief Dixon's twelve-year-old granddaughter Sammie and her friend Amy sprawled on a rotting log, transfixed by the twins, my gate-crashing, pot consumption, alcohol, or all of the above.

"Stay where you are," I yelled. "Don't move a muscle."

I holstered my gun and attempted to lower my heart rate. *Did I need my Taser?* While I know young teens can—and do—kill, these kids seemed unlikely murder suspects.

Dressed alike, the twins wore two-hundred-dollar sneakers and dirt-streaked iridescent mesh shirts cut off to expose nonexistent abs. The crotches of their baggy britches swayed around their knees. Wearing those getups, the boys stood no chance of gathering sufficient knee-pumping speed to outrun me in the rugged terrain.

"Oh, man," Jared whined. "You ruined everything, you bitch pig. We were about to powwow with old Stew's ghost. You freaked his spirit, man."

"Freakin' 'ho," Henry chimed in. "You made me drop my holy blade." He paused then resumed his chant. "She grabbed his head and massaged it a-quiver...I snatched a gun and ventilated his liver."

Though I figured Henry was spouting bad rap lyrics, he was weirding me out.

"I'm snowboarding on blood-stained ice. I yanked out her cheating eyeballs and rolled 'em like dice."

"Knock it off, Henry," I ordered.

"Hey, man, your chrome don't scare my bro'," Jared interjected.

"Shut your traps," I barked. "The nearest 'hood' is at least two-hundred miles away, so ice the attitude. Sammie, cough up an answer now: What's going on?"

"Just a séance," the young girl mumbled. She tugged at the peasant blouse sliding down her skinny arms. The drooping top exposed a strap on what we called a training bra in my day, though this girl had zilch to tutor. The child's attitude was sullen, and the eyes she flicked my way were bloodshot. *Bollocks.*

The aroma of burning leaves made me cough. Marijuana.

"Jared, what's the red stuff?" I motioned at the decanter.

"Tomato juice." He added a theatrical cackle as an afterthought. "It's a hell of a mixer. Like whad'ya think it was, blood? What a dork."

"Bring it here." I grabbed the container and took a whiff. Yes, my nose said, tomato juice. I stuck in a finger and extracted a sample. *A Bloody Mary. Pot and vodka. Great.*

"Okay, party's over. It's way past island curfew. And we won't even talk about the marijuana or booze. I'm taking you home and talking with your parents. If we had a jail, you idiots would call it home tonight. As it is, my decision on pressing charges will wait till morning."

My threat struck no fear in the pubescent quartet. Only Amy seemed abashed.

"Hey, she's going to talk to *Mommy*. This should be fun," Jared smirked.

"We get a ride in a berry," Henry added.

"Can it." I snatched the swaying lantern from a tree branch, then slipped on thin leather driving gloves to scoop up Henry's knife and a reefer as potential evidence.

"You guys, pick up everything else. You're not leaving a mess."

Their nonchalance infuriated me. "Didn't it occur to you bozos that you could be the next murder victims? What were you thinking, sneaking out in the middle of the night when a killer's on the loose?"

"Hey, what are you thinking, coming here?" Henry -

mimicked. "You couldn't find a turd floating in a fish tank."

Would I be found guilty if I took out my pistol and capped him? Unfortunately, jurors would only acquit if they could hear his garbage mouth.

No signs of remorse. The foursome was simply miffed at being caught. The girls kept cutting their eyes to the twins. A case of misplaced hero worship.

We trooped to my patrol car and I shooed everyone inside. Unwilling to leave Sammie and Amy sitting unprotected in the car while I dealt with the Cuthbert boys, I stopped by the security gate and requested another patrol car to ferry the girls home.

"Ask whoever plays chauffeur to make sure a responsible adult answers the door," I added. "Have him tell the parents to expect a call from me."

My fervent hope? That the chief wouldn't answer the knock at the Dixon door. Sammie and her mom lived with my boss, who'd want to tear the twins limb from limb for corrupting his granddaughter.

I wanted the Cuthbert boys locked within their mansion before Chief Dixon heard about tonight's activities.

***

On the ride home, the boys turned uncharacteristically quiet. I marched them to the front of their modern-day castle and rang the bell. I expected a long wait while Grace and/or her boyfriend Hugh gained consciousness. The door ripped open instantly.

Though it was three in the morning, Hugh was dressed like Batman. Black leather pants, a black long-sleeved silk tee, and shiny black boots comprised his kick-ass stealth ensemble. His hair was slicked back with goop. Either he'd just doused himself with cologne or his fragrance-of-choice had more holding power than a pissed-off skunk.

"What?" Hugh barked, eyeing my delinquent charges.

"I found the boys in a clearing at Beach West. We have a midnight curfew for children under eighteen. But that's not the biggie. They were drinking, smoking pot, carrying a weapon, and had twelve-year-old girls in tow. They coaxed those girls into the woods in the middle of the night while there's a murderer at large. I want to talk with their mother. Now."

"Get in here," he yelled at the boys. They moved, but behind his back they choreographed mocking gestures.

"Would you please get Grace?" I asked again.

"Afraid that's impossible," he said. "Her health is fragile. She's on medication. No way I could wake her. Even if I could, she'd be groggy. Tell you what, I'll catch her up when she comes to. You come back, say, five-thirty tomorrow afternoon. Believe me, Henry and Jared won't cause more trouble," he added. "I'll sit on the runt bastards. I don't mean to be rude, but I'm expecting a call. Doin' business in another time zone. Goodnight."

The door shut in my face before I could suck in a breath to protest. Though angry enough to bang on the door, I figured Hugh spoke the truth: Grace would be blotto. Odds were good the boys would stay put the rest of the night. Tomorrow was plenty soon for a roundtable with this dysfunctional crew. By then Chief Dixon would have cooled down sufficiently to join the party.

The radio crackled as soon as my car cleared the Cuthberts' drive.

"Marley," Chief Dixon's voice boomed through the speaker. "What the hell are you doing? Do you still have those pissants in your car? Are you at the Cuthberts? I'm coming over."

It took a few minutes to calm my irate chief. Told him he'd have ample opportunity to kick butt at tomorrow's conference.

Before hanging up, I reminded him of my off-island plans for the morning. "But, don't worry, I'll be in your office by four-thirty."

***

The next hour of my night shift proved routine. Making a second swing by the Cuthbert estate, I drove to the end of Dear Drive and parked in the cul-de-sac overlooking Mad Inlet. The thready sound of a small outboard floated across the water.

Island skippers seldom ventured out so early. Had the Cuthbert twins taken their gangsta act on the water?

A small skiff headed toward open ocean. Beyond Dear's sandbars, it could go anywhere—Hilton Head, Fripp Island, Wilderness Point Park. All were within easy reach when the ocean was calm, as it was tonight. A sliver of cloud-shrouded moon revealed only a blotchy silhouette on the dark water. It was impossible to tell if the boat carried more than one person.

Waves from the wake slapped at nearby pilings. The boat must have motored down Flying Fish Creek. Just prior to bankruptcy, Dear's first developers dredged a tidal creek to create dockable homesites. Grace had purchased a vacant lot cattycorner from her oceanfront estate to conveniently moor boats.

Maybe a check of her dock was in order? No. Wouldn't help. Without knowing the size of her fleet, it would be impossible to determine if a boat was missing.

Water lapped at the top of the riprap that served as the creek's retaining wall. The tide was near its crest. That meant the mystery boat could have launched from any of two-dozen creekside docks or even the marina. At high tide small boats could navigate the full length of the crooked fissure. The waterway ran from the mouth of Mad Inlet to the middle of the island, where it narrowed and meandered due west to the marina.

A glance at my watch provided unwelcome news. Two hours to go. My eyes itched. I poured coffee from my thermos while I stared out to sea. In a blink, the tiny craft disappeared.

What do you think, Jeff? Am I letting my imagination run wild?

FIVE

"What?"

My head snapped back from its full-doze, chin-on-chest position. My mouth felt like the Sahara during a sandstorm.

"We're here," Donna announced. Her head, with its dense crop of gray curls, swiveled toward the backseat. "Ready to pop open a can of balls and inhale the aroma of fresh rubber? Come on. Up and at 'em."

"I snored, didn't I?"

"So that's what you call it?" Rita offered from the front passenger seat. "We thought you were imitating a leaf blower."

"Hey, I'm the one who deserves sympathy," Julie put in. "I had to share the back with Sleeping Beauty."

"You sure you want to go through with this?" I asked. "I'll buy lunch if you'll let Donna and me forfeit." I snuggled deeper into my seat.

"No way, Jose," Julie scolded as she reached over and unlatched my seatbelt. "You gotta suffer with the rest of us."

Though not a regular competitor on Dear's senior—over fifty—tennis team, I owed Donna, the captain, big time. Three days ago, she'd extracted my promise to sub in the Hilton Head match. Had I known about my midnight to six a.m. shift, I'd have declined in a heartbeat. By the time Dixon switched my schedule, it was too late to find a replacement, and I couldn't disappoint Donna.

She was a gem. The first to befriend me after I moved into the house on Dear. My mother-in-law, Esther, willed the house to Jeff. Had she dreamed her son would die so young and leave the abode to me, she'd have set matches to the timbers. Her ashes were undoubtedly still a-whirl at my occupancy.

Esther's contempt for me poured as freely as vinegar. My hair was too short; my running obsessive. I talked too much; my

59

voice was too loud. My failure to procreate was an affront to womanhood.

My first day as a bona fide island resident, Donna welcomed me with a plate of warm brownies. "I know we'll be friends," she chuckled. "I belonged to Esther's bridge club. Anyone who could aggravate that woman as much as you did must be good company."

When the tennis match was over, it wasn't clear I'd done Donna a favor. We lost: 6-1, 6-1. Too many of my potential overhead smashes found the net. Despite the doubles loss, our team won, which put my companions in a celebratory mood.

"I just love it when we tromp those Sea Watch snobs," Julie crowed. "Let's eat at Chez Azure, talk trash, and hope someone's listening."

About one, we claimed a patio table with a smashing view of Calibogue Sound. I was salivating. The trendy bistro served the best shrimp salad in the Lowcountry.

"Don't forget, we have to leave by two-thirty," I said. "I promised Chief Dixon I'd be back for a conference, and I can't show up in sweaty tennis duds."

My friends assumed the meeting had to do with Stew's death, and I didn't contradict them. The Cuthbert family reunion wouldn't be the high point of my day.

The spring sunshine felt deliciously warm. While my teammates nattered on about reaching the regional finals, I floated in that drowsy zone where you hear every word of a conversation, yet the syllables cascade by as a lulling waterfall of gibberish. Then, male voices poked through the wool in my head. The men spoke Polish. The baritone conversationalists occupied an adjacent table; our chairs less than a submarine sandwich apart.

Opportunities to use the language skills gained courtesy of Uncle Sam are rare—not many Poles immigrate to Dear Island—so I deliberately eavesdropped. I picked up random phrases and profanities—curses memorized in the field from sheer repetition. While the gentleman seated at a forty-five degree angle talked, his companion grunted replies. It was clearly a boss-underling relationship. Boss Man barked *murder her*—well maybe he said *she's murdering me,* then something, something *swindle,* and later *his money goes up his nose.* In the next breath, he said *cops are so stupid.*

Was the man hashing over some made-for-TV movie plot?

Then Boss Man mentioned Hogsback Island. Unable to check the impulse, I swiveled my head in the speaker's direction. Our eyes locked. His stare penetrated. It was anything but friendly.

I smiled briefly, plunged my fork into my salad, and focused full attention on my greens. Something told me my best move would be to play dumb. I shivered.

Did this guy sell Gator and Sally the island they planned to market as Emerald Cay? Before last night's real estate banquet, I'd never heard the Hogsback moniker. I didn't even know Dear's tiny island neighbor had a name.

I continued to listen, albeit more discreetly. A sentence or two later, the Pole declared *that's Hugh's problem.* Chairs scraped on the patio's stone pavers. Though dying of curiosity, I ordered myself to keep my head down.

A hand rested lightly on my shoulder. I jumped as if shocked by a live wire.

"Excuse me, miss," Boss Man said in Polish. The broad smile didn't reach his eyes.

"Yes?" I replied in English, trying to sound pleasant but confused by a foreign language.

He switched to English. "Sorry. I had the impression you understood Polish. I simply wanted to introduce myself."

Blue eyes searched my face. They were simultaneously cold and hot, like frostbite. Blond streaks, expertly applied, shot through his thick brown hair. A Roman nose and chiseled chin defined his strong face, making his small rosebud mouth look misplaced.

"Oh Marley, here's a chance to practice your Polish," Donna piped up before I had a chance to avow ignorance. "She once worked as a Polish linguist."

Crap.

I spoke in purposely halting Polish. "I apologize for my half-forgotten Polish—it's been twenty years. My skills are quite rusty. You speak much faster than I can process."

Boss Man's laser eyes skewered me. He was perhaps forty. Big, well over six feet tall, broad in the shoulders, muscular. He wore an expensive silk shirt and carried the sort of leather satchel European men favor. He held the silence a moment, tempting me to blather.

"I'm sure you shortchange your skills." He switched back to perfect English. "Where did you say you learned Polish?"

"Oh, in school," I answered, not about to tell him the school was the Army's Defense Language Institute.

My fake smile faltered when my gaze flitted to Underling. A prizefighter? He looked like someone had used Silly Putty to push his features into temporary lumps, then tired of the face-making game and quit. His complexion had a grayish cast as if the dough hadn't been fired. The man was about my height, five-nine, though he must have outweighed me by a hundred pounds. Not someone I'd care to bump into on Dear's dark roads at night.

"Are you vacationing on Hilton Head?" Boss Man asked. "Perhaps you might join me for dinner?"

"You're very kind, but I'm only here for the afternoon." I didn't offer my name. Exchanging Christmas cards with the man wasn't on my agenda.

"How unfortunate. Who knows, maybe we'll meet again? It's nice to encounter an American who's made an effort to learn another language. I hope you and your friends enjoy lunch.

Good day."

Boss Man and Underling retreated with double-time dispatch.

I sank back in my chair with relief.

"I can't believe you turned down a date," Rita said. "He's very handsome, quite suave."

"Not my type."

"Boy are you picky," Donna complained. "It's time you started dating, you know?"

Rita interrupted. "You speak Polish? Wow. Was it your college major? How'd you get from Northwestern to the Army?"

How to answer? What had possessed me to join the Army? Life insurance, that's what.

On that fateful day, I reached my quota of slammed doors. I got to ten and quit. I knew eleven insulting rebuffs would send me over the edge. Especially in my hometown, Keokuk, Iowa, where selling meant pestering my mom's hairdresser and my old homeroom teacher. Turndowns from strangers were easier to handle.

I headed to the Chuckwagon to sip a Coke and feel sorry for myself in air-conditioned comfort. En route, I peered at the posters in the window of an Army recruiting station, a storefront that hadn't been there the week before. A soldier dressed in crisp khakis walked outside and stood beside me.

Half an hour later, the papers were signed. He'd promised me a year at the Defense Language Institute in Monterey. What can I say? My defenses were lowered. I'd never seen the Pacific Ocean.

Now I sat beside another ocean. I grinned at my audience, parsed the story, and skimmed over my transition from linguist to MI—military intelligence.

"When I finally figured out that working in intelligence might be reducing my I.Q., I retired," I quipped. "Actually I'm joking. I enjoyed my work, if not the bureaucracy."

"Your work on Dear is undoubtedly duller, but you look dead on your feet," Donna commented. "We'd better get you home so you can go to bed. I hope you have the night off."

As the ladies calculated tips, I excused myself, letting my friends assume the restroom was my destination. Instead I hustled to the bistro's entry foyer.

"Excuse me." I touched the maître d's sleeve. "The two-gentlemen who sat next to us—do you know their names?"

The maître d' laughed. "I should collect matchmaker fees. Mr. Dzandrek, the tall, distinguished looking fellow, asked if I knew *your* name. Even asked which car you came in. Want to leave a card? I can pass it along. He eats here two, three times a week."

"No, thanks." I mustered a coy smile to mask my discomfort. "What's his full name? Do you know how to spell it? Maybe we have mutual friends who could introduce us."

I tried to be discreet as I slipped the man a twenty.

He palmed the bill with aplomb. "I've seen the spelling on his charge slip. The first name's Kain—spelled with a K not a C—and Dzandrek starts with a D. Fooled me, I was sure it started with a Z. He just bought that baby blue mansion, the first one on the water after you enter our gate."

The matchmaker paused and winked. "He's loaded, lady. Sure you don't want to leave a card?"

Dead certain. I shuddered.

The ladies joined me at the entrance, and we walked to Donna's car. As we approached, sun sparkled on the windshield, spotlighting the distinctive Dear Island decal.

Had Kain Dzandrek seen it?

***

While Dear and Hilton Head are maybe fifteen minutes apart in a fast boat, the land route is eighty miles plus and can take two hours. Long fingers of water curling inland dictate the serpentine route. In the Lowcountry, it's nigh impossible to get from point A to point B without taking two steps back to cross bridge C.

Awake for our return ride, I enjoyed my car mates' easy banter though my contributions to the conversation seemed sparse. I wasn't married and didn't golf in a couples' league. Never had a facial or a pedicure. My skill at Texas Hold 'Em didn't translate to bridge. I wouldn't know a two-club bid if it clubbed me. I was a decade younger. Never had a child.

While living in the D.C. area was no picnic, I missed the buddies left behind. Women who'd been officers like me. Civilian contractors for the military. Wives of the men who'd served with Jeff and me. Our chatter would have been alien to my new friends. Talk of Army posts, PX sales, VA hospitals, military strategies—a different frame of reference.

Was moving to Dear a mistake? My sister had invited me to settle in her new hometown. But I knew no one there. Maryanne had her own life, thirty years of homesteading. I'd be a squatter.

When we were five miles from home, the radio announcer broke in with a news bulletin. "The Dear Island Bridge is closed to both vehicle and pedestrian traffic. At approximately three o'clock, people near the bridge heard a thunderous roar. Occupants in the sole car traveling the bridge at the time felt their rear tires drop as a hundred-foot span of the suspended roadbed sank six inches below the adjoining concrete segments. Authorities say the bridge will remain closed until engineers can inspect the damage."

"That's just great," Rita huffed. "What in blazes are we supposed to do? Book a room at some high-priced B-and-B like visiting movie stars? I have chicken breasts thawing and a husband laid up from hip surgery. I have to do everything but hold his peewee for him."

"You think there's a chance the bridge'll collapse?" Donna wondered. "I bet it'll take months to repair the blasted thing."

"Who has a cell phone?" I asked. "I'll call security. Maybe I can get some answers."

Julie handed over her cellular toy and I punched in the main security number. I got a steady busy signal. No surprise. I tapped in the chief's unpublished mobile number.

When Dixon heard my voice and location, he tossed off a string of curses and gave me my marching orders. He hung up before I could get a word in edgewise. I hoped the man didn't pop an artery, what with Stew's murder, his granddaughter's hijinks, and an honest-to-God island crisis. *Good thing Dear has a helipad for medical emergencies.*

"Well, ladies, here's the deal. The powerboat squadron is organizing a ferry service. We're to leave our car near the bridge, roll up our knickers and wade to the end of the boat ramp. The first pleasure boat that comes our way will give us a ride."

Julie's stricken face telegraphed her horror. "Heavens to Murgatroyd. Not me. I can't swim, and just look at the water."

Our vantage point from the bridge connecting the mainland to Wilderness Point Park offered a scary view of the roiling bay. The park's flag lanyard snapped rhythmically against its pole. Though the sky was crystal clear, winds had to be gusting at thirty to forty miles per hour. Our ferry ride would be raucous.

"Look," I said, "we must be on the edge of a front. The weather could get worse. It's a short hop. I want to get to the island while the getting's good. Soon the water'll be too choppy for any boat. If you want to turn around, fine, but will you drop me first?

"The chief needs extra hands. He's trying to reach off-duty officers, but some won't make it over in time. Rita, I'll look in on your husband if you stay in Beaufort."

"No, I'm coming." Rita sighed. "I'll never hear the end of it if you go across and I don't."

***

At the boat ramp, nearly a dozen islanders awaited portage. The owner of E. T. Grits, Dear's convenience store, was among the marooned. She'd been on a Beaufort supply run and her Expedition SUV was loaded with provisions. Hollis County snuggled up against Beaufort County, and the town of Beaufort offered the nearest shopping.

"You'll make a mint," Donna muttered. "I'll give you twenty bucks right now for a gallon of milk and a loaf of bread."

"Hey, I don't gouge," the owner objected.

"I'll help you load groceries when our rescuer arrives," I offered.

"Me too," said a familiar voice at my back. I turned to see Deputy Braden Mann. The duffle bag slung over his shoulder gave him a rakish, vagabond air.

"Glad to see you, Marley. I tried to call you earlier," he said. "How was the dinner?"

"No one confessed." I grinned. "But I can fill you in on Dear real estate if that helps. You headed to the island?"

"Yep. The sheriff wants at least one deputy stationed on Dear until the bridge reopens. I was the logical choice. I live alone and have island leads to follow."

Rita stood beside me, openly eavesdropping. "Where will you sleep?" she demanded. "I'd put you up, but we just painted our guestroom and the fumes are awful. Marley lives alone and has two spare bedrooms in her rambler. Isn't that right, Marley?"

"Sure," I fumbled, thinking about Dear's wagging tongues. Oh, hell, why not give the neighbors some juicy gossip? My Tae Bo routine had lost its novelty.

"Braden, you're welcome to bunk at my house till things get sorted out."

"That's a generous offer. But the sheriff's made other

Linda Lovely

arrangements." He smiled impishly and leaned closer for a stage whisper. "Knowing the county's per diem, he probably arranged for a cot in the DOA lobby. Maybe you can help me plan a jail break."

Did his joke have a subtext?

Captain Hook's "Ahoy" saved me from the need to frame a clever response. "Hey, we're in luck," I said. "If anyone can deliver us safe and sound, it's Captain Hook and Tinkerbell."

Braden arched an eyebrow.

I laughed and explained the charter boat captain was Tom Hooker a.k.a. Captain Hook. The retired naval officer had named his sleek vessel Tinkerbell. Every Halloween, he delighted kids by donning a pirate's costume. A camouflage rigging let him hide his sound right leg and clump about on a peg, trickery he'd mastered years ago when _Forrest Gump_ filmed on location in the Lowcountry. Hook had provided aquatic support to the movie crew.

When the jolly captain got within fifty feet, he dropped twin anchors to hold Tinkerbell's position so her bottom wouldn't scrape.

He lowered a rubber dinghy and rowed to the ramp. "I can only carry three at a time. And I'm afraid you'll get your feet wet. Might want to shuck any shoes and socks and roll up your pants."

As Hook finished his spiel, Bea Caldwell marched briskly to the head of the makeshift line. "Surely you can get closer than this. You don't expect me to wade, do you?"

Hook was not amused. "Lady, I'm a volunteer, not your servant. Count yourself lucky I'm offering a ride. You can wade or swim to the dinghy. I don't care. Make up your mind while these good folks ahead of you get on the boat."

Not accustomed to back talk from hired help, Bea got her dander up. "I don't think you understand. My husband expects me. I can't go to the back of the line. You might run out of room.

68

Gator told me to take this boat. You do understand? These are Mr. Caldwell's orders."

"Well, ma'am, maybe ol' Gator can tell you to piss up a rope, but he can't order me."

"How dare you speak to me that way?" she huffed.

"I dare just fine. But don't get your panties in a twist. There's room. You can board right after we load all these folks and the groceries. Now that's what I call *important* cargo."

The young woman's face flushed beet red as everyone in line snickered.

"Way to go, Hook," Rita whispered, as he handed her into the dinghy. "Wish I had the nerve to give the witch her comeuppance."

"Not much Queen Bea can do to me," our ferryman replied. "I spend all my time aboard Tinkerbell and don't give a flip about club membership. But I'll wager I've booked the last company fishing charter."

It took about fifteen minutes to load all the passengers. The boat ride proved wet and wild. At one point Braden's gaze wandered below my chin. He must have sensed my perusal. His eyes met mine and he blushed. Then he stripped off his windbreaker and held it out.

"You're getting soaked," he mumbled.

I looked down and realized my tennis warm-ups were pasted to my body. I was shivering like a newly shorn sheep in a downpour. Braden tucked the windbreaker around me.

"Thanks. You'll have to start carrying two coats if you keep giving one away."

We reached the dock and tramped up the sloped loading ramp. Chief Dixon tossed me a towel and shook Braden's hand.

"Glad you made it," he said to Braden. "Marley, I'll drop you home for dry clothes. The seas are too heavy for more ferries. That means everyone on the island stays here till morning, and no one else can join us. I couldn't reach any of our

Linda Lovely

fellas on the mainland in time to get them on Hook's boat."

Glancing at the white-capped frenzy, I spotted a hulk of a man on the docks. He coiled a rope in hands the size of platters. Something about him tickled my memory. He bulled his way down the rental docks, his hunched back as broad as a billboard. Then he swiveled in my direction, offering a glimpse of his grayish face. It looked like Underling's ugly puss.

Why would Kain Dzandrek's flunky be docking at Dear Island?

***

It was four-thirty and chaos reigned. Stranded construction, service and delivery vehicles jammed the marina parking lot. *The bar will do a banner business tonight.*

Dixon exited against the traffic tide. A line of golf carts clogged the road. The drivers were all sixty-ish with gray hair, glasses and pastel windbreakers. The carts snaking along Flying Fish Drive conjured up a fleeting vision of zombie clones capturing the island. Some drivers were undoubtedly coming to retrieve passengers, others to volunteer for ferry duties. All wanted to check the marina hubbub firsthand. For Dear, this was major excitement.

"We still meeting Grace Cuthbert?" I asked the chief.

"No," he snapped. "Got a call from some hot-shot lawyer. He said the Cuthbert boys' latest prank had traumatized their mother, and she'd gone away to...how'd he put it? 'regain her mental clarity.' Hell, she's at some fancy spa. Incommunicado for three days."

Grace's departure surprised me. "She left the boys alone on Dear?"

"The boyfriend's playing nursemaid. The lawyer claimed he'd keep 'em on a tight leash, bed checks included. Fat chance. If those little bastards come near my Sammie again, I'll kill 'em with my bare hands. Screw Grace's money."

The sheriff sucked in a breath, held it a beat, and exhaled. Anger management? "We don't need to worry about those

70

pissants tonight," he added. "Hugh drove the boys off island before the bridge buckled, and they didn't make Captain Hook's last run."

Braden's face reflected his puzzlement. "What did the Cuthbert boys do?"

I filled him in on the twins' nocturnal escapade.

"I'd sure like to know what those boys were up to the night of the murder," the deputy said. "If they regularly prowl at midnight, maybe they saw something. I need to chat with Hugh Wells, too. Stew's calendar had 'H.W.' penciled in for lunch Saturday."

"Well, you can't grill them tonight," the chief allowed, "so how's about a little patrol help? The three fellas who worked day shift are stuck here, can't get home. But I can't rightly ask 'em to work twenty-four hours straight."

"Sure. I'll help. That's one reason the sheriff wanted me on island. No way to get deputies to Dear in an emergency."

"Right." The chief nodded. "Nobody's gonna swim over if I sound an alarm."

"Can you provide a car?" Braden asked as he tossed a smile in my direction. "Marley introduced me to your wildlife. I'm not eager to walk a beat in a place where alligators have their own crosswalks."

"Cars we got. How about the midnight shift? It's close to five now. Reckon you worked all day. Maybe you can get a little shuteye before then. Same goes for you, Marley. I'm counting on you to pull graveyard duty."

I stifled my groan. Another night without sleep. I was dead on my feet. "Okay. But remember how agreeable I've been when I ask for a month off to visit Iowa."

Dixon pulled into my driveway and Braden cleared his throat. "You mentioned shuteye, Chief. The sheriff said you'd find a place for me to bunk."

"I forgot. Been a little busy," Dixon grumped as his

dilemma dawned on him. "There's usually a free bunk at the fire station, but the EMS guys are stranded. And it's a zoo over at guest reception. Lots of folks who were supposed to leave today went exactly nowhere. And I'm not just talking angry tourists. We've got construction workers, drivers of delivery trucks, maids."

I opened my mouth, willfully ignoring the reasons I shouldn't extend my hospitality.

"Tell you what, Braden, it'll be midnight before the chief gets you settled. You're welcome to crash here a few hours, as long as you don't expect a dutiful hostess. Shut your eyes to the dust bunnies, and my B and B has some fringe benefits—like leftover lasagna in the fridge." *And a woman ready for a remedial course in French Kissing 101.*

"Sold," he said cheerfully. Unfortunately he didn't respond to my mental telepathy.

Braden climbed out of the back seat, and the chief peeled away before my front door unlocked. Inside, I gave my guest a nickel tour, making sure to note all major points of male interest—TV, refrigerator, microwave, and, finally, bedroom and bath.

The deputy was clearly surprised when I led him to the master bedroom. "All yours." I pointed at the king bed with its bright multi-colored quilt and oversized pillows. His eyes searched my face. He appeared confused and hesitant.

"Umm, isn't this your bed?" he asked.

"No, don't worry. I converted the sun porch for myself. It's sunny and cheerful. I prefer it. The master suite is great for guests, and it offers privacy. No skulking down hallways in the dead of night searching for a toilet."

He didn't need to know the real reason for my relocation. The room made me lonely. The bed was too big. The space too silent. I hadn't slept in this room since Jeff died. I cleared my throat and headed for the final tour stop. "Ta da," I said. "Your bath."

"I really appreciate this." Braden put down his duffle.

"No problem. See you in a few hours. I plan to get up at eleven, grab a bite, brew some coffee. Want me to knock on your door?"

The deputy's yawn telegraphed his weariness. "Great."

As I crossed the threshold to the sun porch, my bedside phone rang.

"Can you talk?" Janie asked. "Who's the hunk, and why is he carrying a duffle bag into your house?"

I couldn't help but laugh. "Sometimes I miss city life and having a smidgeon of privacy. Why are you peeking out your window? I figured you'd still be at work with all the excitement."

"I am at work," my friend answered cheerfully. "A real estate agent was driving some prospects past your house when you and Handsome Harry got out of Dixon's car. She asked me what was up. Were you shacking up? As your best friend, I was embarrassed to say I didn't know."

"Nothing's up. The deputy's helping with patrols. We're taking catnaps. Our shifts start at midnight. So don't ring the doorbell or, worse, use your latchkey. For all I know, the deputy would draw a gun if you surprised *him* in the shower."

"Oooh, now there's an idea. From what I hear, deputies come equipped with big guns," she said with Mae West emphasis. "But, hey, you can give me a full report. I hope you're encouraging things. You're not wearing your ratty moose nightshirt, are you?"

"Stuff it. You up for breakfast tomorrow? I'll be starving after the night shift."

"Sure. Golf café at seven? Bring the hunk. It pays to feed 'em. Stamina, you know."

Janie hung up before I could verbally thrash her. With a grin, I pulled on my moose nightie.

A *rattle, rattle* noise echoed in the kitchen, followed by a crash and a muffled curse. My houseguest's foiled attempt at a stealth raid on the fridge made me smile. I climbed into bed and closed my eyes. I wanted to sleep, but the same mental rat kept scurrying through my maze.

Kain Dzandrek. What the hell was he up to? And why was he curious about me?

Forget him. Think pleasant thoughts, I told myself. However, my pleasant thoughts weren't conducive to sleep either. I tossed and turned, wondering whether Braden wore pajamas or slept in the buff.

SIX

I cut generous slabs of lasagna to nuke in the microwave. As Braden walked into the kitchen, the stove's digital clock flipped to 11:15.

"I'm heating enough for both of us. You hungry? I was about to knock on your door when clanking pipes told me you were in the shower. Figured you were up and at 'em."

"Well, up anyway." He tried unsuccessfully to stifle a yawn. "Thanks for giving me a place to crash. The lasagna's great. In case you didn't notice, I helped myself to a big square before my siesta. But I'd love more."

"Sure." I put wedges on both our plates without bothering to offer veggies.

"Is it kosher to ask how the investigation's going? Did the autopsy tell you anything new?"

Braden unfolded his paper napkin. "We're getting nowhere fast. The forensic pathologist from Charleston couldn't pinpoint time of death since the hot tub maintained the vic's body temperature. His best guess—Stew died after midnight. No surprise as to cause. He drowned. No defensive wounds. It looks as if Stew got zapped before he realized he was in trouble. The bruising on his hands and feet indicate the killer probably trussed him up with zip ties while he drowned him. Not sure why he cut them off after Stew died."

Braden raised a forkful of lasagna, chewed and swallowed before continuing. "The crime scene guys couldn't offer much help. It's a public area, so they have tons of fingerprints and baggies filled with stray hairs. But without a suspect, that's worthless litter. They picked up nearby palm fronds, figuring the killer might have used one to scratch out that 'stewed' message. None had fingerprints."

"Maybe you'll get a lead from Stew's papers," I offered.

On yesterday's tour, Braden mentioned the sheriff had retrieved reams of paper and a computer from Stew's apartment.

"Nothing popped. 'Course by the time I'd scanned five appraisals my eyes glazed over. Not exactly riveting reading. Sales reports on comp properties. Digital snapshots. Excel worksheets. We're checking to see if any of Stew's recent appraisals came in so far below the purchase price, they torpedoed sales. But it's hard to imagine someone working up a murderous rage over a decimal point in the wrong place."

"I might be able to tell you something about the buyers or sellers for Dear properties."

Braden frowned. "Actually, I didn't see any appraisals for Dear. They were all on neighboring islands."

"That's odd. I had the impression Stew worked mostly on Dear Island. The agents at last night's dinner told plenty of stories about their dealings with him. All complimentary. Maybe his island work came in spurts."

A glance at the clock reminded me we didn't have time to sit and gab. It was quarter till twelve. "We'd better go. Bet you're excited about pulling patrol duty when you've got a murder to solve."

"I don't mind. It'll give me a feel for what happens on Dear after midnight."

I laughed. "You thought Stew's paperwork was a snooze? Sometimes I count raccoons to keep my brain functioning."

"So why do you do it? Got to admit I'm curious. If you retired as a lieutenant colonel, you're pulling down enough pension to live comfortably without some Mickey Mouse job."

I lifted an eyebrow, and Braden started backpedaling. "Sorry. I have a gift for sticking my foot in my mouth, shoes and all. It just seems, well, a bit of a demotion."

"Hey, I'm not easily offended. Security guard wasn't exactly a career goal. I was at loose ends. Restless. I watched

Law & Order reruns so often I memorized the dialogue. Bridge lessons and golf leagues bore me. Someone mentioned my background to the chief and we talked. Maybe the job is Mickey—or Minnie—Mouse, but it keeps me involved."

Was there more to it? I grew up in an all-female household, raised by a strong-willed woman who'd divorced in an age when it was a scandal. I liked women, trusted them, enjoyed their company. Yet Jeff's death, combined with a move to Dear that stripped away male friends, left a void. I wasn't longing for sex, just conversation, jokes, getting a different take on the world. My security job let me mingle with men while avoiding dating's messy complications.

Braden fixed me with a funny look. I knew I'd missed something.

"Sorry, I was gathering wool. What did you say?"

"I was in the service," he repeated between bites. "Unfortunately, there were no women in my Coast Guard unit."

"When did you serve?" I asked.

"Joined in '89. Needed money for college, and the G.I. bill looked good. I'd pinned my hopes on a football scholarship, but blew my knee out senior year. Back then I was a poor excuse for a student so no academic scholarship. And my folks didn't have the dough."

"You enlisted?"

"Yeah, I had visions of running down drug smugglers in my cigarette boat and hitting the beaches in my off hours. Instead I spent most of my tour guarding the Mississippi River. What a thrill. It's colder than a witches' tit there in January."

I laughed. "Well I'm sure my hometown appreciated your protection. I grew up in Keokuk. It's a river town."

"Hey, I know it. Just south of Burlington near the Missouri border."

The microwave timer's beep interrupted. I'd set it as a last-ditch reminder that it was time to walk out the door. "We need to leave. We'll have to save our *Prairie Home Companion* reminiscing for later."

Braden grinned. "I was a bit of a cad back then. You might discover I jilted your sister."

"Not unless she was cheating on her husband. She had a ten-year-old son by the time you were patrolling the Mississippi."

"Obviously you're the baby of the family. I do remember Iowa girls were very pretty and friendly. No surprise you come from Midwest stock."

Was he interested? It had been so long I wasn't sure. Perhaps his banter was another strange Southern custom. *Dang but he's cute.*

***

Chief Dixon said he'd man the security gate and handle resident calls. He assigned Braden to cruise the island's north end and gave me the south. Since no cars were entering or exiting Dear, Dixon appeared to have captured the plum assignment. But within half an hour, he complained the phones were driving him batty.

Stew's murder and the damaged bridge spooked residents. Every rustle in the bushes suggested a prowler. Every tapping tree branch signaled a sicko Peeping Tom. Naturally, they wanted security to investigate.

We played den mother, too. To hold down expenses, stranded workers pooled their resources to rent villas and buy cases of beer. Whenever the partying pissed off sleepy neighbors, Dixon dispatched us to knock on doors and ask the marooned intruders to lower the noise a notch. While E. T. Grits might still have milk and bread, the store's beer rations had to be dangerously depleted.

By three in the morning, things quieted, and I could no longer blame my procrastination to patrol Beach West on cranky residents. Time to reenter the jungle. Nothing scary—

just an overgrown tangle of vines. Who's afraid of inky blackness or slithering snakes?

While my internal pep talk failed to psych me, it shamed me into launching my patrol car down Beach West's rutted logging lane. After bouncing along for a few hundred yards, my headlights caught the open door of a red Mercedes wedged into a small clearing in the swampy bramble. The bumper sticker read: "My Other Car is a Broom."

Bea Caldwell's car. My mental antenna put me on full heebie-jeebie alert. She'd pitched a hissy fit about the sticker last night, screaming at Chief Dixon about some vandal's vile sacrilege of her vehicle.

When the chief asked if Bea could think of possible suspects, he'd almost choked on his inhaled laughter. The pitiful truth: Bea had nothing but enemies on Dear. I figured high-spirited college interns working at the Dolphin as the probable bumper-sticker culprits. But a sinking feeling told me Bea's abandoned luxury ride was no prank.

I pulled up behind the vehicle. No occupants were visible in my headlights. I called in. "Hey, Chief, it's Marley. If you don't hear from me in ten minutes, send the cavalry, will you? I just drove into Beach West and Bea's Mercedes is ditched in the swamp. It looks abandoned; the driver's door is wide open."

"Want to wait for backup to check things out?" Dixon asked.

"Nah," I said with more bravado than I felt. "Just stand by while I take a peek."

I took a deep breath and checked my Taser and Glock. My heartbeat quickened as I grabbed a flashlight and opened my door. My shoes sunk a couple of inches in the mushy ground as I tiptoed toward the Mercedes. Cold water seeped through the seams in my shoes. I shivered.

My flashlight beam swept the car's interior. Nothing. Then I painted the surrounding landscape with my beacon. Fifteen feet away, my light ricocheted back.

"Oh no." My flashlight lit up Bea's silver-spangled pantsuit like a beacon.

"Mrs. Caldwell?" I called. "Bea? Are you all right?"

No answer. I inched closer to the sprawled body. "Sweet Jesus."

Bea was anything but all right. Her face was grossly swollen and covered with angry red welts capped by white pustules. Tiny red ants crawled in and out of her staring eyes. I watched mesmerized as they exited a mouth that must have opened in a final scream.

Check for a pulse. I leaned forward and picked up a limp wrist.

No pulse. My fingers grasped her wrist for an extra beat to be sure.

She's dead, I told myself. Mouth to mouth will do no good. Get the flock out of here.

Still, I lingered, trying to decide if there was something, anything else to be done. Bea lay on a huge fire ant mound, and her tongue protruded slightly. Something rested on it. The object, small and round like a quarter but darker, appeared to be ant nirvana, the center of a swarm.

A burning pain seared my hand. My proximity had tempted a few of the tiny enemy to forage for fresh meat. Dammit to hell. The ants marched across my hand and wrist, piercing my flesh at will. I beat my hand against my pant legs to squash the suckers.

As I backed away, I viewed Bea's neck from a different angle. Telltale stun-gun burns decorated her skin. Based on the pattern, it appeared the killer opted to incapacitate his victim with a hand-held stun gun this time.

Bea's wrist—the one encircled by an allergy alert bracelet—was flung at a bizarre angle. It looked as if her arm had been posed to point at an open patch of mud.

I drew my gun and crept toward the mini-clearing. Capital letters were scratched in the damp earth: "TO BEA OR NOT TO BE."

Nausea hit me. *Get back to the car. NOW.*

Frantically, I splashed my flashlight high and low, a 360-degree sweep. Nothing.

I ran to the car and slammed the door shut.

"Marley, you there?" the chief's voice boomed out of the squawk box.

"Yeah, I'm here. Send the cavalry. Bea's dead. The killer's probably long gone but I'm not about to search the woods alone."

"Stay in the car," Dixon yelled. "I'm on my way."

My allegro pulse didn't calm, but my mind started to function. Opening the car door, I thrust my legs outside. I rummaged through my wallet, extracted a credit card and used the stiff plastic to rigorously brush off the ants clinging to my trousers and shoes. After jettisoning as many of the suckers as possible, I closed and locked the door.

My metal cocoon felt claustrophobic. Nervous sweat soaked the shirt beneath my jacket and my skin grew clammy. At any hint of a rustle, my flashlight beam probed the canopy of greenery.

Is the killer out there?

My thoughts returned to Bea and Monday night's real estate gala. Everyone at our table knew about her allergies. Yet it was doubtful my dinner companions belonged to an exclusive club. Bea probably vented frequently about insects. That meant lots of folks would realize how simple it would be to sentence Bea to death. Find an ant hill, immobilize the woman, and dump her.

Who wanted to see Bea dead?

The list of candidates would fill an entire notebook. Even Gator's junior partner, Sally, had vocalized her fervent wish that the second Mrs. Caldwell would "make like a frog and croak." Amazingly, Sally never bothered to hide her loathing from Gator. She expressed her sentiments about Bea with the woman's husband sitting at her elbow.

The rest of us politely waited until both Caldwells were absent to hurl our epithets. However, wishful thinking and acting on homicidal fantasies were two different matters.

The minutes in my solo vigil stretched on, leaving time to puzzle over the murderer's choice of victims. Stew was as well liked as Bea was reviled. Stew was male. Bea, female. Stew worked as an appraiser. Bea's sole job was pampering Gator and Feng Shui'ing corporate digs. Stew and Bea didn't move in the same social circles, and I'd wager there were no amorous ties. Bea wouldn't risk her princess status, and Stew had better taste.

Yet the crime scenes shared the same nightmarish signature. Some sort of stunner to cripple victims. Smart-alecky messages printed in capital letters.

While repulsed, I was also intrigued by the killer's M.O. Why stun the victims? His methods were indirect, time-consuming, risky. The killer had to work fast to hogtie his prey before the initial jolt of electricity wore off. Then he had to wait around long enough to make certain there was a final curtain call. That upped the threat of discovery. Did it also give him an adrenaline rush? Who knew?

I cringed, thinking of Stew and Bea waiting to die. Unable to move or scream, trapped inside their paralyzed bodies while their killer manhandled them. It was beyond hideous. Beyond bizarre—it was evil. Who could do this? And why? What did the killer plan next?

A sense of determination gripped me. Since Jeff's death, I'd been floating. The sight of Bea's grotesque face filled me with righteous anger and a surge of energy. No one deserved to die like this. Not nice guy Stew and not even poor, stupid Bea—

their lives reduced to freakish jokes.

We had to catch this sick bastard before he killed again.

SEVEN

The lonely vigil with Bea's remains lasted less than ten minutes but felt like an hour. Bill O'Brien, the former Army medic who served as our fire department's Emergency Medical Service guru, kept his first-to-arrive honors.

Seconds later, Chief Dixon's four-wheel drive Cherokee followed the ruts left by the EMS truck and churned to a stop in the spongy marsh mud. Braden rode shotgun. My reaction surprised me.

Too bad I have my own coat tonight. I need you to wrap those arms around me.

O'Brien pronounced Bea dead and speculated about the foreign object visible on her tongue. Using a sheet of plastic to shield himself from the ants, the medic almost rubbed noses with the corpse as he maneuvered for a closer look. "God, it looks like a Reese's Peanut Butter Cup. My kids eat enough of them. D'you suppose the killer gave her candy? Or maybe she popped it in her mouth right before she got zapped."

I groaned. "Bea was allergic to peanuts. The candy was insurance—just in case her allergy to fire ants didn't provoke a fatal attack."

The chief produced a sound between a retch and a cough. "Jesus H. Christ on a crutch."

We established a perimeter around Bea's corpse though I seriously doubted the forensic whiz kids could uncover usable evidence. The lane we'd traveled provided the only motor access to Beach West. Since noon, probably thirty trucks, SUVs, and cars had boogied in and out, carrying surveyors, DHEC inspectors, workers, gung-ho real estate agents and curious islanders. In high spots, traffic pulverized the sandy soil into shifting dunes, while the muddy low spots boasted more elasticity than Play-Doh. The ooze reclaimed even a heavy vehicle's tire tread in minutes.

The fire ant mound sat atop a hillock, which rose above a bog-like depression bordering the dirt road. An exceptionally high spring tide had already liquefied the impressions my shoes made when I approached Bea and retreated. If the murderer left prints, they'd long since vanished. Bea might as well have been beamed to the spot.

As we waited for Braden to finish his call to the sheriff, Dixon kept muttering. "Dammit all to hell. Pluck a dang duck. How in tarnation did someone coax Bea here in the middle of the night? I sure as hell don't want to be around when Gator learns some sicko offed his wife. Unless, of course, he did it himself."

My jaw dropped. Gator's name didn't appear on my most-admired list, but this was beyond the pale. "Jesus, you can't seriously think Gator could have done this?"

The chief hawked up some phlegm and walked a few paces away before pulling the eject button. "Never know. If it weren't for the murder method and smart-ass note, he'd be suspect number one. I've never struck a woman, but if Bea'd been my old lady, I'd have been sorely tempted. 'Course I hear Bea was a regular Jekyll and Heidi—lovey-dovey and sweeter than molasses at home but a bitch on wheels out of Gator's sight."

Braden ended his call and pocketed the cell phone. "Since the winds are down, the sheriff is going to helicopter over with the coroner and land at the marina helipad. Want me to pick them up?"

Dixon sighed. "No, I'll roust one of the security officers sleeping at the fire station."

In the half hour since my grisly discovery, the water level had crept higher and higher. Soon the marshy off-road area where we stood would be submerged. The encroaching tide would rinse away the murderer's "TO BEA OR NOT TO BE" calling card and any other meager evidence. A nightmare vision of the eddying water lifting Bea's limbs and reanimating her corpse fired goose bumps up my arms.

"Chief, the tide's going to inundate this area—it might even float the body." I glanced at my watch. "The tide tables predicted ten point two feet in Mad Inlet an hour from now. Want me to get my camera and take a few shots?"

"You better," Dixon agreed. "Dammit. If she starts to float before the coroner gets here, we'll just have to grab her."

Braden's frown knit his thick brows into a furry question mark. "Jeez, if the water gets that high, won't it flood the island?" He stood next to me. I ignored my impulse to grab his arm, lean into his body.

"They don't call this the Lowcountry for nothing," I answered. "Dear Drive will have patches of standing water. It'll be up to our hubcaps in the DOA parking lot. With just the right conditions, acres of land you see every day—even at high tide— are swallowed whole. Makes you think about building an ark."

I retrieved the camera stored in the patrol car to document run-of-the-mill problems—like raccoons strewing garbage from the marina to Timbuktu when club trashcans weren't emptied. While snapping away, I provided the chief and Braden a synopsis of the real estate dinner party, including Bea and Gator's seemingly cordial couplet appearance, the lady's loud-mouthed soliloquy on insects and allergies, and her golf course run-in with the Cuthbert twins.

Braden tapped his index finger against his lower lip as he listened. "Can you give me a list of the folks at your table? We'll need to check alibis."

"Good luck. Everyone who lives or works on the island wished Bea dead at least once," Dixon added. "But this is screwy enough to be a teen's wet dream. Maybe those Cuthbert kooks think they can get themselves on primetime TV. Who knows how their hopped-up little brains work."

Dixon appeared ready to launch into a full-fledged diatribe.

86

"Hold on, Chief, you said Hugh and the Cuthbert twins didn't make the last ferry. If so, they're in the clear."

"Maybe." He scowled. "Or maybe they bribed some druggies to do their dirty work."

We all knew the boys—following in mother Grace's footsteps—habitually used alcohol and occasionally tossed marijuana into the mix. We suspected the twins pilfered Grace's feel-good cornucopia and acted as penny ante suppliers to impress other kids.

Dixon's eyes narrowed and his jaw clenched. How much might hatred color his judgment?

"I seriously doubt Henry and Jared could lay hands on enough booze or Mary Jane to buy a murder hit. And if they could, they'd get rid of Hugh, not Bea."

A change of subject seemed prudent. "What do you think the killer used for a writing instrument this time? I'm thinking rebar."

"Yeah." Braden nodded in agreement. "I noticed the corkscrew impression in the mud."

We lapsed into another silence. My wet feet cramped, and I stamped them to restore circulation.

Before the lurking tide could float Bea's arms and legs, we shifted her body. Braden also bagged her hands to preserve any trace evidence that might be washed away.

"How in Sam Hill did the murderer get Stew and Bea to drive themselves to his kill zones?" Dixon wondered aloud as he stared at the corpse. "The victims must have known him. Would Bea have agreed to meet here if she'd been afraid?"

The questions went unanswered as we completed our gruesome tasks. Then we sheltered in the back of the EMS unit until the welcome slam of a car door signaled the arrival of the sheriff and coroner.

"Sorry it took so long." Sheriff Conroy shook hands with Dixon and nodded toward Braden and me. "Our pilot will hustle for medivac runs, but saw no call to put himself in high gear for us to commune with a dead body."

After the coroner did his thing, the men wrestled Bea into a body bag. Less than anxious to touch her again, I didn't complain about the Lowcountry's rampant male chauvinism. The coroner borrowed a shovel from the sheriff's trunk, scooped up a generous portion of the ant hill, and sealed the teeming mass in an oversized baggie. Could the ants chew through their plastic prison? Based on the carnage they'd already wrought, it seemed plausible.

The coroner and sheriff walked to a patch of high ground and conferred.

"The coroner's flying back with the body," Sheriff Conroy reported when he rejoined our group. "That means I'm stuck breaking the news to Gator. Thank God telling family isn't part of my usual job. Braden, you're coming with me. I know Gator's an excitable bastard. Chief, how about joining us?"

"Not on your life." Dixon chewed on an unlit stogie. He'd quit smoking, but still teethed on a soggy cigar when agitated. Bits of tobacco clung to his plump lips.

"Ol' Gator and me aren't exactly bosom buddies. Better if I'm not along." The chief pointed his shredded nicotine pacifier at me. "Take Marley. The man's four-year-old grandson—name of Teddy—is visiting. It'd be good to have a woman along to look after the boy if he wakes."

I considered protesting. In principle, I liked children but lacked practical experience. No kids of my own and, even as a teen, I steered clear of babysitting, preferring to earn my money lifeguarding, waitressing or flipping pancakes. Still, curiosity got the better of me.

How much trouble could a four-year-old be?

***

I sat shotgun. Braden drove and Sheriff Conroy took the back seat. With sections of the road flooded, we adopted a funereal pace. No need for sirens or speed. Braden did a slow head roll and cast a weary look my way. "Thought you said nothing happened on Dear after midnight."

The sheriff wasn't talking. Maybe he was rehearsing his lines for Gator.

"It seems unreal," I said. "Less than forty-eight hours ago, I sat at a table with Bea eating crème brûlée on bone china. Now she's dead. I can't wrap my mind around the fact that someone on Dear did this. I may not know every resident, but I've met most. When these people fight, it's a snit fit over a neighbor's untidy lawn. They get revenge by removing offenders from their party lists. They don't paralyze people on fire ant hills."

Braden looked at me. "You said it yourself, it doesn't take a magician to get past the gate. Why assume our killer's a resident? Maybe it's some homicidal tourist."

I shook my head. "Wish I believed that. But whoever killed Bea knew about her allergies, plus he was able to lure—or trick—her into visiting a swamp, alone, in the middle of the night. The woman was no Einstein, but she wasn't a complete imbecile."

"There are other possibilities," Braden said. "She wore an allergy-alert bracelet. Maybe someone kidnapped Bea at gunpoint, forced her to drive there."

The prospect of a kidnapping never occurred to me. "A lot of islanders never lock their doors—it's some sort of we-live-in-paradise badge of honor. At Gator's house, you might try the front latch; see if it's locked. It's conceivable someone just walked in."

"It's also possible that Bea's murder is a copycat killing," Braden added. "Maybe hubby seized a golden opportunity to offload his wife without alimony."

The sheriff shifted in his seat and snapped out of his reverie. "At least we know where our killer is, what with the bridge blockade. He has to be on this island. That narrows things down, gives us a starting point."

Picturing the killer trapped on the island offered cold comfort. "Yeah, it does remove a few suspects," I said. "Everyone in the Cuthbert household is off-island. Of course, if you made it over in a helicopter, a boat could have slipped across, too, once the winds died down."

The scary face glimpsed on the docks—Underling or his look-alike—flashed through my mind. I couldn't fathom a connection with Bea but wondered if all of yesterday's itinerant boats remained snugged in their assigned slips. The marina might be worth a gander after our call on Gator.

We pulled into the Caldwells' circular drive. Nary a light inside or out. Like most island abodes, the home featured a two-car garage and storage space at ground level with the main living areas on second and third floors. Insurance requirements now dictated the live-in portion of coastal homes be at least fourteen feet above sea level. However, older homes—including my low-slung ranch—had been grandfathered. I was thankful for the reprieve since it would have cost a fortune to separate my house from its foundation and jack it up on stilts.

Something about the shadowy scene seemed out of kilter. "If Bea left of her own accord, she didn't want to advertise it. Otherwise she'd have left a porch light burning."

"Or she left in a panic—or a huff—and didn't think about turning on lights," Braden said.

Together, we trooped up the curving grand staircase to double doors. The etched glass panels featured a pair of egrets, wings unfolded and eternally poised for flight. Braden tugged on a plastic glove and thumbed the latch on the active door. It clicked open.

"What the hell do you think you're doing?" Sheriff Conroy hissed. He'd been zoned out when I suggested testing the lock. "We don't have a search warrant. You want to be charged with breaking and entering?"

"Just checking Marley's theory that a kidnapper could have waltzed in through an unlocked door." Braden gently pulled the door shut. "I wasn't planning to enter uninvited."

The sheriff dismounted his high horse. "Sorry. I'm uptight. You know what they say about bearers of bad tidings."

Braden pushed the bell. A stately chime echoed inside. After the third singsong chorus, we heard Gator hollering. "Bea, Bea. Where are you? If you're downstairs, get the damn door."

Braden tapped the bell again, triggering more trills. A minute later, Gator yanked the door open. "What in blazes do you want? Do you know what time it is?"

The sheriff exhaled deeply as if he'd been holding his breath. "I'm Sheriff Conroy." He used his conciliatory politician's voice. "We met at Jess Hamrick's fundraiser. Sorry to wake you, but we need to talk. Can we come inside? It's about your wife."

"I can't imagine where she's got to. Bea?" Gator bellowed. "Get yourself down here." He turned back to us. "What's so all-fired important it couldn't wait until morning?"

If Gator knew his wife was dead, he was one hell of an actor. He'd thrown on a silk kimono. While a belt cinched it at the waist, it bared a wide fissure of chest above the tie. The developer wore pajama bottoms, but no top. Wiry white chest hairs sprang through the kimono breach. For some reason, I found myself staring at Gator's bare feet. His stubby toes were exceptionally hairy, and the hairs were charcoal black—a striking contrast to his chest's white steel wool. I wondered at what anatomical point Gator's body hair changed color, then shuddered as I decided I really didn't want to know.

"Sir, we need to check on your grandson, make sure he's tucked safely in bed," Braden said. "Could you tell me where he's sleeping?"

"What the hell is this about? My grandson's fine. Don't go bothering him."

91

Though polite, Braden didn't waver. "Sorry but we must, sir. Sheriff Conroy will explain everything. Now where can I find your grandson?"

Gator directed Braden up the staircase. "First room on the left. But you'll answer to me if you wake that boy."

As the deputy hustled up the stairs, Sheriff Conroy gravely announced Bea's death.

Confusion clouded Gator's meaty face. "What do you mean dead? Like she's lying dead somewhere in our house? How the hell would you know? Man, you've got your wires crossed."

Braden slipped back into the room and gave a discreet thumbs-up as Sheriff Conroy walked Gator through the nightmare. No, there was no mistake. Yes, Mrs. Caldwell was dead. Her body had been found in a deserted site in Beach West. Yes, her Mercedes was parked there. No, the death did not appear accidental.

Gator appeared angry, but not disconsolate. No tears, no anguished shrieks. Was it shock? Or maybe Gator couldn't decide on the proper manly response. He didn't ask to see Bea. He kept shaking his head, alternately muttering "that son-of-a-bitch" and "the bastard."

"You came home from dinner at the clubhouse just before nine?" the sheriff probed.

"Yeah, had to get home to tuck Teddy in," Gator answered. "That's my grandson."

"And you never left again?"

"Well, obviously my wife did. I didn't. Never heard Bea take off."

"You had a babysitter tonight?" the sheriff continued.

"Yeah, Mrs. Pope. She left as soon as we came home."

Braden held up a hand as he inserted himself into the interrogation. "Mr. Caldwell, sir. We can't rule out the possibility that someone abducted your wife. Do you lock your doors?"

"No need," he replied gruffly. Gator's mouth had started running before his brain engaged.

"Mind if we look around? Could you show us where Mrs. Caldwell usually sleeps?"

"Bea sleeps with me." Gator exploded in anger, as if the question were a slur on his manhood, then his mouth snapped shut. He must have realized his protestation sounded a tad strange, given that his wife was found miles from his bed, and he hadn't noticed.

"When I went to bed, Bea said she wasn't sleepy," he amended. "Probably went to the den. That's where she piles up them home decorating magazines."

Braden pressed on. "Could we take a look at the den?"

"Yeah." Gator led us up a grand staircase that echoed the front entrance's curved Tara theme. Sheriff Conroy, Braden and I followed single file.

At the top of the stairs, Gator turned right and pointed at the first door. Inside, twin antique fainting couches covered in heavy silk brocade provided the only seating. Plumped pillows left so little space that even an anorexic butt would have been forced to hover. The pillows were arrayed as if *House Beautiful* photographers were expected. If Bea sat here tonight, her exit had been anything but hasty.

Conroy looked around slowly and mumbled, "Doesn't look disturbed."

"Mind if we walk through the rest of the house?" Braden inquired.

"Yeah, okay." Gator slumped down the hallway ahead of us, his shoulders hunched. Maybe he did feel something.

The door next to the den gave way to the master bedroom suite. Gator nodded us in like a headwaiter. The room had two focal points: a king bed and French doors that opened on a private deck with a view of the Atlantic. Rumpled sheets spilled from the bed. Gator's dirty underwear lay heaped on the floor, while his trousers and shirt draped a chair. If Bea had disrobed, she'd been neat.

I flashed on the murder scene and her silvery pantsuit.

"Gator, what did Bea wear to the club last night?"

"I don't know. Some silvery getup."

"Wouldn't she change—put on a nightgown—if she wanted to read before turning in?"

Gator swiveled my way and bared his teeth. "You accusing me of lying, Marley?"

"No. Just trying to get a handle on your wife's state of mind."

After a moment's silence, Gator answered. "Truth is we had us a little spat. I wasn't real happy with something Bea said at dinner. Thought she insulted a client. When we got home, I yelled. She stormed out of the bedroom. I went to sleep. End of story."

The scene he painted certainly had the ring of truth.

"Where does Bea keep her purse?" I wondered.

Gator's irritation was evident. "How the hell should I know?"

Sheriff Conroy cleared his throat, a signal for me to shut my trap. However, I was determined to follow my train of thought. "If Bea left voluntarily, she probably took her purse," I explained. "I didn't see one on her car seat or…umm, near her body."

Gator shrugged. "Sometimes she sets her purse on the kitchen counter."

I turned to the sheriff. "Mind if I look?"

His frown indicated the prospect of ditching me had definite appeal. "Go ahead."

The kitchen gleamed. It should have. Mine would too if I had free daily maid service. *Bet that perk never shows up on their income tax.*

The counter boasted the usual assortment of kitchen

gadgets but no handbag. Of course, Bea could have tossed the purse on a couch or table. Or maybe the muddy ooze near Bea claimed it. Then again, the killer might have wanted a souvenir.

A tug on my pants startled me.

"Who're you?" asked a squeaky voice.

Looking down, I found the instigator, a small raven-haired boy in pajamas covered with friendly-looking dinosaurs.

"You a new babysitter?"

"You must be Teddy." I tried a smile. The boy nodded and rubbed fists against his eyes.

"I didn't hear you come in. You're pretty quiet."

His face scrunched up. Somehow my comment suggested he could be whining. "I'm thirsty. I want juice."

Should I give a four-year-old juice at three a.m. or would he wet the bed? Who knew? But, hey, I wouldn't be here come morning. Figuring my number one mission was to keep the tyke happy, I opened the refrigerator and handed over a Juicy-Juice.

Suddenly the boy seemed suspicious and frightened. "Why you here?"

How to answer? I didn't want to scare him. "Some friends and I came to see your grandpa."

"Why?"

It wasn't my place to tell the kid Bea was dead. How did you break such news to a baby? I hedged. "Your grandfather will explain. Let's go upstairs and he can tuck you back in bed."

Something in my sentence—maybe the mention of bed—brought on a microburst.

"Don't let him tell Bea-Bea," he wailed. "Bea-Bea said not to come downstairs—not ever—after grandpa kissed me goodnight. Bea-Bea yelled. She was on the phone."

Teddy pointed at a wall-mounted phone above the granite countertop.

"I won't tell Bea," I assured Teddy. "Did Bea yell at you tonight?"

If Teddy answered, his words were incomprehensible amidst his sobs. But his shaking head indicated yes.

"Did you hear what she said?"

The boy whimpered. "Can't tell. Bea-Bea said she'd spank."

"I promise. No one's going to spank you. What did Bea say? You play cops and robbers, don't you? If you tell me what Bea said, you can help the cops catch bad guys. You'd be a hero."

For what seemed an age, Teddy sniveled and I coaxed. "Be brave. You can tell me."

Finally he blubbered a reply. "Bea-Bea was mad. She sayin' 'You believed Adam...Adam Spate.'"

I heard a racket and looked up to see Gator storming toward us. The sheriff and Braden followed timidly in his wake.

"What, you're browbeating babies now?" Gator yelled, bringing his red face inches from mine. His breath smelled of garlic and whisky.

I understood his anger and tried not to take it personally. "No, sir."

Gator snatched up Teddy, turned on his heel and headed down the hall.

"We're through," he yelled back at us. "I have to break the news to Bea's parents and tell my daughter to come get Teddy. Let yourselves out. Now."

"Goodnight, sir," Sheriff Conroy said. "We'll talk tomorrow."

"Goodnight," Braden and I echoed.

***

An amused grin played on Braden's face. "Hey, were you grilling Teddy as a suspect? I usually can't get hostiles to crack in a single interrogation. Want to share your techniques?"

"It comes naturally. I have a gift with pre-school perps. Seriously though, Teddy provided a clue. The boy made an unauthorized visit to the kitchen after he was tucked in for the night. When he surprised Bea on the phone, she yelled at him. Teddy claims she was already mad as a hatter. The boy's playback of the conversation seemed muddled but he recalled a name, Alex, no, Adam Spate. I don't know a soul by that name on Dear Island."

Braden massaged the bridge of his nose. He looked as tired as I felt. "I'll run the name, see what we come up with. We'll check phone records, too."

The sheriff sighed. "I'll bet the killer used a pay phone or an untraceable prepaid cell. This guy doesn't appear careless— just freakin' sadistic and weird."

"Did you find Gator's reactions a bit odd?" I asked. "It almost sounded as if he knew which 'son-of-a-bitch' killed Bea."

Braden flicked me an approving look. "I felt something off, too. But Gator could simply have been railing at the anonymous bastard who tortured his wife."

The sheriff phoned my chief, who suggested we convene in his office.

True to predictions, the parking lot resembled a saltwater lake. As the spring tide began its retreat, patches of asphalt rose like tiny volcanic islands.

I turned to Braden. "Drive to the front door so you two don't get your feet soaked. Then I can scoot over and drive."

"Aren't you coming with us?" Braden asked.

"I want to check the marina first. If the killer isn't an islander, he might have arrived by boat. I'll make some notes to check with our harbormaster come morning. Save some hot coffee for me."

The deputy's eyebrows bunched as he frowned. "Okay. But don't take any chances. If you see something suspicious, call. This guy enjoys killing."

Ironically Braden's warning cheered me. His tone spoke of genuine worry.

He likes me.

Jeez, I sound like a teenager.

EIGHT

It was dark, though the approaching dawn brightened the sky with a promise of morning. I parked at the marina and sat in my car for ten minutes, gazing at the pale moon and listening to the breeze rustle the palm fronds. My chromed cocoon felt snug, and I needed to decompress. Could Gator have killed her? Images of Bea and Gator at various public venues chased around in my head. Lovey dovey kisses. Murderous glares. Did either mean anything? Who knew what their marriage was like? Only Bea and Gator.

My own marriage shocked plenty of folks. We met while stationed in Bad Kreusnach at one of the lovely German town's communal hot springs. I could still hear my CO's rant.

"Marley, are you freaking nuts? Marry Jeff and you kiss your career goodbye."

"Sayonara," I replied with a wry smile. *"I'm thirty-four and in love for the first time."*

"How did this happen, Marley? He's a noncom for God's sake."

"Too bad Army regs don't require insignia on bathing suits. I didn't plan it, you know."

Our wedding didn't end my career, just applied the brakes to promotions. We were happy because neither of us tried to change the other. We were old enough to know better. We admired the other's strengths; shrugged off the irritating foibles. We laughed one hell of a lot.

Hey, Jeff. Hope you're still laughing. I miss you, kiddo.

It was time to sally forth. Get this over with, drink hot coffee—and look at Braden. *Look, don't touch.*

After exiting the car, I strode down the boardwalk connected to the floating docks and took a sharp left onto a section reserved for temporary anchorage. All slips were full. If a boat had left, someone else had snatched the vacancy.

With no idea which, if any, of the twenty-odd boats might have been captained by Underling, I began taking notes on each moored vessel. Arched lampposts spaced every fifteen feet pooled enough ocher light to decipher boat registration numbers without a flashlight.

As I bent forward for a closer look at the third boat's bobbing registration number, a board creaked. I started to turn. Pain seared my body as outraged muscles spasmed in series, a head-to-toe cataclysm. I screamed—but no sound came out. My mind fuzzed. Thoughts skittered about like dry leaves. Total blackness descended.

My cheek was planted firmly against slimy decking. Slivers from the rough board pricked my skin.

Maybe sixty seconds elapsed. It felt like an hour.

Before my mind could clear, my tormenter zapped me again. My brain cells registered a single fact—prongs were embedded in my back. I prayed for the torture to end.

As the second electrical assault subsided, my body's movements were beyond my control. My skin felt raw and tingly; I couldn't lift my head.

I'm as good as dead. How will he kill me? No ant hill nearby. An image of Stew's floating corpse invaded my consciousness. *Is that how they'll find me?*

I wanted to see my attacker's face. My neck muscles ignored my mental screams. I couldn't raise an eyebrow, let alone my chin. Positioning restricted my view to the dock and the water and flotsam below. I watched a chunk of white Styrofoam dance on the black water's ebb and flow.

My attacker jerked my arms behind my back. Something sharp cut into my wrists as he cinched them together.

I heard a *psst* noise. It stopped, then repeated. A rhythm developed. On, off, rattle. On, off, rattle. An aerosol can?

The assailant grunted, the first human sound he'd made. Next came a sloshing gurgle, and a pungent, unpleasant odor assaulted my nose. *Gasoline.* An icy liquid soaked my pant legs.

Oh, God. He's going to set me on fire.

My heart hammered so hard I expected to implode before he lit a match. Maybe a heart attack was better.

Don't panic. Think. I'd been stunned before as part of my own less-than-lethal weapons certification. Though he'd zapped me twice, I'd be able to move in a minute—provided he didn't hit me with another jolt. And I felt pretty confident he wouldn't pull the trigger now. Gas fumes could ignite and we'd both go up in a ball of fire. He wouldn't risk it while he stood nearby.

God, please don't let me become a human torch. I'd rather drown.

Could I marshal enough strength for a small roll? My fingertips brushed the edge of the dock. A quarter body turn and momentum would carry me. A sudden plunge into the dark water. Surely more of my muscles would rally before I drowned.

Mustering every ounce of grit I possessed, I held my breath, and heaved. A slight twitching sensation came as a reward. My toes wiggled inside my shoes. The rest of my body parts remained stationary, as leaden and unfeeling as a fallen statue. I was exhausted, frightened, dispirited. *Focus. Don't let him win.*

I channeled all my will, all my hope. *Come on, muscle memory. One small turn.*

The splash sounded deafening in the still night. I gasped as the ocean bay pulled me downward in its frigid embrace. Not a good thing when there's three feet of water overhead. I gagged on the saltwater, but my legs responded. I kicked upward. When my face broke the surface, I sucked cool air in hungry gulps and floated on my back.

"Damn." The expletive came from above. The dock swayed beneath pounding footsteps. Thank God, they were moving away. A motor cranked and an outboard roared to life. The boat's wake flung me toward a piling. I struggled to keep my head above water and wrapped my legs around the piling as if it were my lover. *He's leaving. I'm alive.*

My glee proved fleeting. Before I could think about extricating myself from the drink, the dock shook again. Thundering footsteps headed my way.

Once again an expletive rang out above. "Crap."

For a moment, I wondered at my crazed déjà vu—could electric shock have put my brain in reverse? Would I find myself back on the dock in another minute, only imagining I'd escaped?

"Marley. Where are you? Can you hear me?"

I recognized the voice. Braden. "Here," I yelled. Well, tried to yell. A whimper escaped my throat. I'm not sure how Braden hoisted me onto the dock. My waterlogged uniform, bound hands, and uncoordinated muscles amplified my dead weight.

"Dammit, what happened? I had a bad feeling about you coming here alone."

"He shot me...in the back...with a stunner. Twice." My thoughts erupted like hiccups, a mental stutter. My teeth chattered so violently I thought the enamel might crack.

Braden took a knife from his pocket and cut the plastic zip-tie around my wrists. Then he wrapped his arms around me. "A boat rocketed out of here just as I pulled in. The killer must have seen my headlights. Did you get a good look at the guy?"

I shuddered. "Not his face, and he only said one word, 'Damn.' He planned to kill me. I know it."

"I believe you." Braden shucked his jacket, and cocooned my quaking body inside. He held me tightly, letting his body's warmth seep into my bones. I had an insane desire to smother my rescuer with kisses.

"There's gas all over the dock," Braden said. "And the sick bastard spray-painted a message."

I didn't think it could get worse until I read my intended epitaph. The wet orange paint glowed. The message: "KENTUCKY FRIED COLONEL."

"He knows me? He knows who I am. He never touched me, didn't look at my ID. It wasn't some stranger. I don't go around introducing myself as Colonel Clark."

The deputy glanced toward the one empty boat slip. "His boat was in slip number 23. Dear's harbormaster should have a copy of the boat's registration. Maybe we can use it to trace him."

He stroked my cheek. "It's over. He can't hurt you. We'll catch the SOB. At least we know he's off island."

But he'll be back, I thought, and shuddered again. *I'm unfinished business.* Somehow I knew this failure would infuriate my would-be executioner. I'd screwed up his plan.

"Take me home. Please."

Braden's concerned eyes studied my face. "Maybe we should stop by the fire station, let the paramedics check you out," he hedged.

"No, I'm okay. Or will be. Please, I just want my own house...my own bed."

Braden used the patrol car's radio to call my chief and the sheriff, who were still holed up in Dixon's office. The chief swore at his news.

"Is Marley in shock?" I heard Dixon ask. "Does she need a doc?"

Braden looked at me for an answer. I fiercely shook my head. "I'll be fine. I promise. I just need to get warm."

As the deputy relayed my reply, the chief's loud voice floated back. "She's one tough bird."

They talked a few more minutes as Braden drove, but my ability to concentrate was shorter than their conversation. I was too busy reliving my attack. To divert my mind, I fastened on how strong and warm Braden's arms felt when he wrapped them around me. I liked the feeling and wished he'd pull me to him again with more than comfort in mind.

"Since you've already told me everything you remember,

the sheriff agreed it's pointless to put you through more tonight," Braden said, as we reached my drive. "Said you could give a formal statement tomorrow—actually, I guess it's later today."

He helped me out of the car, draped my left arm around his shoulders, and circled my waist. He pulled me tightly to his side. "Hold on," he whispered. "Take it slow and easy. We'll get you warm in no time."

I felt woozy and weak. At the door, I fumbled in my pocket and withdrew my keys. *Thank God, I didn't lose them in the water.*

Inside, Braden shepherded me down the corridor toward the master bathroom. Though I normally use the guest bath, I didn't argue. My squishy shoes squeaked on the hardwood floors. Leaning against him, I realized my wet clothes were soaking his shirt. "You're wet. I'm sorry."

"I'll dry. Let's worry about you first." In the bathroom, he lowered me to the padded bench beside the garden tub. I'd used it as a towel holder before, never as a seat.

"I'll draw a hot bath," Braden said. My teeth chattered. *I'll sink in hot water up to my neck. Heaven.*

I smelled lilac. He'd added drops of the bath oil I kept on the ledge for guests. A mist rose from the tub. He took off my shoes and socks and rubbed my feet to massage warmth back into them. "Um, do you need any help undressing?"

"Of course not. I'm fine." My voice sounded shaky, even to me. "Leave me and get some dry clothes for yourself."

He looked unconvinced. I made a half-hearted shooing motion and tried to unbutton the top button on my blouse. My fingers felt like icicles, cold and unbending. Braden stood his ground. I fumbled a minute more.

"Oh, for Christ's sake, don't be so stubborn. Let me help."

He knelt before me and gently nudged one pearl button from its nest. His clever fingers dropped lower and the second button relinquished its hold. Hot water cascaded from the faucets. Steam began to fill the room. My blouse was undone.

Tenderly he lifted it away and slid it down my arms. He reached behind me and unhooked my bra. His hands grazed the sides of my breasts as he pulled the fabric forward.

God, how I want to run a finger down his cheek, pull his mouth to my breast.

"Can you stand? Lean on me."

He put my arms on his shoulders and pulled me up. My nipples hardened as they touched the cool fabric of his shirt. *I can't let this continue. I'll do something foolish. He's being kind and I'm imagining scenes from* Sex in the City.

I didn't have much willpower left in the tank, but used it all. I smiled at Braden and gave him a gentle shove toward the door. "I'm feeling a lot better. There are some things a girl just needs to do for herself."

"You sure?" He was trying to be a gentleman, staring into my eyes, not letting his gaze wander below my chin.

"Yes, I'm sure."

"Okay, but I'm leaving the door open a crack so I can hear you if you need help."

Once he left, I wriggled out of my pants and slid into the soothing water. I felt warm and liquid. Steam from the hot water misted the mirror. But with the door ajar, it began to defog. In one clear patch, I could see Braden in the bedroom. He'd stripped off his wet clothes. He was nude and erect. My breath caught. *God, he's beautiful.*

He looked toward the bathroom and our eyes met in the mirror. Neither of us looked away. The doorbell rang.

"Goddammit," Braden swore. He pulled a clean pair of trousers from his duffle bag, and ran to answer the door.

Janie's voice floated down the hall. "I saw lights on. Thought I'd check to see if Marley was ready to go to breakfast."

Braden gave her a quick update and tried to get rid of her.

Fat chance.

Your timing sucketh, Janie my dear. Well, maybe not. Maybe you saved me from acting like an idiot. What if Braden's just a horny bugger? Maybe he'd have reacted the same if he'd seen any naked broad. Doesn't mean he wants ME.

Janie barged in before I could finish my mental debate. She looked down at me with her hands on her hips. "Are you playing with a full deck, girl? You're gonna trot out your women's lib card once too often. Wandering in the dark with a murderer on the loose. I swear."

The irony prompted a smile. A variation on my lecture to the Cuthbert twins and their preteen playmates. But I was a grown-up. In theory, I was able to take care of myself—and trained to protect others. A responsibility I'd failed. A vicious killer had been inches away, and I hadn't even managed to see his face.

"You need hot coffee and breakfast," Janie said. "Don't stay in that bath too long. It'll cool and you'll catch your death."

Maybe I daydreamed or nodded off. It seemed only a moment before Janie was back, ordering me to towel off. After helping me from the tub, she handed over my flannel nightie and a floor-length velour robe. She eyed the robe's shiny caboose with obvious disgust.

"This is a disgrace. When did you shop last? The 1980s? Boy, do you need lingerie. Couldn't find slippers, but I guess these'll do." She tossed a pair of wooly knee-highs on the toilet lid. "They sort of complement your ensemble."

Her diatribe earned an eye roll. "You mentioned breakfast. I can't believe you cooked. What d'you do, nuke the last piece of lasagna?"

"Hell, no. I'm servin' up omelets, pancakes, and sausage. I do takeout well. Called over to the 19th Hole and bribed that waitress, Arlene, to run food over. You gave her a real nice tip by the way. Didn't have my purse on me."

106

I laughed. Janie's levity put welcome space between the night's horrors and the day's promise. Sun streamed through the bedroom window, and the lagoon behind my house sparkled crimson and gold.

"Did Braden leave?" God, how I hoped he was still here.

"No, honey. He's a man, isn't he? We're talking food. Let's head to the kitchen."

The table in my breakfast nook brimmed with our catered feast. Braden stood and pulled out a chair for me. The deputy didn't look me in the eye. Was he embarrassed?

"I feel terrible," he said. "I never should have let you go to the marina alone."

"Hey, it's my job." I tried to smile. "As the chief said, I'm a tough bird."

I figured I'd drink a cup of coffee and choke down a couple of bites to humor Janie. My stomach was on tilt, and I was sleepy, not hungry.

I sat down, accepted the proffered hot mug, and sniffed. "What d'you lace it with, Janie?"

"A wee bit o' the Irish, me lass." Her South Carolina drawl overwhelmed her sorry attempt at brogue. Even Braden chuckled. Suddenly I was famished. I regularly lose many things—car keys, my temper, brain cells—but not even attempted murder could vanquish my appetite.

After we scarfed down every morsel, Braden seemed more relaxed. His eyes met mine and held. He grinned.

"Looks like you're feeling better, the way you attacked your food. Remind me to go Dutch when we go out to dinner. Are you up to talking a bit before you get some sleep?"

Braden turned a policeman's stony stare on Janie. The one that says: "Why don't you leave before I toss you out?" My friend refused to take the hint.

"Might as well let Janie stay," I said. "She'll find out everything in an hour tops."

My neighbor kept her chair. When Braden and I replayed the evening's nightmares—first Bea's grisly death and then my flirtation with the afterlife—Janie gasped on cue and interrupted with the occasional question.

For background, I recounted my possible afternoon sighting of Underling at the marina, and my earlier, very strange encounter with the man's Polish boss on Hilton Head.

"Does his name ring a bell?" I asked Janie. "Know of any link between this Kain Dzandrek and Hogsback Island? Has Gator ever mentioned him?"

"Nope. The MacIsaac family owned Hogsback. They're Scottish, not Polish. Can't see a connection. This is the first I've heard of the guy. And I'd remember a wealthy Polish émigré. I'm an equal-opportunity gold digger."

Next we reconstructed our visit to the Caldwell household. When I got to Teddy's sobbing report of Bea's conversation, Janie shook her head. "You're right, there's no Spate family on Dear Island or any employees by that name."

A light bulb flickered in my brain, but I wasn't quick enough to decode the message. I tried to focus, but the thought was gone. As the adrenaline rush dissipated, my eyelids slid closed.

Braden offered to clean my waterlogged weapon, and my mind wandered as I watched him disassemble the piece. I dozed as Janie catalogued Bea's personality disorders for the detective. Somehow my unlikely wardens half walked, half carried me to bed. For the next four hours, I was dead to the world—a much better proposition than being dead.

NINE

What triggered the nightmares? Maybe I heard voices. Maybe my brain needed to sift through the night's terror.

Back on the dock again—this time on my knees, my hands lead weights. A crowd of people stared at me. Upfront Stew held hands with Bea, while Hugh yelled at the Cuthbert twins. Janie gossiped with a black stranger. Behind them, the Polish thug glared at me. And little Teddy ran in circles, yelling "Adam." Braden shouldered through the assembly to reach me. He grabbed my arm…

Janie shook my forearm like a terrier with a bone. "Wake up. Your boss, the sheriff and Braden are in the living room. I hunted up some clothes for you."

"What time is it? Why aren't you at work?" I tugged on jeans and pulled a sweatshirt over my head. I'd been cocooned in a down comforter, and it was hard to leave my warm nest. My sweatshirt seemed too thin to keep the ocean's chill from seeping back into my bones.

"It's one-thirty. I wasn't about to leave you alone. Besides, Gator isn't in today. Sally said she could hold the fort. I offered to help with Bea's funeral arrangements but Gator said he'd handle it himself."

I slid into a rocker beside the crackling fire. Sun streaming in the windows proclaimed it to be a beautiful day, not cool enough to justify a fire. But Janie must have sensed my craving for warmth. The dancing flames gave me a moment's pause though, as I remembered how close I'd been to becoming a Roman candle. Janie didn't join my inquisitors, though I bet she remained within earshot.

The sheriff inquired about my physical well being while the trio of lawmen surreptitiously evaluated my mental health. Impatient with the Miss Manners ritual, I testily urged them to get on with it. I retold my story twice, but nothing new sprang to mind as I relived the nightmare. I never saw the man, not even his retreating silhouette. His one-word curse wasn't enough to diagnose an accent. The only smell I remembered was gasoline.

When they finished repeating their questions, I had my own. "Did the marina yield any clues? How about the missing boat's registration?"

"Dead ends." The chief shrugged. "The guy rented the slip by phone. Called in a stolen credit card and boat registration number. Folks at the marina were too busy with the ferry to check itinerant boats. Especially since everybody'd prepaid."

"What about Kain Dzandrek?"

"Yeah, Braden told us about your run-in...that you thought you'd seen some Polish thug at Dear's marina," the sheriff replied. "As a courtesy, a Beaufort County deputy accompanied one of our men on a visit to Dzandrek's place. The man's smooth. Said his lunch mate was a stranger, someone he'd heard speaking Polish and invited to join him on a whim."

"Bull hockey. The man works for Dzandrek. I'd bet my life on it. What a crock," I protested.

"Well, it's a crock we have to accept. Dzandrek doesn't have a sheet. There's no proof he's guilty of anything but a fat bank account. Lots of rich expatriates have a soft spot for Hilton Head."

"Did your deputy ask Dzandrek about Hogsback Island or Hugh?" I prodded.

The sheriff rolled his eyes. "Look, we have no call to grill the guy. You overheard some Polish, and you admit you're not one hundred percent on the translation. You didn't like the guy's manners or his sidekick. Doesn't make him a killer."

The chief interrupted. "Are you thinking these Polish wankers might be friendly with Hugh Wells? If so, they didn't visit Hugh-boy on Dear last night. When Bev Collins got off the morning ferry, she gave me an earful about her sleepless night. Said Hugh and the twins were in an adjacent suite at the Beaufort Inn and had the TV blaring till the wee hours.

"That reminds me, our bridge is kaput. Engineers say it'll take at least two weeks to make even temporary repairs. Meanwhile, we can send golf carts over in emergencies—say, porting folks to an ambulance. Otherwise, everybody's stuck with the ferry."

"You still shorthanded?" I asked.

"Not too bad. I talked most of our crew into bunking here for the duration. Bud's the only one who balked. His wife's due with their first baby. Can't blame him."

Sheriff Conroy stood and stretched. "We're going to beef up our Dear presence, too. Braden'll stay until we catch this killer—or we're certain he's moved on. Two more deputies come on board this afternoon. They'll rotate shifts so there's always a deputy on duty. The resort's springing for a villa for our guys."

The news triggered a pang of regret. I'd hoped the handsome deputy would need my extended hospitality. Was Braden disappointed, too? His eyes fastened on his boss. The sheriff's decree didn't provoke so much as an eyelash twitch.

Okay, he's fine with the sleeping arrangements. What's your problem? You hardly know the man. Are you that lonely? You can take care of yourself.

Sure as hell, I'd watch my back—literally. I reached behind me to rub the tender stunner contact points.

"You think the killer will return?" I asked.

"Nah, I doubt it," the chief said. "No time soon anyways. He'd have to come by water, and he knows we'll be watching the marina. Too risky."

Risky, how? If I was wrong to suspect Underling, the homicidal maniac could be anyone. Without a clue as to the killer's identity, how would we ever know if he returned?

"Wish we could lure the sucker back," Sheriff Conroy lamented. "If only Marley had seen the guy's face. 'Course we could lie—say she did." He gave me a speculative look. "We could let it out that Marley hit her head rolling off that dock, that we're hoping her temporary amnesia will clear so she can provide a positive ID. That might interest him."

"Yeah, and get Marley killed," Braden objected. He took a deep breath. "But we could use a decoy, hide Marley off island. With a wig and the right clothes, Ed could pass for Marley. He's slim and the right height."

Oh, great. He suggests a man for my understudy. And what's with the protect-the-little-woman nonsense? I was seriously insulted.

"Hello, I'm here. How about including me in this conversation? The killer knows who I am. It wouldn't take him two minutes to detect a decoy. If you want a trap to work, I'm the bait."

"Don't be crazy," Braden said. "You're retired. No one's paying you to dodge bullets."

The retired reference stung.

Think I'm over the hill, do you?

"I've already earned a permanent spot on this psycho's hit list. Think he'll shrug off a botched job? I don't. If you don't catch him, I'll be looking over my shoulder a long time."

Janie waltzed into the room and took up a guard dog position by my chair. "Don't worry. I'll stay with you, Marley. No way he could take on the two of us."

Janie was someone you pigeonholed at your own risk. She purred like a kitten with real estate prospects but unsheathed razor-sharp claws if anyone challenged office oligarchy. The woman refused to pump her own gas—"not something a lady should be expected to do." Yet she carried condoms in a jeweled Daughters of the American Revolution case. My neighbor played life by her own rules. Rule number one: a fierce allegiance to friends.

"Forget it, Janie. I won't put you in danger," I said.

"Fine." She agreed much too quickly. "Then *you* stay here, Braden. You need a bed anyway. Sheriff, if you're going to dangle Marley's ass out there with a 'come and get it' sign, the least you can do is provide round-the-clock protection."

I caught Janie's sly smile. *Lord, help me. She's using murder to find me a live-in beau.*

"Not a bad idea," the chief agreed. "Marley and Braden can work the same shifts."

"I don't need a babysitter."

I didn't want to be foisted on Braden. My secret fear? I'd do something goofy and inappropriate. My mind wasn't exactly firing on all cylinders. My emotions seemed to be calling too many shots. "I can take care of myself."

"Don't argue," the sheriff said. "Your friend's right. If we put you on the line, we protect you. Either Braden stays in your house or we take you off the island. Your choice."

Braden turned toward me. "You'd be doing me a favor," he cajoled. "Otherwise I bunk with Dan, who plays that god-awful rap."

"Okay, you win."

Or was I the winner? I was afraid to examine my feelings, especially given his naked cameo appearance in my dream. Not to mention the melt down when I saw him nude in living color. Why had Braden's suggestion of a transvestite doppelganger smarted? The answer was as plain as the bruises on my wrists. I wanted the deputy to prefer me as a roommate for reasons other than a fondness for elevator music.

He's too young. I scolded myself. Another part of my mind replied, Who cares?

Maybe I *had* hit my head on a piling when I rolled off that dock.

After testy negotiations about my freedom to come and go

as I pleased, we reached détente. It was Wednesday afternoon. Officially I was off duty until Saturday night though I'd continue to serve as island liaison for Braden's investigation.

I won grudging permission for one off-island excursion—a standing once-a-month lunch date with Beaufort friends. The sheriff balked at first, but finally conceded that a killer wasn't likely to try a hit in broad daylight at a trendy waterfront café. On one point, however, they stood firm. After sunset, I would never be alone.

Never alone at night? I pictured Braden in my room. Undressing. Sliding between cool sheets. His tan skin a stark contrast to the pale linens. I'd given my houseguest the master bedroom. Now I wanted it back. Wanted to share that big bed.

TEN

The men appeared eager to leave: the sheriff to arrange a press conference, Braden to pack for an extended stay and return before sundown, Chief Dixon to meet with Sally.

Janie gave Dixon a pitying look. "She's gonna go batty if you fellas don't offer damage control. Two murders and a busted bridge have reporters salivating. Tomorrow's tabloids are gonna shout *Killer Stalks Marooned Islanders.* Sally's freaked. We can't afford to scare off potential buyers right before Easter."

Always the politician, the sheriff sugar-coated the PR nightmare. "I'll stress the killer *left* Dear and a watch on the marina will ensure he doesn't return. We want our perp to think this island's the last place we'll look for him. My spin should make everyone happy."

Yeah, except for the next poor slob who gets killed. Possibly me.

As the trio exited, the sheriff sketched a salute and promised deputies would mosey by my house on the half-hour, walk its perimeter on the hour. He ordered me to stay inside until Braden returned.

The precautions seemed overkill on a sunny afternoon. Our murderer exhibited a predilection for gloom and had to be as tired as I was—too pooped to sail over for an après-lunch murder spree.

My keyed up state made napping impossible. I paced beside my picture window, watching golfers parade from fairway to green. Though temperatures hovered near sixty, the seniors were girded in Gortex and sported scarlet ear muffs and blue watch caps. Up north, folks wore shorts when the mercury crept this high. But who was I to ridicule? I was more than happy to cower by the fire while the ocean winds sliced and diced.

I picked up a mystery novel but couldn't concentrate. I glanced at a picture of Jeff and me hoisting beer mugs in Munich.

Braden's nothing like Jeff. More serious. Less irreverent. Braden had dark hair and hazel eyes. Jeff's hair was blond, his eyes, milk chocolate.

Oh, stop it. Jeff's dead. And you weren't exactly a virgin bride. You've had relationships with other men.

I looked over at Janie, who flipped through back issues of *Southern Living.*

"Janie, I think I'll shower before Braden comes back. Okay?"

"Sure, it's not like you're Chatty Cathy this afternoon."

I lingered in the shower, hoping the pelting water would clear my mind. It didn't. After toweling off, I rummaged through my vanity searching for perfume. I dabbed on *Obsession* and immediately felt guilty. Jeff had given me the perfume. But guilt didn't stop me from forsaking my usual Chapstick for creamy, cherry-red lipstick. Opening my underwear drawer, I pawed past maybe twenty cotton briefs to locate a pair of black lace panties.

Oh, crimey. Stop this nonsense. Still, it was the silky lace I slid up my legs.

When I rejoined Janie, she seemed even more fidgety. Was my jumpiness infectious?

"Why don't you go to work?" I suggested. "Braden will be back in no time—thanks to your manipulation. Don't think I'm not onto you."

"Hey, no reason your bodyguard shouldn't be male, handsome, and single. Besides you must be blind if you don't know he's attracted to you. Thought I'd choke on the pheromones."

"Yeah, right." Nonetheless, curiosity and a smidgeon of hope prompted me to ask, "Like what?"

"For starters that hungry look every time he glances your way. He wasn't craving waffles this morning." Janie's smile faded. "But I need to tell you something before he returns."

She paused, apparently debating how to start. "Remember how upset I was when Sally dropped that bombshell about Hogsback Island, now known as Emerald Cay? Something's really wrong. I'm scared my tits are gonna be in a wringer if I don't find out what's what."

"Are you worried about your greedy bosses being overextended? Even if the Dear Company goes belly up, some other Lowcountry developer will snap you up. You know the real estate biz. You have contacts up the wazoo and a treasure map to all of Hollis County's buried bodies."

Janie chewed on her lip. "I won't be such a hot commodity if I'm wearing a prison jumpsuit. I have this sinking feeling some members of our glorious 'sales team' are engaged in fraud. Yesterday I caught Woody Nickel sneaking my notary stamp back into my desk drawer. I'm not exactly Miss Goody Two Shoes. If he felt compelled to go behind my back, it's bad. The document in his hand had something to do with Emerald Cay."

"Did you confront him?"

"Damn straight. Afterward, I stormed into Gator's office, demanded he fire the SOB and destroy whatever paperwork the guy dummied with my stamp. I threatened cops. That made Gator sputter. The boss sweet-talked me. Said it was a misunderstanding, promised Woody wouldn't touch my notary stamp again. Said he'd protect me 'no matter what happened.' That 'no-matter-what' line scared the crapola out of me. What are they hiding? Will you help? You can pretend to be a buyer, ask questions I can't."

I laughed. "No way. Your officemates would never believe I've developed a sudden hankering for investment property. Plus my own plate is rather full—you know, acting as bait for a psycho killer."

Janie sprang from her chair. "Don't play hard to get, Marley. I know how your fevered brain works. You're wondering if there's a connection—crooked real estate deals, dead appraiser."

She stopped her pacing, pleaded with her eyes. "Come on. I can't trust anyone else."

I sighed. "Guess I could say I'm helping my aunt...that she wants to build near me. Aunt May would play along. She sells real estate in Iowa."

"Thanks." Janie grinned. "I'll fill you in so you don't waste time turning over old rocks. But you've got to promise—not a word to Braden or any other law-type person."

"You trying to make me an accessory to your crimes?" I asked, only half-joking.

"Oh, don't be such a Girl Scout. Everything I know—well, up until Woody forged my signature—is quasi-legal. Ethical? That's another kettle of fish."

For the next half hour, Janie provided an advanced course in developer shenanigans. Her lecture explained a lot—like why homesites in new corporate developments always sold for more than larger, equally scenic "resale" lots.

To extract the greatest profit per inch of oceanfront, Dear's newest developer had sliced parcels into skinny, zero-lot-line plots with house plans tailored to fit the corseted space. The shotgun homes featured trendy tabby exteriors and Romeo-and-Juliet balconies.

"Here's where it gets interesting," Janie said. "Comparable value plays a big role in the property appraisals banks insist on these days to approve a mortgage. So appraisers check to see if other buyers have plunked down similar wads of cash for neighboring properties.

"Sally and Gator make sure the comps look good. Just before a grand opening, they whisper to select employees, urging them to buy at inflated prices. Corporate money's loaned interest-free so the shills can manage down payments. Sally and Gator promise to unload the properties once suitable patsies are found—before the bogus buyers have to make the first loan payments."

My mouth hung open. "You're kidding. I thought bankers wised up after the last bubble burst."

"Some did, but institutional memories are short—especially when early sales are brisk. The shills start a bidding frenzy. Real buyers decide to snatch up lots before prices shoot higher. Once appraiser comps show several homesites in the new development have already sold at the high prices, the market's set. Bankers rubber-stamp the loans."

I shook my head. "This is legal?"

Janie rolled her eyes. "Sure. Well, sort of... If all goes according to Hoyle, who's gonna complain? Insiders pocket a bonus, and the ultimate buyers think they're Donald Trumps since Sally and Gator ratchet prices higher on each new development. Folks who bought in the last round think they got a steal."

I stood and walked to the window. "What happens if real buyers never materialize? What if the shills have to pony up and pay their mortgages?"

Janie's face, reflected in the window, frowned. "Things get nasty. Foreclosures for sure."

Outside, a golfer jumped, arms raised as his long putt found a home.

"I can't believe buyers are this stupid. Any research would tell them they're paying ridiculous sums for dirt that costs half as much on an older wedge of the island."

Janie smiled. "Real estate agents get a bonus, on top of regular commissions, for selling corporate dirt. Don't forget, agents work for sellers not buyers. Why should they wise folks up about cheaper deals? It would cost them.

"Fortunately for the Dear Company—and me—buyers who've spent sixty winters in Ohio and are sick of snow don't crunch numbers. They tool down I-95, stopping here and there. Compared to many islands, even our high-priced lots look reasonable."

"If this fleecing's legal and works so well, why the hell isn't the Dear Company rolling in dough?"

"Kaboom." Janie imitated the sound of an explosion. "Simple collision of ego and greed. Sally and Gator wanted to be Dixie land barons. Six months ago, they formed another company, a real estate investment trust—R.E.I.T.—and bought a bunch of foreclosed properties for pennies on the dollar..."

The doorbell rang. Janie jumped, breaking off her discourse mid-sentence. She mimed a zipper sealing her lips. "Remember, no tales out of school. Make an appointment with Woody to talk about buying in Emerald Cay. I can play sleuth, too. I'll call April tonight and see if my sister's heard of your Polish émigré. It's amazing what the owner of a gentlemen's club picks up through the grapevine."

Janie flung my front door open. "Hi and bye," she said cheerily as she brushed past Braden. "You'd better not let anything happen to Marley."

"Come in," I said. "Ignore the reception committee."

I heard the quake in my voice. Seeing Braden arrive with suitcase and groceries worked like a defibrillator, kick-starting my heart.

His vintage Samsonite suitcase featured a skin of stamped vinyl veneer and those hinged snaps that let you wedge in forgotten items at the price of pinched skin. He precariously balanced three bags of groceries. Six-packs bulged in bas-relief through one of the thin plastic sacks. I relieved Braden of one bag of provisions. He set the others on the kitchen island.

"Why don't you put your suitcase in the bedroom while I put away the groceries? Your room awaits, unchanged. Hasn't gotten any cleaner since you left."

A crash prompted me to run to the bedroom. Braden was on his knees, picking up big chunks of Jeff's Oktoberfest mug. The engraved silver lid with its thumbed lift clung tenaciously to the mug's broken handle.

Braden looked up. "I'm so sorry. I knocked the nightstand with my suitcase."

A fist of sorrow cut off my breath. I couldn't force words to exit my mouth though I made a noise. So few mementos remained. We didn't take pictures. Didn't collect trinkets. I'd bought Jeff that mug in Munich the month we met. Now one more tie was gone.

Braden put the pottery pieces on the nightstand and walked toward me. Tears trickled down my cheeks.

Stop it. Don't lose it, not over a freaking two-bit mug. You could buy a thousand identical mugs on Ebay.

"What have I done?" Braden asked. "That wasn't just a beer mug."

I managed to choke out three words, "It...was...Jeff's."

The dam broke. I turned to leave, to take my grief private. Braden pulled me against his chest. He defeated my attempt to wriggle away. Holding me tight, he stroked my hair as I cried. Again and again, he repeated, "I'm sorry."

Once I managed to turn off the waterworks, embarrassment tied my tongue. Anger figured into the equation, too. Not at Braden—at myself. My breakdown had to make him feel like a jerk, as if he'd committed high treason.

I straightened and pulled back. "I'm the one who's sorry...and ashamed. Please, accept my apologies. It was an accident. The mug was a silly souvenir. I don't know what possessed me. Just...give me a few minutes."

I walked down the hall to the powder room, closed the door. I soaked a washcloth and pressed the cold compress against my eyes. Sitting on the commode, I sucked in a series of deep breaths. I felt drained. But drained was an improvement. For over a year, thoughts of Jeff left me either numb or angry. Unable to feel anything else. Now, to my surprise, I felt a niggling of hope, a wedge of curiosity about what might come next.

I smiled when I realized my mind had already turned to food. Back in the kitchen, I put away the rest of the groceries. When Braden joined me, I spoke before he could rehash what I'd already dubbed my mad mug lunacy.

"You didn't need to bring groceries." Would a smile telegraph my desire to move on? Let him know I was fine, that I wasn't winding up for a new crying jag?

Braden picked up on my manic clue. "It's the least I could do. Plus I figured E.T. Grits might be out of beer by now."

I grinned. "From the sounds of the partying last night, you're probably right." I found space for the last of three Old Milwaukee six-packs. What had I expected? Neither of us were the wine spritzer type.

"I'll cook tonight," he added. "But I have a limited repertoire."

"What are the chef's specialties?"

"Steak, hamburgers, and scrambled eggs. I bought all of 'em. Steaks for tonight. There's also a salad mix, pre-sliced garlic bread and frozen key-lime pie."

"Sounds great. But if I'm going to eat pie, I need to run first. Listen, make yourself at home. It's only four-thirty. I'll be back in an hour—before dark."

I needed a run to regain my equilibrium.

Braden frowned. "I'd try to discourage you, but I have a hunch how that conversation would end. Give me a minute to change, and I'll come along. I'm not letting you out of my sight."

"Are you a runner?" My question wasn't exactly innocent. I don't do badly for an over-fifty broad, and the thought of forcing Braden to pant a little held a certain perverse appeal.

"Running's not my favorite activity, but I'll try to keep up."

He certainly looked fit, but I didn't picture him as a runner. Maybe bending a Bowflex to his will or hefting dumbbells as sweat popped on his forehead. His hard, defined muscles didn't have a runner's sleek contours.

"I started packing on pounds after I turned thirty-five," he confessed. "Figured I either had to run occasionally or give up beer. No contest."

I smiled in spite of myself. "A strong motive. Me? I love running. I really miss it when I lay off a few days."

"Do you have a DVR?" Braden asked.

"Sure," I answered, momentarily puzzled by the quick topic shift.

"Let's record the news. See how the sheriff handles his press conference."

"Right. Can't believe I forgot about it." I had a vested interest in the sheriff's fictionalized account of my encounter with Dear's killer.

Five minutes later we were out the door. We appeared to favor similar exercise attire—torn T-shirts, threadbare shorts, dingy running shoes. No flashy, form-fitting spandex or designer headbands. My concession to sweat was a man's handkerchief tucked in my waistband.

Braden glanced at the contraption on my wrist. "That's one honking big watch."

"A new GPS toy. We have to stand still a minute so it can acquire satellite signals, then I'll be ready to roll."

"What, you're afraid you'll get lost on Dear Island?"

I laughed. "No. It's got a trip computer. Tells me exactly how far I've gone, average miles per hour, even my maximum speed. I wear it whenever I run so I can set 'waypoints' for the fellow who runs Camp Dear. He's planning geocaching games for his little munchkins this summer. I'm marking points of interest for his treasure hunts. You know, osprey nests, rare plants, alligator hangouts, that sort of thing."

"Give me a heads-up on those alligator hangouts," Braden said as we set off down the leisure path.

The sun hovered low on the horizon, probing the landscape with slanted golden beams. Motes danced in the light, and the slender shadows cast by palm trees and pampas grass looked mystical—cloaked monks stealing silently across the adjacent fairway's velvety winter rye.

I checked to make sure no golfers were teeing off behind us, then sprinted onto the eleventh fairway. The soft grass with its spongy cushioning was kind to rickety knees. A couple of hundred yards later I ducked into a wooded shortcut to the nearest ocean crosswalk.

"Hey, you don't waste time warming up." Braden's breathing, like mine, was audible but not labored. I'd lost any illusion of leaving him panting in my wake. The man could run, even if he didn't enjoy it.

When the ocean cutover took us past Stew's condo, I glanced at his windows. The panes were fiery mirrors. They caught and liquefied the dying sun's glow, turning it into molten ingots. A fisherman in waders stood resolutely in the surf, rhythmically casting his line. The filament danced over the frothy breakers. Half a mile down the narrow ribbon of beach, a woman walked a dog. Lonely silhouettes.

We slowed on the uneven surface. The rhythmic slapping of our shoes against the sand all but drowned out my words. "It's beautiful, so peaceful. Hard to imagine some maniac is murdering people on Dear."

"Nothing to say murder and beauty can't coexist," Braden answered. "It's just easier to accept death in tacky surroundings. Back alleys. Crack houses. Slums. Your island's untouched by that kind of ugliness. It's isolated. You have to cross what, four bridges, to get here from the mainland? How long have people lived here, anyway?"

"That final bridge—the one that's defunct at the moment— was built in the seventies. Before then the island was a hunting preserve. In the fifties, a logging company strip-cut the pines. Hard to believe, looking at the heavy forest that's grown up since."

We lapsed into silence as we picked up speed. Braden almost stepped on a horseshoe crab's carcass. Birds had picked its prehistoric armor clean, leaving only its turtled brown shell and spiny tail. Jumping to avoid the remains, he lost his balance in the ankle-deep sand and accidentally hip-checked me. Reaching out to steady me his grip felt strong, hot and reassuring.

"It's not easy running on this stuff," he complained as he released my arm.

I glanced toward the water. Each wave brought the ocean nearer its crest, almost as high as the spring tide that tried to snatch Bea's corpse. That tide's demarcation line was clear. The sea had deposited reeds, tiny shells, and the occasional Styrofoam scrap in an undulating pattern. We ran uphill of the detritus, hugging a line of chameleon dunes that appeared and disappeared at nature's whim. Braden was right. The sand was too soft for running. Sucking at my feet, it caused my ankles to wobble.

I stumbled against him. "Sorry. I forgot it was high tide. Not the time to run here. You'll have to come back at low tide. Acres of white sand, hard-packed enough to ride a bike. Next crossover we can cut over to a road."

We skirted a stretch of four- to five-foot dunes. Sea grass anchored the shifting mounds. The winter's nor'easters had bent and battered the once golden stalks. My mind floated as I shook off last night's ordeals and surrendered to the cleansing salt air. Then the world exploded.

"Get down." Braden tackled me.

125

We landed in a sweaty tangle. He rolled his body on top of mine.

Boom. Crack. Boom. Crack.

For a second, I shared the deputy's alarm. *Gunfire?* My heart hammered so hard I thought it might crack a rib. Then laughter bubbled up.

"Quiet," he hissed. "They'll hear you."

Braden clearly figured I was hysterical.

"It's okay. Just some touron shooting fireworks." I chuckled with relief as an additional snap, crackle and pop marked the launch of more harmless pyrotechnics. "You get used to it. Fireworks are legal in South Carolina, and people pick them up en route to the beach."

Braden didn't move. He was still on top of me, his weight a pleasant pressure. His mint-scented breath made my lips tingle. I'd quit laughing. I scarcely breathed as I searched his face. I'd never been much on mental telepathy but I gave it a go: Don't move. Kiss me. Messages I'd never utter aloud. It had been so long. How did this work?

God help me, I wanted this man. It had been more than a year since I'd felt the solid comfort of a man's body atop my own. *Forgive me, Jeff. I need to feel alive again.*

The cool sand cemented itself to my legs. I felt clammy and flushed at the same time. Braden toyed with a damp curl matted to my forehead. A finger sauntered down my cheek and grazed my lips. His eyes no longer looked hazel; they'd darkened, a smoldering ash that overpowered the lightning flashes of green.

An arched eyebrow asked the question. I gave the answer in my steady gaze and the tremble of my lips. Slowly he lowered his mouth to mine. The kiss began as a whisper. A promise. Then I felt the liquid heat of his tongue and joined the duet. The song began sweetly, our tongues shyly flirting. But my nerve endings were dry tinder, aching for a match. I felt his arousal and shifted my hips to intensify our contact. I wrapped my arms around his muscled back and hugged his hard body to mine. The sand grinding beneath my limbs was a forgotten irritant.

In seconds, we'd reached the flashpoint. My ferocious longing frightened me. Braden's need appeared just as keen. Our bodies raced ahead of conscious thought.

When he broke our full-body embrace, I felt dazed.

"Can we head back?" he asked between ragged breaths.

"Yes," I answered, my voice husky with want.

Am I nuts? I've got twelve years on this man. We've never been on a date. Yes, but he saved your life. And you're alive...alive like you haven't been in thirteen long months.

My decision made me feel giddy with anticipation. "Race you back," I taunted impishly, wondering if a hard-on would add or subtract from his foot speed.

We were both panting and shivering when we burst through my front door. The minute it shut, we grappled like mud wrestlers, slick with sweat. Encumbered by few items of clothing, we were naked in a flash—and still in my foyer. If Janie walked onto my porch, the glass sidelights would give her an eyeful.

I giggled.

"What?" Braden asked, somewhat irritably.

"I hope Girl Scouts don't pick this moment to make a cookie call. We're in plain view."

"Oh. We can fix that."

I let him lead me toward the master bedroom, but resisted his pull toward the bed.

"Let's do this right," I said. "We're caked with sand. Shower first?"

"Why not?" Braden's lazy grin made me melt. "We have all night."

We stood slightly apart under the pulsing cascade, our

fingers reaching across the steamy divide to explore. My skin tingled from the prickling spray.

Mini droplets clung to his long black eyelashes. Inside-out tears. His eyes met mine, unblinking. They told a bedtime story I'd sorely missed.

I want you.

He reached for the soap. In his clever hands, the slick bar slithered across my shoulders and snaked down one arm. When he reached my hand, he opened it, brought my palm to his face and tenderly kissed it. Then he lavished his attentions on my other arm.

A clean piney scent rode on the shower mist and filled the spare space between our bodies. The drumbeat of warm water painted my breasts the delicate pink of seashells. My nipples hardened though he had yet to touch them. Braden bent his head and licked at a rivulet of water as it meandered from my shoulder to my chest. His tongue, a marriage of velvet and sandpaper, felt even warmer than the shower's cascade. His teeth grazed my flesh and I sucked in my breath. *Oh, God, his touch. A gentle, easing rain after a long drought.*

"Hey, you can't have all the fun." I tried to quell the quaver in my voice.

I soaped Braden's chest and watched as his matted hairs first clung to his skin and then slowly sprang back to life. *Resilience, what a marvel.*

"Turn around," I ordered.

"You want me to turn my back on you?" He laughed. "What do you have in mind?"

I soaped a long-handled brush and made lazy circles down his spine. Then I traced them lightly with my fingernails. He gasped. "May I turn around now?" His voice rumbled, cascading over me like the water.

Braden captured the soap from me and lathered his hands. Now the soap was gone. Yet I could see bubbles where his fingers painted sudsy designs on my skin. My body hummed. He pushed me against the smooth tile, and I wrapped my arms around him once more. As the warm water sluiced over us, it found the few tiny crevices where our bodies were not wholly joined. Trickling into these voids, the water perfected our fit.

This felt wonderful. This felt right.

ELEVEN

Braden proved to be a marathoner, not a sprinter. What more could I ask for in an exercise partner? Strength, endurance. Shared exuberance at the finish line. And the knowledge that warm-down exercises do count.

His caresses hadn't stopped. Now it was light finger exercises, a hand skating over my thigh as I curled against his length. More than an hour had elapsed since we'd entered the shower. As I lay in bed with my eyes closed, I could replay each sensuous moment.

When was the last time I'd felt this good? I almost wanted to burst into song. Not a love song, mind you, but something exuberant and free-wheeling like Jan & Dean's "Little Old Lady from Pasadena."

He yawned, stretched and patted my behind. "Time to get up. I'll fix dinner, but first let's see what Sheriff Conroy fed the newshounds."

In the living room, Braden claimed the recliner, a man magnet if I ever saw one. If I'm ever desperate for male company, I'll just buy a La-Z-Boy for yard art. I curled up on the couch. At least I beat him to the remote control.

The DVD rewound to the start of the news conference. Conroy's voice boomed. "I have a statement, then I'll take questions." I punched down the volume.

"Last night saw another horrible, senseless murder on Dear Island. Beatrice Caldwell was killed after midnight. We believe her killer to be the same person who murdered Stewart Hartwell early Monday morning.

"This vicious murderer left the island by boat shortly before dawn. A Dear Island security officer scuffled with him at the marina. We hope to circulate a sketch of the suspect shortly. The guard suffered minor injuries and a concussion, but she's recovering nicely. Our witness got a good look at her attacker. While her short-term memory remains a bit cloudy, doctors are confident it'll clear quickly.

"We *will* catch this killer. We've got a crackerjack team working the case, including forensics experts from the South Carolina Law Enforcement Division. Our lead investigator has ten years of experience as an Atlanta homicide detective."

The Q&A free-for-all that followed yielded no surprises. Conroy tailored his answers to soothe the citizenry. By the end of the press conference, he'd repeated umpteen times the number of officers, squad cars, helicopters and boats trolling for the killer and protecting the populace.

Conroy deserved high marks for schmooze. But would our killer buy his heavy-handed hints? I turned to Braden. "Was Conroy too obvious? Authorities normally don't spill the beans about an eyewitness."

He chewed his lip. "Let's pray the perp thinks the sheriff's a local yokel who forgot himself. I wish Conroy hadn't sent such a clear message. I have a strong feeling our killer will be back. Sure you don't want to leave the island?"

I teased to keep the mood light. "What? Think the pressure will get to an old retiree?"

"I don't want to take any chances." His eyes were dark, brooding.

Nothing would convince me to abandon the plan. The only way to trap the killer.

When I said nothing more, he relented. "Okay, I'll make a salad and grill our steaks. We can talk strategy later. At least we've settled the question of sleeping arrangements. I plan to stay glued to you until this maniac's caught."

I answered with a grin. "You do 'glue' nicely."

I walked into the great room and checked my answering - machine. I'd heard the phone ring while we were otherwise engaged. The neon counter read "10." Clearly the Dear Island tom-toms had identified me as the "mystery" witness. I fast-forwarded through seven nearly identical messages—callers clucking over my bad luck. I jotted a note to return the eighth call. Tammy Nowling asked if we were still on for lunch tomorrow.

The ninth message came as a surprise. Leyla's rich near-baritone always commanded attention. We shared the same last name, Clark, and, if we were feeling mischievous, we introduced ourselves as sisters. Leyla's skin was dark chocolate while mine is nearer marshmallow, even when toasted. So our banter either drew a good-natured laugh or a bewildered mumble.

The tension in Leyla's voice signaled her call was no laughing matter. "Marley, my niece has gone missing. It's been less than twenty-four hours, and the sheriff's office said we have to wait forty-eight hours before they'll look into it. Can you stop by my office tomorrow? Say eleven? Don't bother calling tonight. I'll be at my sister's."

Though I hadn't the foggiest notion how I could help, I would meet her at Gedduh Place in the morning. I tutored in the center's adult literacy program.

Janie was the tenth caller. How did she always manage to have the final word?

"Listen, I talked to April. My sister says this Kain guy hangs out at her club. Shows up about nine every Friday. Usually leaves with a young chick, but never plays hide-the-salami with the same gal twice. I told April we'd be there Friday. We can bunk at her place since there's no way to get back on Dear after sundown. Bye."

I considered calling Janie to remind her I was joined at the hip with a bodyguard. Of course Braden might not object to visiting a gentlemen's club. Tomorrow I'd spring the idea of a Hilton Head sleepover on my new roommate.

The sizzle of steak and its companion aroma made a sneak

attack. My stomach rumbled. "How much longer?" I called.

"Five minutes, tops."

Time enough to power up my laptop and check emails. Earlier I'd fired off questions to Steve Watson, an Army buddy who'd opened a Web-based "defend-yourself" business. His Internet storefront did a brisk trade in non-lethal weapons from stun guns and pepper spray to blinding LED guns. I hoped Steve could suggest how our killer acquired his weaponry. He'd responded quickly—two lengthy emails.

"Dinner's ready," Braden called.

"Just a minute." I printed Steve's missives to read later and powered down the computer. For the remainder of the night, I had no intention of dealing with modern technology. An easy decision when there's age-old—or is it old age—lust to satisfy.

***

I awoke with a start. Disoriented. I was tucked into the king bed in my master bedroom, not my normal sleeping digs. More important, a warm naked rump pressed against mine. I smiled. *Change can be good.*

The room wasn't so much black as mocha. I could discern the shape of my dresser, the outline of the bathroom door, the picture window where moonlight cast shifting shadows of overgrown oleanders against the shades.

Wind-blown branches scratched against the siding. The sound probably nudged me to consciousness. In winter, I'd have blamed the commotion on a large buck that liked to hone his antlers on my shrubbery. But spring wasn't the season for antler rattling.

A hoarse whisper brought me fully awake. *Should I wake Braden? What if it's my imagination?* I didn't want to appear a high-strung ninny.

I crept out of bed. Nakedness compounded my feeling of vulnerability. I edged to the window and peered out a corner of the shade. A shadow moved. I blinked, then focused where a

133

silhouette darted into deeper shadows. This was no dream. A man moved. He held a long gun. A rifle?

My pulse rate be-bopped up the charts. I backed away from the window.

How could I wake Braden without creating a ruckus? I wanted to catch the prowler, not scare him off. Maybe we'd bag our murderer.

After pulling on running shorts and a tee, I tiptoed to his side of the bed and squeezed his shoulder. With my other hand, I pressed two fingers against his lips. He shot up like a geyser, his breathing staccato. I'd scared the crap out of him.

I whispered. "Someone's outside. In back. By the window. I think he has a gun. A rifle, maybe."

"I'll go," Braden whispered fiercely. "You stay here."

"Fat chance." Though it was too dark for meaningful glances, I was pretty sure the deputy was pissed.

"Come on, let's do it," I urged. "No time to waste arguing."

Braden pulled on pants and grabbed his gun from the holster draped over a rocking chair. I retrieved mine from a dresser drawer. We both slipped on shoes and stole from the room.

I cursed the squeaking floorboards I'd pledged to fix many moons ago. To surprise our backyard intruder, we snuck out the front door and down the three steps from porch to lawn. Braden motioned me to follow him to the right. I resolutely shook my head "no" and pointed left. Making a *Yellow Pages* walking fingers motion, I signaled my intent. My partner wasn't a happy camper.

I'd barely cleared the front corner of the house when my foot landed on a palm frond. I froze, certain the crackle of a tinder-dry frond could be heard for blocks. I listened for fleeing footsteps, a curse or a shot. Silence. Even the tree frogs had stilled their chorus.

The absence of bushes on this side of the property provided

a clear view. No one lurked near my path. I uttered a silent prayer, crouched low and scuttled forward, hugging shadows cast by the house. I peered around the corner. Silhouettes. Plural. Crap.

There were two of them. Only one carried a gun. I inched forward. Since no one ever called me Dead Eye Dick, I needed to creep mighty close to nail anyone. And I needed to make damn sure no stray bullet flew in Braden's direction.

My fear decreased as my anger surged. I was ninety-nine percent sure I knew the identity of the culprits. When I got within fifteen paces, I yelled, "Drop it. I have a gun, and I'll shoot if you don't put yours on the ground this instant."

Boys, not men. They reeked of alcohol. Their lack of sobriety probably explained their bumbling lethargy. No telling how long the Cuthbert twins had been dithering about.

"I've got you covered," Braden yelled from a nearby vantage point. "Don't be stupid."

Jared flung his rifle to the ground, as I was certain he would. Braden rushed to retrieve it.

"For Christ's sake," he yelled at me. "You didn't wait for me to get in position. Are you trying to get killed?"

Ignoring his ire, I turned mine on the twins. "As soon as I got a good look—and a whiff of you two—I knew I was dealing with inebriated dumbbells. Introduce yourself, boys," I ordered as I began patting down the twins.

Hands held high, the teens started to whine.

"Hey, man. No guns," Henry said, his speech a sibilant slur. "Ours wuz just a pop gun."

"Yeah, we only wanted to scare you a little," Jared added. "You really spoiled things the other night. We owed you."

I turned toward Braden and holstered my weapon. "Meet Dork Number One—Henry Cuthbert—and Dork Number Two—brother Jared. Let's take this discussion inside."

TWELVE

I made a pot of Ajax-strength coffee and dealt mugs to all players. Some do-gooder would probably haul me up on charges for over-caffeinating minors. I wanted the boys a lot less pie-eyed. Interviewing drunks is seldom enlightening. Either they're laughing like lunatics or they're so wiped drool snakes down their chins as they stare into space.

Braden and I didn't bother with a good-cop, bad-cop routine. Neither of us was in the mood to play the good guy.

"How'd you get out of your house?" I asked. "Tie Hugh to a chair?"

"He'd probably like that," Henry snickered. "Wouldn't give that kinky mother the satisfaction. You oughta see his porn collection."

When Braden replied, his tone was pure drill sergeant. "Cut the crap. No elaboration. No f-words. No attitude. Just answer the questions, and make it snappy. I just met the two of you, and you already turn my stomach."

Jared's eyes went wide. Then the sneer returned. "Hey, you're a cop. We know our rights. I demand a lawyer. You aren't messing with some lame-brain lowlifes, you know."

His cockiness made me want to smack him. "I know exactly who you are—hoodlums holding a gun outside my bedroom window. Now, think *whom* you're messing with. I'm no cop, just a 'little old widder lady' trying to protect herself. If I get too frightened, my nasty ol' gun could fire by accident."

I switched off my sweet old lady imitation and adopted a sergeant-major's bark. "No jury in the world would convict if I shot you. Got it? You're on my property, carrying a gun. I could plug you right here, but the blood would make a real mess on my tile. Talk."

Though Henry and Jared smirked through my bluff, my

honest-to-God anger planted a niggling seed of doubt. Henry raised his hands in surrender. "Okay, okay."

I repeated my initial question. "How'd you get out of the house—past Hugh?"

"We waited till he left," Jared answered. "He takes off lots of nights after he's poured *Mommy* into bed. He takes The Predator—our fourteen-foot skiff. We followed him to the dock. He went out Mad Inlet. We've watched him before; it's usually three, four hours before he's back. We figure he meets some drug dealer."

Henry butted in. "Yeah, you should be grilling Hugh, not us. I bet he murdered Stew. Dr. Death was out that night. Leave it to some aging lounge lizard to cook veggies with a dead body."

Braden slammed his palm down on the table in front of Henry's face. Silverware jumped, and I feared he'd cracked the sturdy oak surface. Coffee sloshed wildly in the rocking mugs. The deputy had the boys' attention.

"How do you know about the vegetables? We didn't release that detail. Only the killer could know. Guess I should read you your rights after all."

"Oh, man, ask your old lady. This is Dear Island," Jared complained. "How long do you think it took for everyone on this dirt-bag island to hear the news? That's old, man."

After a moment's silence, I sighed and broke in. "Okay, what possible reason would Hugh have to kill Stew?"

The boys shrugged in unison. "He met Stew at the marina Saturday. When he got home, he made a call on his cell. Sounded mad as hell," Henry said.

"That's real conclusive, Slick." Braden's voice dripped sarcasm. "We have better reason to suspect you losers. Who knows, maybe you killed Stew and Bea for thrills."

Henry's head snapped up. "We weren't even on the island when that bitch got offed."

"You were with Hugh in Beaufort, right?" I asked. "That gives him the same alibi."

Jared pouted. "Maybe... But he's still a freakin' killer, and nobody cares."

I looked closely at the boys. "Okay, in the last five minutes you've accused Hugh of being a drug addict and a murderer. Sure you're not just pissed because he tries to make you toe the line?"

While the twins' anger was real, it didn't exactly lend weight to their accusations.

"Maybe he hasn't killed yet, but it's not for trying. The bastard feeds Mom a dozen kind of pills, practically pushes 'em down her throat. Keeps her too blotto to notice he's pissing our money away. When she sobers up, he diddles her till she moans."

"Enough." I shuddered. Good God, was their home life truly this horrific or were they playing us for yucks? For their safety, I wanted the boys locked away until their mom could arrange bail. But there was no way to get them off island, and it wasn't a good time for houseguests. If the real killer showed, they could get caught in the crossfire. I'd figure out how to investigate their painful accusations later.

"We're taking you home. Tomorrow you may have a new address."

After I spoke, I realized the decision to release the boys hadn't been mine to make. Not unilaterally anyway. Did Braden have more questions? Did he want to keep them here? I would apologize...later. I was unaccustomed to having a partner—in any arena.

Braden didn't appear miffed. "You heard the lady. Move it."

In the car, the boys fell silent, just as they had the last time I chauffeured them home. Dreading a return to their pricey prison? Or had acting like brats sapped all their energy?

On this visit, Braden assumed the doorbell honors. No response. The mansion's front door was locked, and a blinking camera light above the threshold indicated the security system was engaged.

"Told you so," Henry said. "Hugh-baby is out on some drug run."

"You boys have a key?" I asked. Jared shook his head no.

Braden wasn't buying. "So how were you planning to get back in? Transporter beam? Or were you going to ring the bell and wake Hugh? What's open—some back door, a window?"

The boys looked at each other. Henry shrugged. "There's a separate entrance to the servant's quarters. It's off the security grid. When Hugh fired the maid, we stole the key."

"Well, here's what's going to happen," Braden said. "I'm going to walk you to that door and watch you go inside. Then Marley and I will sit in your driveway until Hugh arrives. Capiche?"

"Yeah, yeah."

By the time Braden returned, I was as close to horizontal as I could manage, my car seat cranked to full stretch.

"God, I'm tired," I mumbled. "You think the boys are telling the truth?"

"Probably. Though I'm sure their stories are shaded with more than a little malice. Hope my sons don't turn out like those two."

"How old are your boys?"

"Braden Jr.—Brady—is three; Keith, two. They live with their mom and her new husband in Atlanta."

"You have pictures?"

"Sure." He flipped open his wallet and passed it to me with his penlight. I held the light low so no escaping glow would warn Hugh of our presence. The chubby faces made me grin. Shavings off the old block. Both inherited Braden's hazel eyes and killer smile.

"Must have been hard to leave," I managed.

"Um, Brady and Keith already call Jim 'Daddy.'" Pain colored his voice. "My ex made it clear there's no room for me. Says my hanging around would *confuse* my sons. Claims I wasn't around all that much when we were married, so it shouldn't be a hardship."

Braden's forlorn expression spoke of guilt and regret. "You have kids?"

"No. Jeff was ten years older than me. He had two children with his first wife and wasn't anxious for more. Military careers aren't exactly conducive to parenting."

"So who are the kids in the pictures by your bed?"

"Photos of my stepchildren when they were little. Duncan's forty now, a pilot for United, lives in Chicago. He's divorced, no kids. Janice lives in San Diego. She has a three-year-old daughter, Riley. She's the blonde pistol with the sandcastle. The rest are shots of my great-nieces and nephews."

Conversation petered out. Neither of us felt up to talking. I couldn't stifle a yawn. "Hope we don't have long to wait."

Something caught Braden's interest. "Looks like your prayers are answered."

Walking briskly, a man angled across the estate's cobbled driveway. He'd yet to spot our car stashed in a cubbyhole partially screened by twenty-foot oleanders. The man's gliding gait identified him. "Walks like Hugh."

"Let's see if it talks like him," Braden muttered sotto voice. "Stay put this time. But get your gun out and keep it out."

I started to object, and then thought the hell with it. My weariness was so complete I wasn't sure I *could* climb out of the car. I did muster enough energy to open my car window.

Braden's sudden materialization startled Hugh, who jumped when the deputy braced him. The two men stood beneath a nearby lamppost, giving me an orchestra seat. Hugh was decked out in black again, apparently his fave color. The shimmer of tailored silk made me think of a seal. But his chalky face and the twinkle of gold ruined the illusion.

Though neither man raised his voice, I could hear every word.

Braden explained what had brought us to this address: the twins. That put Hugh at ease until the deputy segued into the boys' report of Hugh's meet with Stew. The tattle drew a smirk. "We were planning a fishing excursion. I don't think that's illegal."

Just as easily, the former lounge singer shrugged off the twins' allegations of nocturnal assignations, and their claim that he'd had a heated phone conversation after lunching with Stew.

"I'm not shocked by their wild tales. They hate me. It's their father's doing. He's filled their minds with malicious poppycock. A real loser. Don't know why Grace keeps him on the dole. He gets a ten-thousand-dollar stipend the first of every month.

"But I digress. To answer your questions, yes, I argue with business associates on occasion. Who doesn't? Did I disagree with someone that day? Don't recall. But if I did, it had nothing to do with Stew. And, yes, I go for evening boat rides. I have insomnia. It's peaceful on the water at night. Sometimes I simply need to get away from those boys."

From the car, I sent Braden mental vibes. *Ask about Kain. Ask if he knows Kain.* Finally he did.

This time Hugh fumbled the conversational ball. His face entered a bleach cycle and drained of color. "Never, um...heard of the man." A nervous catch in his voice refuted his assertion.

Abruptly, Hugh ended the exchange. "If you'll excuse me, I need to speak with the boys. If you have more questions—for me, Gracie, or the twins—call John Schmidt in Beaufort. He's our lawyer. I'll deal with Henry and Jared. Goodnight."

The man pivoted and stormed to the front door.

"Better call that lawyer early tomorrow," Braden said in a

parting shot. "I'm going to recommend placing the boys in foster care."

Hugh's response to the Kain question pumped adrenaline into my system. As soon as Braden climbed in, I launched the car in reverse. Less than a hundred feet down the road, I braked.

"Why are you stopping?"

"I'm going to the Cuthbert dock and give The Predator a once-over."

"We don't have a warrant," he objected.

"Oh, but I'm not looking for evidence. While driving by, I heard a strange noise. Had to check it out, make sure everything was secure. Wouldn't want to shirk my duty as a private security guard. You coming?"

A flashlight retrieved from my glove box lit our way along a swaying boardwalk. It bridged seventy-five feet of tidal marsh before culminating in a two-slip dock. A sailboat and The Predator, a small skiff, were berthed side by side. I'd checked Grace's boat registrations and learned she also owned a cabin cruiser. Too big to negotiate the manmade channel, it was moored at the marina.

"What are we looking for?" Braden asked.

"Don't know," I answered. A full-scale rummage under The Predator's seats scavenged meager finds. A tidal chart for Mad Inlet. A marine map of this section of the coast. A sheet of paper with two columns of numbers. I pulled out a notebook and copied ten of the numbered pairs while Braden made a cursory inspection of the bow.

"Find anything?" he asked.

"Some numbers on a sheet of paper. They mean nothing to me. Probably a list of losing lottery numbers. Let's head home."

***

There was no time for nuzzling or post-coital coos when the alarm trilled. After our romp with the twins, we'd set the clock to catch an extra hour of shuteye, and we were pushing the envelope.

Braden had a nine a.m. appointment with Sally, and I'd promised to corner Woody as soon as the office opened. I also had to decipher the ferry schedule, borrow one of the cars parked off-island, and drive to Leyla's office at Gedduh Place. My lunch rendezvous on the Beaufort waterfront was scheduled for one-fifteen.

I jumped into the sweater set and capris laid out the night before, brushed my teeth, and padded to the kitchen barefoot. No time to make fresh coffee. I siphoned two mugs of late-night dregs from the unwashed pot, nuked them to tepid, and returned to the bedroom. I congratulated myself on my steady, non-slosh delivery.

Braden zipped up his pants and grabbed a mug. "Ah, coffee. You're a goddess."

Then he sipped the bitter brew and choked convincingly. "You just tumbled off your pedestal. This is awful. I see you no longer feel a need to impress me. Guess there's no more lasagna in my future. Am I cooking again tonight?"

"No." I grinned. "Fair's fair. It's my turn at the stove, though you'll have to settle for a quick-fix menu. I'll pick up groceries in town."

Braden's smile evaporated. "No way I can talk you out of this excursion? I'd feel better if you stayed on the island. Why take chances?"

"We've been through this. If, somehow, the killer is keeping tabs on me, the outing will set the bait. He'll see I'm alone. No deputy riding shotgun. He won't try a hit today. Heck, if I don't know what car I'll be driving, how could he? And he sure as hell isn't going to stab me with a fork on Plums' patio."

I didn't mention my little side trip to Gedduh Place. While not exactly off the beaten path, it sat on a road less traveled.

"You'll come right back after lunch?" Braden asked.

"Promise. Just one stop at the grocery. What are you going to do about the twins?"

"Ask Deputy Lewis to pick them up at their house and take them to the Hollis County courthouse. Let a judge sort out that mess. Maybe they can live with their father."

When we pulled into the Dear Company parking lot, the scene stunned me. Strangers stood ten-deep on the wraparound Lowcountry porch, waiting for the office's nine o'clock opening—ten minutes away. It was a wonder the floorboards didn't buckle. Dozens of golf carts crowded the pavement. It looked like a gaggle of Shriners had abandoned their miniature vehicles in fright.

My motor idled as I scanned the parking lot, searching for an empty spot. A rap on the driver's side window startled me. Dave Dougherty. The retired salesman grinned ear to ear.

"It's somethin' else, ain't it?" He chuckled. "I'm brokering golf carts and making a killing. Those tabloids must hand out expense money like toilet tissue. I know you don't have a golf cart, Marley, but tell your friends to call me. I have a waiting list for rentals."

"Are those all reporters?" Braden sounded horrified.

"Maybe half of 'em. A real ferryboat captain agreed to moor his thirty-footer here. He's offerin' a regular service from seven-thirty a.m. to four p.m., weather permitting. The skipper's charging six dollars a pop for a five-minute ride. If he gets this many heads per trip, he can retire in a month. Me? I doubled my Social Security check this morning. See ya'll later."

We parked catawampus in an empty niche and approached the circus with trepidation. Bollocks. Joe Reddick stood a stone's throw away, talking loudly to a six-pack of reporters. Spotting me, he pointed an accusing finger my way. A dozen vulture eyes sized me up like fresh road kill.

"Oh, no," I muttered.

Reddick throttled up to full rant. "Some security guards are using these murders as an excuse to bully residents. That *woman* could be Gestapo. The night Stew Hartwell was murdered I was trying to, um…to ascertain facts. The people of this island elected me to the Board and it's my duty to serve them. She practically decapitated me with some martial arts hocus pocus she learned in the Army."

Braden snuck a glance in my direction. If I'd expected sympathy, I was sorely disappointed. Good God, he was laughing. Maybe I *should* demonstrate my martial arts training.

"Am I about to see how a woman performs in combat?" Braden purred, egging me on.

"What's her name?" a reporter asked. "Is she the guard who tangled with the killer?"

Braden ceased to find the scene amusing. He grabbed my arm to hustle me back to the car. That's when Dave called out, "Marley, your friend's a wavin' at you."

The golf cart wheeler-dealer pointed at an office window. Janie pantomimed energetically, motioning us to a back entrance. We made for the emergency-exit door at a dead run and slipped through before any reporters gave chase.

"That was too close," I wheezed.

"Yeah, and you're no longer incognito. Now we'll have to fend off the press as well as the killer." I watched Janie relock the door. "What are you going to do with those reporters? Sally must be beside herself."

Janie grinned. "Nope. She found a silver lining. When our doors open, we'll offer reporters island tours and free lunch at the club. As our vice president so eloquently put it: 'Last week, I could have offered every editor on the East Coast a blowjob and still not lured a single feature writer to the island. Now they're lined up like whores on a Saturday night.'"

I shook my head. "Surely she realizes they're here to report on murders, not vacation property. This can't be good publicity."

"Sally thinks she can win 'em over. Plus she says we've got nothing to lose. They're gonna stay regardless. Personally, I think Sally celebrated with happy pills after she heard our pre-Easter bookings were breaking records. Sure, a few tourists canceled when they heard about a psycho killer at large, but the ghouls are lining up, ready to take their places.

Janie turned to Braden. "If you want to powwow with Sally, you better get in her office and close the door quick. All hell's about to break loose. Marley, you're here to see Woody, right? He's upstairs. His office is one door down from mine."

Braden and I parted in the upstairs hallway. "Call the chief when you're ready to leave," I reminded. "He'll bring a car over. I'll park mine at the marina so I have a ride home whenever I get off the ferry. See you tonight."

I wanted to kiss Braden and hug that delicious body. I settled for a discreet wink.

Woody Nickel's office door was closed. I knocked briskly. "Who is it?" he asked.

"Marley," I answered.

The door swung open. The speed indicated he was standing with his mitt on the doorknob. "Have a seat. I don't have much time. Sally expects me to greet the press. Janie says you're representing a potential buyer?"

"My aunt," I lied, and spun my tale. "After the real estate banquet, I told Aunt May about Emerald Cay. She's been thinking of buying property in the area, and she's a real environmental maven. I'd love to have her nearby. Anyway I wanted to ask a few questions, pick up some literature for her."

Woody sucked on his teeth, then exposed them like a flasher. "These homesites are very special. I'm afraid they are beyond the budget of most seniors."

Too bad Aunt May wasn't representing herself in person. She'd eat this guy for lunch. "Oh, well then. Maybe it isn't the right thing. May didn't want to spend more than a million on a lot. She put a three-million dollar ceiling on her vacation home budget—construction and all."

Woody's Adams apple waggled up and down. He'd swallowed hook, line and fish pole. *Now you'll be a polite little suck-up and answer my questions. Hand over everything I want.*

"That's wonderful," Woody hedged. "I have complete confidence Emerald Cay will meet her expectations. But as Sally explained at the banquet, we can't put the horse before the cart. Our documents aren't ready. We have to dot all the i's..."

Having run out of hackneyed phrases, the smiling salesman spread his hands wide in a helpless gesture. "Can I call you next week?"

"Of course." I smiled back.

Woody's door practically hit me in the butt. Janie's instincts were sound. Something wasn't kosher. I'd picked up a few skills working Army intelligence, including the ability to read documents upside down. Two sales contracts sat on the corner of Woody's desk. Both for Emerald Cay homesites. The selling prices were $500,000 and $600,000. The contracts listed the buyers as Anthony Watson of Columbia, S.C., and John Beck of New York, N.Y.

How in hell could he write contracts if they hadn't completed the offering paperwork?

I stopped by Janie's office. She put a finger to her lips. A signal to keep my mouth shut.

"We'll talk tonight," I said. "Now how do I run your media gauntlet?"

Janie motioned me to her window. "Piece of cake. Most of the reporters are taking Sally's tour, and your friend is entertaining the rest."

Below, Dr. Bride, the ecological evangelist, stood next to his golf cart. He appeared near rapture as he handed out flyers and quoted selectively from the Bible. "Because they have forsaken me, and have burned incense unto other gods, that they might provoke me to anger with all the works of their hands..."

"Hey, get your fanny in gear," Janie said. "The going won't get any better. I'll let you out the emergency exit."

As I tiptoed to my car, Dr. Bride's quavering baritone followed me. "...therefore my wrath shall be poured out upon this place, and shall not be quenched."

THIRTEEN

A barter system had evolved between Dear Island's two camps—folks with cars off island when the bridge failed, and those with cars garaged on Dear. Since I knew Donna's Lexus to be part of the off-island fleet, I called to beg wheels, offering to shop for her as payment in kind. She snapped up the deal, and handed me a lengthy grocery list when I picked up her keys.

On the ferry ride, I fiddled with the taped shoebox on my lap, unsure if portaging my handgun in the closed container violated South Carolina law. Braden insisted I stash my gun in the car's glove box during my Beaufort excursion.

In our state, it's perfectly legal for anyone with a registered gun to keep it fully loaded in a closed glove compartment—a scary thought given increased road rage. However, it's illegal to carry concealed weapons without a special permit, and I'd had no reason to obtain one—prior to my electrifying meeting with our killer.

The gun I kept holstered on my hip while on-duty was a different matter. As SLED-certified crime fighters, all Dear Island Security Officers were authorized to carry on the job.

No gun did much to bolster my sense of security. In the Army I had to qualify annually with a pistol. Basically that meant I could hit a paper target under ideal conditions. Until this past week, I'd never drawn my gun for real.

Inside Donna's Lexus, I dutifully unwrapped my gun and tucked it into its cubbyhole. It seemed silly. No one would attack me in my loaner car, and I wouldn't tote the gun to lunch. Thankfully, even people with concealed weapon permits aren't allowed to pack heat when they enter establishments that serve liquor.

The car ride seemed far more sedate than when my Mustang met the gopher-sized potholes on Sea Island back roads. Several weeks had passed since I'd visited Gedduh Place, and I felt guilty. I hadn't signed up to tutor new students since my last two "graduated." Both could now read what mattered to them. In Alycia's case, that meant tackling schoolbooks with her young children. Willard, in his late eighties, wanted to read the Bible for himself "before he passed." I made a mental note to tell Leyla I'd take on new pupils come May. *If I'm still alive.*

Two years ago, Dr. Leyla Clark had traded a cushy faculty post at a Midwest university for Gedduh's lower pay. After we got to know each other, I asked what brought her here.

"I grew up a thousand miles from the Sea Islands, but my roots are here," she said. "First time we visited, my cousins taught me to cast a shrimp net, and Gran cut me raw pieces of cane. I knew I'd come home. I love the Gullah people, the language. It's unique, you know? My ancestors were isolated here. I want to preserve their culture."

Turning onto one of Gedduh's hard-packed dirt drives, I felt the familiar time warp. A former plantation housed Gedduh Place, and many of the original buildings remained—a touchstone for a disappearing way of life.

Shade from overarching live oaks swallowed my car on the winding corridor. The trees had withstood centuries of hurricane winds in gnarled dignity. And the old buildings evoked a time-capsule sensation. Their thick walls filtered the outside noise and Lowcountry heat, giving the interiors a church-like serenity.

I parked, entered a building that had been partitioned into offices and started down the hall. Today, the cool quiet triggered goose bumps, not meditation. The center had a small fulltime staff. When there were no classes, it seemed downright spooky. I paused to make certain the echoing footsteps were mine alone.

Leyla's office door stood open. She frowned at a large stack of papers as I crossed the threshold. When she saw me, her handsome face failed to light with the usual smile. "Oh, Marley, I'm glad you came. I'm scared something horrible has happened to Sharlana."

I'd met Sharlana once. Leyla's sister, Rena, had married a Gullah native and moved to the island years before Leyla accepted the Gedduh job. Sharlana was Rena's youngest child. My friend came around her desk and we hugged. "Let's walk. I'm so freaking frustrated I feel like a caged animal."

She led me outside. "When did your niece go missing?"

"About six o'clock Tuesday evening." Leyla turned and clutched my arm, her grip as tight as her voice. "Now it's Thursday and no one's seen her. I'm sick with worry."

I matched Leyla's pace as she headed toward a sandy lane that ended at a rickety crabbing dock.

Her voice trembled. "Rena—Sharlana's mom—called the sheriff's department at midnight when my niece wasn't home yet. She'd already phoned all of her friends."

"What did the sheriff say?"

Leyla dabbed at perspiration on her mahogany forehead. She looked ill. "A deputy came, talked with the family. He suggested Sharlana's disappearance was likely teenage rebellion. But, Marley, she's not the type to hook up with some boy and leave her parents frantic. Do you have contacts in the sheriff's department? Someone you could convince to take this seriously?"

I put my arm around her shoulders, and gave her an encouraging squeeze. "I know one deputy. I'll do what I can. Sharlana graduated high school last year, right? Didn't her boyfriend start college at Georgia Tech?"

We reached the dock and stopped. Too many sagging sections to advance any farther. Near the bank a fallen tree provided a makeshift bench. Leyla sat and patted the space beside her.

"We hoped Sharlana would head to college, too, but she -

argued it was a waste until she decided on a career. Claimed she needed to live a little first. My sister tried a carrot-and-stick approach. Told Sharlana she'd foot the bill for college. But if she didn't go to school, she had to pay room and board."

Leyla stared out at the water. The sun's reflection hurt my eyes. "I'll give my niece her due. Sharlana didn't bitch and moan. Got a job and paid rent. Of course, that sent my sister round the bend, too. The idea of her bright daughter cleaning toilets for—now don't take offense—some lazy-ass honkies."

I laughed. "No offense taken. Where's Sharlana working?"

She looked surprised. "I figured you knew. Dear Island housekeeping. Told her mom she was doing graduate studies in racism on an honest-to-God twenty-first-century plantation. Said the lady of the house—Bea Caldwell—was a real witch."

A chill of foreboding swept over me. Bea was killed Tuesday night, the same night Sharlana vanished.

I suddenly remembered four-year-old Teddy's innocent replay of Bea's last phone call: "You believed Adam...Adam Spate." With a sinking feeling, I wondered if Bea, with her affinity for horrid racial slurs, had said something quite different: "You believed a damn spade."

Leyla's head dropped into her hands. "Do you think that woman's killer murdered Sharlana, too?"

Yes, that's precisely what I think. Of course, I didn't admit it. Hope is a powerful weapon, and I wanted to leave my friend armed for the days of waiting.

"Perhaps there's a connection. That doesn't mean Sharlana's dead. You said your niece came home from work, then left again about six?"

"Yes. She changed clothes and tacked a note on the refrigerator, telling her mom not to wait supper. She was headed to town and would be back by nine. Sharlana wrote it, my sister knows her handwriting."

No wonder these folks are terrified.

"Did she drive herself to town?"

"No, she doesn't have a car. Rena assumed a friend picked her up. But she called everyone she could think of. None of her friends saw her that day."

Her eyes brimmed with tears. I helped her up from the stump and hugged her before we began to retrace our route. Leyla moved slowly, as if she dreaded what waited.

Halfway between the crabbing dock and the center's main building, a loud snap startled me. Someone stepping on a twig? The sound came from my right. The woods were thick, choked with underbrush. Leaves rustled and my breathing quickened. I thought I heard a whisper. Who was out there?

"Something wrong?" Leyla stared at me.

I'd stopped dead behind her. "I'm just jumpy. Thought I heard something."

She shrugged. "Probably deer. Sooner or later the developers will replace them, too. Find a breed that poses for pictures."

We walked the rest of the way in silence. I felt edgy as if the woods hid a predator. Were we being watched? *Enough paranoia. Leyla has real problems. Don't project your personal terrors.* It's easy to ridicule hunches, harder to shake them.

When we reached her office, I bid Leyla good-bye. "I'll do everything I can. I know some ladies in housekeeping. I'll talk to them. Did Sharlana have any special friends at work?"

Leyla smiled through her tears. "Yeah, a young girl. Sofia, I think. From Croatia. Her town never recovered from the civil war. Sharlana was teaching her English. Poor girl knew about eight words when she arrived."

Croatia? Another connection to Eastern Europe? The coincidences were piling up.

Leyla walked me to my car. "Sometimes I despair. Did you know the Dear Company let a bunch of housekeepers go? Replaced 'em with a boatload of refugees. I never dreamed

153

people would be elbowing Sea Islanders out of the way to scrub floors."

Leyla's contagious misery fed my certainty that Kain Dzandrek was involved. God, I wanted a go at him.

***

I was late for my lunch date and surprised to find only one of my friends on Plums' patio. Brenda Gerton held down a prime table for four, ignoring the evil eye from people waiting to be seated.

The restaurant overlooks Beaufort's Waterfront Park. As I walked onto the back porch, a sleek thirty-foot ketch gracefully docked under sail at the downtown marina. On terra firma, kids swarmed over the play fort that anchors one edge of the village green. They giggled with delight in the mild sunshine. An added bonus was the breeze—stiff enough to keep no-see-ums, the insect scourge of a Lowcountry spring, at bay.

"It's about time somebody joined me," Brenda sniffed. "I went ahead and ordered for you. Now don't be difficult and make this the first time you study the menu."

I pulled out a chair. "Nope. I'm content with my rut." Lunch at Plums meant a cup of she-crab soup, a chicken-salad sandwich, and unsweetened tea—a nod to my Yankee heritage.

Brenda frowned. "You okay? When the sheriff announced his murder witness was a security officer and referred to 'her,' I knew it was you. If memory serves, Dear's only other female officer is on maternity leave. Did some nutcase really attack you?"

"Yeah, but I'm fine."

Brenda snorted. "Fine? You had a concussion, right? Don't rush things."

"I'm not."

"You shouldn't be traipsing all over creation on your own. I thought the sheriff had more sense. You're the number one topic for Beaufort gossip. If that maniac eavesdrops on the right conversation, he'll know more about you than your own momma."

I laughed at Brenda's colorful phrasing. "Hey, where's Tammy?"

"Beating the bushes for the Hollis County Alliance. Called to say she's running late."

I'd met Brenda and Tammy in a history course on the University of South Carolina-Beaufort campus. We had little in common beyond our age. Brenda, a career wife and mother, had never worked outside the home. She was born-and-bred Beaufort aristocracy. In contrast, Tammy was a private banker on Wall Street who relocated when her much older husband retired. Neither woman had any interest in military matters. Maybe it was our differences—plus a quirky sense of humor—that bound us as friends.

"Well, are you going to tell me about the attack?" Brenda probed.

"Nope. I'd just have to repeat everything once Tammy arrives."

"Speak of the she-devil." Brenda nodded at Tammy bulling her way toward our table. Her pleasantly plump face was flushed, her eyes stormy. She slammed her briefcase on the table then muttered, "Sorry."

Tammy took a deep breath. "Couple more weeks like this and I quit. I used to close multi-million dollar deals, and the A-holes here treat me like pond scum. I need a drink." She snagged a passing waitress and ordered a gin and tonic.

When Tammy arrived in the Lowcountry, she decided her I.Q. would drop faster than her golf handicap if she didn't find something to occupy her mind. She signed on as membership director for the Hollis County Alliance, a private-public partnership aimed at economic development. The area's volatile mix of seat-of-your-pants entrepreneurs, landed gentry and nouveau rich carpetbaggers intrigued her.

"What's got you so riled?" Brenda asked.

"I called on two new businesses, and you'd have thought I gargled with garlic juice. A polite no thank you is one thing, rude and crude another. Zach Antolak—he opened a mortgage brokerage six weeks ago—told me how he preferred to be welcomed."

The waitress slid a gin-and-tonic in front of Tammy and she took a long swallow. "Then I called on Clay Jacobs. He wasn't lewd, just said he had no time for small-town ass kissing. Claimed he had more business than he could handle. Good God, he's an appraiser who hung out a shingle a month ago. With that attitude, how's he getting customers?"

I raised an eyebrow at Brenda. Her hubby was one of the county's leading real estate attorneys. "Has real estate made that big of a rebound? Can any dipwad make it?"

Brenda shook her head. "No way. Ned says the second-home market is improving but not what you'd call robust. Banks are still skittish about exposure to developers. But Ned did check out that Jacobs fellow for Stew, who couldn't fathom how the newcomer had stolen all his Dear business."

Stew's name piqued my interest.

"Jacobs comes from Columbia so Ned called buddies there. Few months back, the guy got slapped on the wrist for ethics violations. The Alliance is probably better off without him."

Tammy looked my way. "Marley, I can't believe I'm blowing off steam when I haven't asked how you feel. The sheriff said you 'scuffled' with a killer. What the hell does that mean?"

Our food arrived, giving me a short reprieve. Between spoonfuls of she-crab soup, I dished out a subtly shaded version of the truth. Yes, I'd been attacked but I now felt hunky-dory. Yes, I remembered seeing the killer, but his facial features were still fogged by my mental mist.

"I'm sure our killer's moved on," I lied. "Let's talk about

156

something more cheerful. Who starts?"

For our once-a-month luncheons, each of us prepared a mini-lecture. Five minutes—or less—on a topic the others weren't likely to know beans about. Tammy usually enlightened us on finance. Brenda offered up colorful local histories. I talked about the military and weaponry.

"I'll go first." Tammy opened her briefcase. "I even brought handouts. My topic? Estate planning."

Brenda protested. "Our friend just pulled one foot from the grave and you want to speculate on how they'll divvy up her jewelry?"

I laughed at the interplay. "Don't get your undies in a twist, Brenda. Retired military broads don't have jewelry."

Tammy cleared her throat to quell further rebellion. "As I was saying..."

I half listened. Couldn't quit mulling over Tammy's brush-offs—first by a shady appraiser, then by a mortgage broker with an Eastern European name. Luckily Tammy didn't quiz me on her info. A waitress brought coffee, and it was Brenda's turn.

"Okay, I'm going to educate you Yankees on how the Turners regained their fortune after the War Between the States. Notice the name: nothing 'civil' about that war."

Since Brenda's mom had been a Turner, she swore her tale of a prodigal son, a mad-as-a-hatter grandmother, a randy papa, and a sprinkling of out-of-wedlock offspring was the absolute truth. When she finished, I teased her. "You sure you didn't add a little southern seasoning to *Days of Our Lives*?"

"You want off the hook today?" Tammy asked. "Don't imagine you had time to prepare anything."

"*Au contraire*. Given recent, uh, events, I had a strong incentive to bone up on what's known in the trade as ECDs— electronic control devices. Nothing like first-hand experience to sharpen your thirst for knowledge."

During my ferry ride to the mainland, I'd culled tidbits

from my friend Steve's emails to create a short op-ed. I began with definitions. "All ECDs, including stun guns and Tasers, use electricity—up to fifty-thousand volts—to stun and incapacitate. That's enough to reduce a three-hundred-pound gorilla to a quivering pile of misfired neurons."

Tammy interrupted. "God, can you electrocute someone with an ECD?"

I shook my head. "Nope. Legit models limit dosage. Once the probes make contact, the ECD sends impulses in pre-set waves. In fact, the Taser I carry at work is preset to deliver a five-second jolt.

"The ECDs won't kill, even if the perp is standing in three feet of water. Some deaths have been reported, but they've mostly been tied to drug overdoses or extenuating circumstances. As a multiple jolt recipient, I'm happy to report studies have found no long-lasting side effects."

Brenda waggled her fingers, signaling a question. "What if the bad guy's a biker dude in a thick leather jacket?"

"No problemo. The probes will zap through two inches of clothing. Tasers have plenty of law enforcement fans. I'm one. Suppose some sky-high PCP addict is about to attack. Shoot the guy with a pistol and you'd better hit a vital organ or it's like popping a bear with a BB gun. These guys can be hemorrhaging and feel no pain."

Tammy cleared her throat. "I'm all for cops having ECDs. But what about bad guys? Can anyone buy one?"

"'Fraid so. Order one over the Internet and UPS will deliver it to your door. But reputable providers do background checks. Plus, in theory, owners are easy to trace. The guns eject a kind of confetti when they're fired, littering the crime scene with tiny shards that identify the gun and original purchaser."

Tammy cut in. "Hey, does that mean the sheriff can track the weapon used on you?"

We'd come to the crux of my research. Steve had reached

the same conclusion as Braden. "No. An East European manufacturer is producing an ECD for police and military that can be fired from twenty feet. It doesn't eject any confetti. Somehow our killer got his hands on one."

"Well that sucks," Tammy said.

My sentiment exactly. It meant our killer was no run-of-the-mill psychopath. He had international connections. That convinced me Stew's and Bea's deaths weren't part of a random killing spree. But where was the motive? The pattern?

We signaled for our checks. As we waited, a man walked by our table, nodded to Brenda and murmured, "Nice to see you."

"Wasn't that Michael Beech, Esquire?" Tammy asked.

Unable to keep all the elite Beaufortonians straight, I chuckled. "You two could publish your own newspaper. I've never heard of Beech."

Brenda arched an eyebrow. "You've never heard of anyone. He's an attorney, but unlike hubby dear, he concentrates on nonprofit and corporate work. You know, setting up C corps and LLCs. His family came here when Robert E. Lee was in short pants. His daddy and granddaddy were attorneys, so he inherited their client base."

She sipped her drink before she continued. "A few months back, he got caught engaging in Superman accounting. He billed a hospital for sixty hours of his time and a local business owner for seventy hours over the same three days. It was his misfortune the business owner joined the hospital board and noticed the double billing. Hearsay has it Beech needed the money to pay a gambling debt."

"Was he disbarred?" I asked.

Brenda shook her head. "He tore up the invoices. Claimed he'd fallen victim to an accounting glitch. My husband's angry. Says he should be penalized for violating ethics. Me? I wonder how Beech paid his bookie. He didn't hit the lottery."

We left the restaurant and hugged before trotting off to far-flung parking spaces. With Beaufort's azaleas in bloom, parking was at a premium. April was the peak month for empty-nester tourists to ooh-and-ah over the quaint downtown and enjoy horse-drawn carriage rides through a historic district made famous by movies like *The Big Chill* and *The Prince of Tides*.

As I walked toward Donna's car, I wondered how long it would be before beachcombing tourists swarmed Dear. This year I'd welcome any visitors with only sun and surf on their minds. They beat hell out of reporters with an insatiable appetite for blood.

FOURTEEN

By the time I bought everything on my dual grocery lists, my cart overflowed, and my checking account had taken a three-hundred-dollar hit. To dazzle Braden with my culinary skills, I'd splurged. The entrée would be filet mignon topped with steamed crabmeat, lobster, shrimp and white asparagus, all slathered in homemade Béarnaise sauce.

I glanced at my watch. Crapola, 3:15. I wasn't used to timing excursions to make a four o'clock ferry. One open bridge could wreck my timetable.

Donna's oversized trunk accommodated the purchases with ease, and I marveled once more at its pristine condition. Though I loved my vintage Mustang, my adoration fell short of a slavish devotion to auto hygiene. If I borrowed her car again, I'd spring for the deluxe package at the Carteret Street car wash where humans actually vacuumed, scrubbed and buffed.

Before I left the parking lot, I witnessed a near collision in my rearview mirror. A green SUV cut off a dawdling oldster to claim a space two cars behind me. It was a wonder the old lady didn't keel over dead. The ranks of belligerent drivers seemed to swell by the day.

Or was someone following me? The thought flickered in and out. Who could know I was driving this car?

Frequent journeys to and from Dear Island meant I could navigate by rote. This freed me to daydream about Braden and obsess on the luncheon gossip. How did a new appraiser steal Dear's business from Stew? What brought an East European mortgage broker to Beaufort? It seemed weird that two newbies turned up their noses at an offer to tap into the local business pipeline.

Did any of this connect to Janie's worries about real estate fraud? I tried to picture the documents strewn across Woody's desk. Had the newcomers' names—Jacobs or Antolak—appeared on them?

A red light blinked ahead. I eased off the gas. The swing bridge had opened for two shrimp boats. They'd already run the steel gauntlet to head up river. Only four cars idled ahead of me. Curtailed travel to and from Dear had definitely taken a bite out of inter-island traffic flow.

I slid to a stop. Donna's well-tuned Lexus purred so quietly I almost thought it had stalled. The wait would be short. I rolled down my passenger-side window to reduce the glare and leaned out to see if one of the homecoming captains was Janie's most recent conquest. The boats moved at too fast a clip to decipher the names painted on the prows.

With shrimping season weeks away, the skippers had probably been after tuna, drum fish or snapper. In the wake of the vessels, sea gulls squawked and dived, quarreling over gutted remains. The scene is picturesque afar, just plain smelly and gory up close and personal.

Glancing in my rearview mirror, I noticed the rude SUV from the grocery had maneuvered directly behind me. The behemoth left a huge gap between our bumpers. That seemed out of character, given the driver's parking lot aggression. The hairs on my neck saluted.

I studied the driver's silhouetted head. Dark-tinted windows obscured all facial details. When the man looked left, my stomach lurched. God help me, in profile, he was a dead ringer for Underling.

Could it really be Kain's lackey? If so, would he dare mount an attack on a public highway?

Slowly the bridge pirouetted to close the yawning chasm between its stationary sections. I was shaken—literally—out of my macabre musings when the bridge clanged shut, and the structure shimmied in momentary aftershock. *Thank goodness, I'd still make the ferry.*

162

The cars ahead coughed to life and crept forward. I inched along behind them. The SUV maintained its wary distance. Not a good sign. My fingers tensed on the steering wheel.

Just beyond the bridge, three of the lead cars turned into the first gated enclave. The remaining auto, a black Firebird, tore off like an entry in the Indy 500. He had to be doing eighty—at least twenty-five miles over the speed limit. *Where are the cops when you need them?*

I was now quite alone with the green SUV, which practically kissed my bumper as soon as the other vehicles in our motorcade split. Coincidence? Not bloody likely.

With my speed pegged to the fifty-five-miles-per-hour limit, I ticked off my suspicious tail's options. He could try to muscle me off the road and into the marsh where I'd be a mired duck. Or he could pull alongside and shoot.

Either way I needed to keep him behind me. Returning fire wasn't an option. Hell, I couldn't even reach the glove box to retrieve my gun—not if I wanted to keep the car under control.

Beyond the next curve, the snaking road briefly righted itself into a straightaway. Afraid the man might put on a burst of speed, pull parallel, and shoot, I straddled the centerline, leaving his giant boat of a vehicle no room to pass.

To my surprise, he didn't speed up. Why? Memories of that Kentucky Fried Colonel message stiffened my resolve. If paranoia had gotten the better of me, no harm done. The fellow on my tail could just write me off as another crazy woman driver. If I was right, well, I had to protect my back.

The straightaway section ended. Rounding a bend, I spotted a black Firebird several hundred yards ahead. Slewed sideways, it blocked both lanes of traffic. It was the same car that zoomed away from the bridge like a scalded cat. A body sprawled on the pavement beside it.

Hell and damnation. Normally I'd play Good Samaritan and stop to help anyone lying face-down on concrete. But the off-kilter scene smelled of setup, a classic pincer movement to trap me. If I stopped, I'd be at their mercy.

I glimpsed Wilderness State Park's homey welcome sign carved into a large wooden plank nailed to two sawed-off tree trunks. I waited as long as I could then stomped on the gas and swerved onto the entrance road. Groceries thudded in the trunk as I fishtailed on gravel. A stray thought wicked its way front and center. *Donna would have a cow if she could see me mistreating her Lexus.*

Another set of tires squealed, and all extraneous thoughts fled my brain. *He's right behind me.* I sped toward the interior entry gate a football field ahead. The wooden traffic arm was hoisted in an open position. In season, a park employee always sits in the booth and collects admission fees. Today it was abandoned. Until the vacationing hordes descended for Easter, there wasn't enough patronage to justify a gatekeeper's salary.

Wilderness Park had been preserved in its natural state. One minute you were in civilization, the next, jungle. As I zoomed through the gate, towering oaks and battered palms crowded the sliver of blacktop. I felt hemmed in, claustrophobic. The State of South Carolina had adhered to a low-environmental impact policy. No wide, two-lane roads. Traffic was one-way, a single-lane asphalt ribbon wound through the wilderness until it exited back onto the highway. Swinging around and flying past Underling wasn't an option. At least there'd be no danger of collision with an oncoming car while I played stock car driver.

As the SUV towered menacingly behind me, the forest canopy plunged me into early twilight. Temperatures dropped to the shiver point.

What could I do?

I had an annual state park pass and visited Wilderness often. I knew the park's points of interest by heart. If my attackers kept in contact by cell phone, the Firebird was either right behind the SUV or—scary thought—coming in the exit to create a new roadblock. If that happened, I'd be squeezed between them.

Note to self: when—or if—you get out of this mess, buy a cell phone.

At the turn-off to the welcome center, I didn't hesitate. Please, please, let a park ranger be on duty. Actually, any witness would do.

I swung onto a side spur and caught a glimpse of the welcome center and its front pond covered with duckweed. Tourists usually congregated on a footbridge over the pond, peering into the ghastly green scum in hopes of glimpsing an alligator. Today there was nary a loiterer. *What is going on?*

The parking lot had not yet come into view. I turned the corner, my speed too high for the twisting road. I caromed forward, roughly jostling bordering underbrush. The sharp fronds of scrub palms scraped the chassis. Brittle vegetation met metal with a sickening screech.

A heavy chain stretched across the parking lot entrance. Red lettering flashed an explanation: *Closed for repairs. Reopening April 15.*

Were folks inside working on repairs? Should I slam into the chain? That was likely to put my car out of commission. A gamble I couldn't afford. The land was too swampy here to risk running to ground.

With my options shrinking, I circled back to the main road and sped toward the lighthouse. The jungle beyond it was dense. With a head start, I could disappear. The footing would be surer on higher ground.

Trying to think while maneuvering the serpentine roads had me panting. *One way in one way out.* Wasn't that the motto for those old roach motel ads: *They check in, but they don't check out.* Not a positive train of thought.

I glanced in my side mirror. Crapola. My racecar

maneuvers had opened up a measly hundred-foot lead. To calm myself, I listed my advantages. *A gun. Knowledge of park geography. Good conditioning.* I could hide in the dense foliage before Underling had a clue. But I needed a few more seconds' lead.

I prayed the black Firebird wouldn't sneak in the exit and cut me off before I performed my vanishing act. My only question was where to jump ship—and how. Leaping from a moving car looks good in movies, but I couldn't risk breaking an ankle. Or worse.

My best bet: stop in the middle of the road, just around a bend. Then dash into the jungle. With any luck, Underling would smash into the abandoned Lexus. A fatal crash would be peachy.

I reached the parking area used by tourists who visit the park's lighthouse. As the white tower leapt into view, I noticed a lone car in the lot. The nearby picnic area and a boardwalk leading to the sandy beach were empty. No sign of life at the base of the lighthouse either. I'd have to follow through on my hide-in-the-jungle strategy.

I heard a loud pop and the car shimmied as if I'd run across a patch of ice. A blown rear tire. Impossible to make the next bend and my planned exit. What now?

I slammed on the brakes, and opened the glove compartment to grab my gun. Empty. My gun was gone. *Damn.*

A minute ago, I was scared. Now I was terrified. I practiced Tae Bo and knew some nifty little kicks and thrusts, but such antics were no match for a bullet.

I took off at a dead run. In a nod to visiting picnickers, rangers had cleared this section of subtropical underbrush. Cover was nonexistent. The trees left standing were mostly palms, too skinny to hide anyone with hips wider than Olive Oyl's.

Weave. Don't be predictable.

I glanced over my shoulder. Two men in pursuit. The driver of the black Firebird had joined forces with his buddy in the green SUV. Firebird's angled trajectory cut me off from the beach.

Nowhere to go. Except the lighthouse. I conjured up old military training protocol. *Seek high ground—easier to defend. Always leave a back door.* Unfortunately, while the lighthouse offered high ground, it was also a trap. No back door.

Flouting tactical wisdom, I scrambled toward the lighthouse. The upside was a single entry. No surprise attack. Constructed of bricks covered with cast iron plates, the lighthouse was designed to be disassembled and moved whenever tides ate too greedily at the eroding shoreline. If the gunmen could be kept outside, the armor would stop any bullet.

I had little hope of transforming the lighthouse into a personal fortress. The door could only be locked from the outside—a bulky padlock arrangement. Within a few feet of my goal, I noticed that a two-by-six wedged open the structure's stout wooden door. This time spring-cleaning worked to my advantage. Yellow caution tape festooned the entry. A sign read: *Caution Wet Paint.* I hurtled through the tape like a mad marathoner using her last burst of energy to punch through the finish line.

Turning, I squandered a second on a visual check of Underling's progress. I'd been right: the portly thug had been the SUV's driver. His black shirt shimmered in the sun and his shoes gleamed with a spit-and-polish shine. He resembled a fat, glistening cockroach. One I had no way to squash. Though I couldn't see his hands, I felt certain he was armed—gun, stunner or both. My back burned in recalled pain. The lighthouse blocked any view of Firebird.

I dashed inside and shivered in the dank base of the tower. Could I jam the door shut? I dismissed the possibility as soon as it crossed my mind. The door swung out. *Forget it. Find a weapon.*

The packed dirt floor was empty except for a few moldy bricks, crumbling mortar still attached. Better than nothing. I hefted one and balanced it on my shoulder. I considered picking up another, but I needed to keep a hand free for the railing.

Staring up at the spiral staircase, I swallowed hard. The stairs and rails were metal, the steps a see-through mesh. A friend in the construction trade had counted the steps—176—and tried to calculate the rise. *How on earth had I remembered that?*

I'd climbed to the top twice. What I remembered best about my last visit was my mistake: looking down as I began my descent, an excruciatingly slow and queasy one.

I'm not a total acrophobe. Whisk me to the top of a skyscraper in a glass-enclosed elevator, and I'll marvel at the scenery. Take me up in an Army helicopter, and I'm okay. The need to upchuck isn't triggered until I look down a shaft, or find myself perilously close to a ledge with nothing substantial between me and a yawning chasm.

The two times guests talked me into a climb to the lighthouse's pinnacle, I clung to the walls like Spiderwoman, while they strolled the circular parapet and leaned over the railing to drink in the view. On a clear day, you could see for miles. Freighters appeared to be toys on the sparkling sea. Dear Island's lush interior looked like a feathery green bouquet. Sandbars poked from the dark ocean like pods of surfacing white whales.

Get your ass in gear. Don't look down.

I psyched myself to dash up the steps. *Don't stop until you reach the top.* I'd climbed exactly four treads when I fell like a ton of bricks. There was a reason for that "wet paint" sign. I'd used my hands to break my fall. They were caked with the sticky goo. Reddish gunk smeared my white slacks. Lifting a sneaker, I saw the jelled goop had oozed into every crevice in my soles. *So much for running*. Get up. Still gripping my brick, I began slip-sliding upward. At least the thug would be climbing the same greased pole if he followed.

But how far did he really need to climb? All he needed was a clear shot.

The tight, winding metalwork offered limited cover. If I were lucky, the mesh treads would repel bullets zinging up from below. I just had to keep as many treads as possible between Underling and me and avoid leaning over the railing at the spiral center. If I could reach the top, I had a chance. Once I walked out onto the viewing platform, Underling would have to come through the door to reach me. Then I'd brain him with the brick, grab his gun, and deal with his sidekick. Piece of cake.

I'd scrabbled a third of the way up the lighthouse when Underling and his cohort made their raucous entry. I didn't dare look down. Vertigo. My pulse rocketed to hummingbird status, and my neck vibrated with the continuous thump of blood.

They were arguing. Hope surged. Dissension in the ranks. *Yippee.*

Pop. Repeated pings followed the loud noise. Ricochets. One bullet dodged. Below me, the thug unleashed a torrent of Polish cuss words.

You may kill me, but you're going to have to work for it, sucker.

The staircase rattled when one of my pursuers started his climb. The metal groaned in protest. Was the overweight Underling trudging upward?

I panted and climbed higher. While the interior was dark, there were openings in the brick foundation every ten to fifteen feet of vertical rise. The two-foot-square air holes served as beacons. Each spot where light pierced the shaft became a concrete goal as I rushed skyward.

Ten steps from the summit I heard a thudding crash. The

stairs shook. My hefty pursuer had taken a swan dive on the greasy metal. His two-hundred-plus-pound frame must have bounced a few steps before it collided with the wall. What I heard next—the sound of a sizable metal object plinking against the metal stairs—made me want to sing a hallelujah chorus. He'd dropped his gun. The musical clangs narrated the gun's fall to the base.

Though not a final reprieve, it was, nonetheless, a cause for celebration. A second later, I burst onto the viewing platform. Driven by a fear greater than acrophobia, I dashed to the railing. Looking over, I spied assailant number two standing guard at the lighthouse door, keeping watch for passersby.

I screamed bloody murder. Looking seaward, a distant beachcombing couple waved at me. No sign of alarm. Did they think my frantic arm flaps signaled elation at making the climb?

I crab-walked to the opposite side of the lighthouse to survey the parking lot. My heart almost stopped as a big yellow school bus pulled in. Good God, I'd prayed for witnesses, but not school kids. The bus doors whooshed open, and Mike, my park ranger friend, jumped out, followed by a middle-aged woman in a pantsuit. A second later, the dam broke and a gaggle of tiny legs flashed down the stairs. An elementary school field trip. Youngsters swarmed over the picnic area, screeching like banshees.

"Call the police," I screamed, trying to pierce the racket below. No luck. The din also drowned out any auditory clues about Underling's progress toward my perch. *How close?*

I flailed my free arm again, like a duck with an injured wing. I lacked the strength to lift the arm holding the brick, my only weapon. I stupidly clung to the notion that I could brain my attacker as he stepped from the interior of the lighthouse onto the viewing platform.

My waving caught Mike's eye. He strode briskly toward the lighthouse.

"Call the police," I yelled again. "Don't come closer. There's a killer in the lighthouse."

He kept walking. Had the ocean breeze whisked my warning away?

FIFTEEN

I didn't have a prayer of making myself understood. It didn't matter though. As Mike advanced on the lighthouse from one direction, my ebony-clad assassin scuttled away at a forty-five degree angle. He met up with the driver of the Firebird near the parking lot. From this height, the thugs truly looked like bugs as they climbed in their vehicles and drove away.

Shaking with frustration and relief, I suddenly realized my feet were planted about an inch from the waist-high balustrade. I inched back from the railing. Mike's angry voice echoed from below. "Who's there? You're trespassing. Come down immediately."

He had to figure an idiot tourist had ignored the wet paint signs and ruined a tedious job. That's okay. Better to be reamed out for being a live idiot than a dead duck.

Mike Willis, the young park ranger, had taken me and a dozen fellow adventurers on an overnight camping excursion. When he caught up with me halfway up the lighthouse stairs, his anger vanished. He knew I wasn't a wanton vandal.

"My God, Marley, what happened?"

Talking helped keep my vertigo at bay as we descended. Still I teetered on the edge of an emotional precipice, hysterics a short step away. I bit the side of my mouth each time a sob bubbled up. I refused to break down in front of a casual acquaintance.

Pride didn't stop me from gripping Mike's elbow as we spiraled downward. He gentled me step by step. The seismic tremors that rattled my body gave ample clues about my fragile state.

By the time we reached the lighthouse base, I'd relayed the complete story and regained my mental equilibrium. Though I sidestepped a sob-o-rama, I now had a violent case of hiccups,

172

Dear Killer

and anger supplanted terror on my emotional roller coaster. I was furious the thugs got away, and even angrier with myself for my idiocy. Why hadn't I listened to Braden this morning? Why didn't I check the glove compartment for my gun before I left Beaufort?

During lunch, I heard a car alarm sound. Could it have been Underling filching my pistol? Car alarms sound so often we become immune. Or maybe I'd pushed the wrong button on Donna's key fob and left her car unlocked.

Finally my rabid speculation addressed more pressing questions. How did the killer get a description of my borrowed car? An island accomplice?

Mike radioed Sheriff Conroy and alerted the other ranger on duty. His compatriot was clearing brush from one of the park's woodland walking trails and hadn't seen or heard a thing.

Mike turned back to me once he signed off. "Sorry I didn't see the creeps running away. First, my focus was on the kids. Then, after I spotted someone waving atop of the lighthouse, all I could think about was a ruined paint job. Never occurred to me you were in danger."

Shaking his head, he bent to retrieve the gun Underling dropped when he slipped. It had wedged between the bottom stair and a pile of discarded bricks. Crap, it looked like my very own handgun.

"Better leave it. Conroy will want to dust for prints."

I figured the forensics would prove pointless. He'd probably worn gloves. If so, the only fingerprints to lift would be mine. I prayed the sheriff wouldn't think I hallucinated the episode. No one else had seen my stalkers. The gun was mine, and my disjointed account sounded demented—even to my ears. Then I remembered the bullet hole in my tire. I hiccupped again and held my breath.

Mike touched my arm. Wallowing in self-rebuke, I'd tuned

him out. "Want me to drive you to the Beaufort hospital? Or do you need to wait here for the sheriff? Since you're out of danger, Conroy says a roadblock is his first priority. He'll be awhile."

Another hiccup escaped. "I want to go home. Conroy knows one of the thugs is Underling and he's got a description. I didn't get a good look at the second guy—too far away. He was about six-feet tall and thin, maybe one hundred and sixty pounds. He had blond hair and wore jeans and a dark pullover.

"Mike, could you help me fix the flat? I don't want to be stranded off island tonight. I'll feel a lot safer on Dear. If we hurry, I can make the last ferry. Besides, I have a fortune in groceries melting in my trunk. I can give my statement to a deputy on Dear."

I didn't mention that I hoped to do so while clinging to his naked body.

"You sure?" Mike scuffed a foot in the sandy soil. "I better clear it with the sheriff. He said I wasn't to let you out of my sight."

Mike rang Conroy and explained my hankering to leave. "He wants to speak with you." He handed me the phone.

After I repeated my description of the thugs and their vehicles, the sheriff okayed my departure. A sketch artist would meet me on Dear tomorrow.

Mike mounted my spare tire and insisted on following me to the boat landing—his muddy Jeep hugging the bumper of Donna's abused Lexus.

We arrived at 3:57 p.m. The ferry wallowed in its makeshift berth. Most of the mainland-bound passengers had already disembarked. Since this was the last ferry of the day, the folks trudging toward parked cars probably weren't Dear residents. I opened my trunk and Mike helped me repack the escaped oranges and errant vegetables spilled during the chase.

"You don't have to stay," I said. "I was trembling like a leaf when you rescued me, but I'm fine now. Looks like the skipper plans to take off almost as soon as I board."

The ranger studied me. My hiccups had subsided, and the hand I held out for a thank-you handshake was steady. "Glad you're feeling better. But I'll stay till the boat shoves off. Besides you can use some help carting these groceries. It's going to take a few trips."

I smiled. "Just one. Publix loaned a fleet of shopping carts. A great PR move. We load the groceries at this end, roll 'em aboard, and wheel 'em to a waiting car on Dear."

I started walking toward the ferry. "I'll get a cart."

"No, I'll go. You stay here and catch your breath."

I leaned against the Lexus and watched Mike head down hill. He nodded a greeting to a group of women dressed in Dear Island uniforms. Three were black, two white. Maids. My nightmare had made me temporarily forget Leyla's plea for help. I considered running to intercept the women, but figured Sharlana's co-workers would be more forthcoming if I were introduced as a concerned friend.

Mike boarded the boat, grabbed a grocery cart, and rolled it across the gangplank. Just ahead of him, Sally Falcon's mother fussed at her ten-year-old granddaughter Molly. Grandma's bulging suitcase banged against her leg with each struggling step. My gallant park ranger rushed to help. "Where's your car, ma'am? I'll carry this."

With effortless grace, he hefted the lady's suitcase into the grocery cart and the procession wheeled my way. When they reached my outpost, I greeted Mrs. Brown and formally introduced Mike to the woman and her young charge.

"What in blazes happened to you?" Mrs. Brown asked as she took in my disheveled state and paint-streaked clothes. Using some rags in Mike's Jeep, I'd wiped the worst of the paint off my skin. But my attempts at cleanup merely smeared the gunk on my slacks and top.

"A little dust-up with some wet paint," I said.

"Little?" Mrs. Brown laughed. "Looks like you rolled around on a wet blacktop."

"Not quite." I didn't elaborate. "Are you and Molly leaving Dear for a spell?"

"Yep. Sally sent us packing. We're headed to Augusta to stay with relatives for a week. I called a rental car company. They're sending someone to pick us up. Hope we don't have too long to wait."

Molly wandered away, drop kicking pebbles toward the bay. "Sweetie, what did I tell you about going near the water?" the concerned grandmother called. "You keep your distance from that boat ramp."

The woman turned back to me. "My daughter wants Molly off Dear until that maniac killer's caught. She has some wild hair that Molly and I might be targets. She's worked herself into a tizzy for no reason. Sure, one of the victims was married to her partner. But it's not like the killer is gunning for our family."

Mrs. Brown didn't expect a reply. I answered anyway. "You can't blame Sally for wanting to keep you two safe. Besides your daughter's got plenty to worry about with reporters, the bridge, and the Easter holiday.

"Who knows how and why this guy picks his victims," I added, though I suspected some real estate link.

Mrs. Brown sighed. "I know, I know. Sally's worried about her little girl, just like I'm worried about mine."

***

A note taped to Donna's front door asked me to refrigerate anything that would melt. Her apology bristled with exclamation points. She'd left to play nursemaid. Gerry O'Grady claimed he'd go nuts if he couldn't escape for a few hours to play golf. So Donna agreed to baby sit his wife, the razor-tongued Maureen, whose disposition had curdled further since she broke her hip.

I retrieved Donna's key from its well-known hiding place under the mat, carried in the groceries, and restocked her fridge. A peek inside the egg carton revealed half the eggs had cracked. I considered writing my own rambling apology but realized my tale of auto abuse and scrambled groceries would never fit on a sticky note. And the authorities wouldn't want me to blab. I took the coward's way out. I'd call later.

By five o'clock, I'd replenished my own larder, trashed my ruined clothes, and showered. Vigorous scrubbing removed the last vestiges of paint and rinsed away the smell of fear. Coming from Iowa, I'm well aware that pigs don't perspire, but I couldn't think of an appropriate substitute for the familiar "I sweat like a pig" metaphor. While scaling the lighthouse stairs, sweat poured off me in buckets, and every trickle carried the stench of terror.

My ablutions came at a price. Purpling bruises bloomed on shins and forearms where I'd repeatedly bashed my body against unyielding metal. I toweled dry, snuggled into a velour warm-up and ambled toward the living room. The cursed answering machine light blinked a visual SOS. Braden's message came first. He curtly informed me that he'd joined the sheriff at Wilderness Park after the roadblock failed. They'd found the SUV and Firebird, both stolen, abandoned at a launch. The thugs fled by boat.

I swallowed hard. The all-points bulletin would be a waste. Nothing to go on except my estimate of both men's height and weight and an antiseptic description of Underling's ugly mug. There was no clue about the true identity of either man. Kain Dzandrek swore the "stranger" he'd lunched with had introduced himself as Jonas Zegan. The name quickly proved an investigative dud. I permitted myself a smug smile. The sheriff shouldn't have blown off my suspicions. Maybe they'd re-interview Kain.

I rewound Braden's message and listened again. His

controlled anger provoked conflicting emotions. I was both disappointed and relieved he wasn't here. Though I longed to be held, I was in no mood for lectures.

Braden said to expect him about seven. A friendly park ranger, undoubtedly Mike, had promised a boat ride since the ferry had shut down for the day.

The voice on my second missed call brightened my mood. "If you want me to call you back, you ought to park your hiney by the phone for more than ten seconds," Aunt May pontificated. "Why in the name of Jesus, Mary, and Joseph don't you buy a cell phone?"

I laughed, reminded of my recent vow to enter the twenty-first century.

May Carr was seventy-nine going on nineteen. Wrinkles and her fluffy white perm verified her age, but her feisty blue eyes never surrendered to the years. When retirement bored the former nurse to tears, May started a real estate career at age sixty. Since she'd helped deliver half the population of Spirit Lake, Iowa, she had no problem getting prime lakeside listings.

At least once a year, I visited May and my cousin, Ross, in the resort community where I'd worked and played every summer from pre-teen through college years. May wasn't a blood relative. She'd wed my mother's brother. But she was family. I adored her and she loved me—something that came through loud and clear even when May was kicking butt, often mine. Since Mom's death, May had been my sole link to her generation.

I postponed dinner preparations long enough to call May. She was just the tonic I needed to quell a case of jitters. She picked up on the first ring.

"Carr Residence." Her voice held a hint of sleep. I pictured her snuggled in the lady's recliner sized to fit her five-foot frame, softly snoring as she took an afternoon siesta.

"My hiney is secured to a chair. I'm ready to listen to your pearls of wisdom."

"Can it, Marley," May barked. "I knew you'd be trouble when you were just a little fart. Nine years old and you scare the bejesus out of me swimming across the lake alone."

"Guess I take after you, May."

She snorted. "What's up? You're not calling your old auntie just to chat, are you? Or did you phone so you could rub it in that you're sunbathing. You know I have snow past the rafters and icebergs floating in the lake. When are you coming to Spirit Lake?"

When May took a breath, I repeated a promise to visit in June and inquired after my three cousins. Then I listened to May's latest tales of real estate daring-do. Finally I got to the point, telling her a dear friend feared her real estate cohorts were engaged in illegal activities.

"Janie's got a toe in something that feels like quicksand. She's afraid her bosses have sunk past their armpits and might reach out and pull her down, too."

To set the stage, I explained how my friend's employers primed the marketing pump by offloading a few choice homesites to insiders.

"They lend employees and relatives interest-free money for down payments and promise to buy the properties back at a profit before the shills have to make balloon loan payments."

May harrumphed. "Pretty slick. By the time real buyers arrive, the market's made. If the patsies have their lots appraised, the comps look dandy. Appraisers look at sale prices, they're not paid to do background checks. Of course, if the same buyer names popped up repeatedly, it would raise questions. But that doesn't sound like their game. They're using real people, not folks who only exist on paper.

"It would be hard to prove the transactions were fishy," she added. "The developers could argue their interest-free loans were perks for loyal workers. Still, I'd advise your friend to type her resume and distance herself from those yahoos."

"Hold on, May, I'm just warming up. Her bosses have been playing this shell game for years. Janie's worried about something new."

I filled my aunt in on the surprise ten-million dollar purchase of Hogsback Island and its hurried unveiling. I detailed Woody's unauthorized use of Janie's notary seal on Emerald Cay documents and Gator's refusal to fire him for it. I noted that Gator and Sally had been strapped for cash, partly because a real-estate investment trust created to snap up foreclosures was draining off dollars faster than new Dear sales could mint them. Finally, I described my visit to Woody's office, including my fib that Aunt May would shell out a million bucks for a homesite close to her beloved niece.

May responded with a hardy guffaw. "Pay a million to get eaten alive by no-see-ums and plot the course of hurricanes spinning my way? No thanks. I'm not that senile. But I'll be glad to play this Woody. Always wanted to pose as a rich dowager. Tell me again about those documents you read upside down."

I told her what I remembered, adding tidbits about a prosperous new mortgage broker and a shady appraiser appearing out of nowhere. I skipped over other details—principally Dear's rash of bizarre murders and the dual attempts on my life. I crossed my fingers the *Des Moines Register* wouldn't fill in these blanks.

"Okay, that's all I know. Any idea what these jokers are pulling?"

May stayed silent a moment, an unusual event. When she spoke, I figured her pause had been intentional. She wanted me to listen and listen hard. "Tell your friend to give notice and find another job. She's an idjit if she waits for the other shoe to drop. The ten million to buy Hog or Pig Island, whatever, didn't drop from the sky. I bet they're laundering money. If not, they may have hoodwinked bankers into loans for a property they have no intention of developing. A while back some high-profile Minnesota promoters skipped town. Defrauded hundreds of homebuyers. Promised a dream lake resort. Built community docks and three model homes, started construction on a clubhouse. Once they sold all the properties, they vanished. It was all over the papers for a month."

My aunt's hypotheses prompted a dozen questions. "Would the developers need a crooked appraiser for a scam like that?"

"Not necessarily, though it couldn't hurt." May chuckled. "Don't know whether I should be flattered or insulted that you think I'm an expert on shady real estate deals."

I laughed. "Be flattered. I figured you'd learn enough about potential real estate pitfalls to make sure nobody fleeced you."

"Okay, a compliment," May said. "I've read up on land flips. A dishonest appraiser's essential. Most scams seem to be big-city though. A crook buys a slum property and immediately resells it to a straw buyer—a fictitious person—for three or four times its value. The straw buyer never forks over a penny, though closing documents show a down payment. Then the loan gets sold to an out-of-town mortgage banker who doesn't know shoelaces from Shinola. The bank gives a half-million-dollars to the land flipper on an appraiser's say-so.

"A land flip requires a greedy attorney, too, to handle the closings. If he's not in on the scheme, the lawyer has to be mortally stupid. I've heard a land flipper can quadruple his money in weeks. One California scam flipped fifty-odd properties in six months. By the time lenders foreclosed, the crooks were long gone—with ten million and change."

I started to ask another question, but Aunt May cut me off. "Marley, my bridge club is due in an hour. I have to go. I'll ask my broker for other ideas. Meanwhile if you're in such an all-fired hurry to become a mortgage fraud expert, look up land flips on the Internet. You're always telling me it's such a wonder. But you be careful, Marley Elizabeth Clark. Don't let 'em catch you snooping. If these guys are running some big-time swindle, they might cut off any nose they find poking in their business."

SIXTEEN

A Google search on mortgage fraud and land flips found a ton of articles. I culled the results and printed six case studies. Then it was six-thirty and time to make supper something more than a good intention. Though my plans for a gourmet feast were flushed, I figured filets and salad might help smooth Deputy Braden Mann's raised hackles.

After gathering a variety of salad makings, I paused mid-reach for the cutting board. Why did I feel a need to appease Braden? His voice on the answering machine message vibrated with anger. Was he blaming the victim for the crime?

Jaw clenched, I chopped the celery into green mush. True, I'd been a tad careless, but the more I thought about it, my nightmarish afternoon had turned out perfectly. For starters, I was alive, and the authorities had justification to hunt down Underling. Before, they'd dismissed my hunch he was a killer. Today I'd seen his ugly face as he fired his—oops, my—gun.

What's more, Underling's motivation to remove me from the planet had lost its urgency. While my pretend amnesia provided incentive to murder me post haste, I'd now identified him. Damage done, and a tenuous link to Kain established.

The doorbell's singsong made me jump. I wiped my hands on a dishtowel and headed for the door. Janie's hands cupped her face as she peered through the sidelight. *I have to buy curtains.*

"So tell me," she demanded as I let her inside. "Did Woody confess?" Suddenly she lowered her voice to a conspiratorial whisper. "Oh, cripes, is Braden here? I keep forgettin' you've got a man in the house. Can we talk?"

Janie trailed me to the kitchen. "He won't be back till seven. But I wish you'd talk to him, off-the-record anyway. Something squirrelly is going on in your office. It's no big honking coincidence that islanders with real estate ties have a high mortality rate."

My neighbor snagged a baby carrot from my cutting board. "Talking would get me fired. How long do you think Gator would keep me if I blabbed? Plus I can't prove anyone besides Woody is involved in any hanky-panky. I caught him with my notary stamp; that's it. Sure I'm suspicious of how Gator and Sally got their mitts on ten million for Hogsback, but I'm hired help. They don't have to share high-finance secrets with the office manager."

When Janie's hand snaked forward for another snack, I batted it away. "Listen, you're not imagining things. My guess is mortgage fraud, a land flip. Today Woody claimed Dear Island Real Estate had to do more homework before it could start selling Emerald Cay homesites. Yet he had two contracts on his desk—for lots on Emerald Cay."

"The hell you say," Janie exploded. "Woody is our sales manager, not the office manager. I handle closings. I'm going to call Sally, demand an explanation. I've a mind to corner Gator down at the funeral parlor."

"Calm down. Don't let Gator and Sally know you're snooping. It could be dangerous."

"Oh, hogwash. These murders are the work of a psychopath. There's no connection."

I seized Janie's shoulders, forcing her eyes to meet mine. "Ever think these murders might be staged? You say you're a hired hand. Well, maybe the killer's hired help, too. My hunch is someone told him how to kill Stew and Bea, what messages to write. Whoever's pulling the strings wants the cops dancing to his tune, looking for mental cases instead of greedy bastards."

Janie rolled her eyes. "Marley, you've plain wigged out if you think Gator or Sally killed—or conspired to kill—Stew and Bea. God knows why, but Gator loved his wife. Plus it's a real stretch to claim Bea was *involved* in real estate. That's like saying

I'm a stripper because my sister runs a gentlemen's club. Bea knew squat about the business. And if Sally's some murderous conspirator, why'd she send her own family packing?"

"Valid points," I conceded. "Gator or Sally may simply be in over their heads. I'm stuck on this Kain Dzandrek. I swear he was talking about Stew's murder when he lunched with the thug who tried to kill me today..."

"What? Someone tried to kill you again? Today?"

At my friend's insistence, I sidetracked to relate how Underling and his pal shot out my tire and chased me at gunpoint. Though not a Catholic, I felt an urge to cross myself while recounting the saving grace of metal stairs and a busload of wee witnesses.

Janie's eyes grew wide. "I can't believe you didn't spill the beans the minute I walked in."

I glanced at the kitchen clock. Five minutes to seven. "Braden will be here any minute. Will you talk to him? Please."

Her golden pageboy swished as she fiercely shook her head. "Let me sleep on it. We're going to Hilton Head, right? If Braden tags along, we can talk. I want to check out some things first. Don't worry, I won't set off any alarms."

I agreed—with misgivings. Even if Gator and Sally were up to their eyeballs in fraud, I couldn't imagine them killing Janie. Gator was off island burying his wife. Reporters tailed Sally everywhere. And Underling and his understudy were on the run.

How many hit men could Kain have at his beck and call?

***

Braden rang the bell at seven-fifteen. As soon as he stepped inside, he crushed my body against his. The fierce embrace communicated more than words. He pulled back and lifted my chin.

"Do you have cat genes or what?" His index finger stroked my cheek. "If you have nine lives, you've blown two. How about going a day or three without cheating death?"

He locked his arms around me once more. "God, am I glad to see you."

He felt so good, so solid. As he kissed the nape of my neck, hot tears of relief welled in my eyes. "Same here," I whispered.

He nuzzled my neck. "I can't believe I almost lost you today."

I tried valiantly to strike a lighter tone. "Yeah, playing hide-and-seek wasn't high on my afternoon agenda. Neither was scaling a lighthouse. I'm not fond of heights."

Determined not to cry, I fought the tears. While I'm ordinarily more likely to rage than blubber, my pent-up emotions resisted protocol. Tears dribbled down my cheeks as sobs shook my body.

"For heaven's sake. I'm crying again. This isn't like me."

Braden slipped an arm around my waist, and walked me down the hall to the master bedroom. I rested my head on his shoulder. "It's okay. Even colonels are entitled to shed a tear or two once the battle's over. I won't tell a soul."

He guided me toward the bed and turned back the coverlet. As I sat on the edge, he tugged off my sneakers. Once he'd tucked the covers around me, he walked to the other side, shucked his own shoes, and slipped into bed. He held me as I cried myself to sleep.

When I woke, the clock's digital readout glowed brightly in the pitch-black room: 8:33 p.m. Braden was still by my side, though he'd extracted the shoulder that pillowed my head. "You awake?" I whispered.

"Yeah." He switched on the reading lamp built into the bookcase headboard and fiddled with the dimmer to soften the light.

We kissed. "Thank you. I'm fine now. My emotions have been kind of raw."

My brisk, all-business tone said the histrionics were over.

"You must be starving. Glad I left the salad in the refrigerator or we'd be eating wilted weeds. I can have dinner ready in ten minutes."

Braden shut me up with a wake-up kiss. Also all business. "We've waited this long, why not a few minutes more?"

I was decades past the randy, can't-get-enough stage when hormones overwhelm good sense. Yet in this opening chapter of our relationship, I surrendered to the tidal pull of lust. Awkwardly we undressed each other beneath the covers.

His hands floated across my breasts, a gossamer touch that left me quivering. He pulled my hips forward and I twined my legs around him. For long minutes, we communed, kissing deeply, almost in a trance, refusing to allow our bodies to bolt ahead to the finish line. Statues a sculptor froze in a final moment of icy-hot anticipation. Consummation a promise just beyond our trembling reach.

Unable to wait a moment longer, I whispered "yes," and we moved to the next plateau. No fevered thrusts, just a long, rocking meld. The molten sensation of joining as one.

Afterward, we lay on our backs, pillows fluffed behind our heads, fingers twined. I thought about my husband then. The hundreds of nights we'd slept in this same bed.

"A penny for your thoughts?"

"Not worth a penny." I doubted Braden would be flattered to learn our lovemaking triggered memories of a dead husband. My gaze wandered to the framed cross-stitch my sister gave me for my fiftieth birthday: *If you're lucky enough to be at the beach, you're lucky enough.* "Just thinking how lucky I am."

"Yes, you are." Braden's tone had changed. He obviously wanted to say more. "I can't understand how that dirt bag found you." His frustration poured out in a torrent, seasoned with a hint of censure. "How did he get your gun?"

Recess was over. He'd launched into interrogation mode. *Dang it.* I angled for a postponement. "Look, time we eat, it'll be nine-thirty. Can we move the cross-examination to the kitchen? I'm starved."

He backed off. "Okay. Sorry. This creep is frustrating the hell out of me. Can't believe we haven't gotten a line on him. And now we know he has an accomplice. But, you're right, no point ruining our appetite."

During dinner, we shared a little about our parents and told funny and not-so-funny stories about our childhoods. Due to circumstances, we'd skipped the usual courting, getting-to-know-you rituals. Now we backtracked to pick up missing pieces. I wanted to know what molded the man who'd seized center stage in my life, virtually overnight.

I sensed Braden felt the same way. I also wondered how the difference in our ages might influence our views. I grew up with *Mork & Mindy, Happy Days,* and *The Six Million Dollar Man.* I watched Bobby Kennedy's assassination, remembered disco.

Braden inhabited another generation. My husband, ten years older than me, could have been Braden's dad. *Did we really have enough in common to remain lovers?*

After supper, Sheriff Conroy phoned to say a police artist would come by at nine the next morning.

Braden helped me load the dishwasher, tidy the kitchen. Once we moved to the living room, he forsook the easy chair to spoon with me on the sofa. My fingers traced the muscles in the arms enfolding me in a loose embrace. I sipped peppermint schnapps and sighed contentedly.

"Can we talk about your lighthouse romp now?" He crossed his heart. "Promise, no bad cop routine."

"Sure."

He returned to the question of my pilfered gun. How did Underling steal it? I recalled the car alarm, admitted my failure to check the glove box afterward.

I walked Braden through the trap and my attempts at evasion tactics.

"There is an up side. I'm out of the woods as far as this madman's concerned." I smiled. "Underling gains nothing by killing me. I've identified him. Any attempt on my life would be extremely risky. The cops are looking for *him* now, not some anonymous bogeyman."

Braden stood and carried our schnapps glasses to the wet bar for a refill. "Wish I saw it your way. But Underling still has a strong motive to kill you. If he stands trial, your testimony will be crucial. I just wish we knew his motive for the other murders."

"We know his motive—he's doing what his boss pays him to do," I interrupted. "Kain Dzandrek. He decides who gets killed."

Braden shrugged. "Okay, I'll bite. What reason could this Kain have to murder Bea and Stew? As far as we can tell, he's never set foot on Dear Island. We've asked dozens of people. I even called the former owner of Hogsback Island—MacIsaac. He never heard of Kain."

"Did MacIsaac sound on the up and up?"

"Yeah, he chummed the waters, writing a bunch of letters to likely buyers. When he didn't get a nibble, he figured he'd sit on the property a few more years."

Braden rattled the ice in his glass. "MacIsaac said the call from Gator last month was a real shocker. The seller's attorney swapped the deed to Hogsback Island for a two-million-dollar certified bank check and a loan agreement. The buyers agreed to pay MacIsaac two million plus interest each January 1 for five years."

I frowned. "Who wrote the check?"

"It was drawn on the account of Emerald Cay, LLC, at a Cayman bank. And before you ask, no—I haven't gotten my hands on any bank or corporate documents yet to see if Kain's connected. A SLED forensic accountant is digging."

With Kain a main conversation topic, the time seemed ripe

to press for a Hilton Head excursion. After I proposed an invasion of a gentleman's club by three unlikely musketeers—Janie, Braden and me—the deputy laughed.

"Say what? You're pulling my leg."

When I shook my head, he crossed his arms. Closed off, but still listening.

Finally, he shrugged. "I can't imagine what we'll accomplish. Regulars at April's club aren't likely to spill their guts to two women and a cop. But I suppose a surprise appearance can't hurt. It could make Dzandrek jumpy. If we know where to find him on a Friday night, he might decide we know a lot more than we do."

I rewarded Braden with a smile, and he raised a hand in a stop gesture. "Three requests. I won't call 'em conditions because you'll get riled. One, you and I spend the night in a hotel, not at April's condo. Janie can sleep where she pleases. Two, we don't leave one another's sight. Ever. Underling and his buddy may be a thousand miles away, but there's nothing to say Kain couldn't decide to do his own wet work."

"And condition three?" I asked.

Braden paused and smiled, "You protect my virtue if any strippers wiggle my way for a lap dance."

I laughed. How I wished we could retire on this note. Sadly, I needed to tell him about Sharlana's disappearance and its possible tie to Bea's murder. Too much coincidence. I also reminded Braden that Eastern Europeans had a booming market in long-range ECDs that lacked the Taser's telltale confetti. "Kain's from Poland. It could be another link."

Braden promised to fold Sharlana's investigation into his double-murder probe.

One other thing weighed on my mind—Dear Island's real estate irregularities. Though sorely tempted to break my promise to Janie, I had no right to play know-it-all parent. Janie was an adult. Besides, I felt confident my friend would come clean tomorrow. Of course, a little nudge from me wouldn't be out of line.

SEVENTEEN

At seven a.m. my alarm buzzed like a horsefly. I groaned and swatted it off. My body ached from the self-inflicted thrashing on the lighthouse stairs, and my head throbbed from multiple nightcaps. It had been years since I'd imbibed beyond a single drink, and Braden poured with a heavy hand. His loud groan implied he was equally groggy.

I made coffee while he showered, then followed him into the steamy bath and showered while he shaved. I'd known the man less than a week, and we acted like an old married couple. The sight of a nude man in my bathroom wasn't the least bit jarring. It seemed…natural.

I raised my voice over the drum of water. "I forgot to ask, what happened with the Cuthbert twins?" I caught Braden studying my reflection in the steamy mirror.

"The lady of the house showed for court yesterday, relatively sober. The judge released the twins into Grace's custody pending a hearing next week."

Braden vacated the bathroom as I climbed out of the shower. "Want to bet how long Henry and Jared stay out of trouble?" I asked. "Think we can get the father involved?"

"Hope so. Those boys are in a bad place." Braden sat on the bed to pull on his socks while I toweled dry. "What are you doing today?"

"The police artist, then a meeting with Hank Jones. He runs Camp Dear. We're scouting kayaking points of interest for teens. We set up the excursion last week before the first murder."

Braden's look telegraphed his opinion: I was bonkers. It killed him not to say so.

I smiled. "Hank was Special Ops. He can handle himself. And, yes, we'll both be carrying. He called while you were in

192

the shower. But the precautions are just that. We're just paddling around the local creeks."

I threw on a robe and we wandered out to the kitchen. Braden poured coffee and I pulled a six-pack of plastic-encased blueberry muffins from the bread drawer. The muffins had survived yesterday's kamikaze ride unscathed.

Braden sighed. "I'll meet you and Janie here at four-thirty so we can catch the last ferry. My car's parked at the boat landing so we can take it to Hilton Head. I'll make a hotel reservation."

I watched enviously as Braden slathered butter on his muffin. "Sound's good. Mind if I talk to folks in housekeeping about Sharlana? After my mother-in-law died, I hired one of the housekeeping supervisors to clean the house. We hit it off. Diana might open up to me."

"Diana? She's yours. You've got my cell phone number, right? Call if you get a lead—or need me."

Butter migrated to Braden's fingers, and his tongue snaked out for a final lick before he carried his plate to the sink. "Be careful." He leaned over to kiss me goodbye.

"I will. Have to live long enough to see if those exotic dancers crank your engine." I winked.

"Yeah? What'll you do if I get excited?" He waggled his eyebrows and exited.

I phoned housekeeping. Diana's crew had already left to clean a group of villas. I asked for a call back when she broke for lunch—about two p.m. according to the message taker.

Finally, I closed my eyes and pictured Underling's face. A disturbing way to begin the day, but I wanted a clear picture in my head when the police artist arrived.

Ten minutes later I answered the doorbell and greeted a dead ringer for Mr. Magoo. The elfin man in rumpled duds wore Coke-bottle glasses. His eyes, magnified to fried-egg dimensions, bespoke vision in the legally-blind realm. *How does this guy tell a cauliflower from a kumquat, let alone suspect A from suspect B?*

I'd fretted for naught. The artist played his laptop like a Stradivarius. With a symphony of keystrokes, he built a frightening likeness of Underling. The details chilled me. Tufts of black hair sprouted from his oversized ears. The smashed nose made breathing look like a snorkeling exercise.

The artist cocked his head. "Ugly sucker, isn't he? Don't worry. Soon he won't be able to show his face. You have a wireless net, right? Can I use it to transmit?"

"Anything to help put that SOB in jail." Goose flesh crept up my arms as I stared at the cartoonish yet evil face projected on the computer screen.

***

I changed into grungy shorts and a ragged, long-sleeved tee, a souvenir from the Beaufort Shrimp Festival's 5K Run. I also donned a pair of ancient sneakers in case we ran aground on a mud flat. Razor-sharp oyster shells slice neatly through bare feet.

Hank beat me to the friend's dock where I store my kayak. He'd been busy. Both our oceangoing kayaks sat in the water ready to shove off.

"Sure you want a human bulls-eye as a traveling companion?" I asked.

He grinned. "Hey, I survived Afghanistan. I think I can handle Dear. But let's try to avoid tipping over. Don't know if my pistolo fires as well wet."

After seeing my GPS, Hank bought an identical model, and this was its maiden voyage. I showed him how to set trip functions to track distance and speed. "Teens can use the speed calculations to see how tidal pulls influence their paddling pace."

With high tide seventy minutes away, we had a perfect two-hour window to poke around the meandering ocean creeks. As we paddled, I told Hank how I'd been stranded between two muddy humps on my first-ever kayak outing. While waiting for the water to inch high enough to escape, a handful of shrimp and one small fish imprisoned in the same landlocked puddle flopped into my kayak. Hank rolled his eyes. No one ever believed me. I should have snapped pictures.

Five minutes out, I realized my neck muscles had relaxed. I *needed* this. Exercise—especially in the great outdoors—was my Prozac. It calmed me, renewed my optimism. What a grand day. An egret soared in the Carolina blue sky. As sunlight pierced its white feathers, the translucent wings glowed. Only the soothing metronome of gentle surf and the calls of quarrelling seagulls broke the silence.

The peaceful illusion shattered when a motor starter coughed downwind. In the lee of tall marsh grass, we were invisible to the frustrated boater. We paddled to a spot that offered a view of the portion of Flying Fish Creek that wound past the Cuthberts' dock to Mad Inlet.

Hugh Wells was the boat's sole occupant. Once the motor caught, he headed out the inlet toward the ocean. Impossible to follow him in a kayak. Still we paddled in his wake. Hugh's skiff bucked over the breakers near the mouth of the inlet, then skimmed smoothly across a calm ocean on course to Hilton Head. Of course, he could be angling toward one of the many tiny islands between Dear and Hilton Head. Or maybe he had no destination, just out for a pleasant spin.

A dolphin surfaced four feet from my kayak. Its black eyes seemed to lock on mine. Oxygen whistled through its air hole and the mammal gracefully dived. When I once again looked toward Hugh's boat, a small craft covered with camouflage paint shot out of the shallows near Sunrise Island. Had it lain in wait? Two heads bobbed above the chase boat as it crossed the breakers. Did Hugh have a tail?

It was a mystery I couldn't solve. Rip tides swirled the

waters of Mad Inlet.

"Hey, aren't we going to stay in the creeks?" Hank asked. "The water here looks like a wicked witches' cauldron."

"Yeah, just wanted to take a quick look-see." With a few swift strokes, we returned to the tranquility of the creeks.

We glided beyond the Cuthberts' dock and set a cross-island course for the marina. Soon our rhythmic strokes built to a soothing cadence. Rounding a bend where the wandering waterway sliced into the new Beach West development, I pointed out an osprey nest and showed Hank how to mark it as a fun GPS waypoint for summer campers.

Further along, we locked in GPS coordinates for another waypoint, a fork in the creek that ended just short of an artesian-fed pool. Winter and spring, it served as an alligator spa. The Beach West logging road skirted the inland lagoon, and I drove by often. If temperatures dipped into the forties, clouds of steam hovered as the earth belched heated water from its belly. Two weeks ago, I counted the snouts of fifteen alligators luxuriating in the spa's warmth. Using the location as a turnaround point, we headed back to my friend's dock.

Hank thanked me for the GPS lesson and offered to serve as bodyguard any time I wanted to escape the house.

His throwaway comment reminded me a killer was still on the loose. *Damn.*

EIGHTEEN

I foraged for food, showered, changed clothes, and packed my overnight bag. Camped on the sofa, I'd just lost my battle to prop my eyes open when Diana returned my call. After stifling a yawn, I explained my friendship with Sharlana's aunt and my promise to help gather information about the missing teen.

"Come on over," Diana said. "Sharlana's a nice kid. We're all worried. Look for me in the break room."

Dear's housekeeping building isn't on any sightseeing tour. Tucked behind trees on a piece of swampland, the prefab metal affair offers no redeeming vistas. With my entry, I traveled from spring to summer in the space of two feet. Hot, humid air blasted from long rows of laundry machines, heating the interior more efficiently than a furnace.

Wandering down the center aisle, I soon spied the break room. Near the entrance four men played cards as they wolfed down brown-bag lunches. Across the room, Diana and two companions sat at a scarred table beside ancient vending machines.

"Hi, Marley," Diana greeted. "This is Gina, Sharlana's supervisor, and Sofia, one of the girl's friends. I'm afraid Sofia doesn't speak much English."

Gina was a middle-aged black woman. Sofia was a blonde waif who looked all of fourteen. I shook hands with Gina. Sofia dipped her head in a quasi greeting, but didn't lift her eyes.

"I explained you wanted to chat," Diana said. "See if we could come up with anything to help the sheriff."

"I appreciate your time." I paused. "Sharlana's last few days at work—did she appear worried, scared, upset? Did she mention any trouble?"

Gina, a talkative Gullah native, needed no additional conversational lubricant. She confirmed Sharlana got the short end of the stick—a one-week assignment at the Caldwells, dusting, vacuuming, ironing and polishing silver while Bea carped. Gina described the missing teen as a happy-go-lucky girl who hadn't confided any fears, although she was counting the days until she served out her sentence at the Caldwells.

"I don't mean no disrespect to the dead," Gina added, "but no one wanted to work in Miss Bea's house if'n there was some way around it. I didn't see Sharlana that last day. My boy, he took sickly with the flu bug that's flyin' round."

The supervisor looked up, her eyes sad behind thick glasses. "Sharlana's a worker bee. I started frettin' when she didn't come or call Wednesday. Then her momma phoned to say she'd gone missing. I prayed real hard Sunday for God to lift the evil that's done got Dear by the throat. I'm downright spooked to walk 'round this island by my lonesome nowadays."

Diana cleared her throat. "'Fraid I have nothing to add. I didn't see Sharlana till quittin' time that last day. Since the bridge was out, our boss hauled us to the marina in batches to be ferried across. Last I saw, Sharlana was huddled with Sofia on Cap'n Hook's boat."

Sofia hadn't uttered a peep. "What did you and Sharlana talk about?" I asked.

The girl didn't speak. She twirled her straight blonde hair, her eyes glued to the table.

"You're not in trouble. No need to be afraid. Don't you want to help us find your friend?"

"No can help. Know nothing." She looked up with tears in her eyes. "English not good."

Though she wasn't facile with English, I figured her understanding went beyond her speaking ability. Her accent sounded familiar. On a hunch, I addressed her in Polish. She flinched as if she'd been slapped.

"You speak Polish." Her response—also in Polish—

sounded like an accusation, not a compliment.

"Yes, I studied it in school. Are you from Poland?" We were both rusty in our common-denominator language and spoke haltingly.

"No, my mother's mother teach me. She lived with us in Croatia. My sponsor…he's Polish."

Kain Dzandrek? I bit my tongue to keep from asking. I couldn't afford for her to clam up before I found out if Sharlana had confided in her. The language shift seemed to put Sofia more at ease. The comfort might have come from increased privacy. Our tablemates couldn't understand a word.

"I hope you'll excuse us for leaving you out of the conversation," I apologized in English to Gina and Diana.

Diana stood. "Sure. Nice seeing you. Hope the sheriff finds Sharlana safe." Though Gina seemed miffed to be missing out on potential gossip, she took the hint. "Already clocked out. Guess I'll head home."

Alone with the hair-twisting teen, I asked more direct questions. She volunteered nothing. Each question coaxed forth a bare-bones reply. I learned Sofia was an orphan. She'd seen a sign at a shelter offering passage to the promised land—America. If I understood correctly, she was a modern-day indentured servant. She lived with other immigrants in a collection of shacks on Sands Island. She never saw a paycheck and believed she'd "earn" her freedom in five years. Her wages were held to repay her boat steerage and sponsorship fees.

The girl and fifteen fellow workers were assigned to Dear Island. Dozens more shipmates from savaged communities like Chechnya had been placed with cruise ships or other resorts needing menial labor. When I asked her age, she mumbled "eighteen." A practiced lie. My guess of fourteen hadn't changed.

"Sharlana is your friend?" I asked.

Sofia nodded. "Yes, very nice. Teaches me ten English

words a day. And brings gifts…foods I never tasted, like sweet potato pie. I miss her."

"Do you know what happened to her?"

A tear dribbled down her cheek. "My fault," she whispered. "I promised Sharlana I wouldn't tell, but I did. She was afraid. I wanted to help. She heard Miss Bea argue with her husband about the man who drowned. Miss Bea said she didn't buy pearls to wear in prison. Begged her husband to pack up and leave before his killer friend murdered them, too."

"Did Bea identify this killer friend? Did Sharlana hear his name?"

"I don't know." Sofia's hands shook. The child had reason to be scared.

"Who did you tell about Sharlana's eavesdropping?"

Sofia shook her head. "No. I can't. Please leave me alone."

"Is your sponsor Kain Dzandrek?" I held my breath.

The waif bolted. I didn't run after her. For long minutes I stared into the dank, overheated room. What could I do beyond sharing Sofia's story with Braden?

Except for Sharlana, only one *living* person knew what Bea said, and that man, Gator, was in Beaufort burying his wife. If Sofia's hearsay was true, Gator had to suspect his "killer friend" arranged Bea's murder. So why didn't he give the guy up? Was he afraid? Or had he given his wife's killer the all clear?

***

I rushed home and found Braden packing an overnight bag. He glanced up as I walked into the bedroom. "I've been running all day," he said. "No lunch, no breaks. Thought I'd pack and spend the next hour returning phone calls."

"First, let me tell you what I've learned."

"Okay, but let's talk in the kitchen."

He opened the refrigerator and retrieved a hunk of cheese and an apple. While he munched, I filled him in on my conversation with Sofia.

"I fear Sharlana's dead," I began. "She overheard Bea and Gator arguing. Sounds like Bea blurted out the killer's name. Instead of calling the cops, Sharlana confided in Sofia, who blabbed to a woman she called her 'housemother.' Anyway, the news got relayed to the girl's so-called sponsor. A hundred to one, it's Kain."

Braden put down his half-eaten apple. "You're tossing out a lot of conjecture. Any facts?"

"No, but that doesn't mean I'm wrong. I figure Bea's outburst prompted Kain to contract her murder, psycho-style, to keep cops looking for a madman. He probably arranged a less spectacular end for Sharlana. Bizarre murders on two islands the same night would puncture his single-madman smokescreen. Especially if anyone connected Bea's death with her maid's. I'll bet Sharlana's body is never found."

Braden hoisted his eyebrows to mid-forehead. "Let me make sure I understand. You're saying the Dear murders are tied to modern-day slavery? And Kain Dzandrek is your candidate for a Polish Simon Legree?"

"Yes." I ignored his mocking skepticism.

He shrugged. "Your so-called slavery may be legit. Think about it: your version of reality comes courtesy of a naive orphan speaking pidgin Polish, and Kain Dzandrek isn't the only Pole on the East Coast."

I tried to interrupt. "But…"

He held up a hand. "Don't get me wrong. I'll grant you that Kain's bent. But I don't buy imported 'guest workers' as a credible motive for murder. Let's say Kain furnished Dear with a dozen workers at less than minimum wage. Profits on a transaction like that wouldn't pay the monthly electric bill on his mansion."

I bit my lip to keep from screaming in frustration. "Okay, maybe there's more to it. But will you please talk to Sofia before something happens to her?"

"Definitely. We'll drop in, see if we can turn up hard evidence to tie the workers to Kain. Do you know how to find the barracks?"

"No, but nuns run a migrant outreach program not far from Gedduh Place. Word about the place would definitely reach the sisters."

The deputy's acquiescence encouraged me to go for broke. "We ought to confront Gator tonight. Bea's funeral is tomorrow. We could drop in during visitation and ask a few questions. Maybe catch him off guard."

Braden held up one hand. "Whoa. I'm not bracing a widower while his wife's casket sits ten feet away—especially with reporters spying and the sheriff stopping by to offer condolences."

He paused. "In fact, we should cancel this Hilton Head trip—it was a bad idea from the get-go. We've got enough trouble north of the Broad River."

I shook my head. "No way. Kain will be at April's club tonight. I'm going with or without you. I don't have to worry about police protocol."

Braden groaned. "You think Kain will confess…that you can trick him into providing some clue?"

I rolled my eyes. "Not exactly. But this guy has a huge ego. I'll bet he's real pleased with himself. Maybe he'll drink to celebrate. Maybe he'll be itching to brag and throw out hints he thinks some stupid rent-a-cop doesn't have the smarts to pick up on. What do we have to lose?"

A few phone calls provided directions to the worker barracks, located at the end of a dusty road christened "Harry" during a push to ID every crossroad for 911 calls. "Harry" had been the best-known inhabitant of the muddy track that circled behind acres of tomato fields.

At four-thirty, Janie rang the bell, right on time for our outing. Braden mumbled a hello. As we walked to her car, she nodded her head toward the deputy. "Seems kind of scratchy. Sure was a short honeymoon."

True, he was irritated but I appreciated his willingness—though coerced—to compromise. As we drove to catch the last ferry, I repeated Sofia's story for my neighbor.

"Surely the girl's confused." Janie frowned. "I write weekly checks to Help-Lease. It's an employment agency headquartered in Washington, D.C. Provides foreign workers who don't complain when they're asked to do manual labor. We pay the agency a lump sum. In exchange, it delivers the crew, houses the workers, and takes care of workmen's comp, FICA withholding—the whole nine yards. Nothing illegal. It's a legit temp agency."

"Could Kain own Help-Lease?" I asked.

Janie shook her head. "You're barking up the wrong tree, Marley. Hugh went on a cruise ship staffed by Help-Lease and told Gator about the agency. My boss followed up, eager to glom onto a source for cheap, docile employees. If a worker turns out to be a dud, he's gone. No lawsuit threats, no grievance cases."

I didn't argue the ethics with Janie. I did wonder about Help -Lease scale of operation. What happened to guest workers after they fulfilled their labor contracts—*if* that's what they were? Were they dumped unceremoniously back in their homelands? Did they have any shot at happy-ever-after?

After an uneventful ferry crossing, we piled into Braden's waiting car and headed toward Sands Island. The barracks proved easy to find. Once painted a dazzling blue, which, in Gullah mythology, wards off evil spirits or hants, the dilapidated shacks had faded to a bluish-gray.

We walked inside. The paint job had failed to thwart evil. Cockroaches didn't bother to scurry; they sauntered, knowing they owned the filthy landscape. Single cots lined the walls; the thickest mattress skinnier than a slice of Wonder bread. Most chilling was the absence of people. A few stray articles of clothing—mostly worn socks—said the occupants vacated in a hurry.

"Jesus Christ," Janie muttered. "I can't believe folks lived like this and didn't gripe."

My fingers itched with the urge to strangle someone. "To people living in worse hellholes, this looks like Nirvana. No one's lobbing grenades. There's food. Their sponsor knows where to look."

Braden shook his head. "Doubt we'll ever find Sofia. By nightfall she'll be billeted in some other backwater shack or maybe on a cruise ship. Who's going to run to the police to protest?"

Janie looked downright ill. "I feel like crap. I never questioned anything. You guys still want to go to Hilton Head?"

"More than ever. I can't wait for Kain to see I'm alive and ready to stick a red hot poker up his ass."

Braden opened the car door. "You're delusional. This guy won't talk to you—or anyone—about anything."

"Want to bet?" I challenged.

He muttered something under his breath. It sounded suspiciously like "freakin' Yankee women." I knew he meant me—and possibly his ex-wife. Not the most promising pairing.

NINETEEN

We spoke little during the first half of our ride to Hilton Head. As we traveled Beaufort's perimeter, a military convoy slowed our progress to a tortoise pace. The young men occupying jump seats in the truck ahead looked more like Boy Scouts than warriors. My perception was a defect of age. Everyone under thirty looked like a kid these days. When the soldiers exited at Parris Island, I mentally wished them well. At least they'd complete basic training before summer's stifling blanket of humidity settled over the Lowcountry.

Crossing the Broad River provided enough emotional distance from the desolate worker camp for us to talk again. Janie broke the silence. "Maybe this labor crap *is* connected to the murders. Stew's job took him to Sands Island. Bet he saw the camp and threatened to report Help-Lease. Could be they killed him before he could blab."

Riding shotgun, I turned and fixed Janie with a look designed to wither.

"Your theory doesn't explain Bea's death. She wasn't exactly a champion of workers' rights. Something more lucrative than imported labor is behind this mess. In these parts, that means drugs or real estate."

I verbally twisted my neighbor's arm, a nudge to tell all to Braden.

Janie sighed. "Okay, I give. Braden, my *friend* wants me to tell you about some fishy goings on in our real estate office. This goes against my better judgment and I'm asking you to be a gentleman. If it's unrelated to the murders, it's out of your jurisdiction, right? Personally I think Marley's nuts. Gator and Sally aren't killers."

"What the hell are you two babbling about?" Braden asked with heat. "Sounds like my *island liaison* has been holding back.

Somebody fill me in *now*."

"Okay, chill out," Janie said and launched into a recital of suspected hanky-panky from Woody's unauthorized use of her notary stamp to Gator's and Sally's mysterious funding of Hogsback Island.

When she finished, I added background on the mechanics of land flip scams courtesy of Aunt May. I also listed the co-conspirator suspects gleaned from Beaufort gossip. I was now convinced the shady and profitable appraiser, the foreign mortgage broker, and the down-on-his-luck lawyer were pawns in the puzzle.

"Let's see if I've got this straight," Braden said. "You're convinced a real estate scam is underway and that Kain, the central villain, somehow cajoled or coerced Gator and Sally to dance to his tune."

He looked my way. I nodded without speaking.

"Doesn't wash. Why would Gator and Sally go along? Every land flip has a foreseeable end, inevitable discovery, right? To profit, the crooks have to skip before mortgages start to default. It would take one hell of a big payday to make it worthwhile for Sally to disappear when she has a kid, family. And, once Bea was killed, why would Gator keep his trap shut?"

I didn't respond immediately, figuring a few moments of silence might dial down the emotional temperature. Keeping my mouth shut for so long about a potential subplot clearly pissed Braden off.

"Maybe Gator and Sally got sucked in gradually—like tar babies, one greedy hand at a time. By the time Bea was killed, the message was clear. If they talked, they were next."

Braden glowered. Though angry, he'd calmed. "Okay, it's a theory. But we don't have a shred of evidence that Gator or Sally ever met Kain, let alone got into bed with him."

Janie chuckled. "Good metaphor, or is it a simile? If nothing else, maybe we'll find out tonight what type of bedmate Kain prefers. What do we have to lose?"

***

Perhaps we'd all begun to think about our losses. Whatever the reason, a funk—and silence—descended. My own thoughts migrated from Kain to Braden. Did we have a future? Did I want one? I speculated on his "Yankee women" barb. Did he see me as too willful? If so, I gave our relationship the longevity of a fruit fly—despite the amazing sex.

At seven o'clock we crossed the soaring bridge over Skull Creek and touched down on Hilton Head during the prime feedlot hour. But luck was with us as we claimed seats at one of the island's popular eateries.

Our table offered an impressive beach view. Though night had fallen, we could still see the white froth of the breakers and hear the rumbling surf. On the flat horizon, a shrimp boat with its arms locked upright looked like an angry bull, its metal horns ready to charge the sea. We could see only one of the boat's running lights—a fierce Cyclops's eye.

The waiter took our drink orders. I requested an O'Doul's, and my tablemates seconded the motion. Though a belt of hard-core booze had definite appeal, nonalcoholic beer seemed wiser given the night's mission. We needed our wits—or what passed for them. We voted unanimously for the house specialty, Frogmore Stew, and devoured the Lowcountry mélange of shrimp, spicy sausage, potatoes, onions and corn in no time.

We kept the conversation light until our plates were empty—edibles gone and shells and corncobs flung in a tin bucket sunk in the center of the table. Janie gabbed the most, telling amusing stories that poked fun without transforming Dear's inhabitants into caricatures. Braden smiled in spite of himself. My neighbor was good company if you weren't on her black list.

With time to spare after dinner, Braden ran Janie by her

sister's condo so she could drop her suitcase in the foyer. She'd already shared her intention to help April close up, freeing Braden and me to leave the club whenever we wanted. Next, Braden checked us into our hotel and schlepped our overnight bags to our room.

We reached April's club a few minutes after eight o'clock. Braden entered ahead of Janie and me. Five minutes later, my neighbor and I staked out a two-person table six feet away from his seat at the long bar.

The night spot—Shore Leave—was a far cry from my expectation. Warm, pleasing lighting made it easy to read patrons' expressions—mostly smiles. April must have spent a fortune on acoustics, too. If Kain did talk to me, he could whisper and I wouldn't miss a word.

Large watercolors in spare wood frames decorated Shore Leave's cream walls. The artwork celebrated the sea and human forms. The tributes were sensuous not graphic. Wax held thousands of tiny seashells prisoner in the candles topping the mahogany tables clustered around the performance stage. Flickering shadows danced merrily across the polished wood. The club was, well…classy.

Janie promised our trio wouldn't stand out. She was right. April did not cater to a strictly male audience. The atmosphere was comfortably cordial, the clientele upscale. Like many South Carolina retail establishments, I noticed this one posted a leave-your-concealed-weapon-outside reminder at the door. I hoped Kain read English as well as he spoke it.

The deputy nursed a dark Samuel Adams beer as he chatted with a middle-aged man on the adjacent stool. I automatically frowned when Braden paused to flirt with the young, top-heavy barmaid.

Though small, Shore Leave had an open floor plan with no side rooms or confessional-style banquets for lap dances. It didn't take long to scan every face and verify Kain's absence.

April sashayed over and greeted us with hasty cheek kisses. A few years older than Janie, she clearly shared her sister's screw-you mindset.

"Hey, Sis. Marley. Welcome to Shore Leave. It's a class joint, huh?" She flashed a smile my way. "What'd you expect, a condom dispenser at the front door? Wait'll you get a load of our new belly dancer. Muscle control like that and I could seduce Prince Harry."

Her laugh tinkled like a bell. "Your pigeon hasn't arrived. Usually comes in alone a little after nine. You have a prime spot to watch the door."

"Are any of his former dates here?" I asked.

She grinned conspiratorially. "Nope. But I'll keep an eye out. If I see one, I'll introduce her to your deputy. He's cute. I'd be glad to tell him my sexual preferences."

April glanced toward a group of arrivals. "Got to play hostess. Will check with you later. Drinks are on the house."

At nine-twenty, Kain swaggered in. When our eyes met, he made a beeline for our table. My stuttering heart hammered my ribs.

"Marley, isn't it? You do turn up in the most unusual places. I can't tell you how pleased I am to see you. And here I was thinking I'd need to engineer our next meeting."

His smug smile hinted at an inside joke. That's when an old Gullah proverb flashed through my mind: "Every grin teeth don't mean laugh."

TWENTY

"May I join you?" Kain bowed slightly.

Shore Leave's muted lights flattered the handsome man. I guessed him to be ten years my junior, fairly close to the big 4-O divide. Blond highlights shimmered in his thick brown mane—a Clairol ad man's dream. Yet his cruel mouth and haughty manner brought to mind the actors who played Nazi S.S. officers in vintage World War II flicks. His chiseled features projected no hint of humanity.

I hadn't answered Kain's request to join us. An under-the-table kick from Janie forced me to focus. My friend lifted an eyebrow in an unspoken question: *What the hell should I do?*

We hadn't scripted this scenario. "I'd welcome the company." I returned Kain's smile. "Especially since my friend has to leave. Please, have a seat."

Though I purposely made no introduction, Janie vacated her seat with a curt, "Nice to meet you." I vowed not to tell the creep anything I didn't want him to know.

Janie nervously fluffed her pageboy. "Be back in a few minutes."

Kain leaned in so close his hot breath assaulted my ear. "I hear Janie Spark's quite the strumpet. Did she have those inclinations before her hubby started screwing her little sister?" His tongue snaked over his lips. "Maybe we should convince her to stay. I do enjoy a spirited ménage à trois. Older women, if they're as well preserved as you, my lieutenant colonel, are quite the treat. So keen to please. Especially widows who've tired of their dildos."

Heat rose to my cheeks. Feeling simultaneously slimed and flabbergasted, I checked a strong impulse to smack the guy. I'd planned to surprise Kain, put him on the defensive. In seconds he'd turned the tables, letting me know he could pen unauthorized biographies of Janie and me, complete with sexual footnotes.

How and why had Kain checked us out?

I recalled his attempt to pump the Sea Watch maître d' for my last name. The Dear Island sticker on Donna's car could have given him a place to dig for dirt. Other inquiries—undoubtedly on Dear—bore fruit. He knew my name, rank and, for all I knew, serial number. My uncommon first name probably simplified his research.

That didn't explain why he'd probed Janie's past. She swore they'd never met.

To buy time, I countered his sexual innuendo even though the gambit made me want to gag. I decided to let him know I could be clairvoyant, too. "Well, Mr. Dzandrek, on behalf of older ladies, I should point out that we're quite particular about our sexual partners."

Kain smiled, though his eyes held all the warmth of a black hole. "Oh? And I'd heard you were screwing that deputy seated at the bar. Does the hotel room Deputy Mann booked for the two of you have twin beds? The cop seems very ordinary, no imagination."

To any passersby, his tone communicated light-hearted banter. His cold eyes spoke of darker emotions. He seemed disappointed when his barbs failed to provoke an outburst.

I sat stone-faced, unwilling to give this bully the satisfaction of revulsion or fear. I sensed these were the responses he prized. Kain's forefinger lightly stroked my arm. While I could censor my words, my body's response to his icy touch proved beyond my control. Goose bumps erupted along the route of his caress like welts rising from the lick of a whip.

Concentrate. I knew how and why I'd come to Kain's attention, but why had he dug into my neighbor's background? And how did he know about a hotel room Braden booked a few hours ago? Did he have us under surveillance?

Kain spoke. "A lot of turmoil has come into my life since our chance meeting. Your police have questioned me not once but twice. I'm a private man. I fear your insinuations and nosiness are to blame. I won't tolerate meddling."

He grabbed my wrist and squeezed for emphasis. "When I was a boy, I ate moldy bread, fought dogs for meat that had gone green. Now I'm wealthy. How do you suppose a Pole like me gets rich, eh? It's not attending Northwestern."

His allusion to my alma mater was more theatrical window dressing. He'd made his point. I chanced a furtive glance toward Braden. Had he seen our villain claim his seat?

"A pity." I shrugged. "Northwestern is a good school."

Kain released the grip on my wrist. "I believe in education, and I love to study language. Want to know how I mastered English? Word games. When I meet someone, I repeat the name, and connect it with a catch phrase. Since you're a colonel, I might associate you with...oh, I know...Kentucky Fried Chicken. Get it? Colonel Sanders."

His chilling nonchalance provoked the desired effect. My bowels turned to ice water. The freaking psycho just boasted he'd authored the leave-behind murder notes and the spray-painted epitaph intended for me. I doubted Kain had *written* those notes or killed Bea and Stew with his own hands. He'd merely dictated the messages and his surrogate killer's MOs.

The sick bastard was directing Dear's murder play and taunting me, implying I couldn't do a doggone thing to stop his production. His carefully chosen words could be interpreted innocently. Even if I'd been wearing a wire, he'd admitted nothing.

"An interesting game." I feigned indifference. "Do you have a similar affection for weapons, say electronic control devices? I hear a new long range stunner has become quite popular in your old stomping ground."

"You do say." He tapped a finger absently against his lips.

"There's always that nagging problem with weapons—they can be turned against their owners. I'll bet you'd be highly embarrassed if someone fired your gun at you."

My Irish temper flared. *Two can play this game.*

A waiter stopped at our table. "May I get you something, sir?" Kain's striking profile and projection of wealth hadn't escaped the junior barkeep's notice.

"Yes, please. A martini—stirred not shaken."

With a tee-hee, the waiter sped on his way.

"I confess I can be a bit of a ham. But I do have a James Bond aura, don't you think?"

No way, you pile of gussied-up manure.

Repulsed by his cat-and-mouse game, I decided to lay down some verbal covering fire. Maybe I'd smoke out a reaction that would lead us down a promising investigative path. "I hear times are tough for ex-patriots," I began. "Especially those who exploit orphans. That might prompt an imaginative entrepreneur—someone with your brains—to choreograph a land flip. You know, mortgage fraud as diversification—multiple product lines?"

Kain took the salvo in stride. He even chuckled. "My, my, what an imagination."

I continued as if he hadn't spoken. "Now me, I'd never try a land flip. Too many mouths to keep shut if the plan goes south. Say, if I tried a land flip with Emerald Cay, I'd need to rope in Dear's developers, plus a mortgage broker. Oh, by the way didn't one of your countrymen just set up shop in Beaufort? Then I'd need an appraiser with a murky past and a compliant attorney. I imagine one with financial woes wouldn't ask many questions."

Kain's complexion signaled I'd scored direct hits. His ears turned scarlet. Dots of red sprang high on his cheeks, making it look as if he'd been lit up with laser scopes. His hands curled into fists. I reckoned he was dying to beat the snaffle out of me.

Too bad there were so many pesky witnesses. I'd drawn blood. The scent made me greedy.

"I've taken a keen interest in real estate," I added. "In fact, I intend to visit the courthouse daily to check Emerald Cay title transfers. If I spot irregularities, I'll pass the word. Nice thing about being retired. I can pursue any passion wholeheartedly. And I have two passions now—monitoring real estate deals and finding evidence to fry one psycho killer."

My pent-up rage spent itself in a quavering crescendo. "Retirement's been a tad boring. Now I have a new lease on life, a mission."

The waiter sidled up to the table with Kain's drink. He gave the raving madwoman—me—a wide berth. I panted as if I'd just finished a marathon.

"Here you are, sir," the waiter said timidly.

"Thank you," Kain replied with a wintry smile. "Afraid I can't stay. I'll pay my tab now."

He placed a twenty on the table. "Keep the change," he said coolly. The waiter grabbed the bill and scurried away.

"You're quite the conversationalist, Marley."

I had to give the guy credit: his teeth still flashed in an ersatz smile.

"What passion and imagination. Too bad you don't have any idea what you're talking about. Nonetheless I'd rein in your wild accusations. They might provoke some psycho to bully you. If he had a defective personality, he might threaten those near and dear to you—your step-kids, your sister, your nieces and nephews. And, just for fun, he might hint about starting closer to home so you could watch. With a neighbor, perhaps?

"Ah, Deputy Braden Mann's headed our way. My cue to leave."

Leaving his drink untouched, Kain rose and strode briskly toward the exit. He was out the door before Braden reached our table.

"What happened? What did the SOB say?"

I bit my lip, willed my erratic heartbeat to slow. "He's our killer, but the bastard didn't incriminate himself. Give me a sec to find Janie so we can talk."

Kain's not-so-subtle threats shook me. If my big mouth placed my own life at risk, I could accept it. Putting others in danger was something else. I elbowed my way across the club to where Janie perched on a stool, gossiping with April. "The ladies room," I said, "now."

My neighbor started to frame a smart-ass reply, then my expression registered. "Sure."

In the restroom, I checked under stall doors to make sure we were alone. "Janie, I don't know how or why, but Kain ran a background check on you. He knows about your marriage. He knows you, uh...play the field. His parting shot was a threat to hurt you—and other folks I love—to punish me, shut me up. I believe him. He's one evil bastard."

For once, Janie was speechless—no wisecrack comeback. She looked scared.

"We're changing tonight's plans," I continued. "You're staying at the hotel with Braden and me. There's safety in numbers."

"Braden won't be happy," Janie replied. "Three's a crowd."

Kain's nauseating reference to a ménage à trois assaulted my brain. Sweat popped out on my forehead and my hands trembled like forgotten November leaves. "Don't worry about Braden. He'll understand."

TWENTY-ONE

Braden checked us into a different hotel. The room was spacious. Good thing. Otherwise Braden's pacing would have worn a rut in the carpet. He never sat, cruising the room in looping circles as we talked. The room featured two queen beds. Janie and I each staked out a personal headboard backrest.

"Are you nuts?" Braden growled.

I had to admit the verdict was out. "Okay, I screwed up. I shouldn't have let Kain know we have leads on a land flip. But how can it hurt? His reaction confirms my hunch. He boiled over because he's vulnerable. That food chain he created is way too long. He realizes one of his cronies might squeal."

"Possibly, and your heads-up gives him time to cover his tracks. Maybe he'll 'disappear' more loose ends. If he hired Underling to kill Bea and Stew—and lest we forget, *you*—what's to stop him from ordering more hits? Maybe he'll wipe out everyone he considers a potential liability. Hell, Hollis County's population may take a nosedive."

Dammit, had I put more lives in jeopardy? Even if they were crooks, I didn't want their grisly deaths on my conscience.

Braden paused, rubbed his temples. "Then again the man may just vanish. Hightail it out of the country and back to East Kingdom Come before we can nail him."

Crap. The idea of Kain skeedaddling hadn't crossed my mind. Adrenaline and hatred had jammed the gears in my mental machinery.

"God, I'm sorry. I was wrong. But maybe it's not a disaster. The man is smart and greedy. He knows we have no proof, and I'm sure he put up firewalls. It's entirely possible he's never come face-to-face with most of his co-conspirators. The ones who do know him must realize he's a stone-cold killer. He'll count on their willingness to take his secrets to jail—or the grave—rather than risk his wrath."

A recall of his whispered threats made me shiver. "Numbing fear, that's his specialty. So, no, I don't think I've triggered a bloodbath. I doubt Kain kills on whim. Stew and Bea were loose cannons, peripheral to his scheme. Their deaths served a purpose. They scared Gator and Sally into compliance. Now that his crazy-killer cover's blown, he'd be stupid to commission more bizarre hits."

Braden nodded. "Maybe. But the man *enjoys* his little games. If he's arrogant enough, he may want to rub our noses in his mess, thinking he can still walk away."

The deputy looped the room again, then plopped onto the room's sole chair. "So where are we? Nowhere. Kain's been questioned twice, the last time by Sheriff Conroy, and he didn't break a sweat. He has no record. On paper, he's a solid, very rich citizen. We don't have a shred of evidence to tie him to any murders, Sharlana's disappearance, foreign worker exploitation, or any real estate scam. Everything's hearsay and innuendo."

Jamie bolted upright. "What about that two-million-dollar down payment for Hogsback Island? It had to come from somewhere. And I've been writing checks to Help-Lease for months. Can't some expert track the money?"

"Yeah, maybe SLED's forensic accountants can penetrate the corporate smoke," Braden agreed. "That might prove he's a principal in Help-Lease and Emerald Cay, LLC. But we also need evidence these companies are engaged in illegal activities."

The deputy slumped in his chair. "Financial skullduggery's out of my league. Despite the clever capers you see on TV, most perps are dumber than dirt. I've never needed to analyze corporate balance sheets to prove a murder motive. Usually the husband or boyfriend's still holding the gun."

He stared at his hands, cracked his knuckles. "If we could only catch this Underling. Flip him and we could prove Kain's connection. Unfortunately I doubt an assassin who learned his trade in some Eastern Europe mob is willing to sing."

Janie cleared her throat. "Forget your cop accountants, Braden. If there are any checks or papers tying Kain to the purchase of Hogsback Island or that labor outfit, I'll find them. And I don't need a stupid warrant. I'm alone in Gator's office for hours every day. I know his computer password. I understand how he thinks, where he squirrels things away.

"My master key opens every door in the building," she added. "I'll ransack the office of that twerp, Woody, too. He must be in the thick of this, right? I can't help you with Sally though. She has a custom lock on her office. A very secretive lady."

My mouth hung open in astonishment. Janie was the most loyal person I'd ever met. If I murdered someone, she'd bring a shovel and bury the body, no questions asked. Yet she was volunteering to play Nancy Drew in palazzo pants to send her boss to prison. It seemed totally out of character.

"Hey, don't give me that look," Janie snapped. "Gator decided it was okay to leave me twisting in the wind, either because he's scared or greedy. Take your pick. My snooping's justified."

Braden gave Janie a hard stare. "This isn't a game. If our theories are right, Kain has killed two, possibly three people. He sicced one of his mad dogs on Marley twice. She's got the luck of the Irish to be alive. Janie, I'm ordering you to stay out of this. If there's a paper trail, SLED will find it. I'll start interrogating the folks on Marley's short list as land flip conspirators."

My neighbor rolled her eyes. "Okay. Unpucker your sphincter. I just wanted to help. But if you expect me to crawl in a hole and pretend I'm not screwed, stop talking and go to bed."

Braden phoned the front desk for a six a.m. wake-up call.

For form's sake, I pulled back the covers on Janie's bed. She deftly positioned her foot against my posterior and gave a firm shove.

"Forget it. I've watched you sleeping. You churn the covers like a Cuisinart. Climb in with Romeo. He's got incentive to put up with you."

I used the bathroom to undress, then Janie took her turn. While my friend was in the john, the deputy crawled between the sheets in his tighty whities. To the best of my knowledge, the man didn't own pajamas.

He pulled me against his body and whispered. "Sorry I jumped on you. If we're going to work together, you can't keep secrets."

"I know. It won't happen again," I whispered back. "And I'll keep my temper. Kain got to me. No excuse for diarrhea of the mouth. Not with lives on the line."

"You're frustrated," he said. "It gets to all of us."

His incipient hard-on pressed firmly against my bottom. "You know we could get rid of some of our frustrations," he whispered. "I can be very quiet."

"Not a chance," I replied, though the heat radiating from his body already had x-rated visions dancing in my brain. *Like sugarplums.* Then I smiled and mentally amended the image, *like a sweet Popsicle.*

Sleep doesn't come easily if you're horny, overtired, or stressed. I was all three. Wide awake, I asked myself the same questions over and over.

Did I believe Janie would butt out and leave the investigating to authorities? Nope. Could I change her mind? No way. What could I do to protect her?

Get her to move in with Braden and me?

Maybe.

***

The wake-up call startled me. Janie's loud groan expressed

her opinion.

"It's Saturday," she griped as she padded toward the bathroom. "Tell me again why we had to get up at six a.m."

"Some of us don't work banker's hours," Braden called after her. His cheerfulness seemed to ratchet upwards in inverse ratio to Janie's irritation. There was friction between them, and Braden relished sticking it to my neighbor, angling for a rise.

We dressed quickly and barely said boo until we zoomed over the bridge and stopped at a McDonald's drive-thru for big coffees, no food. I waited for everyone to ingest a mood-leveling dose of caffeine before broaching the idea of Janie moving in with Braden and me.

My friend yelped like she'd been scalded, then hooted with laughter. The deputy silently brooded, but I caught him doing an eye roll.

"You think I'll be safer living with someone who's been shot at and basted like a ready-to-roast duck?" Janie chuckled. "No thank you. Pussy Galore and I will take our chances on the south side of Blue Heron. Besides you're allergic to Pussy."

Janie'd named her twenty-pound white Persian after one of James Bond's stronger-willed females, the pilot in *Goldfinger*. Braden hadn't even been born when that movie debuted.

Quit harping on his age. He's not asking you to marry and bear children.

I swiveled in the front passenger seat to focus on Janie. She grabbed the arm I draped over the seat and squeezed it like she was making lemonade. "Look, I'll be good—and careful," she said. "I'll play clueless Suzy Secretary at work, and I'll keep my doors locked at night. Don't worry about me, Marley. Worry about yourself.

"Have *you* thought about leaving the island?" she demanded. "Going back to Ohio or Idaho or wherever it is they grow corn. Now *that* would be smart. Deadeye Dick ordered both of us to leave the investigating to the authorities. He doesn't need civilian volunteers."

Braden pounced on the suggestion. "I hate to admit it, but your friend has a point. Given Kain's threats, it might be prudent for you to vacate Dodge."

"No way. I won't turn tail and give him the satisfaction. Besides Chief Dixon needs me—even if the sheriff's department doesn't."

My husband always claimed my jaw jutted out an extra inch when I entered mule mode. If so, my chin now staked out territory well beyond my face. I felt exceedingly stubborn.

We rode in silence. The deputy seemed to be vying for a new land speed record between Hilton Head and Dear Island. No fear about speeding tickets. We arrived at the makeshift dock before the seven a.m. ferry started boarding passengers. Once on the island, Braden dropped Janie and me at our homes then left to call on the chief. Before Janie said goodbye, we made plans to attend the afternoon's joint memorial service for Stew and Bea.

Inside my house, I wandered aimlessly, trying to decide what to do. With little sleep, my mind wasn't firing on all cylinders. Maybe that's why I puttered for two hours—surfing the Internet, doing laundry, and making a grocery list—before I checked my answering machine.

Though the caller didn't identify himself, I knew Henry Cuthbert's whiny voice. The twin appeared to have dibs on speaking first. The background noise featured twittering birds and croaking frogs. Not the type for New Age soundtracks, the boys must be outdoors, calling on a cell phone. Their high voices vibrated with excitement. I rewound and listened again.

"We caught fat-ass dead to rights," Henry gloated. "Followed Hugh when he snuck off in Mom's skiff. He beached on the backside of Sunrise Island, waddled above the high-tide mark and stuck a note in a seashell."

"Hey, it's my turn, give me the phone," Jared wheedled.

"We can lead you right to the killer. Meet us where you crashed our party. Bring the *man*, Deputy Dog. Let's say high noon."

The teens started banging on metal—a car hood?—to hammer out a rhythm for some freebased rap lyrics: *"Meet at high noon, fat-ass Hugh will sing a new tune..."* Laughter erupted and the kids hung up.

The call practically made my knees knock. The twins were obnoxious and loathsome, but that was their job; they were teenagers. They had the right to grow up and out of it. No one should die at fourteen. With no notion of their present whereabouts, I had no way to protect them for the next two hours. A call to their home or a drop-in could make Hugh antsy. Maybe he already suspected the twins of spying. I would have to wait. Meet the boys at noon.

Figuring Braden's consult with the chief would be brief, I didn't call. He'd arrive in plenty of time to join me. However, when eleven-thirty rolled around, I started to worry. Minutes later, Braden's car breached the driveway, and I flew out the door. No time for lollygagging.

He poked his head out the car window. "I know you're glad to see me, but we really should wait until we're inside. The neighbors, you know."

Braden waved toward Janie's house, then frowned when he realized I'd turned to lock the door. "Ye gods, what now?"

"We have business to take care of—two little boys who love to play with matches."

***

"Take your next right."

"Where?" Braden complained. "There's no road."

"Semantics, my dear. It's a logging road. See, the underbrush is only thigh-high. Besides we're stopping in about two hundred feet. We walk the rest of the way."

"Just what I wanted to hear," he grumbled.

It was unusually warm for early spring, mid-eighties.

Nonetheless, I wore jeans, high-topped hiking boots, and a long-sleeved shirt. Haunted by the sight of Bea's bloated face, I was determined to keep a little extra between my flesh and any fire ants. Giant spiders and poisonous snakes weren't on my get-acquainted list either.

We heard the boys before we saw them. I hoped resident reptiles found the racket as offensive as I did. Were they rapping? Whatever, they'd cranked the noise full volume. As we weaved between prickly bushes, I caught glimpses of the teens practicing a dippy slide-shuffle.

A dance? Who knew? Maybe Braden. God, he looks young today.

When we reached the clearing, my youthful-looking deputy proclaimed himself the grown-up in charge. Henry and Jared let loose with a few "oh, man" complaints as Braden ordered them to park their fannies on a rotting log, and talk only when—and if—asked.

The twins complied with astonishing meekness—none of the usual lip. Then it dawned on me: Braden was the missing ingredient in their lives, a take-charge male who didn't stoop to bribery or verbal or physical abuse. His command presence hypnotized them.

With the deputy acting as orchestra leader, the boys performed a perfect duet. They took turns bragging about their feats of daring-do.

"We used Jerry's camouflaged johnboat—the one he takes duck hunting." Triumph laced Henry's tone. "Hugh never saw us. When he beached on Sunrise, we slid into tall marsh grass on that hump of island in the middle of the channel."

I interrupted. "I know the spot. Too far away for you to see much."

Jared bounced on the log seat like he had to pee. "We're not stupid. We brought binocs. Hell, we could have counted the hairs on his butt if he'd bent over. We watched him play Tonto. You know, shading his eyes and looking every which way for witnesses."

Henry cut in. "Hugh went straight to a seashell, a big mother wedged behind a palm. He stuffed something inside. He came back carrying a big cooler. Blue with a white lid. Then he went back to brush out his footprints."

"Yeah." His brother chuckled. "He must think he's James Bondage."

The boys were on a high, convinced they'd cracked the case. "Last thing Hugh did was tie orange tape around some - scraggly pine. Once he left, we motored over and snatched the shell."

Henry jumped in, stealing his twin's punch line. "Inside, we found a message in a plastic bag."

The brothers seemed oblivious to Braden's look of alarm. "Did you put it back where you found it?"

"'Course not," Jared replied with glee. With a flourish, he extracted a folded paper from his pants pocket. The grimy slip looked as if it last resided in a cow patty. Grit and the teens' greasy paws had long since eradicated fingerprint evidence.

Braden sighed and held out his hand. "Did you touch the orange tape?" he asked.

"No. Should we have brought that too?" Henry asked.

I shook my head. "The tape signaled Hugh's pen pal that a message was waiting. By now, he knows the drop's been compromised. What a colossal waste."

For a second, the brothers looked crestfallen, then Jared grinned. "Hey, there's more. We got back to Dear in time to see fat-ass carry the cooler to his SUV. We snuck a look soon as he went in the house. It was full of money. Big wads of bills. We slid some twenties out."

He pulled a bundle of dirty cash from his backpack and thrust it toward Braden.

The deputy looked anything but pleased. He ignored the cash, staring glumly at the note in his right hand. His look made me antsy. "Don't keep me in suspense, Braden. I'm the only one who doesn't know what the note says."

"You don't want to know." He took a deep breath and read: "GUARD & OFFICE MANAGER SNOOPING. URGE EARLY RETIREMENT WITH NICKEL."

I snatched the note from Braden's hand. A soft lead pencil had formed the blockish capital letters on plain white bond. I read the note a second time. Sweat trickled down my neck.

Jared looked at me and grinned. "It means you, doesn't it? You're the guard."

"It proves Hugh's a murderer, right?" Henry piped up. "He's asking some mob guy permission to rub you out. You and some office manager. Is Nickel a hit man or a gun?"

The boys discussed Janie's and my impending demise with relish. Nickel? What *did* it mean? Was Woody Nickel about to be retired, too, or was he a hired killer?

Jared tapped Braden's arm. "Can we watch while you arrest Hugh?"

"Sorry, boys." He pocketed the note. "No arrests today. I can't prove Hugh wrote this. You two could have invented the whole yarn. Everyone knows you hate him..."

Jared yelped in protest. "We didn't. What about the money?" He scrunched his face like a baby primed for a three-alarm wail. "I thought you were different, that you'd stand up to Hugh."

The deputy clamped a hand on the boy's shoulder. "Let me finish. I believe everything you told us. But even if a money-packed ice chest is still in Hugh's car, I need a warrant. We need evidence we can take to court. I'll bring Hugh in for questioning, but even if I could prove he wrote this note, there's no specific threat. You could interpret it six ways to Sunday."

Braden shook his head. "I am taking someone into custody, though—the two of you."

"Hey, we didn't do nothing," Henry objected.

"Protective custody," Braden finished. "Suppose Hugh is a mad killer, you think he'll send you to bed without supper if he finds you tattled to cops? His life would be far more pleasant without you two skulking about."

The brothers obviously thought they'd booted Hugh from their miserable lives. As Braden's verdict sunk in, they slipped back inside their prickly psychic armor. I saw the withdrawal in the set of their jaws, heard it in their voices.

Jared's hands curled into fists. "You're going to dump us in some juvenile detention center with a bunch of unwashed retards while Hugh kills more people?"

"No," Braden answered. "Marley tells me you live with your father part of the year. We'll pack you off to him for the time being."

Henry's lips trembled. He looked ready to cry. "Dad won't want us," he blurted. "He hates us. Says we're bad apples that dropped off Mom's rotten family tree."

Braden and I shared a look. What could we say? For all we knew, the kids had it right. "He's your father," I said. "Even if you're going through a rocky patch, he'll want to keep you safe."

Sullen looks on the boys' faces said they weren't convinced.

"What about Mom?" Jared asked as we trudged toward the security vehicle on loan to Braden. "Hugh will kill her. You gotta tell her to get off the island, too."

The deputy responded to the boys' growing hysteria. "Okay, we'll drive by your house. If Hugh's gone, we'll speak with your mother. Suggest she leave the island."

The boys recited their absent father's phone number, and Braden called on his cell. Hearing both sides of the conversation proved easy. Mr. Cuthbert began to yell as soon as Braden suggested his sons might be in danger. "It's Hugh Wells, isn't it? I hired a detective to check him out. That SOB's tight with the mob. Is he a killer?"

226

Braden tried to defuse the situation. "I'm sorry I can't say more. This is an ongoing investigation. I can't comment. Please treat our conversation as confidential. I just want to make sure your sons are out of harm's way."

The deputy ended the call as we pulled into the Cuthbert driveway. The boys claimed they'd last seen Hugh's SUV in the drive, nose out for a speedy exit. The space stood empty now. Had Hugh finished his errands and garaged the vehicle? Was he home?

"Braden, let me go to the door. You stay in the car with the boys. My face isn't likely to cause any panic. They're used to me showing up when the boys screw up."

Braden squeezed my hand. "Keep it simple—and fast. Just tell Grace we're taking the twins into protective custody. Tell her to head immediately to her lawyer's office in Beaufort so the authorities can fully explain the situation."

My heart hammered as I stabbed the doorbell. Understandable given that the man of the house wanted to commission my murder. After the tenth singsong bell, a disheveled Grace cracked the door. Her face was puffy, her eyes pink. Any self-respecting rat would have fled her matted hair. Though it was one in the afternoon, she wore a robe and reeked of alcohol.

"Are you home alone, Mrs. Cuthbert, or is Mr. Wells here with you?" I asked.

She mumbled she was by her lonesome. After thanking my lucky stars, I launched into a shifty song and dance. I claimed the twins were in danger but declined to name a nemesis. Grace's bobblehead quivered, and she blinked fast enough to send Morse code. She raised no objections to my plucking her sons from their palatial nest.

"Okay, we're taking the boys into protective custody now," I said. "Please head to Beaufort as quickly as possible. Go to your attorney's office and ask him to phone the sheriff once you arrive. The authorities will meet you there and explain everything in more detail."

Grace's muddled look told me I might as well be wearing a space suit and speaking Vulcan. Was she safe? As she swayed on her feet, I considered grabbing her arm and tossing her bathrobed body into the backseat with her sons. That would only split open a new hornet's nest.

I bid the lady goodbye and walked back to the car. A glance at the boys broke my heart. Their eyes remained locked on their mom, who swayed in the doorway, her face clouded with confusion. Henry put knuckled fists to his eyes, while Jared bit his lips.

Despite everything, they still loved their mother.

TWENTY-TWO

Braden drove the car part way down the boat launch ramp, opened his door with the engine idling, and signaled the captain. "Wait, please. It's police business."

The captain looked up from untying lines. "Don't have a coronary. We'll wait."

Braden swung back into the driver's seat and started to close the door.

"Go on, get out," I urged. "I can park it. I'll even walk home so you have a car waiting when you get back."

His head snapped up. "What? No. You're coming with us."

I shook my head. "Sorry, I can't. I have to warn Janie. Someone knows she's snooping."

"We'll phone her from the ferry," he countered, "and I'll have the sheriff assign a deputy to protect her. I'll tell him to keep an eye on Nickel, too, since we don't know if he's a hired gun or on someone's hit list."

I bit my lip. He wouldn't like my answer. "There's nothing for me to do in Beaufort. You can handle the boys alone. The chief and Janie need my help here. The memorial service for Stew and Bea starts in forty-five minutes. Janie's picking me up, and I promised the Condolence Committee I'd bring brownies."

The set of the deputy's jaw suggested he was grinding his teeth, attempting to stay cool in front of our young charges. "Brownies? You're worried about brownies? Boys, go on. Get on the ferry, Ms. Clark and I need a minute alone."

The twins didn't move. Probably figured I was in for a verbal thrashing and didn't want to miss the show. "Move!" Braden barked.

Before they could close the car doors, he whispered fiercely, "You are the most stubborn woman I've ever met. I sort of understand why you refused to pack up and leave before. But

229

now you're a sitting duck. Hugh's note wasn't subtle. Do I need to take you into protective custody, too, handcuffs and all?"

I raised my hands, palms out, fingers spread. "Calm down. Remember, Kain didn't get Hugh's note. Nothing's changed since morning except we now know Hugh's the island snitch and someone caught Janie snooping."

I paused for a breath. "Nickel? We knew he was a player before the note. If Janie and I put our heads together, maybe we can figure how Hugh and all that cash might tie into a land flip or some other real estate scam. She's got her finger on the island pulse."

"I already told you what that cash means," Braden whispered. "Kain's laundering money through Dear Island. I'd bet on it."

"All the more reason for Janie and me to compare notes. She has more than a nodding acquaintance with Dear's cash flows. Look, it's broad daylight. Kain's thugs won't attack the two of us at a memorial service in a crowded chapel. If it'll make you happy, I'll even take my gun to church. Just hurry. Go get your warrants and reinforcements, then hightail it back here before sundown."

Braden's prolonged sigh sounded like air escaping a punctured pool float. "You win...about this afternoon. But I'm not letting you out of my sight tonight."

"Deal." I leaned across the car console to kiss him. The minute our lips locked I shoved him toward the open door. "Don't think I'm a pushover though. Chief Dixon already gave orders for us to ride together tonight."

"You're going on patrol—tonight? Good God, woman, you're driving me nuts."

I watched as the deputy race-walked toward the ferry, his muscular backside eye candy for any female who wasn't cataract-impaired. A second after he jumped aboard, the ferry shoved off and I was alone. At least I hoped so. My courage was part bravado. Kain was right about me having an active imagination. I could populate any landscape with bogeymen.

A perusal of the marina parking lot revealed no unusual commotion. In fact, there was a total absence of activity. I figured most islanders were getting ready for Stew's and Bea's wake. No ghoulish reporters were visible either. Probably napping while they waited for the next spate of murders.

I locked the car and walked briskly down the leisure path. The pleasure of warm sunshine and the twitter of birds momentarily lifted my mood. When a horn tooted, I jumped.

My friend Rita pulled her golf cart onto the verge. "Want a ride? I just bought milk at the marina store. It's a lot less crowded than E.T. Grits."

I smiled. "I could use a lift."

Should I ask her to run me by the real estate office for a quick tête-à-tête with Janie? No. Someone might overhear us in the office. Besides it would be quicker to call.

I phoned the minute I walked in the house. Janie had already left. Figuring she'd ring my doorbell in a matter of minutes, I took a perfunctory shower. The speed made me feel like I'd entered an automatic car wash: soap, rinse, dry, exit. Too bad I didn't have a heat lamp—my headlights were still damp when I tugged on my bra. A squirt of perfume, a brush through my wet hair, and a pair of earrings later, I was ready to whip up icing.

Long ago I discovered I could pass off store-bought brownies as a gourmet treat so long as I smothered the results with Aunt May's scratch icing. I draped a dishtowel around my shoulders to keep splatters off my funeral duds then mixed sugar, butter and milk in a saucepan. I stirred patiently until the mixture erupted in a roiling boil. When the bubbling brew threatened to escape the pot, I pulled it off the stove, dumped in semi-sweet chocolates and "beat like hell" per May's recipe instructions.

If only I knew how to pull the boiling Dear Island pot from the fire.

***

Janie honked five minutes ahead of schedule. I juggled the pan of brownies while I locked the deadbolt behind me.

I slid into the pink Caddy's front seat and glanced at Janie. "You look pretty." My friend's ruby red dress featured a mandarin collar, a slim oriental drape and a slit halfway to China. Hardly conventional funeral attire, but it suited. She'd twisted her blonde hair into a conservative chignon. Somehow the overall impression came closer to demure than come-hither.

"Thanks. I figure I better play dress up while I can. Who knows when I'll be living out of a dumpster and dressing like a bag lady? My best guess is I'll be out on the street next week."

Primed to do an information dump of my own, I bit my tongue and waited to hear Janie's news. Once I scared her, she might forget something, a detail that mattered.

"What are you nattering about?" I asked.

Janie looked past me to my porch. "Wait. Where's your cop? Is he coming? I ought to tell you both at the same time."

"Tell us what? Braden left for the mainland. He'll be lucky to make the last ferry." The deputy would have a busy afternoon what with phone calls, interrogations and search warrants. I prayed Grace had enough functioning brain cells to phone her attorney and head to Beaufort without Hugh.

"Well, guess the deputy will have to wait for the skinny," Janie continued.

"Okay, you've got my full attention. What?"

"With Sally and Gator both off island for Bea's funeral, I had a perfect opportunity to nose around, especially when Woody didn't show for work. The office was like a candy store. No worries about some yahoo walking in on me while I rifled desks.

"But Bea's memorial service proved briefer than a pair of

low-rise panties. Maybe the minister was stumped, trying to say something nice. Whatever. Gator and Sally came back while I was rummaging through my boss's files. When I heard him say, 'Janie's not here. We can talk,' I panicked and hid in the closet."

My friend's hand left the wheel to make a cuckoo motion at her temple. "Can't believe how loony that was, hiding. I'm in and out of Gator's office a gazillion times a day. No reason to hide. But I did, and I sweat bullets, afraid to breathe. Then the two of 'em started discussin' this secret rendezvous with Kain. They met him in the basement of the mortuary."

"They what?" I was flabbergasted.

"Hold on, it gets better. At first, Gator and Sally talked normal—like they were comparin' 401K funds. But they always whispered Kain's name. Gave me the willies. It was as if he were some demon who might spring out of the closet. Glad they didn't check."

"All right, already, spit it out. We're almost to the chapel. What did they say to wind you up like a top?"

She took a deep breath. "Woody's dead. Murdered." Janie paused. "Guess that sort of explains why he didn't come to work."

"You're sure? Where? How?"

"I don't know. Neither do Sally or Gator. Kain simply ordered my illustrious bosses to keep their traps shut or they'd join him. That sick Pole even reminded Gator that his nickname suggested intriguing options for an epitaph."

Janie shivered. "This guy plays the godfather role to the hilt. A horse's head here, a carrot there. You know those notes left with the bodies? 'Stewed'... 'To Bea or Not to Be.' Gator said Kain uses them to confuse the cops and scare the crap out of anyone he's got by the short hairs. Who's going to cross a guy with a mind that works like that?"

"That's it? Everything you heard?"

"No. I didn't track all of the conversation. They said

something about laundry, and Sally was pissed that Kain refused to write off the two million he fronted to buy Hogsback."

My head pounded. Kain's illegal businesses—undoubtedly legion—generated cash that needed laundering. I got that. And it didn't take much of a mental leap to assume that two million of his money had wound up as a down payment for the purchase of Hogsback Island a.k.a. Emerald Cay. But I couldn't help but share Sally's wonder at Kain's chutzpah. I'd personally promised the guy the authorities would examine every Emerald Cay document. How did he think he could pull off an extended land flip?

When I shared my train of thought, Janie chewed on her lip. "Kain plans to bury all the fraud mess with Woody. He told my bosses Nickel could still be the fall guy—just like they planned from the get-go. He signed all the phony documents. Now that he's dead, Kain said they could play innocent, develop Emerald Cay for real."

My brain was stuck on double-dealing overload. How many crooks were involved?

What happened to honor among thieves?

I stopped Janie's monologue with a question. "Wait a minute, weren't Gator and Woody fraternity brothers? Are you saying Gator set him up from the beginning?"

"Guess so." She shrugged. "Kain ordered Gator to bring in a sales manager who couldn't refuse a bribe. His old school buddy fit the bill. Then one of Kain's pals bribed Woody to let him handle all the Dear Island appraisals. Once Gator could prove the bribe, Dear's new sales manager had no choice. He had to play along with the land flip. Of course, the slime bucket might have agreed anyway."

"So how does Hugh fit into this mess?"

"Best I could tell from Gator's string of obscenities your Polish mystery man met Hugh and Grace on a cruise ship.

Hugh gambled while Grace drank. When our island gigolo lost a pile of money, he turned to Kain, who canceled his gambling debts in exchange for enough insider information to blackmail Gator and Sally."

My mind teemed with questions. What kind of blackmail did Hugh offer on Sally and Gator? Would Janie's testimony be enough to put these scumbags away? No.

We reached the chapel and Janie—ever the optimist—made a slow circuit of the packed parking lot. Not a single opening.

"Cripes, I'm gonna ruin these shoes, traipsing through the outback," she complained as she whipped her Caddy onto the grass median a hundred yards down the road.

I retrieved my brownies from the backseat before Janie locked the car. "You know where we're headed as soon as this service is over, don't you?" I asked.

"Yeah," Janie replied. "I figured you'd tell me it was time to have a long chat with the chief or one of the deputies. Now unknit those brows or you'll have wrinkles the size of plow ruts by sundown. Not the way to impress your new boy toy."

At the nondenominational chapel, well-dressed islanders shuffled forward in meandering queues. The crowd at today's memorial service was the largest I'd seen. Memorial services for Dear departed are a traditional rite of island passage. Often the official funeral services are held in distant cities—Akron, Pittsburgh, Chicago, Albany—the places where retirees once worked, raised children and bought cemetery plots.

Local memorials gave islanders a venue to reminisce and grieve. After the services, the Condolence Committee provided refreshments in an adjacent community center. The whole shebang had the feel of a wake. Though alcohol was officially banned, the Irish and their kissing kin frequently snuck in flasks to baptize their coffee.

By the time the line of mourners snaked inside the chapel, all the pews were full. Round rumps were wedged into place like stuffed decorator pillows on an overloaded settee. We'd stand for the entire service. I was glad I'd worn comfortable shoes.

A dozen people took turns at the altar, remembering Stew's kindnesses and virtues. Shifting from foot to foot, I wondered if anyone would eulogize Bea. Finally one woman came forward. Her bland comments seemed more a matter of courtesy than conviction. The contrast made me wonder: *Will anyone give a flip when I'm gone?*

As the visiting minister revved up for the benediction, my beeper vibrated. *Uh-oh.* In these circumstances, the chief only rang in an emergency. I whispered in Janie's ear and edged toward the exit. Then I noticed others in sneak-out mode. A dozen reporters who'd come to scribble notes for human-interest follow-ups skulked toward the exit. Somehow these mainlanders had tapped into the island tom-toms.

Once outside, I moseyed to a remote corner of the deck that surrounded the chapel. The chief's message was terse. "Ninety-nine," he said. "Check point BW1."

To thwart eavesdroppers in our murderous new era, the chief had developed a code to communicate what and where. "Ninety-nine" was his code for homicide. "BW1" told me to hightail it to the Beach West entrance—the first street in this section of the island.

As people streamed from the chapel, Janie fought her way to my side.

"There's been another murder," I whispered as I holstered my radio. "Will you drive me home? I need my car."

"Nope. But I'll drive you to the body. Has to be Woody. Come on."

We made a beeline to the Caddy. Since she'd looped the parking lot before settling, we were pointed in the right direction. I feared reporters might notice our retreat and follow. Couldn't be helped. You can't lose a tail on a five-mile island.

236

"It's Beach West again," I said. "Head to the entrance."

Three security cars bracketed the scene, and yellow tape circled an entrance fountain that shot water like a bi-polar geyser, twenty feet with one pulse, two inches with the next. The fountain and its reflecting pool were designed for ambiance, an aesthetic billboard for coming attractions. There were no footpaths in this undeveloped section, and the fountain was two hundred feet from the road. That made it unlikely passersby would spot a foreign object floating in the reflecting pool. Even a big one, like Woody. Perhaps a maintenance worker found him.

Janie parked, and we walked together to meet Chief Dixon. He wouldn't complain about Janie's presence just as a city cop wouldn't think twice about the mayor's top aide showing up if a crime promised to be a political hot potato. On Dear Island, Janie wore the equivalent mayoral mantle.

"It's that Nickel fella," Dixon said. "I'm no coroner, but he looks like he's been floating a spell. Several hours at least."

The chief gave my gray pantsuit, pink silk blouse and skimpy leather flats a disgruntled once over. "Since you're not dressed for duty, take my car and play chauffeur. Go pick up the coroner and sheriff at Dear Island's helipad. They should land in ten minutes. Deputy Mann's on the chopper, too. He was leaving the sheriff's office when I called in a new body."

Janie stared at the corpse, all hint of wry amusement gone. "I'm leaving," she said abruptly.

The comment prompted Dixon to deputize my friend. "Hey, Janie, I don't want to go on the airwaves. How's 'bout you find Sally and break the news? Gator, too, if he's back on the island. I don't want 'em to hear this secondhand. The guy was some buddy of Gator's, right?"

"Yeah," she answered. "Some buddy."

Janie seemed mesmerized by the corpse. Electrical probes had caught Woody in the throat, leaving vampire-like aftereffects. He appeared to have suffered Stew's fate—stunned, bound and drowned. However, while Stew bobbed face down in a steamy cauldron with assorted veggies, Woody floated on his back in the shallow pool. He was fully dressed in chinos, a Ralph Lauren polo shirt, and Gucci loafers, no socks. Silver dollars covered his eyes and mouth. The coins, glinting in the bright April sunshine, were secured by see-through packing tape wound tightly around his head.

"Did our killer leave a calling card?"

"Afraid so. He spray-painted the retaining wall. This bastard is one sick mother."

Janie and I walked the perimeter until the Day-Glo paint came into view: "3 COINS IN A FOUNTIN."

Kain must not have checked this hit man's spelling acumen. Still the message was clear: the man orchestrating the killings was a monster.

As Janie fought a gag reflex, I whispered urgently in her ear. "Listen to me, Janie. I want you to talk to the chief this minute. Tell him everything. When you climbed in the car, I had some news of my own. Your story sidetracked me. This morning Hugh sent a note suggesting that Kain kill you. It appears that Sally and Gator know you've been snooping. Do *not* go looking for either of them. Stay here with the chief until I get back."

Little hiccup noises escaped Janie's mouth. "I feel awful. Woody's death wasn't real to me. Not until I saw his body. I can't believe I was cracking wise. I wanted Woody off the island...behind bars...out of my face. But this is awful. He's someone's son. He has a five-year-old kid in Florida. I'm ashamed."

My friend spun and raced toward her Caddy. "Come back," I yelled as I sprinted after her "Talk to the chief."

She turned as she opened her car door. "Not yet. Marley, please, I need two hours. Then I'll do whatever you ask. I think

I've figured a way to nail Gator, Sally and Kain. I'm going to the office. As soon as I leave, I'll come talk to you and Braden. Then I'll do whatever you ask."

A second later, Janie was gone, her Caddy's wheels flinging gravel.

Dammit. Goddammit.

TWENTY-THREE

Time passed in a blur after I picked up my charges at the helipad. The first moment I had Braden alone, I shared Janie's story. The glint in his eye said he welcomed a break in the case, though Janie clearly vexed him.

"That woman's certifiable. What makes her think she can swim unmolested in Dear's cesspool?"

"Should we head over to the office and pick her up?" I asked.

Braden tossed me his cell. "Call and order her to stay put while I let the sheriff in on the latest developments. Tell her we'll be there in a matter of minutes."

The receptionist recognized my voice and launched into a breathless rundown. "Janie's in a big powwow with Gator, Sally, and all the agents. You heard about Mr. Nickel, right?" she asked in a stage whisper. "They're talking a moratorium on sales and an official mourning period."

The woman took a breath. "Do you know how he was killed?"

I politely sidestepped her invitation to gossip and put in a request for Janie to call as soon as the meeting ended. I covered the receiver and asked Braden for his cell phone number.

"Please, make sure Janie phones the absolute second she's free." I pushed the cell's End button.

"She's in a meeting with all the agents, so no immediate danger. Want to head over and park outside her door?"

Braden massaged the bridge of his nose. "Since she's safe for the time being, I'd like a few more minutes with our bosses."

While Braden huddled with the sheriff and my chief, I helped corral the horde of reporters jostling for photo ops and shooed away the tourist rubberneckers buzzing about in golf carts. Ten minutes ticked by. I caught Braden's eye, tapped my

240

watch. He mimed listening to a phone and shook his head. Janie hadn't called. He held up his hand, his fingers spread wide, a promise we'd leave in five minutes.

Dark clouds scuttled in from the sea, bringing with them a premature dusk. The crowd thinned as darkness heightened anxieties about the identity of the next victim.

Braden touched my arm and held up a set of keys. "Your chief said to take his car and bring Janie to his office—in handcuffs, if necessary."

"Suits me," I said. "I bet Nickel's killer is still on the prowl. Are the twins okay? Did Grace show up at her lawyer's?"

"Yeah, she actually turned up without her boyfriend. When she couldn't find Hugh, Grace tagged a neighbor to drive her to the courthouse."

We approached the real estate building. I looked for Janie's Caddy. It wasn't parked in its reserved slot. The entire lot sat empty. "Uh-oh, where did everyone go?"

We parked and ran up the steps. The building was locked. I inserted my security master key beneath the door's solemn black wreath. Inside, I called Janie's name. My voice echoed in the tomblike quiet. We checked every room. Not a sound, not a soul.

Braden handed me his cell phone. "Call her." After a couple of rings, Janie's chirpy recorded message announced she was out having fun and would return the call soon—if she didn't get a better offer. The leave-a-message beep cut her off mid-laugh.

"Janie, call me. Right away. This is serious." Once again I provided Braden's cell number.

I returned his phone. "Now what?"

"We search." He notified our respective bosses Janie was missing and told them we'd begin a search.

Since there were no lights on in Janie's house and her car wasn't in the garage, we made a two-minute pit stop at my

Linda Lovely

house. I stripped off my mud-splattered Sunday-go-to-meeting clothes and slipped on a uniform with sensible shoes. Since neither of us had eaten since breakfast, Braden threw together ham and cheese sandwiches to wolf down in the car. As we headed out, I grabbed two Cokes and a family size bag of potato chips. He smiled at my additions.

"What? I munch when I'm nervous."

I took a second peek in Janie's garage. Her golf cart was stabled, but no Cadillac. We tried the doorbell once more. Silence. No signs of life.

"Any ideas where to look next?" Braden asked.

I knew where, but wasn't anxious to say so. "Her Caddy isn't an easy car to hide. Let's take a quick ride through Beach West, then check her house again."

On our drive, we speculated why Hugh had used a boat to haul an ice chest full of cash to the island.

"Someone probably delivered the money by car until the bridge went out," Braden said

"And I think I know when the money laundering started," I added.

Braden looked at me in surprise.

"Until two months ago, any charge at a Dear facility—golf course, restaurants, tennis shop—had to be put on a club charge account. You couldn't pay cash for anything. Sally wanted to make sure the folks using Dear amenities were bonafide, dues-paying members. Then overnight she made a one-hundred and eighty-degree policy reversal. Cash was hunky-dory."

Braden nodded. "Sounds right. To deposit Kain's cash, they simply needed to phony up cash receipts and mix them in with legit ones."

The next part of the transaction was a bit hazier for me. "I'm guessing the new Dear largesse was invested in Emerald Cay LLC. Assuming Kain was a principal, he'd have easy access to his money."

As we bumped along Beach West's logging roads, I sucked in my breath at every turn, fearing our headlights would bounce off a pink Caddy. I slumped in relief when we exited the untamed wilderness without spotting any sign of evening trespassers.

"God, I wish Janie would call," I grumbled.

At seven o'clock, we passed her house for the third time. I was beyond worry. Her windows were black holes that swallowed all light and energy.

"Let's stop. I want to check the garage again. See if Janie's Caddy is back," I said.

I'd taken only two steps when Pussy Galore streaked past me, headed for the woods. The overweight Persian was still light on her feet. Too quick to catch. I spun around and motioned Braden to lower his window.

"Get out and bring your gun." Fear roughened my voice. "Something's wrong. Janie never lets her cat outside. Too many alligators."

Braden radioed the gatehouse we were leaving our car. We tiptoed to the garage window. The Cadillac now sat beside her golf cart. *When had she come home?* If she was inside, why was her house blacker than soot?

"Let's not advertise our arrival," I whispered. "No knock, no doorbell. If we scare the bejesus out of Janie, I'll apologize later."

"Agreed." Braden thumbed the front latch. Locked. He raised a boot to kick in the door.

"Wait." I scurried down the stairs, upended a fake rock in the flowerbed, and retrieved Janie's spare key. Half the island knew where she kept it—including Gator and Sally. That realization raised icy prickles on my scalp.

As we rushed in, Braden's penlight splayed across the floor and walls. My pulse tap-danced as we cleared the living room with guns drawn. In the kitchen, I heard a faint sound. A keening noise. I broke into a run. I barely heard Braden's hissed, "Wait."

Anemic moonlight filtered through the skylight. My friend was naked. Scarves bound her writhing form to the four corners of her poster bed. Her head tossed furiously. Braden's light swept over her face. Dilated pupils crowded out all but a slender rim of blue iris. I could tell Janie didn't recognize me.

Gibberish outbursts intercut her moans. "Golf course...oh God, no blue...gurg...uniform."

I untied one of her wrists. Before I could undo a second knot, she beat at me with her freed fist. The stream of verbal gobbledygook continued non-stop. "Blue uniform...blue death."

"Janie, please, I'm trying to help. It's me. Marley."

Braden flicked on the bedroom light.

She shrieked in agony. "No, no....Lasers. Burning eyes. On fire."

The light increased her torment. Janie quit hitting me to cover her eyes. Her squirming made it even harder to loosen the knots crimped in the slippery silk. I recognized the scarf I was untying—swirls of purple, green and pink. My flamboyant present for Janie's last birthday.

Hot tears ran down my cheeks. I wanted to bawl like a baby. Rage and impotence are a repugnant mix.

Braden swept the house, making certain the thug who tied Janie was gone. I slumped in relief when he returned and holstered his gun. "We're alone. I called the paramedics. They'll be here any minute."

"Water!" Janie shrieked and bolted upright. "Desert...thirsty."

"What did they do to her?" Panic made my voice catch. "Will she be all right?"

I attempted a bear hug to minimize the damage to both of us. Janie's fists pummeled my back like berserk jackhammers.

She pivoted and I turned with her. That's when I saw the mirror's rhyme, printed with one of Janie's crimson lipsticks: "Trumpet for a Strumpet."

I blinked and read it again. "What the hell does that mean?"

Janie gave a strangled cry as her body convulsed. Braden wound a blanket around our twined torsos, then pulled out a knife to cut her thrashing feet free. My cheek pressed against Janie's neck. Her racing pulse danced a tattoo on my skin. It was off the charts. Her skin had turned a frightening, illogical shade of red, like a cartoon character who'd eaten a jalapeno pepper.

"Dammit. I think they gave her Angel's Trumpet," Braden mumbled. "That's scary. Last year in Atlanta, idiot teens made herbal tea from the weed and a thirteen-year-old died. You can get high on the stuff but an overdose can cause delirium, photophobia, even coma, and the victims become combative. Her symptoms are classic. I found a baggie filled with seeds on the kitchen counter next to her teakettle."

I rocked my friend in my arms. "Hold on, Janie. Help's on the way."

"What are her odds?"

Braden shook his head. "There's no antidote. Maybe the paramedics can induce vomiting. The hospital will pump her stomach and give her something to absorb the poison. It's a crap shoot."

The sound of a siren vaguely registered as I pleaded with God. Minutes later, paramedics rushed in. I knew these men, and they knew Janie. They'd do their very best. Braden had described Janie's condition when he radioed, so the paramedics came prepared.

We helped the men wrestle her into a soft restraint jacket. During the struggle, I crooned comforting words and tried to stay clear of her windmilling legs. My shins felt like they'd been whacked repeatedly with a shovel.

Braden turned to me. "I'm going to hunt down that bastard. The teakettle was still too hot to touch. He can't have gone far. We'd have seen a car. He must be on foot. Any suggestions where to look?"

"A blue uniform...Janie mentioned it a couple of times. It might have been pure delirium, but she could have been describing the maintenance uniform. Light blue coveralls with names sewn on the pockets. Coveralls could help the killer disappear in plain sight. He could hole up in the golf maintenance shed until the crews start mowing fairways and prepping greens. The uniform would make him invisible. He could walk away unnoticed."

"Where the hell is this shed?"

"Across the eleventh fairway. Take Janie's golf cart and cut behind my house. It's quicker than driving a car. Everyone calls it a shed, but it's a big metal building tucked behind trees by the water treatment plant. Be careful. Wait for backup if you spot anyone. I'll head over as soon as we get Janie in the ambulance."

"No, you won't," Braden ordered. "Stay here. My backup is on the way."

With what he considered a final edict, he split. I heard the grinding sound of the garage door opening. Then Janie shrieked, and I returned to her plight.

Please, God, let Janie live.

***

I gripped Janie's hand as the paramedic wheeled the gurney through her house. "Don't worry, Marley," Bill O'Brien said. "Beaufort Memorial was preparing an airlift for a car crash victim. He died, and they diverted the chopper here. The pilot may beat us to the helipad. I bet Janie's herself and chewing someone's ass in the E.R. inside an hour. She'll make it."

"Thanks, Bill," I answered.

In a flash, the paramedics loaded her into the ambulance

and warmed up their siren for the cross-island race to the helipad.

Staying at Janie's side was pointless. She didn't know me, and Bill made it clear there was no room for me aboard the chopper. While I couldn't help Janie, I could help Braden. There is no such thing as too many eyes, ears or guns when you're searching for a stone killer.

I set off at a dead run across the eleventh fairway. By road, it was a convoluted route to the golf maintenance compound, at least five blocks. The fairway shortcut put it within easy reach of a three-wood—even mine. A golf cart would have been handy, but the deputy had commandeered Janie's.

My lungs pushed air in and out like leaky forge bellows. I was on overload—adrenaline, fear, anger. My breath puffed out in smoky white clouds quickly dissected by the chill breeze. My oxygen uptake was so noisy my brain almost failed to register the first gunshot. The ping of a bullet striking metal makes a distinctive sound. The ricochet created a bouquet of firefly sparks less than fifty yards away.

Squinting into the darkness, I recognized Janie's distinctive golf cart with its faux Mercedes hood. A tall, lean man—Braden?—crouched beside it.

"Might as well give up." Braden's yell confirmed his identity.

"You have the high ground, but backup's on the way. You're on an island. Where you gonna go? Kill me and you're dead. You know how cops treat cop killers."

The shooter let his gun answer. I saw the muzzle flash. Thankfully, a companion metallic chink told me this bullet also missed its soft-bodied target. But how long would it take a pro to correct his aim? Braden was pinned down, and Janie's golf cart provided piss-poor cover.

The assassin's position on the thirteenth hole's elevated tee handed him a distinct advantage. The developers had molded a giant manmade dune—a virtual mountain on our pancake island—to reward golfers with a panoramic vision of ocean and beach. Tonight it gave Kain's henchman a killer view of the twelfth green and Braden hunkered below. Braden curled his powerful body into a compact target in an attempt to compensate for the cart's ineffective shield. He had few choices. If he wriggled beneath the cart, his field of vision would narrow to zilch, and he'd lose all mobility. If he ran, he'd be an easy target on the open fairway.

I had to distract the shooter. But how? The muzzle flash suggested the assassin lay on his stomach, flattened on the tee. No profile, nothing to aim at. The minute I fired a gun, I'd give away my position, doubling options in the sniper's shooting gallery: two ducks for the price of one.

I had one advantage—knowledge of the geography. I'd played this links course a hundred times. From the front and sides, the elevated tee resembled a cliff. Golfers parked carts at the bottom and trudged up a flight of stone stairs cut into its south face. But the grassy dune's sloped back was gradual enough for a riding mower to mount. Yet it would be sheer stupidity to dash up the incline on foot—a suicidal cavalry charge lacking the romance of a horse. *If I only had a mower.*

Then came the "aha" moment. Horsepower aplenty sat a few hundred feet away, locked inside the maintenance compound's steel fence. All I had to do was slip in and steal a mower. *Yeah, right.*

The notion seemed lame-brained, but I couldn't think of a better one. I tiptoed out of the fairway shadows and into the rough, then darted from skinny palm to fat water oak. In seconds, I reached the gate and prayed some dunderhead had left it unlocked. Tonight a jumbo padlock proved a perfect foil. I couldn't pick it on a bet.

Damn. I eyed the fence again. *Okay, do you really need a sergeant yelling at you to scale a little fence? Are you going to let*

Braden die while you dawdle?

Reaching as high as I could on the twelve-foot chain link fence, I stuck my fingers through steel loops. The toes of my shoes wedged between chinks for footing.

I inched upward six feet. Then I lost my tenuous toehold and gravity staked its claim, sucking my body down. The drop yanked my arms so hard I thought they'd pop out of their sockets. Never mind how many pounds dangled mid-air. For long seconds, I scrabbled like a big-footed puppy on a freshly waxed floor. Then the toe of one shoe found traction. Harkening back to my basic training days, I urged myself on with silent drill sergeant screams: *Move your flabby ass. Don't be a wuss.*

Nearing the top, I tried a mighty heave-ho to roll to the opposite side. A graceless belly flop impaled me on the fence's crimped metal ends. The mini daggers poked at me with cruel intimacy. I wrestled free and dropped to the ground. Too hastily. My left ankle crumpled under my weight. I tested it. Painful but functional.

Inside the fence, I stared with consternation at the padlock. If I wanted to liberate a mower, I had to open the gate. I - remembered the head groundskeeper hung his spare keys on a pegboard. I found a match for the padlock and swung the large gate open. The screech of metal assaulted my ears. Had the killer heard?

Time to pick a steed. I scanned the metal carcasses littering the landscape and marched toward the mowers. Then I saw the Bobcat. A huge one. Perfect. I'd actually driven one of these suckers on field maneuvers. Crank them up and they could boogie eight miles an hour, forward or backward. The steel mesh wrapping the sides and back of the cab even provided a modicum of shelter from flying bullets—if someone didn't fire them head on.

Best of all, someone had outfitted this machine with a trencher, designed to slice and dice rock-hard soil with merciless efficiency. Its wicked, heavy-duty blades glistened under the green glow of the yard's fluorescent security lights. The blades attached to a five-foot boom. Could I figure out how to raise and lower it? If so, I could impersonate a charging rhino. That would spell distraction with a capital D.

Another gunshot pinged against metal. Don't think, move. I clambered onto the cold plastic seat and fumbled overhead, groping for the ignition key. I sighed in relief when I felt it. One flick and the Cat purred.

I grasped the twin joysticks with a death grip. *Right hand forward to go right. Push with the left to swing left.* I rammed both joysticks forward, a double whammy, and hit the gas. The cat bucked once and rocketed straight at the open gate. It felt as if I were moving at eighty miles an hour, not eight. *Here goes nothing.*

Outside the fence opening, I careened past trees and sideswiped a palm or two as I got the hang of the controls. The touch of a gorilla.

The raucous engine broadcast my approach to the back of the mounded tee. So much for a sneak attack. The sniper could track every foot of my progress. If I ran the Bobcat dead up the hill, he could take his sweet time as he aimed for my heart or head. Degree of difficulty for a marksman: zero.

Okay, let's turn tail. At the bottom of the incline, I swiveled the Cat one hundred and eighty degrees then jerked hard on both levers to scale the hill in reverse. I prayed the metal cab would deflect any bullets. Of course screaming up the hill ass backward posed its own dangers. The tee platform wasn't large. Failure to stop in time meant I'd overshoot the tee and plunge into the lagoon below. The backward motion seemed dizzyingly fast and disorienting in my dark cage. I hadn't heard another shot, but would I over the Cat's earsplitting racket?

The Bobcat lurched and I sensed I'd crested the hill. Now came the tricky part. I eased off the gas as I swung the Bobcat and raised the trencher boom. I squinted into the darkness, searching for movement, looking for something to tell me the shooter's position. He fired again. The flash nailed his position. To my right, crouched. I thrust the right joystick forward and lowered the trencher boom. A scream pierced the night.

My own scream melted into his. Gears ground but the Bobcat refused to reverse. I had too much momentum. I plunged over the precipice.

***

"Marley...Marley." The voice seemed distant but loud. The left side of my body burned. Pain shot down from my hip and up from my ankle, reaching a crescendo at my twisted knee. The stinging skin on my forearm made we wonder if I'd been sandblasted. My head throbbed. I pried my eyelids open. Braden knelt at my side. I blinked.

"Thank God," he said. Realizing I'd rejoined the conscious world, he tenderly pushed a curl off my forehead.

"What happened? Did you get the shooter?" I asked.

Braden chuckled. "No. You did. You saved my life. Which makes it hard to be mad at you for being such a cowgirl. You nailed the sucker just before your Bobcat crashed over the hill. The guy must have slipped. The trencher blades sliced into the back of his neck. Severed his spinal cord. Dead in a minute."

I'd never killed anyone. Yet the only emotion I felt was relief. Not one iota of remorse for the sadistic bastard who'd attacked Janie. And tried to murder Braden.

"Was it Underling?" I shuddered at a mental picture of his smashed nose and lecherous smirk.

"No. If Kain's behind this, he found a new henchman to parade as a psycho killer. Wonder what he pays—and where he finds them? Course these guys don't have much of a stretch to pose as psychos. The dead guy had a pair of Janie's panties tucked in his pocket as a souvenir."

Noises uphill prompted me to lift my head. I lay sprawled

halfway down the steep embankment on the tee's south side. The Bobcat rested nose down at the bottom of the hill, just shy of the lagoon. I didn't recollect any attempt to parachute free. Yet somehow I'd been thrown clear.

I started to sit up. "Stay still," Braden ordered. "The paramedics are en route, and Bill O'Brien gave specific instructions you weren't to move."

"I'm just woozy," I protested. I shifted and winced as pain pinballed with laser intensity through my limbs.

"Yeah, right," said Braden. "You were out cold. This time Bill insists—you're going to the hospital. Forget any protest. I'm on his side. The doctors need to keep you overnight for observation."

Exhaustion sucked the fight right out of me. "What happened to the other deputy? Talk about cowboys. You promised to call for backup."

"If you'll quit fidgeting, I'll tell you." Braden chuckled. "I was approaching the maintenance shed when I heard a splash and climbed out of the golf cart to investigate. I pulled my gun, took out my flashlight, and spotted footprints in the soggy ground leading to the tee.

"That's when our killer spotted me—a lone cop with a drawn gun. He figured he had the drop on me. I kept waiting for back up, wondering why it was taking so long. The cavalry galloped off to the golf clubhouse instead of golf maintenance. Static bleeped out a key part of my message."

Braden smiled. "You know the rest. I was plain lucky he didn't hit me. Felt the breeze from that first bullet. When your Bobcat roared to life, I didn't know what the hell was happening. You're...amazing."

A flashlight played over us. Braden stood and Bill O'Brien took his place, squatting on his heels at my side. "My, my, I didn't expect to see you again tonight." He added a tongue cluck for emphasis. "Lay still."

He took my pulse. Next he played a visual follow-the-bouncing-ball game with his penlight. Finally he probed my hip and leg. I swore. He chuckled.

"Don't think anything's broken, though it's not for want of trying." His fingers danced over my scalp. "You're going to have one hell of a goose egg."

He looked at Braden. "How long was she unconscious?"

"A minute or two."

The medic frowned. "Well, it's off to the hospital with you. I called and told the emergency room to expect another inbound. While I was at it, I checked on Janie. She's stabilized. Gonna be okay. Maybe you two can get a group rate."

I twisted to lever myself upright and Bill pinned my shoulder with an extra-large paw. "Oh no you don't." He yelled for a litter. That's when I wished I hadn't been packing away so many desserts. I'd heard these guys at the firehouse grousing about lifting island chubbos. I wasn't anxious to take the heat for someone's hernia.

Braden touched my cheek. "Marley, I'll head to the hospital soon as I can. Meanwhile, rest easy. It'll be over soon. I found a note in the dead guy's pocket. It read 'five a.m., Mad Inlet.' Our guess is a rendezvous with a getaway boat. I'll keep his date. We need to grab one of these suckers alive. Get someone to talk."

After regaining consciousness, I'd been giddy with relief to find Braden alive. Now dread tightened my throat.

I can't take another funeral, another lover's body moldering underground.

Stop it.

I kept my tone light. "Hope you have someone covering your backside."

"Yep." He kissed me. It wasn't some prudish thank-you-for-saving-my-life smooch. Not very professional, but necessary. For both our psyches.

Bill whooped with delight. "Now I have a tale to tell. The boys at the firehouse are always interested in hearing about the latest island romance."

"Stuff it," I said as Bill and his buddy hoisted my litter in the air.

"Jeez, how much do you weigh, Marley?" Bill parried with an exaggerated puff.

"I lift weights," I said deadpan. "It's all muscle."

"That's my girl." Braden chuckled. "Weighty but well-toned."

TWENTY-FOUR

I opened my eyes to a sea of white. *Where am I?*

I felt the irritating starch of hospital sheets, and my fingers explored the smooth, cold bed rail. The sun pumped light into the room despite the drawn blinds. *Must be morning.*

I rolled my head to the other side of my pillow. Janie, Braden, and April popped into view. Any more people and it'd be standing room only. Janie's sister was the only non-sleeping member of the trio. She'd draped her long shapely legs over the side of a spine-bending visitor's chair and looked almost comfortable with her pretzel impersonation. She winked, nodded at Janie, and threw me a triumphant thumbs-up. We both grinned. Janie snored softly. Her color had returned to a healthy pink, and her face looked almost angelic. No trace of the frenzied lady who pummeled me with her fists.

Braden's head was cocked at a neck-wrenching angle, but he slept, too. Dark circles shadowed his eyes. Otherwise he appeared none the worse for wear. In fact, the emerging stubble looked sexy, a dash of Miami Vice to flavor his rough-and-tumble good looks.

Thank God. They're both alive.

I fumbled for my watch on the bedside table, and noticed Braden's wallet, lying open. His young sons grinned at me. Was he studying their photos before he fell asleep, using the hospital's tepid nightlights to memorize their happy faces? My watch clattered to the floor and woke Braden. Fortunately, Janie kept snoring.

"Am I glad to see you," I whispered. "Everything went okay last night?"

He stood and leaned over my bed. He cupped my chin in his hand, and for a moment simply looked into my eyes. "Yeah. Good news." He kissed my forehead. "We caught Hugh red-

255

handed. And the sheriff arrested Gator and Sally. I'll tell you everything but let's not wake sleeping beauty." He nodded toward Janie and awarded April a brief smile.

"I'll get a wheelchair and take you for a spin."

"I don't need a wheelchair." I flopped my legs over the side of the bed and prepared to stand.

"You know that, and I know that," he answered as he ran a playful finger down the drafty opening at the back of my hospital gown. "But it never pays to piss off a nurse. Besides I might get turned on if I walk behind you. Your bare ass hanging out for all to see, just asking to be grabbed."

He dashed off before I could clobber him. His absence gave me an opportunity to peek under the hem of my hospital sackcloth. *Holy Toledo.* My leg and side looked like a Jackson Pollack painting—massive blotches of purple shot through with a vile green. I twisted my arm to bring my elbow into view. More colors—bright red scrapes with contrasting brown scabs. I licked my dry and cracked lips.

Oh my, I'm SO sexy.

When Braden returned with a wheelchair, I eased onto the leather seat, more interested in hearing his story than winning a fight. We waved goodbye to April, and Braden rolled me down the hall to a tiny chapel. "It's empty," he said. "I checked."

"You said you caught Hugh. Did he confess? What about Kain?"

Braden didn't answer. The hospital setting apparently gave him an itch to play doctor, and the deputy concentrated on parts of my anatomy Dr. Danner had totally ignored. *Now this is my idea of physical therapy.* Yet I forced myself to swat his industrious hands away.

"No fair," I protested. "You brought me here under false pretenses. Talk. Besides I'm not sure I feel comfortable playing kissy-face in a chapel."

"God is love," Braden murmured, his hands clasped in a

prayerful pose.

"Come on. Tell me what happened. Don't tease."

Braden twirled one of the chapel's padded folding chairs around and straddled it. "Okay, okay. I must say you're a rather testy patient."

He kept his story short and sweet. In fact, I had to beg for every tidbit. Maybe he felt uncomfortable telling a story in which he starred as hero. Or perhaps he didn't want my heart to fibrillate over dangers past. At any rate, I finally wrenched a barebones synopsis out of him.

To disguise himself for the rendezvous, Braden donned a maintenance uniform and pulled a cap over his buzz cut. Then he'd skulked in the riprap shadows at the marshy intersection of Dear Island and Mad Inlet. A few minutes before five, a boat coughed to life and chugged down Dear's manmade canal. When the skiff reached the inlet, the driver cut the engine and floated in the shallows. Figuring that was his cue, Braden hunched over to shrink his silhouette to the dead guy's height and splashed ahead.

"I heard a voice say, 'Hurry up, will ya? We have to get out of here.' I couldn't believe our luck. Our water taxi driver turned out to be Hugh. By the time he realized I'd taken the place of Asshole Assassin, it was too late. The sheriff and Chief Dixon roared in like a Coast Guard SWAT team making a million-dollar drug bust.

"Unfortunately the idiot ignored the sheriff's order to put up his hands," he added. "When Hugh reached in his jacket, Conroy shot him. He's alive but in a coma. They took him to Charleston for surgery."

No real need to ask my next question. If Kain were in jail, Braden would have led with the headline. "You said you arrested Gator and Sally. What about Kain?"

Braden frowned. "Gone. His house was empty. The sheriff found nothing—until he looked in the freezer. Your Mr.

Underling was inside, a bullet hole in place of his left eye. Kain wrapped butcher paper around the head and printed a note: 'One Polesicle. Employees should aim to please.' Guess he was unhappy his hit man missed you."

Bile rose in my throat. "He killed his own man? And left him where it would incriminate him? That makes no sense. He's been super careful to make sure evidence points away from him."

Braden shrugged. "We figure he's disappeared for good—at least in his Kain Dzandrek incarnation. Gator and Sally were no help. Lawyered up and didn't admit a thing. Said they'd never met anyone named Kain.

"Sheriff Conroy wants Kain real bad. We heard a man fitting his description chartered a private jet to Miami. Conroy must have made twenty calls to friends in Florida. And, just in case that plane was a decoy, he phoned every law enforcement buddy up and down I-95. He has folks looking high and low, covering boats, airports, train stations. No one has a clue."

I read the verdict in his face. "You don't expect anyone to find him, do you?"

"No. He probably called in some chips of his own. It's tough to catch homegrown mobsters, especially rich ones. With Kain's international connections, it's worse. From Miami, he could have flown anywhere in a private jet. He could be drinking vodka martinis in Chechnya or Uzbekistan."

I hesitated to ask my last question—unsure I wanted an answer. "Will Kain come back?"

"Not if he's smart. Looks like he had a big operation. In all probability Dear was one of several money-laundering options. He can afford to leave some money on the table. I think it's safe to say we've seen the last of that monster."

Neither of us spoke for a minute. Braden sighed, and I reached out to touch his cheek. The bristles were softer than I expected.

"Thank you," I said softly. "I know you're exhausted. The last thing you needed was to doze in a hospital chair. Why don't we see about springing me? Who knows, maybe we can engage in some physical therapy—the mutual kind?"

"Now you're talking." A slow smile rekindled the warmth in his eyes.

***

At the nurse's station, we badgered a young woman into phoning Dr. Ernie Danner. He was not only ex-Army, but the big brother of my Beaufort-bred friend Brenda. Small-town living has its privileges, and despite the county's rapid expansion, Beaufort still functioned as an upscale village. I unabashedly exploited my connections.

It was early Sunday morning, and the hospital was as quiet as a morgue. That made Janie's scream sound like a tornado-warning siren.

Braden drew his gun, and I kicked aside my wheelchair for a sprint to her room. A trailing nurse came in dead last in our heat.

As we burst through the door, I scanned the room for danger. The stark white cubicle offered no hiding places for a new hit man. Janie and April were the sole occupants.

Sobs racked Janie's body.

Her sister rhythmically patted her back. "You're okay, Janie. You're okay."

When my neighbor looked up and saw Braden and me, her agitation intensified. "He tried to kill me. Did you catch him? Oh please tell me you caught him. And Gator—that pile of manure—he lent him my spare set of keys."

Realizing her patient was in no immediate danger, the nurse turned a withering scowl on Braden and his gun. "You should all leave." She wrestled a blood pressure cuff on her patient. "She doesn't need this excitement."

Braden peered at her nametag. "Ms. Johnson," he began,

his tone even icier than the nurse's. "This is police business. We'll leave if a *doctor* tells us to."

He turned to Janie, and his voice softened. "You can stop worrying. Your attacker's dead. Marley made sure he won't hurt anyone ever again. Gator and Sally are in jail, and Hugh's in a coma, locked in a prison hospital ward."

Nurse Johnson glared at us while she timed her patient's pulse.

"Thank God," Janie muttered with an involuntary shudder.

Braden eyed her carefully. "You up to telling us what happened? Or do you want to rest? This can wait."

Janie shook off the nurse. "I want to talk." She bit off her words as she pushed herself upright. "I know I should have returned your call, Marley, but I figured it'd be almost as quick to drive to your house. That cocksucker was hiding in the back seat of my car. He put a gun to my head and told me to drive to the golf maintenance shed. Once the car was hidden by the building, he clubbed me." She cast a surly look at the nurse. "How do you crank this bed up? I want to sit."

Miffed at her rebellious patient, the nurse plunked the motorized control in Janie's hand, turned on her heel and stomped out. "I'll give you five minutes," she called over her shoulder.

Janie took a deep breath. "When I came to, it was dark. I was naked, tied to my own bed, and scared spitless. He told me I had a choice. I could drink some nasty concoction or he'd slit my throat. The miscreant said he'd prefer the latter. The way he licked his lips, I believed him.

"So I drank the crap. He'd poured it into my 'I may rise, but I refuse to shine' mug. It tasted like boiled manure. It was so hot I scalded my throat."

She swallowed hard and pulled the blankets tighter around her.

April interrupted. "Sis, you don't need to talk about this.

260

It's upsetting you."

"Upsetting me?" she exploded. "Talking about it is nothing. I can still see his freakin' yellow teeth, grinning while he tightened the scarves around my wrists and stared at my boobs. I kept asking what he wanted, what he was doing. He just smiled."

She shuddered. I walked to the bed and squeezed her hand. When she looked up, her face communicated rage and terror. The kind that washes over you in uncontrollable tremors after you realize that tractor-trailer missed flattening you by an inch.

"I was certain he'd rape me. All I could think about was staying alive." She spoke in little more than a whisper. "Once I was bound, he took out a knife. He slid it over my skin like he was imagining carving me up. He kept smiling. Oh, man, he enjoyed me being helpless. I'm glad he's dead."

Janie stopped. She gave her head a tiny shake as if that might dislodge her hellish memories. "I'm not sure what happened after that. It's muddled. Next thing I remember is waking here, and April saying, 'You're okay. No one can hurt you.' Then some doctor took my pulse and told me I was a lucky, young lady. I thought 'yeah, right.' But I guess I am."

When she paused, April poured her some water. "Sis, come stay with me for a few days. My manager can run the club. Hell, it runs itself. I'll keep you company."

She gave her sister a wan smile. "Why not?"

Perhaps it was Janie's window-rattling scream or maybe it was Braden's fast draw with a gun, but the staff at Beaufort Memorial seemed eager to expel us. Dr. Danner gave a special dispensation to hasten our departure. Of course, we still had to sign stacks of disclaimers reproduced in seven-point-type.

Midway through the paperwork, Janie let out another anguished yelp. "Oh my God. I just remembered my attacker booted Pussy outside. She must be frantic. I have to get to Dear."

"No you don't," I said. "Go home with April. We'll find Pussy and take care of her."

"That's a promise," Braden added. "Let April look after you. The sheriff's going to need an official statement, and the logistics will be easier if you're not marooned on Dear."

He paused a beat. "I do have one question though, why did Kain decide you needed killing?"

Janie barked a short laugh. "I was so intent on snooping it never dawned on me that someone might poke around *my* office. I'd doodled questions about Kain, Gator and Sally. Drew little arrows between victims and my suspects. And I made a list of real estate documents to dredge up and study. Gator found the notes tucked under my blotter. He wasn't amused.

"The creep who attacked me did pass along my boss's regrets," she added. "I hope Gator rots in jail. I'll send the bastard notes once a month, saying how I *regret* that he's a slimy son of a bitch and that Ralph Lauren doesn't do prison stripes."

Braden's question prompted one of my own. "You told me Kain paid off Hugh's gambling debt in exchange for ammunition to blackmail Sally and Gator. What terrible secrets did Hugh know about your bosses?"

Janie smiled. "Hugh and Gator were fishing buddies...and you know how Gator likes to play big shot. While they trolled for drum fish, my old boss yakked about his wheeler-dealer doings. He told Hugh how he and Sally bumped up property values, using employees as shills. Worse, he spilled the beans that he and Sally were set to bail out of their real estate investment trust before other investors realized it was in the toilet."

She shrugged. "Gator and Sally knew they'd go bankrupt if word got out. They'd lose Dear and a chance that the Beach West profits might make them whole again. Based on what I overheard, Kain roped them in gradually. First with the guest worker gig, then money laundering and the land flip. He promised millions in profits and Woody as an expendable scapegoat when the mortgages proved bogus."

TWENTY-FIVE

Braden and I caught the eleven-thirty ferry to Dear. The passenger seated across from us seemed engrossed in a tabloid story. I read the headline—"Widowed Granny Steals Bobcat, Beheads Killer"—and groaned.

Geesh. My Bobcat assault didn't sever the guy's head, and "widowed granny?"—puh-leese. Though happy to claim Jeff's grandchildren as my own, the verbal packaging suggested a frail old lady with loose dentures and a walker.

Since it was Sunday, I half expected the island to be quiet. Unfortunately, word of our return had drawn out the reporter vultures. To save our carcasses, we literally ran for our car, and barricaded ourselves in my house.

While I exchanged my bloodied uniform for jeans and a sweatshirt, Braden gave the heave-ho to a brazen hussy who pressed her nose against a windowpane on my back deck. Next he called Chief Dixon, who took pity and ordered security to chase away stalkers. The deputy also taped "Trespassers Will Be Prosecuted" warnings to the front and back doors.

Once the reporters slunk away, we tiptoed outside to look for Pussy Galore. Janie's cat snoozed in a patch of sunlight on my neighbor's stoop. The Persian eyed me suspiciously when I opened Janie's door and shooed her inside. But she purred approval once I perfumed the air with tuna treats.

I immediately rang Janie to say her kitty was safe. My friend appeared on the rebound. Though seventy miles from Dear, she'd begun orchestrating the island's resurrection. "I had our Sunday receptionist post a sign that our real estate office will reopen tomorrow," she told me. "I also asked our resort manager to pretend it's business as usual. Renters need to check in and out no matter who's in the pokey. I'll drive to Dear tomorrow to help sort things out."

I laughed. "You're a marvel. Just don't overdo it."

"Hey, I have an ulterior motive. I've seen developers go under before. Some creditor eventually stakes a claim, and the guy who's put in charge is always clueless. I plan to make sure the bumpkin realizes I'm indispensable. By the by, our resort manager says the bridge is opening to one-lane traffic tomorrow. Life is returning to normal."

With Pussy safe, Braden and I returned to our hermitage. I turned off the telephone ringer and set the answering machine to pick up first ring. Then we closed every drape, reluctantly shutting out the comforting warmth of the April sun.

I felt tired and sore, a little closer to that little old widder lady than I wanted to admit. Braden was on his cell phone tying up loose investigative ends.

He smiled when he hung up from his last call. "They served search warrants on all the suspected off-island crooks—appraiser Clay Jacobs, mortgage broker Zach Antolak, and Michael Beech, Esq., attorney at law—and they even found a paper trail. Best of all, Beech played the fool and acted as his own counsel. He sold out his co-conspirators."

"Terrific," I replied. "But still no promising leads on Kain?"

"No." He shook his head.

I tried to keep my expression neutral. No need for him to see the fear mixed with my disappointment. "I'm going to soak in the tub. Try to work out some stiffness."

"I have to make one more call," Braden said. "Then I hope to get rid of a little *stiffness* myself. How about we meet between the sheets in, say, fifteen minutes?"

I slipped out of the bath and gingerly patted myself dry. Having caught another glimpse of my multicolored hyena hide in the mirror, I avoided further scrutiny and hurried to my horizontal refuge. I'd stripped the bed yesterday and now reaped my reward. When I purchased Egyptian cotton sheets, I felt a twinge of guilt about the extravagance, despite the eighty percent off price. Today the cool caress felt worth every penny. Braden's voice floated in and I smiled, thinking delicious thoughts about his mischievous grin, sexy hint of a beard and bedroom eyes.

That's how I fell asleep, and Braden, a gentleman through and through, didn't wake me. I had no such compunction when I crawled to consciousness and realized I was as randy as an eighteen-year-old. Naturally, it was the deputy's fault. We were tucked in a lover's spoon, nude, of course. His arm draped across my waist, and my bottom snugged against his body. His dream had to be erotic. Unconsciously the deputy pressed me tighter against a silken hardness each time he drew breath. If he was having one of those dreams, we might as well both enjoy it.

Slowly I lifted his arm and shifted to face him. I keep my fingernails neatly trimmed, but they're plenty long enough to skip tauntingly over warm flesh. I hop scotched a wicked little tap dance down his chest and continued the sensory wake-up call along his thighs. Meanwhile I used my tongue to dash out an added SOS on one of his nipples.

I knew Braden was awake when one of his hands slid unerringly into a retaliatory position. As he began an exploratory foray, he didn't need to be De Soto to discover I was ready, willing and able. My low moan and greedy grasp of a most-favored appendage gave the game away. I can't recall the last time I used the word "swoon"—if ever—but I may have done so when his soft but slightly prickly beard led the charge of his counterattack. Then all my troubles, all my bruised flesh and banged limbs, were forgotten in a warm electric rush that sent twitching impulses of pleasure scurrying to every nerve ending.

When the tremors quieted, I sighed my contentment.

"I'm sure going to miss you," I said.

"What do you mean?" Braden looked hurt. He brushed back my hair and twirled a finger in an unruly ringlet glued to

266

my damp forehead. "Are you kicking me out—slam, bam, thank you, Sam?"

I hadn't intended to delve into our relationship at this moment. But my thoughts had popped out. No way to stuff them back in the box.

"No." I smiled. "You're welcome to stay as long as you want—or visit whenever you like. It's just that Janie mentioned the bridge reopens tomorrow. So it won't be long before Sheriff Conroy recalls his deputies. No need for you to bivouac here once you can drive on and off the island."

"Oh," Braden stayed quiet for a moment. "If I don't clear out, Dear's gossip fires will rage, right? Would that cause you heartburn?"

"Not really. I quit fretting about other people's opinions about the time I screwed my military career by marrying a noncom."

I nodded toward a watercolor that occupied four feet of bedroom wall space. It pictured three middle-aged ladies on a beachcombing expedition. "Do you like that painting?"

"Uh, it's okay. Not very flattering. Are you deliberately changing the subject?"

"No, it's relevant. I think the artist loved those women. Sure their thighs are dimpled with cellulite, but it doesn't stop them from sallying forth in bathing suits. Look at that lady on the right, her rump is so plump it's stretched her suit to near transparency. Do any of them give a hoot? No. They're merrily collecting shells and laughing. Content inside their own skins."

I stopped and kissed Braden's fingertips. "So am I. Most of the time anyway. I'm a poor candidate for Botox and unlikely to care if my neighbors approve my sleeping arrangements. But we have a sizable age gap and we didn't really plan this…arrangement. I'm not looking for a commitment. In fact, I think another commitment is tearing you up."

Braden interrupted. "What are you talking about? There's

no one else."

"Sure there is. Your sons. Your boys are calling you back to Atlanta. I saw your wallet lying open at the hospital. You'd been studying their faces, right? If you want to be part of their lives, don't take no for an answer."

He took a deep breath. "I've been thinking a lot about Brady and Duncan. I keep hearing the Cuthbert twins, how they believed their dad didn't love them. I want my sons to know I'm crazy about them. I want them to come to me if they're ever in trouble or just troubled."

"Sounds like you've made a decision," I said.

"Yeah, about my involvement in their lives, not about where I'll live. Who's to say I can't be a good dad and live on Dear Island? And what happens to us if I leave?"

I tried to keep my tone light. "We're fine. You're kind and brave—not to mention tender and sexy. For the past year, I've been sleepwalking. You've been a wonderful wake-up call. I don't want to say goodbye. But I don't want you to stay out of inertia. If you think you can handle long-distance parenting, we should be able to juggle a long-distance romance. It's something to think about."

"Okay," Braden answered. "But I sure as hell don't want this to end."

We had both avoided the "love" word. Was I in love? Or just grateful to be back among the living?

***

Braden slipped his arms around my waist as I turned an omelet for a final browning. "If you think I'm moving out of this bed-and-breakfast any time soon, you're nuts." He kissed the back of my neck. Then he poured us coffee, and retrieved a Diet Coke from the fridge to set beside my placemat. Already the man had adjusted to one of my idiosyncrasies.

I forked a generous mouthful of eggs, and my gaze snagged on a cooler collecting dust in a kitchen corner. "Remember that blue-and-white cooler the twins watched Hugh haul from Kain's Sunset Island drop to Dear? Was it ever found?"

"Nope, and deputies searched every inch of the Cuthbert mansion as well as Gator's and Sally's houses. They also looked in likely cubbyholes on company property—restaurants, clubhouses, resort and real estate offices."

"Well, wherever it is, I bet it's still flush with cash," I said. "Gator and Sally had no time to launder anything—money or undies—between Kain's order for fifty thousand clean bills and their arrest. So where do you suppose Hugh hid it?"

Braden's fork wavered mid-air. "A rental property? Kain must have told Hugh not to foul his own nest. With the boys snooping around, Hugh needed a neutral hidey-hole."

"Well, it wouldn't take long to check out active rentals," I said, "especially ones rented for a month or more. I doubt Hugh would be the renter-of-record though."

He shrugged. "Unfortunately, I doubt a judge would give me a warrant to search a couple dozen rental properties based on a hunch."

I smiled. "No warrants needed. Every Dear rental agreement includes a waiver giving island housekeeping, security guards, firemen and emergency personnel the right to enter the premises at any time for any reason. And, guess what, yours truly is a security guard."

After breakfast, we called Chief Dixon to get his okay for our treasure hunt. He grunted a "yes" so long as I didn't bill my hours. "Hey, my budget's toast with all the freaking overtime. I think you're on a wild goose chase, but who cares if I'm not in range of the buckshot."

Dixon's foul mood probably related to his employment picture. While he worked for DOA and not the developers, the Dear Company paid fifty percent of security salaries. Given the financial morass bequeathed to creditors by Gator and Sally, the new regime might arrive swinging a broad budget axe.

I assured the chief my efforts were gratis. "Okay," he said. "I don't have you down for any shifts this week. Pressure's off. Relax a little. Lord help us, I think the excitement's past."

The consensus was that all the bad guys—with one horrible exception—were dead or behind bars. A charter pilot had identified a photo of Kain, confirming his Saturday night flight to Miami. By now the mystery man could be anywhere. Braden's bet was in one of the "stans" in what was once the USSR.

I got goose bumps thinking about the man creeping back and trying to extract a pound of flesh from my hide one sliver at a time. I didn't want him at large—anywhere.

With the chief's nod to enter rental property, Braden and I suited up for duty, strapping on holsters and guns. As I pocketed my wallet, a slip of paper fell out. The note held the numbers I'd scribbled the night we tossed Hugh's boat.

"You ready?" Braden asked.

"Yeah, let me grab my GPS. Remember that list of numbers Hugh stashed with marine charts? While we're cruising around, let's see if any of the numbers might be island coordinates."

***

Eager to help, the Dear Island resort manager showed us how to work the rental software. In ten minutes, we compiled a list of twenty-four properties meriting a look-see. All were rented after January 1 for extended periods, and none of the vacationers were repeat guests. Sue had already culled the list of Canadians and other snowbirds who returned to Dear year after year.

With a roster and duplicate keys in hand, we headed to the north end of the island. We decided on a surprise knock-and-search operation. No advance calls to see who answered. Though all of Kain's collaborators appeared to be hospitalized, handcuffed or fugitives, we saw no reason to take chances.

Our canvass proved time-consuming. Most of the houses

sat empty. It seemed strange for so many renters to be AWOL on a Monday morning, especially a cold one that felt more like January than April. Yet Dear's newly reopened bridge acted as a powerful magnet. Long lines of cars queued to take turns snaking over the jury-rigged one-lane connector. While some residents headed to grocery and liquor stores to stock up on staples, others simply relished the freedom to drive wherever they pleased. The jailer had opened Dear's gates.

By late afternoon, we'd crossed eighteen houses off our list. Rummaging around in thirteen empty houses had brought only one discovery—tourons leave lots of disgusting stuff strewn about, from plates smeared with spaghetti goo to soiled boxer shorts.

The people who did answer their bells were clearly not in Kain's thrall. Braden's ID checks didn't even scare up unpaid traffic tickets. Still, we searched their haciendas in case Hugh had hoodwinked them.

At four p.m., I rebelled. Prior attempts to badger Braden into taking a break had failed. He belonged to the finish-before-you-relax school. Our first incompatibility issue. I could not last six or seven hours without a caffeine and carbohydrate fix. If I skipped lunch, I invited one humdinger of a headache. My noggin now felt like a bowling ball being drilled for new finger holes. So I refused to use my magic security pass again until I was issued crackers and a Diet Coke.

My snit fit delivered us to E.T. Grits. Braden, who insisted on saving his appetite for an early T-bone, slouched against a pillar at the front of the convenience store while I speed-walked to the refrigerated cases at the back. I grabbed a Diet Coke and started downing it as I made my way to the junk food display. While gazing longingly at a king-size Butterfinger, I felt eyes boring into my back. I spun and spotted an elderly lady one aisle over. Her angry brown eyes, magnified by thick glasses, lasered me. I felt like a bug. *Was my blouse unbuttoned? Did she think I wouldn't pay for the pop?*

A second later, she moved on. I watched her hunched back as she scurried away. Her gray poodle hairdo swayed from side to side as she crab walked down the narrow aisle.

By the time I reached the checkout, the disgruntled oldster was out the door. Sheila, the check-out clerk, tallied my debt. "Do you know the woman who just walked out?" I asked.

"No. She's not a regular. But I saw her with Sally last week. Why—should I know her?"

I waved off Sheila's puzzled look. "No. The lady just looked at me as if I'd farted and tried to shift the blame her way."

Sheila laughed. "Probably needs to eat more prunes. Maybe she can't fart."

Braden sauntered over. "Happy now? Can we get a move on? I'd like to finish our little exercise in futility before the sun sets."

***

"What the heck is that thing?" Braden asked.

We were en route to the twenty-second house on our list, a mushroom-like villa on Blue Crab Point, the last of four homes sprinkled along a slender wedge of forest that protruded into the marsh. A rickety wooden bridge linked the marooned point to the island proper. The desolate spot was as remote as you could get on Dear.

The end villa had not aged well. Separated thermopanes made the glass walls look milky, like the sides of dirty fish tanks. Our long-term rental was secluded and eerie.

"If Hugh wanted a setting to discourage guests, we're here," I said as we parked. Untrimmed oleanders crowded my Mustang and shrouded the cave-like entryway. Braden rang the bell. Once. Twice. No answer. Big surprise. We hadn't seen a car or lights. No sign of occupancy.

He unlocked the warped front door. It funneled visitors

directly to a circular staircase that led to the living quarters above. I shivered. The tubular entrance was damp, clammy. "Braden, I'm getting a bad feeling. Maybe we should call for backup?"

He laughed. "For mold? Go back to the car if you want. I'll take a quick look. We only have two more houses to check. I want to finish up."

I didn't turn back. The stairway proved too narrow for a side-by-side ascent, so Braden took the lead. For some reason, he decided to show off his stair-climbing speed. In contrast, my recently battered legs stuck in low gear. He disappeared from view as I chugged up the stairwell's last spiral kinks. A minute later, I heard his disembodied voice. "All clear. No criminals - except the decorator. The rug's an orange shag."

Relieved, I stopped a minute to catch my breath. Then I heard Braden's voice again—"Oh, sorry ma'am"—followed by a loud thud.

"Braden," I yelled. "You okay?"

Silence. I drew my gun and crept up the last two stairs, my back tight against the slender banister. "Braden?" I yelled.

My call echoed, unanswered, in the hollow stairwell. My heart raced. What's happening? Had some lady beaned Braden with a frying pan, thinking she'd surprised a burglar?

Indecision immobilized me. Should I call for help? Oh no, Braden had the radio, not me. You have a gun, I told myself. So did Braden, my alter-ego answered. Yeah, but he wasn't expecting an ambush.

The door to the living room canted slightly ajar. I kicked it and rushed inside, my gun arm leading the charge. At first, I couldn't make sense of what I saw. Braden was on the floor, propped in a sitting position. A small rivulet of blood meandered down his forehead. His eyes were closed. A woman crouched behind Braden, shielded by his body. All I could see were a few wisps of frizzy gray hair and the gun she held tight to his temple.

"Hello, Marley," a voice boomed. "You don't have a shot. Might as well drop the gun. Otherwise I'll kill lover boy."

Kain's amused voice.

Oh, God. He'd slipped back on the island in drag. Why? He'd been home safe.

"Everyone's so nice to old ladies," Kain said. "We're so *disarming.*"

Sweet Jesus, he was actually enjoying himself. I took a deep breath and considered my options. Kain's assessment was correct. I had only one clear target—Braden.

We were dead. I couldn't shoot Kain without hitting Braden. And Kain could take me out any time he wanted. Why hadn't he?

"Marley, did you hear? Listen up. Put your gun on the floor and kick it over. I'm serious. You've got one minute or I'll kill him."

Though terrified, I was beyond anger and felt mulishly stubborn. If I had to die, so be it. I was going to take this scumbag with me.

"Not a chance, Kain." I was pleased to discover my voice didn't quaver. "If you shoot Braden, I can shoot you. No way am I giving up my gun."

I hoped Kain would pop his head up to argue and give me a clear shot. He didn't. I felt as if I was conversing with the Mad Hatter or a demented puppeteer hiding behind a live prop.

After a moment of silence, Kain answered in a reasoned manner—though the macho voice floated up from a pile of gray curls. "Normally your assessment would be quite accurate, Marley. You lose the gun; I kill you. But there are extenuating circumstances. I need your help. It's in my best interest to keep you and your detective alive. I want your cooperation."

"Why?" I infused my voice with sarcasm and tried to anticipate his answer. Did he want help getting off the island? Did he need transportation? A hostage? Was this another perverted trick? A new game?

Kain sighed. "I see you're skeptical. I'm not any happier about the circumstances than you are. Hugh left me in a quandary. After he learned the twins tailed him from Sunrise Island, he phoned to say he was afraid they might have followed him to this rental, too. He promised to find a safe place to relocate some of my, shall we say...property previously stored here.

"Unfortunately, the stupid ass got himself shot before we could speak again. I hoped he hadn't had time to move the items. Instead, I found a note. Hugh knew my fondness for word games, so either he was trying to impress me or confuse the police. Regrettably, his note makes no sense. I assume I'm missing a clue—probably related to Dear's landmarks or inhabitants. That's where you come in, my dear colonel. I need an interpreter, a linguistic sherpa."

I actually laughed. Talk about your unholy alliances. "Oh, Kain. Even if I believed you, what's the point? As soon as you claim your *property*, Braden and I are dead. You'll shoot us both."

"Gentleman's honor, I won't. No matter what you think, my offer buys you time. I'm sure that overactive brain of yours is already figuring ways to outsmart me. Maybe you can. It's your only chance."

Damned if he wasn't right. I *was* frantically plotting ways to thwart the sucker. But, at the moment, I wasn't even certain there *was* a note. Maybe the note was a creative lie.

"Where's the note? I want to see it."

"Look at the door."

I glanced sideways at a note Scotch-taped to the back of the door. The printing was large and childlike: THE KING'S HOME. COLD CASH.

I lowered my gun. Kain was right. He needed help, and I needed to buy time.

TWENTY-SIX

I yanked frantically against the handcuffs as I screamed at Kain. "You lying bastard. You want my help? Forget it. You can go straight to hell."

Across the room, Kain chuckled. "My, my, such language. Calm down. Is this any way to talk to your new partner? I didn't tell a single lie. I said you could buy time. I didn't say how much. And I promised I wouldn't shoot your cop. I haven't, and I won't. This little incendiary device is set to go off at midnight. Almost seven hours away. If you're efficient, and we find Hugh's hiding place before then, you can untie him before this glass silo goes boom."

Kain gave an exaggerated shrug. He was still in drag and looked harmless, almost silly in his Q-tip wig and pink velour leisure suit. Now that I knew it was Kain, I couldn't believe I hadn't recognized him in E.T. Grits. I had to hand it to the guy, he knew his costumes. In addition to the wig, he'd donned brown contacts and thick glasses. He was also decked out with a prosthetic bra and leg padding that made his thighs look like an ad for anti-cellulite cream. The get-up helped him perfect a waddling gait. A slouch disguised his true height.

"Marley, are you listening? I really don't care whether he lives or dies. My only concern is getting my property back and escaping this sandpit without a police escort. The bomb, well, it's an added inducement for you not to drag your feet. For me, it's insurance. If I don't find anything, I want to make sure no one else does either. The fire will offer a little distraction for the cops and security while I make my getaway."

Perhaps twenty minutes had elapsed since I'd surrendered my gun. Once that power issue was resolved, Kain used my own handcuffs to secure my arms around a pillar that served as a ceiling support. No way could I pull free. I'd watched

276

helplessly as he trussed Braden. Sturdy rope. Expert knots. When—if—Braden regained consciousness, he would never be able to untie himself.

Up to the moment Kain returned from the kitchen with his homemade bomb, I figured faked cooperation could at least save Braden. My plan revolved around luring Kain a safe distance away from Braden before staging a last-ditch insurrection.

The bomb, sitting five feet from the detective's body, changed everything. The device appeared homemade and not terribly sophisticated, but I assumed it was serviceable. Kain showed me the timer. Made sure I saw the midnight setting.

Heaven help me. What had I done? I should never have given up my gun.

Kain glanced my way. "It's dark now, almost time to start our treasure hunt. I hope you've been thinking real hard about 'the King's home.' Any bright ideas? If your efforts appear insincere, I'll kill you. No gun. I'm a man of my word. But you'll die wishing I *had* used a gun. And once you're dead, you must realize your lover's chances to survive are gone, too.

"You have ten minutes," he added. "I need to change clothes. When I come back, you'd best have a brainstorm."

Repeating Hugh's word puzzle over and over in my mind hadn't helped. I was stumped. For decades, a King family had owned a home on Dear. In fact, it was only a few doors from the Cuthbert estate. However, using the King name seemed way too obvious—even for Hugh. Could I gain anything by suggesting the place? Maybe. The house would be empty. The family only visited in summer and never rented it. Kain would be distracted while he searched.

My captor's reappearance rattled me. Somehow he'd seemed less menacing ensconced in pink velour. He'd ditched his drag disguise in favor of camouflage fatigues. With his spine uncurled, his bearing became military, menacing. The icy blue

277

eyes were back, cruel as ever. He radiated evil.

"Time's up," he said. "Do you have an idea or do we end it here?"

I shared my thoughts about the King family abode.

"How dumb do you think I am? I looked in the Dear Island directory. There's no listing for a King."

"True," I replied, licking my lips. "That's why you need me, Bozo."

My one psych class in college hadn't offered advice on how to talk to megalomaniacs. However, knowing Kain got off on people's fear, I figured a little attitude might put him off balance—or earn me a quick ticket to eternity. His face registered shock at my hubris. Then he smiled. "My, my. You do plan to entertain me, don't you? Let's hear it."

"My last name is Clark, but I don't live in the 'Clark' house. I live in the 'Sherman' house—my mother-in-law's name. It'll be another decade before it's the Clark house. Island etiquette. Jack King's daughter inherited the family vacation house. Her married name is Winchester."

He nodded. "Okay, I get it. Let's go. Hugh's dumb. It wouldn't surprise me if that's the best he could do. You'd better rev up your gray matter though. You're the one on the clock if this doesn't pan out."

Kain proved exceedingly careful with his gun when he freed me from my pillar embrace and recuffed my hands behind my back. He nudged me with the pistol as I stole one last look at Braden. Except for the ropes, he looked peaceful. Like he was sleeping. Kain hadn't even bothered to gag him. No need. No one could hear him if he screamed.

I didn't fare as well. When we walked outside, I figured we'd head to a car—mine or Kain's. Then he told me to turn right, away from the driveway and my Mustang. The absence of a car in the drive had been one reason for the ambush's success. Overgrown bushes concealed the golf cart.

"Your car's too recognizable. We'll take the golf cart. I liberated it from the Cuthbert house after I tied up at their dock. Didn't figure anyone would miss it with Grace, Hugh and the twins gone."

Kain ordered me to describe our destination then instructed me to sit—an awkward position with my hands locked behind me. My discomfort had only begun.

"I'm not taking any chances." Kain tightened a noose around my neck and tied it to a roll bar at the back of the cart. "Don't want you to get any ideas about jumping free or screaming for help." That's when he stuffed a rag in my mouth.

How the hell does he plan to drive around the island with me gagged and hog-tied? He's crazy to risk someone's headlights.

He wasn't crazy. He pulled a tarp over me and tucked it securely in place. Now if anyone saw the cart moseying down Dear's dark, quiet streets, the tarp would blend into the shadows. A passerby might notice a shape on the seat next to Kain, but it was unlikely to arouse suspicion.

"Comfy? Ms. Bozo?"

I was getting my comeuppance.

He threw the golf cart into reverse and the noose sawed into my neck as I bucked on the seat. Under the tarp, I was virtually blind. Using my arms to brace myself proved impossible. It would be a rough ride. The graveled roads in this interior section sprouted potholes every few yards.

Each time we hit a rut, my body shot forward, then recoiled. With every bump, the coarse noose sliced a little deeper into my flesh. Suddenly the ride smoothed. The cart swung right. Kain had turned onto Dear's main boulevard.

We were headed south, toward the King house. We bounced over something sizeable and the whiplash tightened my choke chain. I wheezed in a breath.

I guessed we'd left the road and jumped the grass median separating the street from Dear's leisure trail. After a few smaller jolts, the cart leveled and shot forward. We were tooling down the walking path, avoiding the main road's traffic and headlights. Though motorized vehicles aren't allowed on paths, we'd be invisible at night, especially if he kept his headlamps switched off.

We were minutes from the King's, and what I felt certain was a dead-end. Minutes for me to manufacture a new lead.

***

Kain flung off the tarp. I gulped in fresh air, relieved to be free of my sweltering hothouse. I shivered as a cold ocean wind buffeted my sweat-soaked limbs. I glanced about. He'd driven the cart behind the King house where it couldn't be spotted from the street.

He left me tied in the cart while he picked a backdoor lock. I had no illusions about Kain's forced entry setting off an alarm. Ninety percent of the islanders believed alarm systems were a waste in a gated community complete with roaming security guards. My only hope rested with a security patrol. When properties were placed "on watch"—listed as vacant—guards periodically strolled around the house and rattled its doors and windows. Of course, the odds of security showing up at this precise moment were slim to none.

"You're coming inside." He led me like a dog by my hemp leash. Inside, he tied the rope end of my noose to a refrigerator that anchored one end of a galley kitchen. As soon as he ran up the stairs to search the top floor, I made a stab at getting a weapon. The rope gave me a three-foot radius to open and rifle kitchen drawers. Since my hands were locked behind me, I couldn't look and grab at the same time. Besides it was too dark to see. Kain used a penlight to search, eliminating the need to turn on any house lights.

Damn, damn, double damn. My fingers scrabbled around in the first drawer I opened. Fabric, quilted. It was stuffed with hot pads. Great weapons.

280

I pushed the drawer closed with my butt and groped for the next handle. I slid a new drawer open. *Aha, silverware. Much more promising.* Unfortunately the knives I fingered would have made safe toddler toys. They were duller than Bea.

I heard Kain padding down the carpeted stairs and palmed a fork. Slightly more lethal than a butter knife, it was the best I could do. I slid it under my waistband. Knowing my luck I'd fork myself in a kidney before I could stick it to Kain.

I scooted the drawer closed with my bottom just before my nemesis rounded the corner and walked over to threaten me with hot garlic-laced breath. "There's nothing here. So do I get to kill you now, or can you postpone your death a little longer?"

He looked at his watch. "Six hours left for Deputy Do-Right. Tick, tick, tick. What's your answer? Any more bright ideas?"

I think it surprised him that I had one. "'The King's h-house,'" I stammered. "It's usually a palace, right? Well, one street over is a house with white marble walls and a turret. Islanders think it's pretentious. They call it the palace."

I was jabbering too fast and forced myself to slow. Mom always said she could tell my fibs—I sounded like a record played at the wrong speed. And I *was* fibbing. *Yes*, there was a white marble house with a turret. *No*, I'd never heard it called a palace.

Luckily, Kain lacked my mother's sensibilities and bought into my whopper. A scooch more time purchased. *Hang in there, Braden. I'm trying.* I prayed the "palace" was unoccupied. This time of year, it tended to be a weekend getaway. I had no desire to drag innocents into danger.

Kain allowed me to climb into the golf cart on my own. I did so with careful posture to avoid a poke in the back from my pilfered flatware. He reinserted my gag and threw the tarp over my head. Back in the dark. But not for long. The "palace" sat right around the corner.

***

My heart sank when Kain peeled back the tarp. The palace was flamboyantly occupied. Though blinds were drawn, light oozed from every window.

"Guess someone's home, so we play it differently. You're the one in uniform so you'll do the talking. Tell 'em someone saw a burglar sneaking around their house. Say we need to check their place to make sure it's safe. I'll stay glued to you.

"Remember, I've got the gun. Do anything to raise suspicion and I kill you *and* them. Understand?"

This time, he angled the golf cart behind a dune near a beach crossover. He yanked the gag from my mouth so I could answer. My mouth was so dry my "yes" sounded like a squeak toy. He was super-cautious as he removed my noose and handcuffs.

"You know what I'm looking for, right? A blue cooler with a white lid."

"I figured that. But I don't understand. I've seen how you live. Crime pays, and you're good at it. So what's fifty thousand cash to you? A week's profit?"

"Not even that." Kain snorted at the insult. "I could care less about the money."

Oh. It was beginning to make sense. That cooler held something more.

"What are you after?" I asked.

"Move it." Kain shoved to emphasize his point. I staggered and the pilfered fork slid down my pant leg. At least the loss was quiet. My captor never noticed the utensil poking from the sandy soil. The mansion had his full attention.

Built in the last year, the dwelling's living quarters floated on piers positioned the required fourteen feet above sea level. That meant we had to mount an acre of steps to reach the front door. With every tread, I tried to think of a feint, some way to take Kain down without endangering strangers. But my Tae Bo

282

moves were more defense than offense. Even if I were Jackie Chan, I'd give the odds to the guy with his finger on a trigger. Kain made sure I knew his gun was in his jacket pocket, cocked, and ready to fire.

I pushed the bell. Kain crowded me. The tip of his gun poked my ribs.

A reed-thin girl flung open the door. Blaring music assaulted our ears. Flickering images from the living room TV replayed in miniature on the front door's glass inset. The girl, fourteen at most, looked anorexic and bored. I started my spiel. She cut me off.

"Mom, someone to see you," she shouted and shuffled back to her music video.

For a moment, we stood orphaned in the hall. Then a middle-aged woman rushed to meet us, apologizing for her uncouth teen. While I recited my load-of-crap story, the lady ignored me, preferring to offer Kain a come-hither grin. She liked what she saw and repeated her name, Sherry. Three times she mentioned she was alone with her daughter, a respite from a nasty divorce.

Kain made sympathetic noises. The woman accompanied us on our rounds, striking provocative poses in her midriff-baring yoga getup. She kept up a steady patter for his benefit. I hoped her attraction didn't prove fatal. I was invisible to her, though not to my warden, who kept me lassoed in his peripheral vision.

I reconciled myself to the fact I couldn't jump him here. However, I decided the woman's banter and his focus on the search might offer enough distraction for me to leave a plea for help. With a fingernail, I probed a scab on my wrist, one of several deep scratches from my Bobcat freefall. Blood quickly welled up from my probe. We walked into the woman's kitchen. While Kain surveyed the pantry, I smeared blood on my finger, backed up to the white marble countertop and wrote

"911." My body shielded my scribbling fingers from Kain's vigilant eyes.

"Everything looks fine here, ma'am," he said. "Thank you, Sherry, for your help."

She cooed her appreciation. While he flirted with her, I charged out of the kitchen as if I suddenly had to pee. I wanted their eyes on me, not on my bloody message.

In a minute, we were out the front door. I sighed my relief as I fast-walked, forcing Kain to trot to catch up. I wanted us out of Sherry's range when she returned to her kitchen and discovered my entreaty. *Hope to God she doesn't misinterpret and call us back to help.* I feared she'd decide our fictitious burglar had bloodied her white marble, not stopping to wonder why he would scratch out "911."

Back at the cart, Kain stared at me. He was angry, suspicious. "What's your hurry? Two strikes. You know what happens on strike three. You're dead. I'll cut my losses. Maybe I should kill you now. You don't have a single idea, do you?"

"No, but you're not exactly helping, *partner*." I'd played to his enormous ego. "You say Hugh's not very bright. Well, that must mean *you* aren't either. You *know* the man. I don't. Tell me about him. Give me something to work with."

Kain raised his hand and smacked me hard across the mouth. My lip split open and I tasted blood. *Uh, not the best tactic.*

Then he smiled. "First things first. I want to make sure you understand me. One more smart crack, and you're dead. But you make a point; let's talk about Hugh, *partner*."

Moonlight peeked from behind a cloud and plowed a golden road out to sea. I blinked away the beauty, a mirage with this murderer at my side. I imagined my watch ticking. Seconds, minutes disappearing—along with Braden's chances. Ask questions, I ordered myself. Buy time. Think.

I questioned Kain about Hugh and his lifestyle. Did he

have friends on the island? Did they ever meet anywhere besides the villa on Blue Crab Point? Where did Hugh like to fish? What did the gigolo do before he met Grace, his golden goose?

An epiphany. Bingo. The King's home. Of course. Hugh had been a Vegas entertainer. *If you're a singer, who's the king? Elvis. The King's home is Graceland.*

Only islanders knew about Graceland. Its formal name is Cuthbert Park, a tiny pocket of green that Gator and Sally set aside to honor their benefactor, Grace Cuthbert. Islanders called it Graceland. The park's pavilion featured kitchen facilities, including a large trough to ice down soft drinks and beer. A place for cold cash? The pavilion closed in winter and had yet to reopen for spring picnickers. Had Hugh put the cooler in the trough? The King's House. Cold cash. A possibility. A strong possibility.

"Okay, what are you thinking?" Kain demanded.

I'd gone quiet while my creaky mental wheels spun. A clear giveaway. Should I tell him? *If his property's there, he'll kill me. Period. I don't have a damn thing to gain by taking him to Graceland. Or do I? When we left the palace, Kain cuffed my hands in front.*

"Let's go to the King's home," I whispered. As soon as I finished my directions, the gag returned and the tarp fell, once more obliterating the moon and stars. In my black cocoon, I tried to visualize every crevice of the picnic pavilion, fix in my mind the exact position of the rusty hatchet. A small one for splitting wood, kept handy by a fire pit. The last time I'd been to Graceland—a shrimp boil—the axe leaned in a shadowed corner. Not far from the ice trough. *God, help me.*

TWENTY-SEVEN

I rotated my cuffed wrists and wiggled a finger into position to illuminate the dial on my watch—7:14 p.m. The iridescent green numbers kept marching. The bomb would explode in less than five hours. I could reach Braden in plenty of time—if my plan worked.

Kain whistled a tune I didn't recognize. I wasn't sure what made him happier, the prospect of reclaiming his treasure or killing me. My Graceland leap of logic definitely cheered him.

"Sounds like Hugh," he said. "Let's hope it's there."

Oh, let's.

I rehearsed the moves in my mind. Wait till he peers in the trough, opens the cooler lid. Grab the axe and swing. Aim for his head? No, he might sense movement and duck. The torso's a bigger target. Better chance to immobilize. You want him down. Dead can wait.

The golf cart shuddered to a stop. We'd arrived. My heart skipped a beat; my hands trembled. Under the heavy canvas wrap, my body manufactured heat like a stoked fire. Sweat streamed down my face. My shirt plastered itself to my body. *God, he'll know I have something planned.*

Kain whipped the tarp off with a flourish, like an artist unveiling a masterpiece.

His eyes gleamed. "I wondered when it would arrive—the fear. I see it in your face. You're shaking with terror. Sometimes I smell it on people. An odor, bitter like almonds. You lasted longer than most, Marley.

"Come. Show me this ice trough."

Thank, God. He read my shakes as fear of death not the flood of adrenalin before a battle. The nearness of his quarry and my perceived fright excited him. Still he took care. His fist tightly gripped my tether as we crossed a spongy patch of grass to the pavilion's graveled apron. Moonlight bright enough to cast shadows silhouetted the building. Shadows pooled at the intersection of walls where I hoped to find treasure. *Was anything there?*

Kain recognized the rectangular ice bin and walked faster. The noose tightened around my neck as he jerked me forward. The rope was a spare four feet. Not enough to maneuver. The trough was six feet from the fire pit and hatchet—if it was there. I strained to separate a shape from the shadows. I saw it. *Hallelujah.*

Kain reached the trough, my tether wound round his left hand. With his right hand, he reached to lift a metal cover designed to keep out animals and leaves. He'd almost forgotten me. *It's now or never.*

I grabbed the rope upstream of my throat and yanked as I lunged toward the hatchet. Kain lurched sideways. I dropped the rope and staggered to the hatchet. I closed my manacled fists around the handle. *Swing now.* As I followed through, I realized my target had shriveled. The man crouched, reaching for his gun. I saw a glint of metal. My aim was off. Kain screamed as the hatchet connected with flesh. A second later, the blade bounced on the dirt. A glancing blow. *Oh, no.*

I tried to lift the hatchet, swing again. Kain copied my rope trick. He jerked my leash and toppled me. I collapsed flat on my face. I saw his boot coming at my head. Black, ugly, huge.

***

I came to sprawled on a dock, my head painfully canted at a ninety-degree angle to my spine. A shift brought instant pain. My choke chain now anchored me to one of the dock's steel piers. However, I'd seen enough to identify our location. The Cuthbert dock.

Kain leaned over and slapped me lightly on the cheek. "Colonel Clark, how disappointing."

He held up a USB flash drive encased in a bulky plastic

package attached to a lanyard. He slowly swung the computer memory device before me like a hypnotist with a pocket watch. "It's even waterproof." He chuckled as he stashed the gizmo in a jacket pocket.

"As a reward for helping me recover my property, I'd planned to let you die quickly. Now, well, infractions must be punished. You cut my thigh. Quite a bit of blood, no permanent damage.

"Wonder why you're alive? It would have been no fun to kill you while you were unconscious. Besides, you have value as a hostage—until I'm safely off the island."

His slow, singsong words smothered hope. He didn't expect an answer. Had he wanted one, he wouldn't have left the wadded rag in my mouth. I snorted like a pig trying to inhale enough oxygen to fuel my frenzy.

My tormentor looked down at me and rocked contentedly on his heels. He grabbed a fistful of my hair and yanked upward, hoisting me to a sitting position. My scalp burned.

"Stand up," he ordered.

I felt woozy. My head throbbed. Oh my God, Braden. What time is it?

I glanced at my watch. The round face confused me. Digital ants marched in circles. Oh. I was staring at my GPS, not my watch. In my groggy condition, I looked at the wrong wrist. It seemed a lifetime had passed since I'd strapped on my GPS to check Hugh's coordinates. I looked at my left wrist.

My God, nine o'clock. Only three hours left.

Despair crept in and threatened to swamp me. I wanted to cry.

Kain's words hit me like ice water. "Sunrise Island. That's my first stop, your last. We'll have a private party. You, me, and the crabs."

He hummed a little ditty.

"Wonder who'll find you? Maybe someone you know. I

288

was surprised to learn you were friends with that black girl's aunt. America's chaotic social structure often amazes me."

He glanced at me. "I didn't kill Bea's maid, you know. Just drugged the girl and shipped her off. Piece of ass like her is worth money. Never hurts to tend to the bottom line. After all, I am a businessman.

"But even a capitalist needs entertainment. Once I'm off the island, I could just dump you overboard. But what fun would that be? We won't part company quickly. No, ma'am."

I'd passed panic. My stomach heaved at the thought of this miscreant torturing me for hours on an uninhabited island. My brain ceased to function. A short-circuit caused the same prayer to play over and over, like an old recording with a skip. *Dear God, please help me... Dear God, please help me... Dear God, please help me...*

Not very helpful if you believe God gave us brains so we can help ourselves.

But I can't do anything, I mentally whined.

Think ahead, dummy. He still has to wrestle you into his boat. What are your options? Another swim?

The doomsayer side of my brain answered: How long can you hold your breath, genius? You're gagged and handcuffed. You'll be lucky not to sink like a stone.

I refused to give up. My kayak waited right around the bend, one dock down.

Kain quit humming and started whistling.

"I haven't had much fun lately," he chortled. "This makes up for it. What message should I leave beside your remains? Notice I said 'remains' not 'body.' What's left won't be readily recognizable.

"Maybe I'll let you vote on your epitaph—while you can still talk. It's hard to find a pun using Marley or Clark, and I've already done Colonel. Perhaps I should combine a pun with a visual. How about *She-Crab Soup*?"

The gag quelled my sudden impulse to scream. Besides, no one would hear. No occupied homes within earshot.

Kain limped slightly, his only souvenir of my axe attack. I'd blown my one chance to save myself and Braden.

My tether offered little play. If I so much as nodded my head, I choked. Kain disappeared down the dock ladder and into the flat-bottomed skiff. He pulled the motor starter and revved the engine. Oily fumes belched from the two-cycle engine, adding to my nausea.

"Okay, showtime." He sounded like a carnival barker.

Cautious before, Kain was doubly wary now. He pushed a switchblade against my throat as he undid the knots that tied me to the pier. After freeing the rope end, he gathered the excess and wound it round his fist. He jerked until I gagged.

"So far, so good," he said. "Move slowly. Walk to the edge of the dock and kneel. Then put your legs over the edge so you're sitting and drop into the boat. I'm right behind you. Any stupid tricks and I'll jerk this rope so hard your eyes will pop out. But don't worry: I won't let you die. Not till we party on Sunrise."

Unfortunately, my frazzled brain couldn't think of any stunt—stupid or otherwise.

It's hard to talk with a giant wad of cotton flattening your tongue. Yet my involuntary silence seemed to irritate Kain. He kicked my leg where I'd filleted it playing demolition derby with the Bobcat.

"Nod that you understand, bitch."

I winced and nodded.

The moon rode high in the sky, offering ample light to scan my surroundings. My mind raced as I tried to think of a ploy. *Anything. Come on.*

"Walk forward," he ordered. He treated me like a dog he wanted to heel. From the corner of my eye, I watched his gaze travel over the bruises that covered my left side from haunch to ankle. Under the garish dock lights they resembled ripening eggplants. To Kain, they were magnets, tempting bulls-eyes. He kicked my calf. My strangled vocalization, the high-pitched product of intense pain, brought a smile to his lips. He'd really enjoy himself once he could remove my gag and hear my unmuffled screams.

My pathetic compliance turned Kain on. He was addicted. The vulnerable skin on display through my shredded pants must look irresistible. I sensed his overpowering need to kick me again...soon.

That's when it came to me. *Wait till he lifts his leg to kick. Charge him while he's off balance. Force him into the water. It may be your last chance.*

I'd barely completed the thought when I caught movement out of the corner of my eye. Kain hauled his foot back to land a stout blow on my calf. I coiled all my energy into one explosive full-body thrust. I locked my elbows, pivoted at the waist and used the power in my legs to land the blow to his face. My handcuffs worked like brass knuckles. I carried through with all my weight. Our bodies collided.

"Bitch," Kain screamed as our momentum took us sideways.

My feet left the dock. Yes! I felt myself suspended in air. Then I met the icy water in a graceless belly flop.

I had surprise going for me. I'd planned to land in the drink; Kain hadn't. He flailed like a drowning man. He made a desperate lunge at me. I weaved and ducked out of his grasp. His heavy camouflage weighed him down. Blood spurted from his nose where I clocked him with my heavy-duty bracelets.

Good. Where's a shark when you need one?

Even without the handicaps, the man didn't appear to be a swimmer. Me, I was Red Cross certified. Never mind that was thirty-odd years ago. I'd never stopped swimming. I could evade him—if we both stayed in the water. And if his hand weren't still twined around a rope that terminated in a noose circling my neck.

I pulled the gag from my mouth, tearing my skin in the process. While doing a modified float, I wiggled my cuffed hands between the noose and my neck so he couldn't choke off my air. Kain was smart. In a minute, he'd quit thrashing and reel me in like a hooked fish. I couldn't give him that minute.

I heard the whine of the skiff's motor and made a decision. I sucked in air and dived. Kicking with all my might, I pulled the rope and Kain with it. My body went numb with cold. My lungs burned.

I kicked harder. My eyes opened. I might as well have been swimming in ink. Sound offered the only guide. Had I gone far enough? I jackknifed to the surface and gave a fierce yank upward on the rope. The motor whined; I was thrilled. The dead weight on the other end was gone. The rope floated free. The motor blades had sliced it in two. *Hallelujah.*

Kain's screams failed to penetrate for a moment. My tug had brought more than the rope in contact with blades. I'd hauled some part of his anatomy into the motor's twirling maelstrom.

"You're dead, you whore," he yelled. The swear words and female slurs that followed were in Polish. Apparently English could no longer express his rage.

That's when I saw a swatch of red and blue, bobbing my way. The flash drive. I grabbed it. Kain saw me sweep the prize into my hand.

Treading water, I gasped to inject oxygen into my burning lungs. Saltwater stung my eyes. Barely six feet away, he pulled himself up the ladder one handed. Darkness wouldn't let me assess his injuries. He was down, not out.

"I'm coming for you," he yelled.

That got me moving. My rope trick fouled the motor. He had to free it before he could start the boat. And he was injured.

But as cocky as I was about out-swimming Kain, I knew better than to think I could outpace a motorboat—or a bullet. He still had his gun. I had to hide, then find a way to reach Braden.

I knew of no swimming stroke to adapt to handcuffs. At least my hands were secured in front. I stretched my arms ahead and flutter-kicked for long yards. When exhaustion set in, a frog kick carried me the last few feet to the dock where my kayak waited.

I'll choose waterways too shallow for his motorboat. Ditch the kayak upstream. Then head for civilization.

Climbing the ladder proved a challenge. No way to separate my cuffed hands to reach the next rung while I clung to the step below. Finally I used my chin as a lever. I heaved myself onto the dock, then shoved the kayak into the water. The splash sounded deafening. Had Kain heard it over the cough of his starter?

I held onto the ladder frame and slid into the seat. I undid the bungee-style clip to free my paddle from its cradle.

Bollocks. From the first stroke, I was in trouble. With handcuffs, I couldn't spread my hands far enough apart to gain leverage on my down stroke. And shifting the paddle from side to side proved a coordination nightmare. Fluid movements that seemed second nature with unfettered limbs became jerky comedies of error.

Maybe I could dog paddle faster.

Kain's motor caught. Our game of hide and seek had begun. I veered from the main creek into an unfamiliar feeder rivulet. I needed less than a foot of draft. I prayed it was too shallow for his motor to clear.

I paddled to a Y, one of dozens of idiosyncratic dips in the meandering creek, and set off down the narrowest passageway. Where would it lead? Moonlight glittered on the waves. Still it was difficult to pick out landmarks. At this tide, the grass towered three feet above my head. Good for camouflage, not for navigating. I brushed against the decaying marsh grass. It felt surprisingly soft. In two months, the brown vegetation would vanish; a sheen of chartreuse would signal the marsh's rebirth. If I lived to see it.

The chug of the motorboat engine sounded close, too close. My feeder creek ran right back to the main waterway. *Damn.* Only a small strip of marsh separated me from Kain. To my dismay, I realized this portion of the channel, though narrow, was plenty deep for a skiff.

I could track Kain's progress as he poked along, methodically probing hidden nooks and crannies. His searchlight beam projected a tiny halo of light above the marsh.

How long would he stay with the main creek? With the paddle I pushed deeper into a little cove of grass. The fecund, slightly sweet smell of rotting marsh made me queasy. Inches away the pluff mud teemed with tiny crabs waving pincers twice the size of their bodies. On the opposite bank a pile of oyster shells gleamed. If I abandoned the kayak here, I'd sink in mud or cut my feet to ribbons on razor-sharp shells.

I fumbled with my paddle to angle my wrists and check the time. Ten-thirty. *Less than two hours to reach Braden. Get moving.* Unfortunately, Kain and his gun stood between me and civilization...phones...Braden. While checking the time, I inadvertently glanced at my GPS first.

Hmm. I had a vague notion of my whereabouts within Beach West's undeveloped heart. My mind flashed on the image of a structure, one Kain couldn't possibly know. One he was unlikely to see at night. Long before Dear became a nature preserve, it served as a poacher's paradise, and ambitious locals built a hunter's blind in the top of a huge oak. A place to drink beer and shoot wild turkey and alligators.

Strips of wood nailed to the oak's trunk formed a ladder. The blind overlooked the island's alligator spa—the deep, dark pool fed by artesian hot springs. The structure was in disrepair.

Rotting floorboards punctured by gaping holes. But it was the best place I could think of to safely hide from his searchlight. He'd be unlikely to look up.

It took a little handcuff maneuvering to work the GPS buttons, but in a couple of minutes I was set. I'd already marked the alligator spa as a geocaching waypoint. Now I set it as my destination. A row of glowing digital breadcrumbs flickered on as a reward. The blinking ants marched steadily, showing the shortest route.

My mind was working again, logic reasserting itself over primitive fear. It wasn't enough to hide. I had to come up with a plan. If I didn't, Braden was dead. I prayed Kain hadn't lied about when the bomb would go off.

By the time I reached the first dry hillock, the outline of a scheme presented itself. Crazy, risky, insane—it was all I had.

I abandoned the kayak on the sandy rise. I ran fifty yards or so, then yelled. I tried for a blood-curdling scream—as if I'd been injured in a fall. Something to get Kain salivating.

The subtropical forest was dense, dark and confusing. I checked my GPS regularly to see which way the green digital ants headed. I picked up a fallen tree branch to use as a probe and poked the ground ahead like an Army grunt testing for landmines. The blind was close by, but I needed to circumnavigate the neighboring lagoon. I wasn't anxious to take a dip with the alligators.

The lagoon proved easy to spot. White vapor rose steadily from its oily black surface. The tall oak loomed above the water, its silhouette quite distinctive. Light scissored the woods above my discarded kayak. *Good.* Kain was following. I ran to the base of the tree and swore. The first ladder rung had rotted to little more than splinters. Were more steps missing?

I grabbed hold of a rung well above my head. My feet scrabbled against the trunk for purchase. After gaining a queasy purchase, I maneuvered for the next notch. Sweat ran into my eyes. Thirst made me dizzy. While I'd been free of my gag for half an hour, it felt as if it was still in place, siphoning off saliva faster than a dentist's suction tube.

I climbed faster using my elbows for leverage. All of the higher rungs felt sturdy. My hand touched the blind's decaying floor just as Kain's flashlight speared me in its beam. *Pure rotten luck.* I'd planned to drop on him, a banshee descending out of the blue. Surprise was no longer an ally.

Kain's discovery prompted a bellow of rage and euphoria. The hunter had run his quarry to ground. I pulled myself through the blind's entry and lay panting on the rough boards. The board nearest my hands teetered when I moved. The nails that once held it to the joist had popped. Only the imbedded heads kept the rusted protrusions in place. *Careful.*

Kain closed to within a hundred yards. I stared at the ground below, where an audience gathered for the coming confrontation. Beady red eyes glowed in the dark. At least six alligators had congregated at the edge of the hot lagoon.

Hell and damnation.

I hid myself as best I could in the foliage of the live oak—a tree that never loses its leaves. My best wasn't good enough.

"Oh, Marley, you do like to play games. Unfortunately for you, I have the trump card." He held his pistol high in the moonlight. "How many shots will I need to wound you? Want to wager?"

The first shot gouged a branch inches from my shoulder. Splinters of bark exploded around me. The second bullet buried itself in thick wood just shy of my torso.

"I'm getting closer," Kain crooned. "Bet I wing you with shot number three."

I didn't want to take that bet. I seized the loose, nail-studded board at my feet. It would have to do. I tightened my grip on my makeshift club and let out a war whoop. A second later I dropped onto Kain. His body cushioned my fall. He screamed and staggered to his feet. The collision had ripped the gun from his grasp.

Now I had the only weapon. *Batter up.* The floorboard with its rusty nails found its mark, and Kain fell to the ground, shrieking. Only this time he rolled down the incline, headed directly to the waiting alligators.

An animal roar filled the air, followed by an unearthly scream. "Help me. God, help me," Kain pleaded. Was he talking to me or God?

Was it a trap? What would happen if I went closer to the lagoon? Had he recovered his gun?

I thought of Braden. The deadline. I turned my back on his screams and ran. I checked my GPS. The logger's lane entered nearby. I sprinted, ignoring the jarring pain in my twisted angle. Yet every woodland rustle prompted a backward glance. I'd watched too many flicks where the heroine assumes the villain's down only to have him materialize with an axe.

Kain didn't materialize.

At eleven p.m., I streaked out of the woods and almost collided with a security patrol car. I pounded on the window with my fists. For a moment, I feared Chip would shoot before he recognized me. My lip was swollen and bleeding. My wet hair matted to my skull. Mud caked my ripped clothes. Panic drove my screams toward a glass-shattering pitch.

"There's a bomb. He locked Braden in a house with a bomb."

Chip radioed for help as we sped to Blue Crab Point. The next few minutes vanished in a blur. Chip beat me to the villa's door and raced up the stairs. I heard Braden's voice before I saw him. "Where's Marley? Kain took her," he yelled. "You have to find her."

"Don't worry. I'm here." I panted as I fell into the room. "Oh, thank God. You're okay."

With Chip's help, Braden shed the last of his ropes, and we

held each other. I cried as Braden muttered, "Thank God. Thank God."

After a minute, Chip cleared his throat. "Folks, didn't you say that's a bomb?" He pointed at Kain's handiwork. "What in blazes do we do?"

"Get the hell out of here," I answered. "Do either of you know squat about bombs? I don't. Try to disarm it and we may set it off. This place could use a little redecorating."

The chief's booming voice startled me. "Damn straight. Let's go. Nothing here worth risking lives. We may not know about bombs on Dear, but we know plenty about evacuations."

I didn't see the explosion. But the firemen, who waited half a mile away, weren't impressed. They doused the flames inside an hour. Of course, the villa was toast.

The chief, Braden and I had unfinished business, finding Kain.

The alligators did not eat him. Even they had better taste. But one of them, startled or aggravated by his uninvited drop in, had chomped through an artery in Kain's leg.

Occasionally I wondered what Kain's last thoughts were as he bled out. I hoped he died cursing me.

When we found his body, my wicked mind thought of a fitting epitaph: *Kain wasn't Able*

.

TWENTY-EIGHT

When did I last attend an Easter sunrise service? I couldn't remember. This year it felt essential. Braden groused about setting the alarm, but sensed the celebration's importance. As we stood on a sandy rise, he leaned down to whisper in my ear. "You warm enough? Want my jacket?"

An ocean breeze rustled the dune grasses in the damp pre-dawn. The air held a chill. "I'm fine." I wrapped my arm around his waist and burrowed into his sweet warmth.

Two weeks had passed since Kain bled to death.

Thank God, the killer told me of his decision to spare Sharlana. Before carting Kain's body away, the coroner emptied his pockets and found a slip of paper with a Miami address. When police searched the address, they found Sharlana. A pimp was softening her up with drugs before putting her on the street. Doctors thought she'd make a full recovery.

The rescued flash drive proved a bonanza. Loaded with data about Kain's criminal enterprise, it sparked dozens of arrests up and down the East Coast. It would be years before Sheriff Conroy collected all the favors law enforcement officers now owed him. The only puzzle was why Kain had entrusted the data to Hugh. Was Hugh acting as a courier, taking the data to another lieutenant? Or was it insurance—a way to keep potential traitors in line? No one knew. Hugh never came out of his coma before he died.

Janie landed on her feet. Grace Cuthbert's lawyer, who headed the creditor delegation rushing to Dear's rescue, named her Managing Director. Now Janie had her chance to be the head cheese.

Braden ran his hands up and down my arms to keep me warm. His touch thrilled me. I couldn't wait for our vacation to begin. We both had a week off, starting tomorrow. We planned to explore the Lowcountry in style. Carriage rides through Beaufort's historic neighborhoods. A boat cruise to Fort Sumter. A day poking around sprawling Middleton Place. Candlelight dinners in Savannah and Charleston. Lots of time in bed.

I felt happy. We'd barely begun to share our pasts— bedtime stories told a little at a time. The future? Who knew? We agreed it would take care of itself.

But, ah, the present was magic. Our deep affection eroded the guilt we'd each stockpiled. I helped Braden realize he shouldn't be bullied by his ex-wife's blame-game. He'd come to a decision. He would not let regret strip his sons of their birthright: a father's love.

In turn, Braden urged me toward my own absolution. My husband was dead. That didn't make my desire wrong. With words and touches, we reassured each other: we were worthy of love. I closed my eyes to say a little prayer.

Braden nudged me. "Hey you're not going to sleep, are you?"

"No, I just remembered the Gullah word for dawn. Do you know it?"

"No, but I'm sure you'll enlighten me."

"It's *dayclean*," I said. "A wonderful image. A fresh start."

Bright reds and oranges danced in the clouds as the sun inched over the horizon. The choir began to sing. It would be a beautiful day at the beach.

***

BOOKS BY LINDA LOVELY

Brie Hooker Mysteries
Bones To Pick (2017)
Picked Off (2018)
Bad Pick (Coming April, 2019)

Smart Women, Dumb Luck Series
Dead Line (Previously titled Final Accounting, 2012)
Dead Hunt (2014)

Marley Clark Mystery Series
Dear Killer (2011)
No Wake Zone (2012)

Stand Alone Titles
Lies: Secrets Can Kill (2015)

Audiobooks
DEAD LINE, DEAD HUNT, DEAR KILLER & NO WAKE ZONE
ARE AVAILABLE IN AUDIOBOOK FORMATS.

ABOUT THE AUTHOR

Linda Lovely majored in journalism and has made her living as a writer, primarily in PR. She now focuses on her first love—fiction. Her published fiction includes novels in three series—**Brie Hooker Mysteries, Marley Clark Mysteries,** and **Smart Women, Dumb Luck** romantic thrillers, as well as **Lies: Secrets Can Kill**, a stand-alone historical romantic suspense set in 1938.

Her manuscripts have earned final spots in 15 contests, including RWA Golden Heart and Daphne du Maurier contests. **Dear Killer**, the first Marley novel, was a finalist in the RWA Golden Quill published novel competition. **Dead Line** made the finals of the National Readers' Choice Awards for Romantic Suspense. **Bones To Pick** was nominated in the mystery category for the Southern Book Prize.

Linda actively supports the Upstate SC Chapter of Sisters in Crime, which she served as president for five years, and she works as volunteer staff for the renowned Writers' Police Academy. She also belongs to Romance Writers of America and International Thriller Writers. A popular speaker, Linda teaches genre fiction classes and often visits with book clubs.

An Iowa native, Linda now lives with her husband beside a South Carolina lake. Her hobbies include reading, swimming, kayaking, tennis, and gardening.

To learn more, visit: www.lindalovely.com.

NOTE TO READERS

Hollis County, South Carolina, and its inhabitants are fictional. However, in creating this county, I tried to be faithful to the charming character of the Lowcountry—its landscapes, wildlife, ecology, colorful Gullah culture, and vibrant yet checkered development history. I lived in the Lowcountry for more than a dozen years and loved every minute of it.

To anchor readers, I mentioned a handful of real locations—the Town of Beaufort, Hilton Head, Parris Island. Even in these locales, I detoured from reality. The Hilton Head establishments are imaginary.

I took more liberties regarding non-lethal weaponry. I needed an electronic control device that provided no hint of ownership when fired. I reasoned an Eastern European manufacturer might produce such an item.

While I have no first-hand knowledge of the illegal activities in DEAR KILLER, my plot taps interviews I did with experts on measures to thwart would-be scam artists.

My best friend from childhood, Major (Retired) Arlene Underwood spent most of her Army career in military intelligence. She generously provided background on her Army days, including her training as a Polish linguist, to add depth to my heroine's biography. Any errors in my portrayal of military life are mine alone.

I love writing fiction. It frees the imagination in ways nonfiction never allows. Yet novels do attempt to portray characters, their challenges, and conflicts truthfully. I hope readers, especially those over age 50, will identify with my 52-year-old heroine, applaud Marley Clark's zest for life, and want to join her for future adventures.

Linda Lovely

ABOUT WINDTREE PRESS

Windtree Press sees writers in all their artistic complexity, individuals who may wish to pursue more than one genre, more than one publisher, and more than one distribution mechanism.

Founded in 2011, Windtree Press is an author publishing cooperative that fills the gap between traditional and independent publishing with promotion, distribution, shared expertise and a supportive environment for publication among proven published authors.

Direct sales of ebooks are available on the Windtree Press website. Windtree digital books are also available from a variety of major distributors and our print books can be ordered through most bookstores.

For more information, visit our website:
http://windtreepress.com

49934038R00173

Made in the USA
Columbia, SC
01 February 2019